A GRITTY DARK FANTASY OF MYTH AND MADNESS

DARKNESS AND BLIGHT

DAP DAHLSTROM

Gardland Books

1

LYDARC, NOW

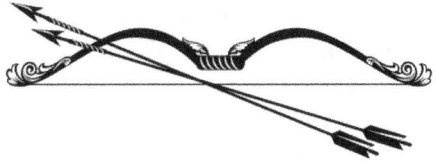

I am Lydarc, the shaman. I hunt the bitterwood, even as it hunts me. It stalks me with frostbite and heatstroke, starves me with the stale jerky feast I choke down on the run. From flood to drought, deep freeze to desert heat, the bitterwood will end you, no matter who you think you are.

My arrow sings, bringing down an eight-hundred-weighter. He spins in the air, his last leap for freedom, then collapses, my barb splitting his heart. An exquisite elkin beauty a moment ago, now a pantry staple for my clan. We'll dry it, mostly. The rest will feed us well, at least for a blastweek or so.

I might be showing my lack of maternal instinct, but I imagine, at the feast to come, another hungry mouth being conceived; another ale-spawned, caterwauling brat, another growling belly likely to go hungry when the cervid herds migrate to the leshii-infested forests of the northern Siletz, where I dare not follow. I may be insane and drug-addled, but not even I will test myself against the leshii.

As I approach, the elkin shudders where he lies, his powerful legs thrashing. I nock a second arrow, but only in an excess of caution. My aim was true. His remaining half-life has fled to the underlands. His body just doesn't know it yet.

I pull a piece of raw rubellite tourmaline from my medicine bag and conjure a glowing flame to illuminate my work.

Placing it gently on a petrified stump, I draw my freshly sharpened blade.

When gutting a stag, one must be wary of slicing a bowel. Only neophater hunters are so willy-nilly in their execution, spicing the meat with excrement's vile taint.

Once I split the hide from rectum to chest, I reach in to slice the esophagus, freeing the mass of viscera. It plops out, a steaming pile at my feet.

As I wipe my bloody hands on a rusty tuft of belchgrass, it squeals like a baby grundle, and a rare, pleasant memory tickles my thoughts. I open my mouth to laugh, but the sound catches in my throat, as if I've inadvertently sucked in a dungfly. Splattering, squishing sounds surround me. The ground shudders and the lovely aroma of a disturbed grave forces my nostrils to close in self-defense.

Carrion ghouls.

A full nest, by the number of exit plops my oversized ears have registered. Despite my visceral reaction, fortune has smiled on me this blastnight. At least they're not wendigos or biddlewites or, even worse, a swarm of skin-burrowing bloodspore ticks.

The carrion ghouls sound and smell hungry. But I've never known them to lack that saliva-dripping desire to feed, oozing from every orifice. Usually, they prefer their prey long dead before deeming it sufficiently ripe to feast on. Perhaps their dinner plans were influenced by the fact that I brought down the elkin in the middle of their nesting grounds. Lucky me.

They exit their holes and creep toward me; horrid nightmare shapes dripping mud and slime. Huge curving fangs gleam in cavernous maws that gape even wider, drool running in rivulets as their desire to feed lures them in. Each limb ends in a mass of blackened claws. They twist and scrabble at the dirt as they crawl with unwavering focus toward the body of the elkin.

My eyes water at the stench as I survey the clearing. All it offers are a few boulders, cervid beds and trampled sedge, a couple of desiccated spine trees and the ubiquitous belchgrass.

This could get interesting.

Grabbing my bow, I climb the nearest tree, venturing as high as I dare in the brittle, thorny branches.

A razor-sharp arrow alone will not do for the Over-spawned ghouls. Oh no. I must bloody each arrow tip with a bit of myself, a gobbet of spirit meat cut from my peri-soul. I only hope there's enough left after the protracted stalk and taking of the elkin. I'll need time and rest, and perhaps a draught of poppy-seed tincture to replenish it.

Tearing my tunic open, I pry my chest apart with a cry, angled up at the ring of lunar debris, and stick a trembling finger into the glowing mess. It comes out covered in a goop as radiant and warm as firefly honey, a dollop of which I apply to each arrow, finishing just as the ghouls reach the elkin carcass.

Ignoring me on my perch, they dig into the animal's guts and organs, rending and slurping as their long tongues lap up the contents of the intestines. Not especially picky eaters, I see.

Their backs arch, revealing scimitar-shaped blades of bone that decorate each exposed vertebra. Their skin is a muddy, mottled mix of charcoal and umber, with stray tufts of hair and weeping sores adorning their gawky limbs.

"Leave off my dinner, you materfucking bastards," I yell, but my voice breaks. I realize these are the first words I've spoken to another being in blastdays. No matter. There's little chance these monsters understand me.

As if in denial of this observation, one beast turns to snarl up at me. She is larger and more grotesque than the others, and her eyes have an awareness the others lack.

The queen.

I aim my first arrow at her, but she skitters aside. The point slides past and into the shoulder of another ghoul, who falls spasming to the dirt with a screeching yowl, then is still.

My aim is sure, or fortune is at least not shitting on me this blastnight. Twelve of the beasts soon lie dead or dying. Only two remain, one of which, the queen, glares up at me with murderous intent.

It's a little-known fact that carrion ghouls can climb: a lesson I now learn. The second ghoul, as if heeding the silent command of his furious queen, struggles up the tree toward me. His claws arch to dig deep into the ashen wood. Angular elbows jut at the swirling sky, and his yellow custard eyes are glowing pits of promised misery.

As this horror creeps closer, I fumble for my knife, but my hands tremble—not from fear or fatigue but from peri-soul depletion. The bow falls from my shoulder, tumbling to the forest floor.

"That had better not be damaged, you fucker," I snap, "or I'll take from you more than your two cursed lives." What more the beast might have to give, I have no idea, but I'll think of something.

If the ghoul understands, he doesn't show it, but continues to climb, glowering at me with bestial focus. As he nears my position, I swipe for his neck, but he twists away from, then under my knife with uncanny speed, clamping my right ankle in iron jaws. His fangs feel like forge-heated knives burning through my flesh. Ignoring the pain, I strike again. This time, my reward is a muffled howl of agony as my blade slices across his twisted features. Now blind in one eye and blinded by blood in the other, my attacker scrabbles for purchase and falls from the spine tree.

Unfortunately, his jaws remain doggedly locked on my ankle, and he drags me down with him. We pause for a moment, adrift in the dirty air, grasping for it as if it would support us if we asked. It does not.

As I land on top of the beast, a ragged hole in his chest whooshes with a gusty exhalation that reeks of blood, bile, and rotting meat. His ribs crack with multiple snaps, one jagged spear piercing his heart. My knife skitters away out of my reach.

I learn a new truth: if you're looking for a soft place to land, don't choose a bony carrion ghoul.

Even before I can coax my lungs to resume their life's work, agony erupts in my arm. The queen has my forearm in her teeth and is worrying it like a stray blastform puppy playing with a greasy bastle bone.

Realizing there will be no escape from her iron grip, I do the only logical thing; I get closer, clasping her around the neck with my free arm and pulling her to me like a sex-starved lover. When her contorted face is nearly touching mine, I channel my inner ghoul, sinking my teeth through the fetid hide and into her neck. Her claws lacerate my belly and her jaw clenches ever tighter on my shredded arm.

Resisting the overwhelming urge to gag, I search for her throbbing carotid with my teeth. Thanking the Overs for adhering to at least some basics of afterarthly anatomy, I yank my head back, simultaneously thrusting the monster away from me. I bite down with all my remaining strength. Her artery bursts, and hot purple blood splatters my face and chest. But she isn't escaping this realm quickly enough. One of her claws rakes my face and searing pain explodes in my head.

Perhaps I've lost an eye, but no matter. That's why I have two, after all. Optimist all the way. But that's just me.

At last, the brute is still, and I stumble to my feet, blearily surveying the gory scene. Thirteen ghoul carcasses, plus one coughing up its last breath, litter the clearing. Dizzy, I stand and sway slightly, cracking my shoulders one after the other. My shirt sticks to the long gashes in my abdomen as blood drips from my arm in a rhythmic cadence to match the *thump, thump* of my straining heart.

At the worst possible moment, and with only a drop of my peri-soul left, a vision intrudes. I fear they will one day take over entirely, and I'll be lost to this world.

Before me poses my warrior friend: short, stout, and surprisingly brutal when she needs to be.

"Always cutting it close, just to best me any way you can," Jarly says with a wide grin. Our captain, Wayland, sits beside her. As my sight clarifies, I see we're in the nameless bar, in a town called Nameless, but that's a vision for another day.

"You in trouble again, probie?" he asks as he raises a dark ale to his lips.

Ignoring his unintentionally sensual smile as best I can, I grit my teeth. "I've survived worse."

"Well, just try to survive this one. I need you."

I can feel my blood vessels throbbing as rage burbles up inside me. "If you'd really needed me, you would have said or done something—anything—to convince me to stay."

Wayland stares at his hands and grips his mug with perhaps more force than required.

"I'd just gotten back with Cassander. Everything was a mess. Look, I screwed up. I know that. Can we just get past all that? Start over?"

"Start over? What're you fucking talking about? You're at least two thousand widder-widths away and—"

"No, no, I'm not. I'm right outside your blastform, waiting to be let in."

Before I can say more, Wayland fades. Not gently, as if in a dream, but with a stomach-turning, disorienting level of detail that I would prefer to un-remember. His expression goes first, then his skin, followed by layers of muscle and bone. Gray matter is amazingly grotesque when you see it in the flesh.

"That's more of you than I ever want to see again," I grumble, as the forest returns.

Shaking my head to clear it, which only makes me more blightheaded, I snake trembling fingers to my chest, and my newly healed ribs crack open again with a sickening, pulpy crunch. As I groan, the remaining sliver of my peri-soul swells and flickers. At my touch, it drags me from the brink of forever with a bright, brittle flash of being.

I wake on my back, unsure of where, or even who, I am.

Regrettably, it all comes back to me.

The tribe depends on my return. And, just maybe, Wayland will be there too. I'm not sure how to feel about that. I reach into a pocket and retrieve the vial of poppy-seed tincture. I take a deep draught, then, considering the extent of my injuries, down another.

After binding my seeping wounds and bloody eye socket with strips of my extra shirt, I resume my work on the elkin.

My knife glides at a careful angle as I work the hide back from the flesh, so as not to break through the fat layer and put a hole in the precious expanse of furry warmth.

The thought makes me chuckle, thinking of Harbinder the Huge. The surly Siletzon wears a coat of many holes that everyone makes blight of—once he's out of hearing range, of course—because he's a quick-to-anger and slow-to-forgive breed of curmudgeon. Curmudgeon. Wayland taught me that word, plus a few others I abuse in his honor.

Harbinder lumbers past, shoving me aside with a hunched shoulder. He emits a guttural snort, as if my thoughts both rile and amuse him. Whether his presence is a drug-induced hallucination or actual timesmear is unclear, and I care not which. If it's the former, I feel no guilt. The poppy seed, psilocybes, and dreamweed feed and soothe my peri-soul, all so I can survive another blastday in this exquisite pleasure garden.

As he passes, he turns abruptly, gazing into me with accusing black eyes. "It's coming. You brought this down on us, witch. Happy now?" he snarls at me, then turns away to fade into the trees. A massive shiver runs through my body, but I shake it off. It's not as if I haven't heard this before, over and over in my visions of late.

Turning back to the job at hand, I kneel before the elkin and set to carving into, through and around each slick hip, shoulder joint and greasy tendon with a speed and accuracy born of seasons of practice in my craft. Once quartered, I will construct a makeshift travois to haul the meat out of the bitterwood, then hoist the shanks by block and tackle up to our blastform, where we will hang it to age.

Several trips it will take, with the hide and horns the last precious bounty to be removed, but a most necessary one. The hides keep us warm, and from the antlers we fashion tools, instruments and smoke pipes to survive the bitter, merciless seasons of afterarth.

As the sky weeps darkness, I hoist the first elkin quarter to the travois with a grunt of misery, followed by a snort of amusement. It's only pain, after all, and I've lived with that every moment since the Over violated me.

I gather my weapon to one shoulder and raise the leather harness to the other.

Stout, grim clouds erupt and belch out a savage, biting sleet. Tiny barbs of ice prick my bloody face, creating delicate rivulets of pink as they melt, trickling down my neck like miniature, writhing snakes.

Without warning, desert highburn bursts from the jump with a thunderous clap. The searing infrared heat and blight burn unbearable orange fire into my remaining retina. The spheres shriek, shuddering as they're torn from their orbits and forced into another space and time. A moment later, with a howl of cosmic torment, the sky flips back to grimshade, reverting to the chill, cloaking gloom of the bleakest of our two hopeless seasons.

A sweaty shiver wracks my tortured frame. Are the jumps coming more often and more erratically now, or is it just my admittedly fuzzy, drug-impaired judgment?

Ignoring the looming apocalypse, I lean into my burden with a grunt until it moves an iota, then two.

It promises to be a long, punishing blastnight, but aren't they all?

Optimist, all the way. But that's just me.

2

LYDARC, NOW

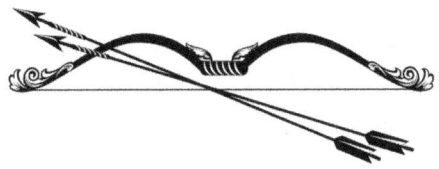

Destiny isn't written in stone, but rather etched into our tortured flesh. We draw our future destiny using the inky fluid of our own blackened hearts.

— WAYLAND PETERS, AS QUOTED BY SITKA SANGASHEE, *A SHAMAN'S JOURNEY*

The blastform bends and twists around me like an exceptionally limber lover.

The Siletzon's attempts at building walkways are thwarted by its constant squirming and turning and contrary "up is down" way of thinking. I say "thinking," but the blastform is not conscious, at least not in any afterarthly way. It confounds and transmutes our every attempt to domesticate it. It's a wild, untamable mustang trying to buck us off.

As I walk the rippling, tubular hallway, I realize it's spiraling at an almost imperceptible rate, until I'm upside down, looking up—or is it down?—at the blastnight sky through the trace-work of ebony branches. Gravity tends to stick to the limbs, following the whims of the onyx matter, but when it fails, a concussive head injury is just as likely as arrival at your destination. Navigating the blastform requires a certain level of bravado, a willingness to take risks. Fools and the stupidly fearless apply within.

As I approach the lookout, I hear hushed voices.

"It's not just the ears," whispers the ill-named Elkhart. "His eyes are buggerish, too."

"Buggerish no a word, an if it wa, you wouldn' wan know wha it mean," says Sitka. "Besides, Lydar's a 'she.'"

"Only just," the boy snorts.

I speak from the shadows. "Why do you mock me? I provide for the clan. Will you brave the bitterwood instead?"

Elkhart's features scrunch up. He blubbers as he sees I have approached silently and tower over them, callused hands on ample hips. The patch on my eye must make me look like a mythical pirate captain from one of Sitka's ancient books. Does the addled boy think I'll force him to walk the plank? It's tempting, I must admit.

Sitka says, "If he prov...provide fo us, we all well an total fucked."

For some reason, *fuck* is one of the few words she pronounces perfectly. She aims a taunting smirk at Elkhart, who glares back at her with furious eyes. Gathering himself, he lashes out at Sitka with the sharpest barb he possesses.

"At least I ain't some dumb cripple what'll never see the bitterwood, much less hunt it."

The lookout is eerily silent, and Sitka's expression freezes. A thorny owl hoots in a distant blastform, and a winsome breeze whistles through the obsidian branches.

I step forward and point a finger at the boy. "Elkhart, go help your granphater with the meat."

"But it's late, and I—" begins the boy.

"Now." My voice is deceptively calm.

Elkhart scampers from the lookout without another word, as

if he's heard this tone from me before and knows better than to risk another word. He's right.

When he's gone, Sitka grimaces down at her shriveled leg.

"Girl—" I begin, realizing that my words are far gentler with my apprentice than anyone else in the clan. I wonder if I'm starting to care, or if perhaps I passed over that rickety bridge a long time ago.

"Don bidder...bodder. Fuck. No wordin working." She runs a hand through her sleek chestnut hair in frustration.

"Hang on." I kneel beside her, taking her small, cool hand in mine. I call up the spirit realm as Sitka does the same. We meet in the middle.

That's much better, she thinks at me with an internal sigh. *Anyway, he's right. It's pretty obvious how useless I am.*

"Hasn't the wolfsbane helped with your leg and hand?" I ask out loud.

Sitka rubs her lifeless leg.

Oh sure. Now it tingles and hurts up here. She slaps her upper thigh. *That helps a lot.* Then she adds, *But I don't mean to be ungrateful.*

"You need to be patient. Roma wasn't built in a blastday."

"An Roma, if still exists, is five thousand, eight hundred widder-widths tha way," she says out loud, pointing east. Numbers are another thing that Sitka's dysphasia-ridden speech produces accurately.

She's very bright, but people underestimate her constantly. The idiots will shout in her face, thinking having a stroke also made her deaf and stupid. It's a little-known fact that strokes can affect children as well as old fuckers like me.

I realize that I'm curling my lip almost imperceptibly, the expression as close to a smile as my face ever approaches. "You know your archaic geography; I'll give you that."

Sitka waves her good hand like a butterfly flitting away.

Concise Atlas of the World, fifty-fourth edition, but I only have seventy pages. The rest is black mold. Lot of good those useless facts will do me, anyway. When the solstice gets here, I'll be purged, ended and maybe forevered.

"You don't know that. Besides, no one alive now has lived through a solstice change. The myths and legends have probably been exaggerated over time. I believe it will be a time of change, but not total upheaval."

I still think I'll be a goner, as Elkhart and his cronies are fond of reminding me.

"Nonsense. You'll be the next shaman of our clan. We need you more than anyone, especially that blowhard fucking little weasel."

I don't know. I still don't have a spirit animal. How will I ever be as good a shaman as you? What the Overs did to you—I don't think I could survive that... Sitka fades off, her gaze soft and distant, as if trying to imagine the unimaginable.

I frown and my healing eye is shot through with a bright twinge of pain. The dreamweed takes the edge off, but a good percentage of the agony still throbs, a constant shamanic drumbeat competing with my thoughts. I finger the clear quartz tower in my pocket. The stone is healing my eye, but its power comes with a price, paid in unrelenting pain.

"You don't need a peri-soul to become a shaman. In fact, you might become a better one without it. Besides, you're stronger than you think."

It's just that I'm too old for a spirit animal to show up in me. What were you, thirteen or fourteen, when yours appeared?

"That's different. I was under duress. The bastard bird was torn from me in a moment of dire need, and—"

Before I can say more, Elkhart is back, panting.

"There's a...there's a couple..."

"Spit it out, boy. Sitka's easier to understand than you, you little fuck." I regret my tone, only because it isn't helping get the facts out any quicker.

"Visit—visitors."

So, my vision in the bitterwood was accurate.

"Yeah. A couple men. Pegram says they're here to see you, Lydarc."

My expression turns even grimmer than usual, and I finger the multicolored crystals that hang from a string around my neck. "Take me to them." My words come out as a snarl; Elkhart takes an involuntary step back. He trips, ending up on his ass. "They're...They're in the meeting room on the lowest level, but I, I—"

"Never mind. Just make sure Sitka gets into her cart and back to her bedform. Can you do that?"

I push past him and down the spiral arm of the long-dead forest behemoth, its crystalline blast structure flickering with sparkling reflected stars as I descend.

At the bottom, the trunk is widest, the walls thick and the exterior rooms windowless and doorless. Openings would only weaken the structure where it most needs support and allow unwanted access to our enemies: animal, man and other.

At a wide oak door, I take a deep breath, fingers tight on the handle.

I force open the heavy door to find two men in the room. They smell of campfire smoke and their cloaks are speckled with many days of accumulated grime and mud. Their shoulders slump ever so slightly with fatigue. To my equal pleasure and disdain, one of them is Wayland.

"Wayland? Rapha? What're you doing here?"

Wayland steps forward. His riot of black dreadlocks, I notice with surprise, is speckled with spots of gray, gleaming like silver fireflies in the lantern blight. His face is as sculptured and handsome as I remember.

Wayland studies the floor. "I need your help, Ly. Cassander's gone. They're both gone, taken by an unseeum. Cassander was forevered, but Eva was only ended, and has a half-life in the underlands. I believe we can bring her back. You're the only one I know who's been there and returned. Will you help us?" He takes my hands in his rough palms almost gently, igniting my senses, just like in the old days.

His face collapses and I'm terrified that he might start to sob. Beat me to death, dig my heart out with a spoon, just don't spout tears in front of me.

"You owe me this, Lydarc."

"Almost anything I would do for you, but this? I just can't. You don't know what it's like down there."

The big man sits with a grunt, slumping into a maplewood chair that creaks in protest at his bulk.

Pegram, the elder, speaks from the shadows. "This is highly unusual, Lydarc. Have you put the clan in danger by inviting these warriors here?"

"I didn't invite them and—"

"I'm no warrior anymore, Overs curse it," interrupts Wayland.

The little man looks Wayland up and down with a frown, obviously noting the sword, bow and quiver, the knives in his belt and leather armor that has, over time, melded to his frame, becoming an even browner second skin.

I lean forward, realizing that irritation is igniting my flashfire temper.

"Please don't interrupt me." I point at Pegram. "Leave us." And then more gently, "Don't worry. No harm will come to the clan."

"Your clan?" Wayland asks when the man is gone. He tilts his head and sneers at me. I consider how I will dispose of his body.

"This is my home now. These people depend on me."

He harrumphs. "As we depended on you until you disappeared without saying goodbye."

"Leaving was not my choice, and you know it. You don't know what you're asking. Think life here is a shitshow? Well, it's a fucking paradise compared to down there. Even if we find her, Eva could be any kind of monster now. Go home and start over. Find a new wife and have more children. It's the only advice I can give."

"But I believe there's a hope for our half-lives, a way to retrieve them."

"I really doubt that. Besides, I'm needed here. There's nothing you could say or do to change my mind while I still have the tribe to feed and defend."

I see a movement in my peripheral vision. Rapha makes the slightest nod of his head.

Wayland groans as he rises. "I knew it was a long bowshot, but I had to try. If your people will allow us to spend the night, we'll be on our way in the morning."

"Of course. Stay as long as you need. I'm sure my apprentice would like to meet you both. She hungers for news."

The other man rises and approaches, controlled power in every movement. Short black hair gleams in the lantern blight. His eyes, always a disturbingly bright shade of blue, glow with a depth I've never been able to fathom. He hasn't aged a blastday since I last saw him.

"Rapha, it's good to see you."

"I will mince no words." His speech is stiff and formal. "You must accompany us to the underlands to restore Wayland's daughter. Your shamanic abilities and peri-soul will shield us from the vagaries of the weather, the egregores and other dangers."

I rub my forehead, where the next migraine is being born. "My blastdays of adventuring are long over. I'm sorry. I can't help you. You've wasted a trip."

"Ah well, it was worth it just to see you again," says Rapha, beaming his charismatic smile. "Besides, Wayland cannot boil water and might have starved had I not agreed to serve as cook."

This, we all agree to be true.

Wayland and Rapha stay several blastdays, and I have to admit that it's good to hear the old stories and catch up on the lives of my former compatriots. Sitka enjoys the animated tales that Wayland spouts, sitting patiently to listen, urging him on, until I'm forced to interrupt them for meals. As usual, Rapha listens more than he speaks.

Finally, it's time for me to restock our larders. The coho are running in the Luckiamute. I stride from the blastform with my nets and spear over one shoulder, looking back at my home. That it had once been called the Valley of the Giants, I can well believe. Still giants, but now bowed into their crouching, twisted forms by a centuries-old Over blast, the old-growth Douglas firs now resemble rocky outcrops more than the vibrant, living things they once were.

In the morning blight the blastform retains some of its tree-like qualities, even though it's now as shiny and impervious as onyx. The split branches spread out from the shredded central trunk, curling and wrapping around themselves like the locks of a giant black goddess, providing the intricate passageways and chambers that the Siletzon have adapted into our homes.

Sitka waves at me. Wayland and Rapha have lowered her cart and are pulling her out onto a grassy hillock, where she will no doubt have them recounting their adventures until I return.

I'm in a daydream on my way back, remembering the (almost) good old times with Wayland, so I'm not too surprised when my feet stop of their own accord.

I'm home. Except home is missing. The other blastforms rise in the distance, like haze-shrouded, arthritic giants, but the haven of my clan is gone.

Did I take a wrong turn after the river? This is the right trail, I know it. Confusion grows to dawning horror as I turn, dropping my catch and running with abandon.

As I approach, my fear morphs into screaming reality. Around me lie shards of curled blastform and reddish pieces of flesh and shredded bone. There is Master Pegram's pipe, sitting on a ragged stump of meat, but it's a woman's naked hip, not Pegram's shriveled lips on which it lies. My own words come back to me, how I assured the elder that no harm would come to the clan.

I would scream, but what good would that do me, or Pegram, or the tribe?

There in the brambles lies Elkhart's head, his expression less twisted and sour in his end than it had been in life. It's almost peaceful now, as if the bitterness leaked out of him with his blood.

Pieces of the people and onyx shards of blastform decorate the ground. A breeze, ripe with the grim perfume that draws carrion, assaults my nose. The carrion-eaters themselves, the giant valley vultures, gather above, circling and gauging when I will leave so their grand feast can begin.

I lean over to throw up, then stand, shuddering, shocked and disbelieving at the utter destruction that surrounds me.

A sudden, even more fearful thought occurs to me.

Sitka.

I search until almost highburn, but can find no trace of the girl's body, or even pieces that look like they once belonged to her.

Another thought then creeps over my addled brain, like a slow-moving miasmic sludge. Only *my* clan's home was attacked. Only *my* home.

"Wayland, you bastard," I yell at the bitter sky. "The Overs must have tracked you here." Then softly, I make a deadly vow, "If you still live, I will forever you, using the most painfully protracted method I can devise."

I stare off into the distance, then look down, searching for tracks. I find a partially obscured double-wheeled track that leads me into the dense, brush-shrouded forest. There are more than two sets of footprints, but it's jumbled. Are those the tracks of oversized boots? Did someone else survive the blast? The trail leads me east, the way I came when I found the Siletz Valley many seasons ago. Back when I actually believed I could escape my past to find peace.

3

LEISIL, BEFORE

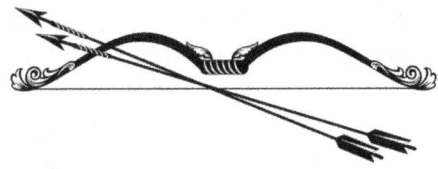

But the stars that marked our starting fall away. We must go
deeper into greater pain, for it is not permitted that we stay

— DANTE ALIGHIERI, *INFERNO*

L eisil killed for the first time when she was only four
seasons old. Though it was an accident, the Great
Balance does not consider intent, but only result, when
adjudicating the master ledger of guilt, forgiveness, accountabil-
ity, and self-blame. So, that blastday, the count was forgiveness,
zero, self-blame, two. Why two? Well, there was the lie that
followed the heinous act to consider, or at least so Leisil judged.

Her brothers were the hunters, stalking off proudly with their
bows and knives, bringing home bloody squirrel carcasses, dead
rabbits and buckets full of solfish from their nighttime fishing
expeditions. She wasn't invited and had no desire to spend the
evening being prey to mosquitems and the other, larger after-
dusk monsters she imagined must populate the woods. Her
brothers could have it; the harvesting, the butchering, all of it.

It began for her like any other blastday on the farm. Life was sweet and free. There were no useless afternoon naps or lessons to deal with, as yet. There was the curiosity of rain filtered through sunblight, the lamb-shaped clouds and the big red barn with its never-ending interests and puzzles, not to mention the heady scents of sweating hay, ripe manure, and cooking silage. The animals were her favorites; even the young bullywinx, who chased her, as yet hornless head lowered, from the courtyard, or the pearly gosems with their constant ruffled-feather honking gossip.

In the loft was the litter of semi-feral bidles, who had to be the cutest creatures in all of creation, though to Leisil, at this point, creation comprised the tiny farm, a stretch of languid river and a dome of cyan sky.

The mater bidle's bidden babies counted seven, three in black, three in black and white, and one the purest white. The white bidden was Leisil's favorite, as it followed her around the farmyard, mewing and purring and pouncing in an amusing way on every shadow.

Even early on, Leisil fell prey to egotism, or so she remembered. Later, she realized that the source of her sin was only the need to be wanted, or, if the skies were to open and toss forth miracles, loved. This blastday, her need turned from vague unease to disaster, as she flew aside the scritching, whining screen door of the farmhouse. It opened into the enclosed porch with its usual off-key squeal of protest and, unknown to Leisil, the tiny bidden followed her in.

Inside, her ears pricked up at the muffled conversation between her mater and visiting uncle. She paused at the heavy oak door to listen.

Her uncle was speaking. "She's smart and athletic enough to get in, eh? I sense the talent in her. Even though she's as yet too young for the trials, you need to start her training now. Competition is fierce these blastdays. Five children you have, Urpine; one girl is obese and, let's face it, lazy. The other lacks the drive and unfortunately, the last two are male. She's your best chance."

"Don't let Artur hear you say that. The boys are his pride."

"And does Artur know he's not really her father?"

Leisil heard the rustle of fabric and barely audible words.

"Hush! He must never know."

"Then the decision is made for you. It will only become more obvious what she is as she gets older."

Leisil heard her mater sigh in exasperation. "All right, but what will it actually mean for us to have one in the Resistance? Do you really think it'll get me out of this contract, or off this miserable cesspool of a farm?"

"No—at least not at first, but if she agrees to enter the training—"

"She will go if I tell her to go."

Her uncle chuckled. "Leisil has a mind of her own, in case you haven't noticed. In that, she's much like you. But if she were to fall in battle—"

"There's a bonus?"

"Quite a substantial one."

Leisil fumed. Even though she was too young to understand much of what was said, she could already sense that her mater and uncle were planning for her a future she probably wouldn't enjoy.

In childish anger, she pulled open the door and entered the kitchen, slamming it behind her. But something didn't sound or feel right. The huge wooden door closed softly, with a muffled thump, instead of the usual satisfying bang.

Looking behind her, she was forced to suffer the most terrifying sight of her young life. The baby bidden squirmed and mewled on the cold tile floor, in obvious agony. She'd caught the poor thing in the closing door, and now it was dying, right there in front of her. She could have leaned down to help it, she could have called out, but instead, in panic, she closed the door against the creature's misery and ran. To the girls' bedroom she fled, to hide under the covers of the bunk bed until her life was over, or someone told her that what had just happened hadn't really occurred, and she was just having a bad, no, a terrible dream. That never happened.

Instead, her dad came to her bedside later and asked if she wanted to come down to dinner and was she not feeling well, and almost nonchalantly, did she know anything about the dead bidden baby on the back porch?

Leisil wanted to die, but instead she said calmly, "No Papa, I didn't do nothing. I'm just not hungry right now."

She didn't remember what her dad said then. In fact, she didn't remember the next few seasons of her life. It was as if that time was lost in a fog of sorrow, regret and unwishing.

It was her first time ending another being, and it would stay with her throughout her long, troubled life

4

LYDARC, NOW

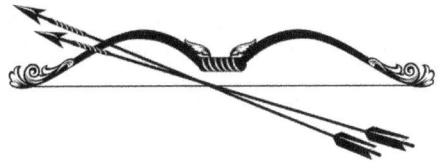

Necessity is the motherfucker of invention.

— WAYLAND PETERS, AS QUOTED BY SITKA
SANGASHEE IN HER PERSONAL JOURNAL

I follow the trail all blastday, having expected to catch up to them sooner than this. How can Wayland and Rapha haul a poorly constructed cart with sticking wheels so quickly? What's gotten into them? What're they running from?

But I know what is making Wayland move like he's being chased by a giant russet bear. It's because he knows when I catch him, I'll forever him.

What happens now, I blame on the fact that I'm hot, tired, midgebitten and just fucking pissed off at life. There's no other logical reason for them to get the jump on me. I'm too good a tracker, but somehow, I've lost the trail. It's just dawning on me why when an incredible weight hits my shoulders. I find my face in the forest detritus, breathing in dust.

A voice says, "Now, just calm down, Lydarc."

"Waywan, you ocksucker, I gonna foweva you." My words are muffled by leaves and fir needles. Wayland has landed on top of me and is trying to hold me down, but I twist like the Overs have me by the gonads (if I had them, though it makes no sense to me why you would want to store your fragile organs on the outside). I turn on him, reaching for my knife, but his big brown hand gets there first. We roll in the dirt, me kicking, yelling, and biting for all I'm worth. Wayland seems only to want to hold me off, as if waiting for something else to happen. We pause, both struggling to get control of the weapon. For a second, we balance there, teetering between the end of one of us.

"Wait, Lydarc, you fucking idiot. It wasn't the Overs, and it wasn't me."

I spit up a disbelieving grunt. "Right. So, who then? Who else knew you were coming here besides Rapha? I know he'd never betray us. You sure did it this time, didn't you, leading the Overs right to the only home I've ever known, and sending a lot of good, innocent folk to their ends."

I finally wrest control of the knife while I distract him with these words that matter little to me. He's probably already seen my intention by the dark rage in my eyes.

I thrust the blade, but something huge and furry swipes my arm aside. Hot breath that reeks of rotting meat and, incongruously, ripe gosemberries, washes across my face. A ragged roar deafens my sensitive ears.

A giant russet bear towers over me and says sweetly in the voice of a young girl, "Are you done, Lydarc? Ready to listen to reason, or do I have to show you what I can really do with this body?"

It's Sitka's voice, but without the distorting dysphasia. So surprised am I that Sitka has found her spirit animal at last that I drop the knife. And what a spirit animal it is!

"Sitka, that's incredible! How'd you do that? And she seems so—"

"Obedient? Yes, she's nothing like your beast. She's actually a part of me, instead of trying to tear me apart, as your lovely falcon seems inclined to do. It happened at the blastform. You said it might take a trauma to bring it out. I just didn't think so many of our people might need to die to..."

The big bear's voice breaks. A single tear trickles from one beady brown eye.

"I'm so sorry, girl. If I'd known this asshole was going to bring the Overs down on us, I'd have ended him as soon as he showed up." I glower at Wayland, who seems oblivious as he struggles to his feet.

The bear sits back on its haunches and puts its front paws together, as if in prayer. It's charming, if you consider six hundredweight of deadly force "cute."

"That's just it," says the bear, gesticulating with its paws in a very unbear-like fashion, "It wasn't the Overs. I saw it. It was as if a star fell from the sky and hit the blastform dead center. There were no winged monsters, or however the Overs are supposed to look. No attackers at all."

"I can't believe it."

Wayland, who has regained his feet and is rubbing the spot on his side where I kicked him, says. "Believe it. I've never seen anything like it, but it wasn't an Over attack. I'm sure of it."

"Are you saying it was just a coincidence? A natural phenomenon? Some kind of cosmic karma raining down on me for all the harm I've caused in my life?"

Wayland gazes at me and his rich brown eyes soften. Is that pity? I can't handle that from him. Not in our dark past and surely not now.

When he speaks again, his tone is resigned. "Lydarc, there are many, far more violent assholes in this world than you, and fucking stars aren't falling on *them*. Besides, I never saw you end someone without absolute necessity, or do it for fun, as some I've seen."

I suddenly giggle, and the sound is shocking, even to me. The bear tips its head curiously, causing me to laugh even louder.

Wayland frowns deeply. "Lydarc, are you all right?"

Holding my sides, I say, "Ahh, I was thinking, as I was tracking you guys, that you were running like you were being chased by a giant russet bear. But it turns out you were being towed by one instead."

My mirth morphs into a sob that I quickly suppress. Grief sneaks up on you at the most inconvenient of moments.

Something else occurs to me. "Why were you running?"

"At first, we didn't know if more attacks were coming," says Wayland. "I just wanted to get Sitka to safety. Until a bit ago, we didn't know who was chasing us, either. Sitka sent her spirit animal back and found out it was you, and we set up this trap, knowing how you can jump to conclusions and be hotheaded, at times."

"At times?"

Wayland examines his shirt where a seam has split from the struggle.

Sitka the bear says, "Well, the truth is, your actions are pretty consistently rash. You tend to react without thinking, and your temper is incendiary. But you know that, right?"

If Wayland said this right now, I would take his head off. But Sitka is my friend, my apprentice, and she is stating fact, after all. I mumble a reply that's unintelligible, even to me.

Rubbing a dirty hand on my sweaty, grit-encrusted forehead, I say, "All right. I'll put off ending Wayland until we can find out more about this attack."

Wayland snorts, turning it into a muffled cough, but says nothing. I ignore him, for now.

"In the meantime, Sitka, you need to return to your own body. I've warned you what can happen if you spend too much time as your spirit animal. You need to take it slow, especially at first."

The russet bear lets out an extended, dyspeptic burp. "I don't know. Would it be so bad to end up like this permanently?" The bear glances back at its massive hind legs. A pan-sized paw wriggles its deadly claws in an endearing manner. "To run, to be free...You have no idea how wonderful it is."

"I can't believe what I'm hearing. Surely you have listened to nothing I taught you. You wouldn't last a fortblight, girl. The spirit animal cannot sustain your consciousness forever. Returning to your body to renew it is essential. Are you so eager to be ended?"

The bear lowers its head. "I know. I'm sorry, and you're right; it's time to take a break."

As I watch, the air flickers around the giant animal and the form shrinks. I'm not sure if I imagine it, but a series of creatures flash into being and out again as fast as I can catch sight of them: a stag, a wolverine, a giant eagle, a fox, and finally, a tiny tundra mouse. I'm stunned.

A female voice from the trees says meekly, "I'm ova here."

Rapha erupts from the brush, pulling Sitka forward in her cart. She looks tired and, if possible, even more frail than before.

My mouth is hanging open. "How did you do that? Somehow, you progressed through a succession of spirit animals in an instant. Is that even possible?"

"Apparently so," says Rapha. "I watched her do it the first time." His proud, glowing expression turns Sitka's cheeks red. Is the stupid girl falling in love with him already? Oh well, everyone does, I guess, until they really get to know him. Back in the blast-day, Rapha was known for his philandering as much as his shamanic talent.

My thoughts return with wonder to her spirit animal transformation.

"Can you take any of those forms?"

"I haven't figure tha ou yet. I alays end up as the bear, bu working on it."

I've only ever had one spirit animal, and mine is far worse than having none. "Yours is obviously under your command, as I fear mine will never be."

Even though she's still a blushing teenager at heart, I'm

forced to revise my opinion of Sitka as a shaman-in-training. She may no longer be my apprentice, but my teacher.

"Only one drawn...drawback. I don have physica strength to be awake while spiri animal is. Mus be ina trance."

"That's all right. Preserving your energy in a trance state may allow you more time as the bear."

We camp for the night in a wood I've never hunted, but it doesn't take me long to bring down a brace of conies. Wayland insists that's what you call a couple of rabbits. Strange man. While the rabbits cook on a makeshift spit over the fire, I place a few root tubers in the coals and nibble on the ripe huckleberries we gathered for dessert. As I cook, I analyze our situation. We all left the blastform in a rush, with limited supplies except for what I carry with me and a few things Sitka had in her cart, which are mostly books. We'll need to find a town to stock up on supplies, then decide our next move. I'm lost for ideas. This trip into the underlands seems dangerous and foolish beyond imagining. Yet, what else are we going to do?

Sitka sits beside me, reading one of the books she found in her cart.

"It's lucky you always have a few books with you," I say. "At least you were able to save those. I'm sorry about the rest. I know what they meant to you."

Closing her book, she touches my arm, and her words come into my head.

I've read those books so many times I can quote every line in here.

She points emphatically at her head.

Have you thought more about taking me to the Fallen City, to the library there?

"Forget that journey. The route to the Fallen City is a nasty, rough slog that no one makes willingly. It's many widder-widths across Over-blasted terrain, with minions, egregores, timesmears and underland breaches everywhere."

And you think I couldn't make it? I can feel the heat of her indignation.

"No, that's not it at all. I'm not even sure that *I* could make it. And there's no guarantee that this ancient library is still intact. Even if it is, the books have most likely turned to dust by now. I should never have told you about it."

But they're preserved better in dry climates, aren't they? I wish you had explored more when you found it.

I grunt. "Recreational reading wasn't exactly a priority for me back then."

Wayland steps up, and perhaps seeing my thoughtful expression, asks, "Are you reconsidering our journey into the underlands?"

I bluster, "Are you kidding? No. Forget it. No, no, no. It's out of the question."

I learn a new lesson: The more you vehemently deny a thing, the more likely the bloody thing is bound to happen. They both look at me with wide eyes, as if I hold the keys to their happiness. I rub my face and sigh.

"All right. But Sitka stays behind."

"No!" she cries. "You gotta le me go wi you."

I give her the look, and she's silent, no doubt planning to work on me as we travel. I'd say there was no chance in hell that she'll talk me into taking her with us, but recently I've learned to keep my mouth shut.

After dinner, Wayland tells me he needs to see a man about a horse, then he disappears into the brush. Normally, I would take this statement literally and wonder where he was going to find a horse trader out here, but I've learned the true meaning of some of Wayland's odd sayings over the seasons. He merely means he needs to take a piss.

I spend a restless night on a fir-bough bed with no blanket and the cold seeping through my leather and fur layers.

I wake as dawn peeks through the trees, a mellow soft blight that paints the edges of the evergreens the color of warm honey butter. With a yawn, I look around to check on my companions. They're all here, huddled against the cold, still asleep.

Except for one. Wayland is missing.

A rushing noise spills out of the woods, like a hundred horsemen or a tornado bearing down on us. The wind makes projectiles of the leaves and twigs it carries on its foul breath. As soon as I see what's at the eye of the stinking storm, I turn to the others, yelling, "Close your eyes unless you want to lose one!"

"Wha?" says Sitka, her face a jumble of questions as she rises groggily from her cart. Rapha is a little slower to rise, but quicker to grasp the situation. He turns his head away.

"Just do it," I say. "I'll take care of this."

Rapha grabs Sitka's hand and I can't hear what he's saying, but she too turns away.

A horseman storms forward, pulling up his ink-black mount with the barest touch to the reins. The powerful animal sets his back legs, skidding to a halt in the dirt. Dust billows up and there is silence as the cloud settles.

"There's nothing for you here, Dullahan," I say, striding forward with more bravado than I feel. "You can't take from me sanity I no longer maintain, and I've already lost an eye this blast-week. Two is just beyond the pale, don't you think?"

The Dullahan grunts. The sound erupts like a sickening burp from his seeping neck. His mouth, attached to his severed head—which resides in the crook of his arm—is perfectly still, the eyes closed, as if his head is napping.

The neck speaks again, a single word, spluttering up through the spouting blood.

"Wayland."

My face loses all color. I can feel it draining away as the ground floats up toward me. With all my will, I resist the urge to feint, to fall away from this moment and this life, just pretending that it never happened.

"No." I croak the word but it lacks all credibility, whereas the voice of the Dullahan is undeniably certain. The powerful steed rises on his back legs and screams like a banshee. His livery appears to be made of mercury, liquid silver swirling and sparking as he shakes his massive head. Silver spittle sprays from his muzzle in slow motion, setting the weeds to sizzling flame as it hits the ground.

The Dullahan unfurls a whip made from a human skeleton. He snaps it and the air crackles with the sound of popping vertebrae. I'm tempted to mention the impossibility of this; that a spine without tendons and ligaments won't hold together under such abuse, but I realize that there is no time left for my useless observations of what should and shouldn't be possible in this fucked-up world. I have not even a second to spare. Wayland is dying right now.

Then, suddenly, there it is. It's a timesmear, but it's one that I can control. It's as if I'm just now remembering a forgotten skill, one that I possessed all along. It's that easy. Almost. I reach into my pack, pulling a worn lava pebble from my medicine bag.

Life's great achievements are sometimes born of dire need. That's what Rapha once told me. This is the moment I discover the true nature of time and the power of probabilities, and my life changes, both future and past.

The stone takes me to the veil in the lava caves, and from there I go back in Wayland's time. I choose a different path for him from the many possibilities offered by the veil.

Unfortunately for Wayland, I'm new to this whole business, and I miscalculate ever so slightly.

5

LEISIL, BEFORE

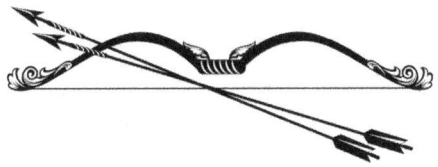

The life of a Resistance fighter was not an easy one. Though he shared little of his early time in that regime, others have related to me some of it, and it's a miracle he survived at all, much less thrived, in that cruel, militaristic environment.

— SITKA SANGASHEE, *EVOLUTION OF THE SHAMAN MASTER*

Leisil paused on the steps of the academy. She stood where her mater had abruptly dropped her off, letting the girl slide from the back of their aging mare Fioner, saying, "Find your own way to class. I've got errands to run in the village."

Even at eight seasons, Leisil was capable and self-assured, but the vast stone building was daunting. Ionic columns framed a massive entry porch. She counted fourteen wide granite steps, each of which she had trouble reaching, especially since the support rails were widder-widths away and she was stuck to the expanse of open steps whose rise and run didn't align to the length of her young legs. Had this school been built for the children of giants?

As she struggled at the heavy double doors, the left side opened next to her and a tall figure in a floor-length cape strode through. Allowing her only a quick glance, the gray-haired man rushed past her, saying, "You're late. Get to your classform now or face detention. You don't want that, trust me."

"But where—"

The man continued down the steps, ignoring her.

Musty darkness met her as she slipped through the closing door. Leisil stood with a frown until her eyes adjusted to the gloom. Before her stretched a long hall with doors running all along one side.

Which one?

It turned out it didn't matter. She opened the first door she came to, only to find that the entire side of the building had been blasted away by the Overs, and all the doors opened onto a muddy, debris-littered field filled with dirty canvas tents. Shaggy horses grazed, hobbled in the distance, and hooded minion-finder falcons grasped wooden perches. Bales of hay supported rough targets that must be for archery practice. A rusty two-cycler sat buried in the nettles and twistweed beside the nearest tent. It looked as if its wheels hadn't turned in a very long time.

Several children Leisil's age and a bit older stood in crooked lines before an adult, the only large person in view. The adult was yelling at them in a bombastic, echoing voice. It was deep and harsh, a voice that threatened harm and demanded obedience with every syllable.

Leisil rushed over and took her place at the back of the group, trying to become invisible. It didn't work.

"You there. Do you know what happens if you're late to a battle with the minions? I'll tell you what. *You die.* Got it?"

"Yes, Madam," squeaked Leisil, her voice sounding weak and pathetic, even to herself.

"What was that? Do I hear a baby sprink? Or maybe it's a bitty bidden that has wandered onto the field by accident?"

Her tone had become farcical, teasing, but Leisil wasn't fooled.

The others snickered, turning to look at Leisil as if she were dog shit on their shoes.

"Or perhaps you were headed for the kitchens. We need another grunt. Only warriors are allowed to train out here with us."

Leisil was getting angry. At this point, she had yet to learn that her temper never seemed to get her anywhere she wanted to go. Had she ever truly learned that lesson?

"My name's Leisil. I'm a warrior, and I'll fight any fucking one of you to prove it!"

The drill sergeant chuckled, but it had a tight, controlled sound.

"Well then, Borcine, perhaps you would like to show our young recruit what to expect if, on the off chance, she lasts the blastweek."

A much older, stout teenage girl—or boy, Leisil couldn't be sure which at this point—stepped in front of her. She looked down at Leisil with a neutral expression, as if she'd performed this duty many times before and found it tedious.

Leisil, to her credit, didn't flinch, but stood her ground with her chin up. Borcine pounded this protruding feature first, with amazing speed for one so large.

Leisil found herself on the ground, and tasted mud and blood. She crawled to her feet, only to be hit again before she could even raise her fists. Blights flashed behind her eyelids as she went down again. This time, she wisely stayed down. The sounds of cruel laughter faded to silence.

When she came to, the field was eerily quiet. She was alone. Where had everyone gone? Had there been a timesmear? She didn't think so. She couldn't remember anything happening twice.

She struggled to her feet and wandered into the largest tent, where she found her fellow students finishing their dinner. They ignored her. When she walked stiffly to the back to get her own food, she found that there was nothing left save a lone, stale biscuit and a few pieces of moldy cheese. Taking the meager fare, she turned to face the room, searching for an empty table. Finding none, she went over to the tent wall and slunk to the ground, trying to be inconspicuous as she ate. It didn't work.

"Back for more, are you, runt?" Borcine stood over her, grinning inanely.

"I don't want to fight you," said Leisil.

The bigger girl cackled. "Ain't that convenient, since you don't seem to be much good at it, eh? Let's get some things straight, right off. These is the rules and you're gonna abide to them strict like, get me?"

Leisil had no time to answer as the girl continued. "You eats last, shits last and sleeps last. You'll be up first and you'll be doing the morning chores afore anybody else. Got it? And you're gonna be my personal bitch. You'll make my bed and empty my piss pot every morn, and anything else I might be desiring. Yeah?"

When Leisil said nothing, Borcine kicked her.

Leisil was tired and frustrated. Was this going to be her life from now on? "All right. Just leave me alone so I can get this slop down."

Borcine eyed the rubbery biscuit in Leisil's hand. With a deft strike that a journeyman kicker would have been proud of, she knocked it away. Leisil watched it roll across the floor, collecting dirt as it went.

"Don't be littering, now, you stupid cunt. Pick that up and eat it."

Leisil had two brothers, so she'd learned early when to fight and when to fold. This time, for a change, she chose wisely. With a sigh, she crawled over and recovered the biscuit, cleaning it as best she could on her sleeve. When she took a bite, it tasted a little gritty, but she was too hungry to let even dirt go to waste.

Borcine turned away, apparently bored with the game, at least for now.

Leisil watched the bully waddle away, wondering what joys would greet her tomorrow.

She didn't know how or when, but Leisil knew as certainly as the fact that life sucked until you met your end that, one blastday, Borcine would pay for every humiliation, slight and bruise. And she would pay with interest.

6

WAYLAND, NOW

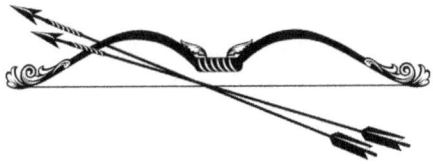

Mostly it is loss which teaches us about the
worth of things.

— ARTHUR SCHOPENHAUER

I wake gradually, my head throbbing. Shadows flicker and
dance around a robust campfire, but darkness owns the rest
of the world. I struggle to release the tightness in my shoulders. After a while, I realize what's causing the constriction; I'm
tied to a tree. I groan, eliciting a chuckle from my captor, who
hunches over the fire, his features hidden. The man-shaped thing
is massive, bald, totally naked and covered in brown stains I hope
are dirt.

"Letth thee," croaks the creature. "Are we in the mood for cold
cutth, or perchanth a leg of man with mint thauth?" It chortles,
then chokes. After a protracted coughing fit, it spits up what looks
like a human finger bone dripping in a pool of viscous yellow bile.

I struggle frantically against my bonds.

"Ah, don't botha, little man. I know my knotth. You won't be leavin' here, exthept in my thit." The beast cackles again. He turns and I can see what he's been digging at the fire with; a wide-bladed knife as big as one of my swords. It too is splattered in umber, and I feel my resolve that the blotches are merely dirt begin to slip away.

"Wendigo." I croak, hearing the hopelessness in my voice, a cavernous pit growing in my stomach.

"Oh, aye, thatth the nathty epithet with which thome aim to hurt me, but I'm thenthitive, you know. I ain't nothin' but an innothent fellow in dethperate need of a good meal. I won't be keepin' you long, mind. I got thimpathy, you know. Just got ta keep you alive ath long ath I thtill got edible bitth. Keepth the meat freth longer, ya unnerthtand? I'll be havin' you over for dinner an' breakfast too, if you geth my meaning."

Suddenly, the beast turns, rising to an impressive height, then bends down to stick its face right in mine. A gust of rotting carcass breath makes me gag. Eyes like buried lava pyroclasts smolder in deep pits of swollen flesh. Its lips...well, there are none, just ragged tatters of blackish skin ringing the gaping cavity of its mouth, as if it has chewed off its own lips in a fit of hunger. A smile splits the chasm and rows of needle-sharp teeth jut in all their rotting, yellow glory.

The beast man lifts an arm, and I notice just how skeletally thin it is. Mottled gray skin stretches tight over very little flesh but shows to good effect a panoply of jutting bones. It moves languidly, as if in no great hurry. The arm comes around: too late, I realize it's the one that holds the oversized knife.

With a frown of supreme concentration, and the tip of a wine-colored tongue just peeking out of its ragged mouth, the wendigo lifts the weapon and brings it down with the accuracy of a master butcher to my arm, severing it neatly at the elbow. It falls with a plop to the dirt.

I scream.

I wake some indeterminate time after dawn to an incredible

throbbing in my forearm. Which is impossible, because I can clearly see my blackened arm smoking on a spit over the fire.

Staring wide-eyed and disbelieving, with drool dripping from my open mouth, some part of my hindbrain still functions, as if I am observing all this from a safe distance. I note the tourniquet above my stump, and the dirty rags that have been haphazardly wrapped around the wound.

Oh great, He's trying to keep me alive. What luck.

Thankfully, I lose consciousness again. When I wake, I think I hear familiar voices but decide I'm hallucinating. For a while, I spend my thoughts on figuring out what part of me will become dinner next. Or was it breakfast time now? Perhaps brunch. What body part goes best with champagne? I giggle.

"I think he's coming around. Rapha, hand me the willow bark and poppy seed tincture."

Now I'm sure it's a hallucination. That was Lydarc's voice I just imagined. I open my eyes and note with horror that there's dark blood everywhere. The headless corpse of the wendigo sprawls next to me on the ground, sporting three arrows in a neat pattern at the center-left of its chest. I start and struggle, trying desperately to wriggle away from the grisly thing.

"Sitka, please get rid of the corpse. It's upsetting our patient."

I finally exhale, realizing the wendigo is beyond forevered and can no longer cause me any harm—except for the memories I will harbor forever. I watch distractedly as the russet bear drags the stiffening body into the woods, batting the head along with one paw.

"It's all right, Way, you're gonna be fine. Drink this. You'll feel better in a bit."

"No, I won't." I rasp. I look down at my arm. Still missing.

Lydarc gives me her best almost-smile. "Well, at least it's your right arm you lost. You're left-handed, as I recall."

"No, no. I'm right-handed. I mean, I *was*." I know I must have the empty-eyed look of someone beyond rational thought, as, of course, I am.

"Your bedside manner could use some honing, I think."

I turn my head slowly to see Rapha kneeling on the other side, grimacing at Lydarc.

She raises her hands. "Well, what am I supposed to say?"

Rapha sighs deeply. "I do not think it matters. He probably will not remember this, anyway. He is in shock."

Rapha is wrong. I remember. I remember every moment of it, and I'm sure it will constitute the bulk of my nightmares for the rest of my life.

The bear returns and looks down at us with a curious tilt of its head, asking, "Is he going to be all right?" When Lydarc nods cautiously, the bear asks, "What was that hideous thing back at the wood?"

"What, the Dullahan? Oh, they're Irish in origin, I think, of the genus *gnomis demonica*. It's said that they speak the name of a person who is about to die. If you look him in the face, he will take your sanity and one eye."

The bear nods her massive head. "So that's how you knew Wayland was in danger. But then you disappeared. You just vanished. Then we were here, and the wendigo was dead. I thought I was in the weirdest timesmear I've ever experienced."

Lydarc frowns. "I'm not exactly sure, but we ran out of time, so I had to make more. I can't explain it right now, but it has to do with probabilities. It's something Rapha was trying to teach me when I studied shamanism with him back in the day."

Rapha says, with a broad smile, "Finally, you understand. You have come into your power."

Lydarc frowns, rubbing her forehead. "It doesn't feel like that. It feels like I just cost Wayland his arm. I was too late, and now I lack the reserves to go back and try again. And too much time has passed, anyway. History is set."

"You saved his life," says the bear. "Try to see the brighter side, just once."

"No thanks. I think I'll stick to the dark. It's a lot less glaring. Besides, optimism is for nincompoops and the hopelessly naïve."

The bear, shaking her head, says, "Can't you heal him like you did your eye?"

My hopes rise, then fall like an avalanche as Lydarc frowns.

"I don't think so. When I healed my eye, I had something to work with. His arm is gone. Eaten. I can't heal what no longer exists."

As Lydarc's potion takes effect, I'm feeling better. A lot better. Tiny, winged unicorns cavort around Lydarc's head. They're wearing saddles, and in the saddles are even tinier buxom naked fairies, each with a different color hair, ranging from purple to puce to incarnadine. They wave at me in unison, like toy princesses waving to their subjects.

I try to wave back, but something is constraining my arm. I look down, only to reel back in horror. A giant crocodile has my arm in its mouth and is crunching away, working its way up toward my shoulder.

I scream.

7

LYDARC, NOW

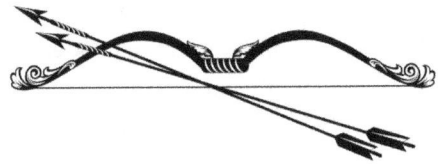

This awareness has been described in many ways over the eons of man. It may be called vision, or inner sight, or even witchcraft by the misinformed. The spirit journey of the shaman opens them to a larger reality, where dreams take the leap from impossible to merely improbable.

— SITKA SANGASHEE, *A SHAMAN'S JOURNEY*

I am Lydarc, the shadow shaman, the warrior who fights no more. I sink below my surface into the sparkling astral lake. A million bubbles boil up from the ebony water, each one containing its own sun, stars, and eternity. I'm gloating over my facility with the spirit world, when gaseous indigestion distracts me. Welling up within my guts is a foul breath that needs to be released, or I will surely explode. The pressure of its hate is more than even the water's massive weight. The two-headed falcon rips open my abdomen and tears out and up with a screech of agony and rage, amid a cloud of my spreading blood. He swims to the surface, swift as a harpy seal, and vaults into the sky. Soon the vile bird is tiny, just a fading speck on my spirit vision that I would as soon forget.

"Good riddance, you worthless avian curse, you plague-infested cock-a-doodle-doo-doo fucker," I scream, but my not-so-witty curses are gargled through blue blight and drowned beneath the ancient waters.

Turning from my senseless rage and diving deep, I inhale liquid probability. It forms me, heals me and forces me to take on its shape, which is nothing and infinity, sprinkled with everything in between, all bound tightly and neatly in my own sweetly wound Gordian knot. Whatever is and could be and that which was, unfortunately, swirls and swiggles and naggles inside the maelstrom of my tumbled thoughts. I toss and turn, resisting the inevitable, as I always do. But it takes me. As it always does. The knot falls asunder, revealing a cluster of former and future probabilities. I choose one.

Evening's blight wanes, and it's storming as if the weeping stepmother from hell has come to call and long outlived her unwelcome. Between sobs of thunder, she bitches about the muddy footprints, while throwing blightning barbs at our dancing retreat. The plain of tall grass is weeping wet and bright with reflected blight, but it's angled, bowing to the coming dark. Even the sun is giving up on our sorry asses.

We're running, panting and grunting, from the grundle, a big fat farting cow whose aroma precedes her. She's too close for comfort in any sane person's reckoning, except perhaps for the baby grundle, who must have no sense of smell at all.

"Way, wha tre furk?" I yell unintelligibly between panicked gasps, but somehow, Wayland always understands me. Mud patties fly and rain splatters as we barely evade the rampaging bovine and her offspring.

This vision occurs before I meet Wayland, which makes it doubly strange, since I have also not yet been introduced to a grundle at this point in my, so far, sad and pathetic life.

"This way," he yells, after he's already turned away and left me with the massive-chested beast painfully close on my heels. I make a jarringly abrupt adjustment in my direction, and my ankle twists beyond its accepted peraminters. "No, no, no," says Wayland, the teacher, in my head, rapping my knuckles with a metaphorical stick. "It's parameters, you daft, silly bitch."

Wayland of this present grasps my arm and pulls me out from under the rampaging hooves of the angry mother grundle, who is so stupid—or smart, she doesn't even pause but runs on and away in a cloud of stink and sticky flying clumps of mud. Her baby trundles past, his little legs giving everything they've got to escape the alien threat and reach the safety and succor of his mother's teat. Despite my pain and disbelief at surviving, I giggle.

"He's so cute! I want one."

"No, you don't. They only smell worse as they get older. Let's get out of here, before mama develops an intellect."

"Is that likely?"

"Perhaps, in an eon or so, but I doubt it. A prey animal is not predisposed to evolving discerning thought, or the ability to avoid danger. If they were, us predators would starve."

"Ouch!" I stumble as my ankle screams in outrage at the disrespect I've lately shown it.

"Come here. Let's have a look at that." He leans down and twists my ankle, none too gently.

"Ow! What're you doing?"

"Yes, definitely sprained, but you'll heal. Can you call up one of your probabilities and get us out of here?"

"My what?"

"Oh, fuck. You may be here too soon, or I'm too late…"

Wayland frowns as his body separates into strips, falling apart into sparkles and threads, delicate waves of snot spreading upward on the electric air. The ribbons of wasn't and couldn't dance away willy-nilly on the chaotic breeze. Frizzled shreds of long abandoned dreams.

I'm alone.

The world is dark, darker than it can be. Gradually, blight

seeps in. My eyes are level with the sand, which goes on forever. It's a desert, but not a desert of hidden life, as I have known and loved them, but one devoid of everything, screaming for a hope or future that is no longer willing to enter the room.

The ultimate end is near, but ever so slightly in the past.

Then, Simply Waites stands over me, grinning inanely.

"Waites, what're you doing here? You haven't been born yet." His first name is John, but since he was a toddler, he's been called Simply. The Overs know why, and I don't ask.

I rise to a sitting position with a groan and sway, scratching my scalp. It always itches in dry air. "Or maybe you're long dead. Perhaps we're all ghosts in this time."

I speak clearly, but my words come out far away and long gone. I'm dull and separated from myself, hanging in the air far above our bodies. Looking down on us, I ask, "Why the stupid grin?"

His wide mouth stretches beyond possibility. Pulling up his leather pants with aplomb, he says "I died for you, you know. At least the first time."

"Wait, what?" My confusion and guilt soak the air with a cloying, noxious syrup that is also infinitely bitter. Sharp spears of regret poke through the sand all around us. It hurts. "You died because I failed you, failed you all." Am I admitting this to his ghost or to myself? "I should have kept the blastform and the Siletzon a better secret. I shouldn't have been there at all."

"You can't change destiny's menu. It's already been cooked," he says, throwing back his shoulders with a jaunty air of self-importance. "All you can do now is try to retrieve our half-lives from the underlands, even though we're broken beings. You could make us whole again."

"But I can't—"

Simply Waites is gone, lost with a snap to the future dark like all my hopes and dreams.

I wake to now, or so I must believe.

8

LEISIL, BEFORE

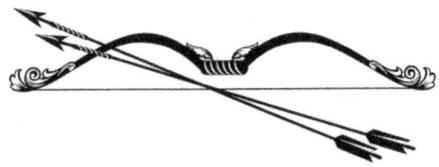

Turning and turning in the widening gyre
The falcon cannot hear the falconer;
Things fall apart; the centre cannot hold;
Mere anarchy is loosed upon the world

—W. B. YEATS, *THE SECOND COMING*

L eisil fought on, despite her fatigue and pain. Sweat and blood caused the staff to slip, almost sliding from her clenched fingers.

She'd gained weight and muscle in the last few seasons, though she was still no match for the older trainees—especially Borcine, who seemed to grow larger and more malicious every time Leisil saw her. Borcine took every opportunity to harass and ridicule her, as she was doing right now. Leisil's nemesis stood at the sidelines, her taunting words and harsh laughter making her sound like a yowling bidle in heat.

"That ugly little bitch is gonna lose. Just watch her. Can't fight worth a fuck, that disfigured little whore."

Leisil almost pointed out that Borcine herself was largely the reason for her ugly face but thought better of it at the last moment. She knew she was no delicate beauty and was almost thankful for it. Though she'd once dreamed of having kids of her own some blastday, it seemed unlikely now; the fantasy of a girl child. Most of the trainees were female. She had yet to figure out why so many more girls than boys were chosen for the training. The males they did accept seemed more effeminate than the usual boys, like her two brawling brothers.

Love or a relationship seemed out of the question now. Though she'd been propositioned a few times, she couldn't alter her natural inclinations. She could find someone of her own gender attractive, but it just didn't elicit the jump in her heart rate that thoughts of the opposite sex brought on. Leisil understood everyone was different and bore no prejudices against those who varied from the norm, whatever that was, since Leisil herself had never fit into any pattern she had thus far found.

Nature had given her wide hips and shoulders, a plain, square face, and a contrary personality. Borcine had given her the twisted nose she would bear for the rest of her life, a life she assumed she would not need to suffer much longer. Her only comfort was that Borcine would undoubtedly go to fight for the Resistance long before Leisil did, and probably die before her, too.

It turned out that bullies didn't make the best warriors. When faced with real opposition, their natural cowardice made them more likely to run than fight, and any soldier found running from the conflict would be quickly dispatched by their own lieutenants to discourage any further defections.

Leisil vehemently hoped that Borcine would run and felt no guilt for this.

Borcine carried a rusted metal device that she'd named Glock, an odd, before-sounding name. She loved to point it at anyone she didn't like, which was pretty much everyone, and make little popping noises, despite nothing coming out of the barrel. The projectiles needed to power the thing had once been manufactured, but factories had gone the way of electricity, cities, civility and the bulk of the population a long time ago. Though Leisil had been poorly educated in history—and any other academic subject, for that matter—she assumed the arrival of the Overs and their minions had occurred long before her birth.

While Borcine treasured her useless metal artifact, Leisil coveted the crossbow the master bowyer carried, a beautiful weapon made of mahogany wood and shining metal, sporting elegant lines and the tight joinery of a master craftsman. She dreamed of designing her own bow one blastday, a piece that would embody the best attributes of all the projectile weapons she so loved, though that dream seemed a long way off, if not impossible to achieve.

The one thing she'd excelled at was longbow practice, even fletching her own arrows to increase her accuracy. Quality archers were in demand in the Resistance, so she assumed she would soon be called up to serve, perhaps in the next few seasons, despite her young age.

She'd yet to see an Over for herself but had eagerly inhaled every rumor about them. Some said they had wings. Others said they had no wings but could fly anyway. They were hideous, otherworldly abominations, so ugly that if you looked straight at them, you'd be turned to ash. They were giant worms with twelve red eyes. They were two-headed coyotle-like creatures who could shred you to pieces with a single swipe of their venom-tipped adamantine claws.

She knew the stories couldn't all be true, and perhaps none of them were. It seemed that everyone saw the Overs as their own personal version of hell's master. She wondered if anyone had actually seen one, after all, because the Overs were said to be unable to enter the human realm, despite the blasts of destruction they regularly sent to ravage the human realm. There was no guarantee she would ever see one, as they sent their minions out as advance troops, creatures said to be almost as fearsome and deadly as the Overs themselves. The minions had no trouble wreaking havoc and death wherever they materialized.

Leisil hoped she was brave enough to fight them and not shit herself the first time she saw one. Survival wasn't a serious long-term concern. Warriors of the Resistance rarely reached retirement age. The one advantage of the service was the ample allotment that went to the families of those who died in battle. She cared little about that. Her family had not once been to visit her since the blastday her mater dropped her off. Her only wish was to survive as long as she could to spite them.

Distracted by her thoughts, Leisil dropped her guard, and her opponent knocked her from the chalk-outlined ring. She lay in the dirt, rolled into a fetal position like a centrapede. The other recruit, called Flossy, was, despite her name, mean as hell and more muscled than most boys her age. Flossy would make a great warrior, Leisil had no doubt. The other girls yelled and hooted as Flossy paraded around the ring with her staff raised in victory.

On the ground, Leisil pretended to be dazed so she could catch her breath. It didn't work. She felt a pressure on the back of her collar that tightened around her neck and made her gag. Borcine hauled her to her feet by her shirt.

"Don't bother faking it, Leisil. We know you're awake, Leisil the weasel."

"That's a terrible rhyme, you know," Leisil croaked, rubbing her throat. "It seems you flunked poetry class, along with the test to find out if you're a human being or not."

A titter erupted from one of the girls but halted abruptly when Borcine turned her livid face toward the sound.

In answer, Borcine rapped Leisil across the temple, causing blight to flare behind her eyes. She knew better than to talk back to the beast, so why did she do it every time, without fail?

Borcine raised her hand again and Leisil winced, but the next blow never landed, as a bellow erupted from the field behind them. Voices stilled and heads popped up to listen.

"Fall in! On the double. Not a moment, not a second from now, but right NOW!"

Leisil scrambled to obey, along with the other girls.

Mrs. Ghandi, their sergeant, eyed them up and down before she spoke again. Her gnarled hands held a wrinkled piece of paper that the woman squinted to read.

"Oh, no," said someone behind her, "it's the new list."

Leisil cringed, despite her certainty that she was too young to be chosen. When the sergeant spoke, the names that followed were a blur. She heard Borcine being mentioned under the ground troops call-up list, then names she didn't recognize. All older girls, she was sure.

She was getting bored and sleepy in the heat when Ghandi said, voice raised, "And we have an unusual request from the archery regiment. Apparently, one of our own has qualified with the highest archery scores in the history of this camp, despite her young age."

Leisil wondered who could have been so stupid as to excel and get called up early.

Mrs. Ghandi continued, "Our young Leisil Frandling has been called upon to serve as a bowman pro tem in the fifth regiment of archers on the front."

What? She hadn't even shot her best. She'd deliberately missed two bullseyes.

There was a weak spattering of applause, and a chuckle from Borcine. The look on her face made Leisil cringe. It wasn't anger, her habitual expression, or even envy. It was almost...joyful. That unsettled Leisil more than anything aggressive the other girl could have said or done.

Leisil rushed away from the congratulating handshakes and bemused looks, using the excuse that she needed to pack her scant belongings. Somehow, Borcine got there ahead of her. She cornered Leisil between two tents, grabbing her wrist.

"So, which fingers are the most important to an archer?"

When Leisil only stared, struggling to pull her hand away,

Borcine said, "Well, that's all right. Maybe we'll just break them all."

Leisil pulled back, but she couldn't match the power of the older girl. What would happen if she showed up to archery duty with broken fingers? First, they would blame her for harming herself to avoid being sent to the front, but Leisil would never do that. She suddenly realized she wanted to go, to have the chance to prove herself. She strained to remember what had happened to other trainees who tried this gambit. Most of them just disappeared. Whether they were sent to other duties or to the Remedial Training Center, Leisil was never sure. Some of the girls whispered, late at night, that the Remedial Training Center was nothing more than an underlands pit where bodies were dumped.

"No!" she screamed, but it was too late. She felt and heard the snap of bone. Nauseating pain shot up her arm. To her infinite surprise, searing rage ran down to meet it, surging from her and releasing a blightning bolt. Was it something dormant that had crouched unseen and unused within her? No. It wasn't within her, it was within the clouds, the sky, even the boulder that Borcine slumped against, rubbing her hands, which had turned as foul and putrid as rotting bat guano.

As the power flowed through Leisil, she felt another presence, like a bad gas she'd always sensed yet had never been able to release. For a second, she and the beast shared bodies.

Borcine shrank away in horror as a huge two-headed gyrfalcon loomed over her, talons extended and powerful wings shaping gusts of howling wind. Both its open beaks bore down on the terrified student with the unwavering focus of a natural predator about to taste the orgasmic sweetness of shredded flesh and spurting blood.

Leisil watched all this from a distance, as if it were happening to someone else. As much as she wanted revenge on Borcine, she knew that this wasn't the place or time. With aching regret, she tried to pull back the falcon's rage, but instead, it turned on her. As the twin beaks from hell spiked toward her, she saw her own bloody end encroaching. Instinctively, she understood the nature of the danger facing both her and the falcon.

"No, you stupid fucking bird! If you end me, you end us both."

Gradually, the soul fire in the gyrfalcon's eyes cooled to mere boiling rage. With a screech that echoed across the training grounds, it took to the sky and flew away at hellish speed.

Staring at her trembling hands, Borcine blubbered and fell from the rock. She stumbled to her feet and ran without grace or a backward glance.

At the medic's tent, a healer leaned away from Borcine with a look of horror on his rangy, acne-scarred features.

"I've never seen anything this bad. What did you get into? Borgeweed? Blacktongue? Or did you somehow ingest pistledung spores?"

When Borcine spoke, her words were almost respectful. It sounded very odd to Leisil, as if someone else, an almost reasonable human being, was talking in Borcine's voice. "No, nothing like that, sir. That recruit did it. She became something, or something came out of her and it—" She pointed at Leisil with a trembling, charcoal-crusted finger.

"Come now. No recruit could do something like this. It's obviously of fungal or bacterial origin. Let's just hope it doesn't spread around the camp. Just to be safe, we'll hold you here in quarantine until you're over it, though."

Hovering over Leisil's cot, a pudgy, red-faced healer *tsk-tsk*ed at her. "Do you think I was born on Dumbday, girl? That it's the first time a trainee damaged herself to avoid activation? Well, it won't work. I'm sending you up anyway and you can just bear the pain. Serves you right."

"But I—"

"It's not broken, anyway. It might have been at one time, but it's pretty well healed now, so you'll be fine, in my professional opinion."

"But Borcine, she—" whimpered Leisil, pointing.

The healer interrupted her, enumerating the many amusing

excuses trainees tried to get out of their or their family's commitments, but Leisil stopped listening. All her thoughts focused on what had just happened. Had she imagined the whole thing? Then she glanced back at Borcine's blackened fingers. Something strange had erupted from her, but what was it?

She found no answers in the next couple blastdays, and the terrifying gyrfalcon didn't show itself again, though she sensed it. It hovered in her nightmares, showing itself in her frequent indigestion. Borcine was released from quarantine; thankfully, she left Leisil alone, scampering away with her head bowed whenever Leisil approached.

Her tenuous sense of victory lasted only until she and the other draftees were herded to the wagons to begin their perilous journey to the front lines.

As they traveled through the ravaged terrain, Leisil reminded herself why she'd never attempted to escape from the academy. The landscape was littered with burned, twisted forests, blast-flattened towns, and ancient, crumbling highways that left the roadway and traveled over open sky, or led you down into the smoking, oily crust of the deadly discontinuities that appeared without warning. Fortunately, they didn't run into any of the egregores, the mythical beasts whose favorite food was raw human. The afterarth was a chaotic, dangerous hellscape, and no place to survive on your own. Besides, despite the daily misery, the Resistance was the closest thing she had to a family after her biological one had so cruelly abandoned her.

Up to this point, she'd thought her life had been filled to the brim with trials she didn't deserve, but it appeared now that it had plenty of room to expand and make space for the truly unbearable.

9

LYDARC, NOW

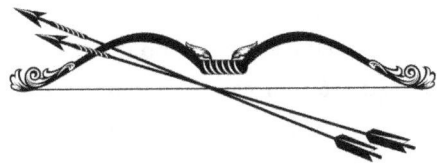

All the world's a stage, and all the men and women merely players.

—WILLIAM SHAKESPEARE, *As You Like It*

"You fucking bastard!" I yell at Rapha, who eyes me blandly, an unmoving and unblinking statue whose head is about to be splattered to mush by the twisted alder stick I call my staff.

The spine trees are sparse here, the air brisk, and the sky hyper-blue. We've almost reached the summit of the Cascade Range. Lost Lake shimmers to the left of the trail. In the thin air above us, snow-frosted peaks pose, almost painful in their clear, sharp beauty. It's highburn and I can only hope that I can hold it a few moments longer, as I much prefer to kill in pleasant weather.

"Now, now," soothes Rapha, his arms raised in a vain attempt to prevent the mortal damage I am about to inflict upon him. The grinning bastard. "What could I possibly have done to make you this angry?"

"You were born, for starters," I hiss.

"But after that—"

Rapha's delaying tactics have given Sitka's spirit animal time to rush in. She inserts six hundredweight of ursine intransigence between us.

"Please," says the bear in its girlish voice, "It's my fault, not Rapha's."

"I sincerely doubt that."

"It's true. It was my idea to summon them, not his. Look at us. We're all exhausted. You all can't haul me in that cart another widder-width before it breaks down completely. Rapha has already repaired it to the point that it's more patched parts than original. We'll never make it to the lava caves on foot. We need them."

When I say nothing, she continues, "Look at Wayland. He can't take another step. He should be in a med tent, not tramping across the wilderness."

I gaze at Wayland where he slumps on a log, his eyes vacant. He's not just exhausted, but lost in some realm far beyond that. His usually sublime brown skin has a gray cast. His stump has bled through the dressing again. He's been hiding it poorly, and I haven't paid attention as I should. In my defense, the weather has been unusually erratic and hard to control of late.

I rub my back and sigh. Sitka is right, but just not *them*. "We could find horses or tame grundles," I say, "Anything but begging help from those bastards. You know I don't trust them, not a one of them. They're Over-born for one thing."

Rapha says, "It is more than that, is it not, Lydarc? There is something else bothering you."

"Thank you, Sergeant Obvious," I snap. A brief, quickly suppressed look of pain crosses his features; guilt at hurting him nudges out a fraction of my anger but fills in the space with irritation.

I plop down on a fallen log near the trail. Beside me, salal and Oregon grape are flirting. They slow dance and rub up against each other in the warm breeze. Rapha sits down beside me. The bear pulls Sitka's cart and Wayland follows, dragging his feet. They fade into the trees, as if knowing I need some space.

I hide my face in my hands and try to explain. "I had a miserable out-of-body experience last night. Not that they're ever that pleasant anymore. I went back to the old blastdays, to the beginning of the grimshade surges, fighting the minions. I had a vision, in two times at once. The same vision I had then, I also had in the present. Except I never had it back then. I'm sure of it. History was changed, somehow."

He says, "I am not sure that is possible, at least by the laws of nature that rule this world, even with the chaos that the Overs and their minions have caused. You must be mistaken."

I stand too quickly, and a dizzy spell takes me. Dragging in a deep, if shaky breath to clear my head, I say reluctantly, "There's more. This ludicrous quest to the underlands you and Wayland talked me into, it's fated for failure. I saw her body. She will die. Sitka..."

"I must point out a flaw in your usually excellently engineered train of logic."

"What flaw?"

Rapha smiles, leaning back and bracing his arms on the log. My first inclination is to beat the smug expression off his face.

"I will attempt to explain," he says. "First, you say that time has become malleable and events that did not happen have now happened. But if that is possible, then how can you be sure of Sitka's untimely end? Is it not possible that, if history can change, then the future might be in flux as well? That perhaps you may be the one who changes it?"

"Your convoluted logic is giving me one hell of a headache, but I see your point, I guess. Still, it's just not worth the risk."

Rapha rises and faces me. "What if going is the only way to save her? There is something I have failed to tell you."

I harrumph. "Isn't that your S.O.G.?"

"S.O.G.?"

"Standard Operating Grundlecrap. It's a Waylandism."

"That sounds like him. You think I have kept secrets from you. It was not my intention. In fact, I will tell you only the truth from here on."

"Unless you're lying, even now."

Rapha gives me a wide smile and his ultra-white teeth shine. "You are a tough one to please, Lydarc. Shrewd as ever. So, I will tell you now. The others in our group know nothing of this, and I would prefer we keep it so."

I've run out of my meager supply of patience.

"I can't agree to that until you tell me whatever it is you're taking your bloody fucking time to spit out."

Rapha rubs one elegant black brow. "All right, all right. Here is the truth. You were right about time. There are anomalies occurring that should not be possible, even considering the fucked-up things the Overs have done to this world in the past. The solstice is approaching."

I'm surprised. Rapha rarely swears. Perhaps I've been a beneficial influence on him. He continues. "We have been communicating with them."

"With—?"

"The Overs."

Now I know he's lying.

"Oh, yeah, right. You forget, I've seen one. There is no talking to those...things. They're just too far above—or maybe it should be *beyond*—our existence."

"That is just it. I do not think they truly understand what they are doing. Perhaps they are just attempting to communicate."

"They have a strange way of chatting, then; end most of us, warp and destroy our world—our universe."

"Perhaps time and reality are different for them. Perhaps they are just now coming to understand how direct contact affects humanity."

I touch my chest involuntarily. The peri-soul. Is it but one example of this ugly fact? I feel that he still isn't telling me everything.

"So, what does that have to do with our luxury vacation tour of the underlands?"

"We believe we have deciphered what they are trying to tell us. The coming solstice is an opportunity to unite the world, to eliminate the underlands and heal the rift that its existence has caused."

"How?"

Rapha hesitates. "When I told you seasons ago that the underlands were being taken over by the demon lord Aamon, I didn't realize how quickly and completely he would dominate them. We believe he has located the veil that exists there. It has now become imperative that we find and eliminate him. If we can accomplish this now, on the cusp of the next solstice, the underlands will fall, restoring peace and continuity to the world."

"Sounds lovely. By the 'we' you keep referring to, I assume you mean the Shamanic Council. But why, if this is so crucial, would they send just one warrior shaman to accomplish such an important task?"

"Well, actually, counting you, there are now two."

I advance on him with threat emanating from my every pore. "Fuck it, Rapha! You had better come clean on this, or I'm walking away right now. With your severed head in my hands."

Rapha raises a hand to defend himself, saying quickly, "All right. I am sorry. Please calm down. It is just that this needs to be a clandestine mission. Only you and I must know what we intend."

"Why?"

Rapha grimaces. "Because Aamon is practically omnipotent and omniscient. He will sense the threat coming, and the closer we get, the more danger we will face."

Despite myself, I laugh. "This just gets better and better."

I pause for a moment, thinking hard.

"You wouldn't be telling me all this unless you had something to offer me, or hold over me, to get me to join you on this suicide mission. I know how the Council works. Which is it?"

Rapha grins apologetically. "Both, I fear."

"Both?"

"The Council has agreed to allow your apprentice Sitka to be initiated into the shamanic tradition, including giving her access to the veil."

"I assume that's the carrot. And the stick?"

Rapha pauses for a long moment, and his expression is dark. I think he might just walk away rather than tell me. Finally, he says to the ground at his feet, "If you refuse, they will put out a bounty on your lives, with instructions that it be carried out immediately, without recourse or mercy."

"That's just lovely." I speak pleasant words, but they don't sound pleasant to anyone's ears. "And I suppose you're the one tasked with carrying out this little assignment." I advance on him.

"Wait, Lydarc. No, of course not. I will do anything I can to protect you both."

I pace the meadow with authority, only to trip over a branch.

Rapha ignores my buffoonery. "There is another fact that you have perhaps not yet considered. Your clan members still have half-lives in the underlands. Like Wayland's daughter, they could be retrieved."

"Were you not listening when I explained this to Way? The underlanders are only half alive. They're the worst of us: our basest instincts, our cruelest intentions, our weak sides. They are the thralls of the Algean witches, the three sisters of the underlands."

"But that is just the legends. Perhaps they are more than we know."

"Is that your certainty, or your guess?"

A feral scream echoes across the mountains and three black dots grow out of the bright sky. Elegant wings, long necks and barbed tails become more obvious as they approach with alarming speed.

"It seems our friends have arrived," says Rapha as he squints into the sun, a hand shading his eyes.

"We're not done with this, you bastard."

"Please do not murder the messenger," he says. "I was utterly against it, but I was outvoted. That is why I volunteered to come. To save you both, if I can."

I spit the words in a harsh rasp. "Your overarching concern for our welfare is duly noted. I'll take it under consideration when I'm deciding for you what method of torturous ending will be most painful and prolonged."

The three figures land, creating a blinding dust cloud as they adjust the angle of wings as big as ship's sails to slow their descent. As they settle to the ground, they curl in their massive foils and appear smaller, but not small. Still, they tower over us.

To me, their wiry bodies look more like skinny, plucked chickens than powerful reptiles. I remind myself that, like birds, dragons have hollow bones to reduce weight and facilitate flight.

I make a note to my warrior self: If you can get past the fiery breath, their bones are easily broken.

The three dragons' hides come in different, luminous colors, but are hard to define or describe, as their scales resemble flashing, iridescent mirrors, dancing in the blight and forever changing color. The first dragon might be black or indigo, the second magenta or rose. The third is more easily described: it gleams, as if sparkling melted gold and sunblight have been stirred together into swirling, molten beauty.

The black is the largest. She addresses me. Her voice is a rumble that you feel in your chest before it even hits your ears. Impressive, if you are easily swayed by such inflated theatrics. I am not.

"Lydarc, my old friend. How good it is that we meet again."

I don't remember us ever being friends but decide to go along with the charade. I have learned how easy it is to rile these irascible, unstable beings.

"Faustina, the pleasure is all yours. I confess, it wasn't my idea to summon you. I'm afraid my friends did that all on their own."

I glance back at my companions with a glare; I note they are standing behind me rather than beside me to face the beasts.

"Ah," says the dragon in her booming voice. "I had wondered why you would choose to allow me to repay my debt with such a small request. But it is a done deal now, is it not? When we drop you at the lava tubes, we'll be even-steven. Long have I awaited this blastday. I don't like owing my life to anyone, least of all a sneaky shaman with an unseeable destiny." She *cluck-clucks* deep in her throat, a sound I know from experience indicates draconic amusement.

Faustina's head bends down on a graceful, spine-ridged neck. She studies me with eyes of the deepest jade and just a pinch of infinity. I smell snake, with a hint of barbequed game hen. Perhaps she is attempting to emulate a human smile, but all I see are rows of ragged carnivore's teeth. I refuse to be intimidated, but my heart rate jumps an iota, and the dragon senses it.

"Worry not, shaman. No harm will come to you or your companions."

"I'm not worried," I lie, "only eager to fly again. Let's get on with it. I will ride behind Sitka to prevent her from falling."

Faustina turns her head slowly to observe the girl in the cart. I'm worried that the dragon will make a disparaging comment on Sitka's outward disability, and I'll be forced to test my theory about the hollow bones, but she surprises us all by saying, "You've chosen well for a change, Lydarc. Your apprentice is strong and unusually talented. Smarter than you too, though that is admittedly a low bar."

"Ha, ha," I say in my own stage voice. "Can we just get this over with?"

As we fetch our gear and secure Sitka on the dragons, Wayland draws near and asks quietly, "How did she know Sitka is your apprentice?"

"How does a dragon know anything? Your guess is as good as

mine. I don't trust her, but no one would accuse Faustina of stupidity."

He snorts, "More like she's psychic."

Before I can mount, Faustina leans down to me and whispers in a conspiratorial voice totally unlike her bombastic stage presence, "Do you think our act fooled them?"

"Faustina, why do you care what anyone thinks? If you really wanted to, you could torch us all to overdone barbeque."

"Yes, but you know I've turned vegan these blastdays and I've always been a pacifist at heart, my dear. I wouldn't hurt a dungfly, much less a human. I'm just such a huge fan of your kind. So soft and vulnerable, with such impassioned hearts. It's so alluring, so sensual."

At these words, the dragon's scales flush a deep maroon. After a hormone-scented pause, she continues, "If only we could have been created more like you, instead of being plated in these insensate metallic scales. But thank you, my sweet, for maintaining my cover. You're just a doll, you know that?"

I've never been sure if Faustina is schizophrenic, or possesses the soul of a showman, or both. Either way, I can't trust her. Did I mention that already?

As we fly, the mountains turn away behind us, vain divas that they are, and the high desert awakens far beneath our feet, a flat land with so much depth—I know this because I've traveled it on foot—that it is unparalleled even by the Fallen City, whose upside-under skyrapers now tease the topknots of hell.

In the almost-desert, hares run and eagles chase, dragging the poor jackrabbits up into the sky, even though the weight of their prey exceeds their own. Mule and whitetail cervids turn and stand, eyeing the wolf and coyotle, tempting their predestiny. Fires rage across the grasslands, only to be thwarted by their instant—at least in geological time—regrowth.

The land is perfectly balanced, not too much moisture nor excessive solar blight. This land was my land once, before I trekked onward to the Siletz; my home until that too was ripped from me.

Without warning—there never is any—blightburn flips to dark murkfall and thunder booms. The sky flashes and shudders as blightning bursts from the newly hatched clouds and a thick downpour drenches us. I resist the urge to be defensive and use my magic to suppress it. The world can still be so beautiful in its petulance. Sitka cries out, but I lean close to yell in her ear over the tumult of the storm. "It's all right. Dragons can't be hit by blightning. Their bodies act as Faraday cages and repel it, somehow."

"An I ass...assume you learn tha from—"

Behind her, I grimace. "Professor Wayland, yes. The bastard talks too much." That gets me thinking about the old blastdays in the Resistance, and the stories he would tell.

I'm dragged back to the present by the twisting and squirming of the great beast beneath us, as we turn and descend sharply. The rain is over without any intercession on my part, and bitterblight is being birthed in the east. The sun peeks up with a self-conscious blush from behind the horizon, and long-legged shadows stretch their limbs across the plains below us. If I didn't know my world better, I might be uplifted by the sight.

The fact that something is very wrong wiggles and waggles at my subconscious as we approach the lava tubes.

When we grow closer, I understand why. The caves are gone. Well, perhaps the caves are still here, but their entrance has been blocked by many hundredweight of rock. Was that the crashing I heard, when last I flew away from this place on the back of a mule-turned-dragon? All this time, thinking it was thunder. But now, I remember more rumbles of thunder than blightning that blastnight. Did I cause this?

"Can this blastday get any worse?" Not realizing that I've

spoken out loud, I jump in our makeshift saddle when Faustina responds.

"Don't even tempt the spirits, girl. You know it can, and *always* will, get worse."

In front of me, Sitka laughs. "She as a way wi words, this dragon fend o yours."

I can feel the exhilaration beneath her words, from this girl who's never left her blastform, now freed at last, and flying, of all unimaginable outcomes.

I'm happy for her yet fear what terrors may await us on this journey. I can't protect her from her own life, but vainly I wish I could make her wiser than I was. Well, that's a low bar, as I've already been told.

The dragons pull up and I cling to Faustina as if she is life itself, while Sitka clings to me in kind. When the commotion is over, we find that we have survived the landing of our living craft. I crawl down from our perch and stand on unsteady legs, lifting Sitka down behind me to the cart that the others have already laid out for her.

Out of the pile of rock, an ancient metal object protrudes. What I can read of it says, *Lav...River...C.* Lava River Cave. I know this because I've seen it when it was whole, if rusty and bent even then. Before the landslide. Back when I was not yet a shaman, or a Siletzon, for that matter. My heart, what there is left of it, aches for my lost tribe, my friends. Sure, I occasionally got impatient with them. Well, all right, a lot of the time. But they were good people at heart, and I miss them. Is Rapha right? Is it possible that they could be brought back from the underlands and made whole again? Hope wriggles in my subconscious, a deeply buried, sleeping worm of probability, slowly eating its way through my resistance.

Rapha and Wayland are there, frowning with hands on hips at the massive rock impediment with a gravitas to which only the macho males of our species can hope to pretend. Turning away from my overwhelming sorrow and loss, I chuckle.

"You guys go ahead and start digging."

They look at me as if I've gone completely over-under, and I break out in a merry laugh.

"All right," says Wayland, "Have your fun at our expense. It would take a hundred seasons to dig out that entrance, and that's assuming that the collapse doesn't go even deeper. We're going to need a plan 'Z' as the befores used to say. Any ideas?"

"Well," says Rapha, as he kicks at a pile of lava rocks. "This and the Fallen City contain the only two safe access points to the underlands near us."

Suddenly, the frail veil of mirth falls away from me. I look back at the dragons with a frown. "I know. We may need to renegotiate our fare."

10

LEISIL, BEFORE

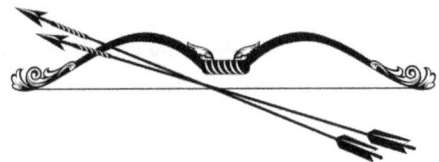

It's always darkest before the dawn of your worst blastday in hell, just before it turns to total shit.

—Lydarc, as quoted by Sitka Sangashee
in her personal journal

L eisil was directed to a long tent in the middle of a dirty camp. The camp looked a lot like the academy training grounds she'd left just a few blastdays ago, except that it was positioned on a flat, open plain filled with odd, twisting black shapes that rose above the terrain in grotesque, deformed patterns, and pocked with deep pits filled with a smoking black liquid that she would later learn was called the hell smudge. This was a substance you must never, ever touch, unless your one desire was for your shredded carcass to be pulled down into the disruption fissure with the suctioning power of a giant anteater on an overdose of ephedra weed.

At first, she wondered how they could defend such an exposed site. Then she realized that any approaching danger would be seen long, long before it reached them. Proving her assumption were the guards who scrutinized the horizon in every direction, including and especially "up."

At the far end of the camp, the terrain rose and bled into a confusing jumble of collapsed buildings and rusting vehicles, cables, tarps and garbage. She wondered why it hadn't been cleaned up.

The camp structures were mainly tents. What permanent structures that existed looked like they could be quickly dismantled if needed. The reason for this, she had learned, was that the minion attacks had been known to shift, and the Resistance forces had to be nimble in response.

Inside the tent, she found her own personal paradise. Racks were lined with longbows, both compound and recurve, flight bows, crossbows, and horse bows of every size and design. There were even a few massive wood and metal projectile weapons that she couldn't name. Other racks held quivers of arrows, bolts, and quarrels. Beyond, there were stations for a bowyer and fletcher.

Paradise.

She wandered back outside and was eventually directed to the baracks of the fifth regiment of archers. Finding an empty cot—there seemed to be more unoccupied than in use—she threw her pack on one tightly made bed. The canvas bag bounced.

"You'll want to make sure it's like that every morning. Peters can be a real bastard about a perfectly made bed. Can't imagine what that has to do with surviving this shithole, but there you are."

Leisil turned to face a short girl, perhaps a few years older than her, with a riot of curly cinnamon hair and a freckled pug face.

"I'm Jarly. I'll be your orientation coordinator."

"My what?"

The chubby girl chuckled. "I'll show you around, that's all. Help you learn the ropes."

"Oh, all right, I get it." Leisil studied her shoes, embarrassed that her vocabulary was so obviously wanting.

"C'mon, let's take you to the archery master and get you set up with your weapon of choice."

Leisil's eyes glowed. "Oh yes. Let's!"

The head of archery supplies was a tall, gaunt man named Cuspis, who had a face as pinched as a bite of bitter green pucker fruit. He looked Leisil up and down with a critical eye.

"Good shoulders, I'll give you that." He pinched one of her biceps with long, cadaverous fingers.

"Ouch!"

"Enough strength for the bigger recurve bow, I think. How's your aim?"

Leisil stood up tall. "Excellent, sir, at least at medium range. There wasn't enough distance at the academy to test myself out at longer ranges. Though I—"

"It doesn't matter, girl. We'll start you out at the front, anyway. Everyone starts there. Jarly!" he shouted unnecessarily, and both girls jumped.

"Get her the Howard Hill Longshot Master, Mark Two. No, it's there on the top shelf. Yes. That one, and the arrows and quiver to match. That's it." When Jarly delivered her precious gifts, Leisil looked down at the bow and quiver in her hands, with a look approaching that of love at first sight.

"Thank you, sir."

"Don't be thanking me now. Thank me tomorrow, after the surge."

"The surge?"

"Yeah. Lucky you. It happens every mid-scattermoon, and you were unfortunate enough to arrive the blastday before. It's one of the few events we can actually predict in this god-smacked fucking world. Let's hope the protesters don't show up this time, those materfucking Over lovers. Go and practice now. Good luck."

He turned and left the tent without a backward glance. Leisil got the impression that he didn't really want to get to know her, just in case.

Leisil stared at Jarly. "What does he mean about the surge? And protesters? What protesters?"

Jarly looked uncomfortable. "Our job here is to hold back the minions. While we get random attacks occasionally, they appear en masse at regular intervals. I know you haven't been trained yet, but we need every archer we can get right now. No one expects you to be a hero. Just do the best you can and try not to get ended.

"You're lucky to be an archer, you know. We get the best rations, and leave is two blastdays every half scattermoon. The ranks of archers are always grouped in front of the mud soldiers, to prevent anything reaching the ground. You'll be at the front of the archers."

"What? You mean I'll be in the front of...everything? Why is that?" she asked, not quite believing what she was hearing.

"Well, we wouldn't want a beginner accidentally taking out one of our best archers, now, would we?"

Leisil would have laughed if she wasn't quite so terrified.

"All right. Got that, but what about these protesters?"

"They call themselves the Followers of Enoch. They believe the Overs are fallen angels, and the minions are their Nephilim. It's a pretty fucked-up ideology, but these people are zealots and terrorists. Sometimes, we end up fighting them at the same time the minions are attacking. It really sucks."

"What? You mean we have to end real people?"

"I'm afraid so."

"I don't think I can do that."

"Well, ultimately, it's up to you, but the first time a drugged-up fanatic comes at you screaming with a sharpened shovel aimed at your neck, you might change your mind."

11

LYDARC, NOW

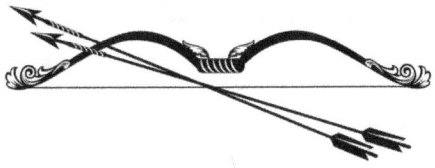

Through me you go into a city of weeping; through me you go
into eternal pain; through me you go amongst the lost people.

DANTE ALIGHIERI, *THE INFERNO*

"My dear, I'm afraid a trip to the Fallen City was not part of our bargain," says Faustina as we stand gaping at the lava cave's blocked entrance. "That's many widder-widths out of our range, and I'm missing my pedicure as it is." Faustina glances down at her scaly legs, now covered in a delicate veil of volcanic dust. She lifts and shakes one giant clawed limb daintily, like a bidden shedding unwanted water from its paws.

"What deal?" I ask. "I never summoned you. It was Rapha and Sitka who went behind my back." I glance back at Sitka, absorbed in conversation with Jin, the smaller golden dragon. The red dragon, Krimsena, is taking a nap. Older dragons sleep about three-quarters of every blastday. If dragons had a second name, it would be *sloth*. Eventually, as they approach an ancient age, they stop moving altogether, sitting like statues in their lairs, turning to a substance like rock, though somehow still alive. You can't end a dragon—they're immortal—but you can bore them to stone.

Dragons also have incredible hearing and can call upon super speed when they choose, though they need to eat several additional meals to pay for one such jump. Before I can register that he's moved, the gold dragon is beside us. I hope *human* isn't on the extended menu tonight.

"Faustina, please!" whines Jin, as he curves his elegant neck down to examine me. Jin is a relatively young dragon and still curious about the world. I envy him that. He turns to Faustina and his violet eyes glow. "I've always wanted to see the desert."

"My dear boy, you're in the desert right now."

"But it's not the same. Sitka says this is high desert, with totally different flora and fauna from the actual desert, where they have things like gila monsters and cacti, worstmongers and carbonbacks. And she says there's a real library there. Oh, please, Auntie! Can we go?"

Faustina hisses under her breath, "I told you not to call me that in public, Jin."

"Sorry, Auntie—I mean, Lady Faustina. I meant no disrespect. Quite the opposite, in fact. So honored am I to be related, in any small way, to her majestic self. Please forgive me for my egregious slight." Jin's gilded scales fade to sand, and he hangs his head melodramatically.

I can see that he's manipulating her, but hold back a chuckle, as I slightly prefer my head being on my shoulders, rather than in the dirt at my feet or in the belly of a dragon.

Faustina sighs and lava dust billows up around us. "Oh, all right, but we can't stay long. I've got an appointment with my mechanical masseuse later this blastday."

Jin dances in a circle, and I jump back to avoid his gyrating tail. The dragon hops off to Sitka, where they again engage in animated conversation. I worry about this new friendship. Should I discourage it? Probably, but I just don't have the heart to tear Sitka away from a kindred spirit, even if that spirit belongs to one of the most untrustworthy beasts on this whole fucked-up world.

After extensive negotiations, the dragons agree to take us to the Fallen City. I'm a teensy-weensy bit excited, though I'd never admit it. My previous visit was a highlight of my life so far, albeit not necessarily a happy one. Then I remind myself that "pleasantly ever after" was never in the cards for me, anyway. I'll settle for "interesting" being the height of my life experiences.

You'd expect a city to show up at a distance. Uh-uh. The Fallen City is mostly underground: its towers, pyramids and hortels lost in the underlands below. How it managed to flip and stay relatively intact is a mystery for the ages of man, or Overs, since they were the determining factor in its upendishness. Or so I assume.

It's only as the dragons start to descend that I see we're close.

Sitka asks from in front of me, "Can I ride wi Jin on a way bac?"

"I prefer not to watch my promising apprentice splattered like a dropped melon on the desert floor."

"Jin woul take care, I know. He very deeper depen...dependable, fo a dragon."

"You need to know someone for at least twenty seasons before you can say with any assurance they are truly dependable. And even then, they can and probably will change, just when they have your life in their hands."

Sitka grimaces. Even sitting behind her, I can feel it. "Fuck. Lydar, you nee to truthin...trust."

"Why? It's never done anyone any good that I can tell."

She twists in her seat to look around at me with a frown. "Will save your li...life, one blasday."

"Is that an augury, or something you picked up from reading tea leaves?" I ask with a stupid grin.

Sitka turns away abruptly and is silent for a long time. Finally, she says, "I goin down ino the unerlans wi you. You nee me, either my know...knowledge, o the strength o my spiri anim...animal."

"What? No way. You should stay at the library until we get back. If..."

"*If* you ge back? Fuck tha. I hafa help. You gon nee me."

"No. The answer is no. What if we get stuck there longer than a blastweek? Your spirit animal would be ended. You would be ended."

Sitka is quiet as we approach the landing, but I can tell it's not the quiet that speaks of agreement.

I've directed Faustina to land as close as possible to the spot where I discovered the library all those seasons ago. Little has changed, but there isn't much that even time can do to depreciate the fortunes of sand and rock and wind-tossed scrub. At first, I think we picked the wrong spot, until Wayland wanders over to a depression in the dirt and begins scratching with his scabbard. Four angled ridges emerge as he scrapes the sand away.

"Is this it?" he asks, looking to me. I know what's expected: I've been preparing myself as best I can. Still, I grimace as I gaze down toward the hidden floor of the library basement, which is now the roof to us. Rapha frowns. He knows what it takes out of me.

"Everyone, get out of the way and let Lydarc proceed."

The dragons, Rapha, and Wayland step back. Rapha offers to help, but I wave him off. This is my specialty, and it's just easier to do on my own. The golden dragon cradles Sitka delicately in his claws. He holds her as if she's something precious, which, of course, she is. I may need to change my opinion of this dragon. This one only.

I lower myself into a cross-legged position beside the depression, ignoring the pops and squeaks of my not-so-young joints. I pull out my medicine bag and sort through my options. Finally, I choose a shard of clear quartz crystal, a selenite worry stone and Herkimer diamond—not a diamond at all, but it still cost me five elkin hides. I add black tourmaline for its grounding, arthly power. I consider the moldavite but put it back. There is such a thing as overkill, after all.

To enter the spirit realm, my thoughts must settle like brittle grimshade leaves on the floor of the bitterwood, until they turn to dust and I'm nothing. Once empty, I'm ready, and have room for the power to flow through the crystals and into me from all around. It comes from the rocks and dirt. It breathes down on me on the wind and out of the powder blue sky. From the smallest particle to the star-encrusted blastnight bleak, it all feeds into me and through me. Even so, it takes me longer than usual to call up the afterarth spirits from below, but when they arrive, they burst out with a little more *oomph* and brouhaha than I intend.

When the dust settles itself, I check to be sure that everyone has survived. Looking down, I see that I've perhaps done a more complete job than was entirely necessary. Before us, a huge pit yawns. The entire side of the before-building is exposed. Good thing I didn't add the moldavite. Through the grimy clear partitions that aren't shattered, and the jagged holes where they are, I can see that the whole bottom/top is filled with broken furniture, fixtures, shelves, and books. Thousands of books. I never understood how the Overs could make a building think up is down yet let the innards hold to their old way of falling.

Behind me, I hear a sharp intake of breath. I expect accolades at my skill, my crystal knowledge, my artful air and afterarth spirit management. Have I learned nothing in all my seasons about the nature of ego and expectation?

As Jin sets her gently into her cart, Sitka says in a voice made for church, "Awe those all *b...books?*"

I would laugh, but dizziness grabs my head, making the desert spin. When it stops, I find myself on the ground with Wayland sitting next to me. We're alone, except for Faustina and Krimsena, who are curled up, again napping.

I try to rise, but Wayland puts his one hand on my shoulder. "Wait. There's no hurry. Hell of an excavation job, by the way.

You've learned a bit since last I saw you work your shamanic magic."

I snort. "Apparently control wasn't part of my extended education. Where are the others?"

"Sitka couldn't wait for you to wake before exploring her library."

Her library?

Now I make a more concerted effort to rise. "She shouldn't be going down there alone."

"Alone? She's with a dragon and a master shaman. How much more security could she need?" He gazes at me curiously.

"What?"

He hesitates. "It's just that, for someone who professes zero desire to have children, you seem to have developed a very maternal concern for this apprentice of yours. She'll be fine."

Seeing that he has a point, I relax. But only slightly.

"Ly, since I have you alone, I just wanted to tell you I'm sorry."

I wonder what he regrets: arm-twisting me into this impossible mission, or breaking my heart a lifetime ago? It turns out the answer is neither.

He fiddles with the handle of his sword with his remaining hand. After all this time, he still does this when he's nervous, even with the loss of an arm. "When you were thrown out of the Resistance—"

"Honorably discharged."

"Yes. When you...left...I should have stood up for you. What they did to you was wrong; just tossing you out without a hearing or anything. They could have transferred you to a non-combat role, perhaps away from the front."

"It's long ago. There's no changing it now."

"Sure. I just wanted you to know. Plus, I had the feeling that the Shamanic Council might have had something to do with it."

"Why? How?"

"I heard that Rapha met with Griffin the blastday before you were discharged."

"No, that can't be right. He told me he visited the blastday *after* I was discharged, looking for me, not the blastday before. I don't entirely trust the Shamanic Council, but Rapha is like a brother to me. He pisses me off on occasion, but what brother doesn't? Besides, I wouldn't have found the Siletzon had I stayed with the Resistance."

"Yes, your apprentice is special. I've listened to some of Sitka's conversations with Jin. They have some ambitious ideas. Perhaps it is the young like them who will repair what's broken with our world. Look, Ly, if there's even a chance we could return the arth to what it used to be...they say it was a paradise."

"I doubt that, but it probably wasn't quite the fucked-up shit show we enjoy these blastdays."

We follow the trail of the others down the sides of the hole and into the roof of the library, which is now the basement. Stepping over broken glass and debris, we hear a squeal and hurry forward, only to find Sitka on the floor surrounded by books, disks, and box-like shapes of unknown purpose. Sitka has a book in her lap and is turning pages reverently.

"Loo a this, Jin. Fuck. A complee copy of *The Hishiker's Gui...Guide to Galaxy*. I alway wonerd how it ends."

"That's great," says Jin, who is forced to curl his neck to fit in the confining space, "But I was hoping to find some scientific journals. We could really use an instruction manual for creating a hydroelectric system, or better medical techniques, or—"

"Oh, sure."

Looking around her, she says, "This mostly fiction ere. If the otha sec...sections fell like is, the non-fiction shoul be oer there." She points into the gloom.

With a nod of his elegant head, Jin lumbers off, ducking under hanging wires and debris, and stepping over metal boxes and broken dark glass panels. What possible use could the befores have made of this junk? A book, you can at least read. These things are useless now, just shattered, empty shells, remnants of a civilization that didn't have the foresight to find a fool-proof way to transfer their knowledge to their own children.

There's a banging, crashing noise from the direction Jin has gone.

"You awe right, Jin?" yells Sitka. A distant voice replies, "Yeah, I'm fine. I think I found the romance section."

"Fuck. Gonna be real elpful rebuil...rebuilding civiliz...ation," she replies too quietly for him to hear.

Wayland sniggers, "You never know. It depends what kind of culture you want to rebuild, I guess."

He turns to grin inanely at me. I return his look with a scowl and crossed arms.

His expression turning serious, he says, "We're on a bit of a deadline here. I'd like to get moving soon."

Sitka closes her eyes and sways where she sits.

"No!" I say, but it's too late. A giant bear materializes in front of Sitka, who now sags over in her vision sleep.

The bear turns its head and says in Sitka's voice, "Ironic, isn't it? To be surrounded by all these books, and I won't be able to read a single one of them until we return."

"I told you, no," I say firmly.

The bear turns to me and growls. It actually growls at me! My temper threatens to erupt, Vesuvius style.

Wayland puts his hand on my arm. I wish he wouldn't do that. "You can't really stop her, you know. She's practically an adult. You see her power. If we don't let her travel with us, she'll just follow. If she's anything like her mentor, nothing can stop her once she sets her mind to a task."

Rapha says, "Also, time flows more slowly up here than it does in the underlands. We should be back in plenty of time to rescue your valiant apprentice."

With the sound of crashing shelves, Jin appears, his claws filled with books. One drops from his grasp and makes a resounding slap as it hits the dusty floor. I notice the title: *Supercolliders for Dummies.*

Turning to me, he says, "Uh, please excuse me, madam—"

"Cut the crap, I'm not your aunt. Just tell me what's on your mind."

Jin begins to dip his head even more, then, as if realizing he's dealing with someone very different from his aunt, he stands up straight, or as straight as he can, in the confines of the broken library. I have to give him credit for adapting quickly. Perhaps this is no vapid or vain dragon after all.

"Forgive me. I just wanted to say that I would be honored to stay here and guard Sitka until you return. In the meantime, I could begin to categorize and organize the books. Then we'll need to figure out how to protect them. I mean, obviously, they've survived here all this time, so I have to assume that this falling city of yours is relatively stable. I'm wondering if—"

"Fallen City, not falling. It fell a long time ago."

"Yes, of course. Forgive me. It's just that the books are crucial to our future. This could save us centuries of scientific and cultural development."

"Us? Why do you care, Jin? You're a metal-sheathed dragon, not a human being. Just a fantastical creature created by a whim of the Overs. Being mortal, we'll all be dead before this renaissance of yours can ever reach fruition—if it's even possible with the Overs, the minions, the egregores and the underlands haunting us."

Jin tips his head, as if surprised. Perhaps he is unaware that I have been listening to his conversations with Sitka. He pauses longer than I would expect. When he speaks, his words are halting, as if he considers each one carefully. "If I could transform myself into one of your kind right now, I would, without another thought. Please don't tell my aunt I said that," he adds quickly. "There's so much potential in mankind. The accomplishments of the past were incredible. I don't understand what happened to human drive. No one seems to care that there are books on how to build a hydroelectric plant right here in this library, and not a single human has tried to advance civilization since its collapse and the arrival of the Overs. It's a mystery I would like to solve one blastday.

"I know I just met Sitka, but I think she's special. She has dreams for your people, and I want to help. I'll defend her with my life while you're gone. It's important that her spirit animal goes with you."

"How do you know that?"

"How does a dragon know anything?"

12

LEISIL, BEFORE

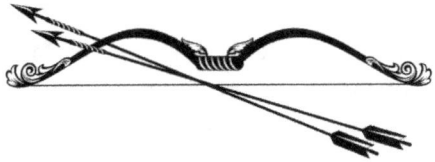

If you know the enemy and you know yourself, you need not fear the results of a hundred battles.

—Sun Tzu, *The Art of War*

They called them mud soldiers, though Leisil wasn't sure how they were any different from the archers, mounted troops, or facilitators. They all lived in the dirt and mud, breathed, ate, and shit out the muck every blastday. Although the facilitators avoided the brunt of it as officers, having been born into families rich enough to keep them out of actual combat, but not quite wealthy enough to avoid the involuntary servitude all together.

Borcine was a mud soldier. Leisil, as an archer, seldom encountered her, except for the occasional sighting in the mess tent where Borcine always turned away, pretending she hadn't seen her former schoolmate. Either Borcine had stopped being a bully or was diligently avoiding Leisil. Knowing what she did about human nature, Leisil favored the latter reason.

Leisil had survived her first surge battle with the minions thanks to Jarly and Peters: the captain could be a real asshole but also possessed a wealth of knowledge on how to stay alive in this hellhole—an invaluable skill for certain. Thankfully, The Followers of Enoch were no-shows that first blastday.

Halfway through her second experience with the surge, Leisil realized that she'd been lucky the first time, and her initial experience had been a mild one by comparison.

Now she faced the real deal. Jarly was there, and Leisil felt the calm resolve as the other girl shouted out instructions and warnings. Thousands of minions filled the sky. Screams of pain and fear grated on her ears and distracted her from her job: skewering as many of the strange beasts as she could before they reached the ground. On top of that, the Followers of Enoch were there, mostly carrying signs, but some with weapons.

Hearing a familiar voice yelling behind her, she turned to find Borcine on her back in the dirt behind the line of archers, poking her staff awkwardly at a bizarre creature of purple, salmon, and rust. It looked surprisingly like the tiny, dried seahorses that her father had brought home after a trip to the Oregon coast, only this one was huge, menacing, and very much alive.

Borcine was obviously tiring, and the seahorse thing—Leisil had learned that they were called "nags," she assumed, for their resemblance to horses—was getting closer every time Borcine took a wild swipe at it. It was only a matter of time before the minion got close enough that its lethal spit could reach the fighter.

Without thinking, Leisil turned her aim on the nag and loosed a whistling shot straight into the breast of the beast. It screamed, an eerie whining noise that caused the hair to stand up on Leisil's arms. The nag fell beside Borcine, scrabbling and twisting, its elegant snout spewing poison spit into the dirt.

Borcine jumped to her feet and swung her staff with renewed strength, almost beheading the nag with her enthusiasm. Purple blood sprayed the ground, and the minion lay still. Then it exploded into a cloud of gray-blue dust that wandered away on the breeze.

Borcine spared Leisil only a passing glance before moving away to help another mud soldier who was struggling with a willywag, seemingly unable to cause it any harm with her sword. The strange collection of gray cubes and spheres just parted for her swipes, recombining around the motion as if it wasn't even threatened, but was only playing.

Leisil left them to it. Willywags had to be beaten and pried apart. Arrows and swords only passed through them, appearing to cause no harm whatsoever.

She hadn't expected Borcine to fall prostrate at her feet in gratitude, but even a nod of acknowledgment would have been nice. Borcine would never change. Had Leisil?

Later, she realized that she'd missed the chance to get her revenge on Borcine. But why? Was it wartime camaraderie? A knee-jerk reaction? Neither seemed likely. She couldn't imagine any kind of fellowship forming between her and the bully, and she had deliberately aimed and shot her weapon. She'd always been like that. In the moment where life and forever hung together in the air, everything stilled. Time slowed for her, giving her an age to aim and reach a deadly certainty of hitting her target. It hadn't been an accident, saving Borcine. So then, why?

Her thoughts were interrupted by a scorching scream right behind her. She turned, only to face a wild-eyed protester who'd broken through the line and was thrusting a kitchen knife at her chest. With a speed she didn't think the big man possessed, Peters drew his sword and deftly relieved the man of his head.

"Wow," she said, her voice trembling. "Good job. Thanks."

"Forget it. Just pay better attention next time."

She braved a look at the bloody scene at her feet. Gushing fluid was being ejected in a pulsing rhythm from the neck. The headless body twitched like a fish drowning on land. Leisil thought she might throw up but steeled herself and raised her bow.

Life goes on.

She thought about Jarly telling her she could decide to end her opponent or be ended herself. She was pretty sure that when the time came for her to decide, she would choose to live.

⁓

Peters stood over the bunk where she sat fumbling with the laces on her boots.

"Passable work today, Frandling," he said. "We'll chisel an archer out of the hulking golem the academy sent us eventually, eh?"

Leisil wasn't offended, because she didn't have a clue what he was saying. Peters had a strange manner of speech, perhaps a result of his eastern roots, but there was more to it than that. The man had been educated to within an inch of his life, as Leisil saw it. It could be a burden to deal with him and his endless stories, but Leisil listened because the knowledge he meted out between implausible tales could be invaluable. He'd saved her life when the unseeums attacked, and again with the protester.

"Thank you, sir. I did my best."

"That's all we can ask. Hey, some of us are planning a perhaps ill-advised foray to the downtime tent later to risk our continence on Gerkin's latest batch of ale. Any interest?"

After translating what he'd said, Leisil was surprised. Peters had never asked her to the downtime tent before. In fact, no one had.

"Well, I—I don't know if..." Leisil spluttered and stopped, staring at the ground.

"Good. We'll reconnoiter after mess. See you then."

The way he said it left little room for objections. When Jarly showed up later to haul her along, it left no room for objections at all.

"Come on, girl. We're off duty till Fuckleday, so let's celebrate." Jarly was a bundle of some unknown substance that you just couldn't deny. Before Leisil knew what had hit her, she was settled on a bench beside Jarly with a sour-smelling, dirt-colored drink in her hands.

Leisil said, "You were amazing out there. How do you stay so calm? I almost lost my shit a bunch of times. If it weren't for you and the captain, I wouldn't be here enjoying this fine drink." She took another sip of the bitter ale and grimaced dramatically.

Jarly laughed. "Oh, you get used to it—the ale and the job. Pretty soon, you'll be the same as me."

"I'm not sure about that, but thanks for having my back."

"You're welcome, but it's my job, right? I get deducted down-time points for every recruit I lose in their first season."

"You do?"

Jarly laughed again. "No, silly. I'm just messing with you. I've just kinda taken a liking to you—not in a romantic sense, I mean —but you could be my sister. All I have at home are brothers, the big nincompoops."

Leisil was flattered and relieved. She'd wondered about Jarly's sexual orientation and didn't want the embarrassment of having to tell her that she tilted in a different direction. She was grateful that the ever honest and open Jarly had eliminated her fears and solidified their friendship, all in a couple sentences,

"Thanks. I really appreciate that. It's been tough being the new kid. Did you hear the captain yelling at me?"

"Oh, don't worry about that; he yells a lot—at least at the ones he thinks have a future."

"Well, that's comforting."

They shared a grin and looked up to find the captain beginning one of his tall tales.

"So, this is a fascinating story about the time I rode a wild grundle—" he began.

A few groans met his words. Someone in the back said. "Heard that one twice. Didn't believe it either time." There was a spattering of laughter.

"All right, all right. I've got a new one for you. I've never told this to anyone." He spoke softly, but he had a rich, resonant voice that even those in the back of the tent could hear clearly. "The first and only time I fought an Over, it spoke to me."

The room was silent for a moment, then a rush of words filled the air, along with some tittering laughter. It grew in volume until Peters raised a hand.

"It's true. It was during my first tour. I can tell you, I was pretty wet behind the ears back then."

Leisil wondered what his personal bathing regimen had to do with anything.

"I was out on blastnight patrol. It wasn't surge time or anything like that. Everything was quiet, and I was spending the time reciting from memory an epic poem that I read at university, called *Paradise Lost*. Quite a beautiful work, if you can get past the vernacular and antiquated speech patterns." Leisil didn't mention that Peters had enough ancient speech patterns of his own.

"Just get on with the story, Peters," someone said from the group.

"So, I was quoting the first lines. Let me think. It goes like this, 'Of man's first disobedience, and the fruit of the forbidden tree, whose mortal taste...' Then, a voice responded from the darkness, speaking the rest of the line in a strange, halting voice, 'Whose mortal taste brought forever into the world, and all our woes. Is that what the before ones did, brought forever to the world? That was not the intention, I'm sure. As for ourselves, we only seek a place to rest, to mend our tortured half-lives and bring peace to the garden again.' Something like that. I couldn't see where the voice was coming from, but let me tell you, I was terrified."

"What did you do?" Leisil asked. She hadn't meant to speak, but his story fascinated her. It had the frightening ring of truth.

"Well, if I'd had a brain in my head, I would've hightailed it back to camp, but I was young and green and eager to prove myself, so I stepped into the dark and yelled for whoever was speaking to show themselves." Peters paused and rubbed his chin.

"After that, it was a bit of a blur. It was as if I was being pulled into some kind of alternate space to our own. I was disoriented and dizzy. There was a rustle of white all around me, like wings, or sails, or sheets on a clothesline flapping in a high wind. An intense blight blinded me, and something touched my cheek, here. It was so strange. I felt...I felt almost violated, like this thing was in my head, messing with it. Then I saw it. Really saw it." He paused, looking into the distance.

"What did it look like?" someone prompted.

Peters took a deep breath. "It was the ugliest motherfucking thing I've ever seen, but I can't tell you what it looked like, not really. It's almost as if it was so abhorrent that my mind forgot the details later, just to protect itself. I remember a little, and it wasn't pretty. Like with the willywags, I just couldn't pin down a shape. It kept morphing. I remember things like tentacles, or hyper-flexible arms, and some kind of bulbous head, but maybe that was its ass. How could I know?"

Someone snorted an incredulous laugh, then asked, "So, what did you do then?"

Peters smiled, but Leisil could sense a slight hesitation, as if he wasn't completely sure that what he'd done had been right. "I pulled my sword and tried to hack the cocksucker to pieces. I don't think you can harm them with a weapon, but the thing faded away. No, that's not right. It was as if it set me back down in my own reality, like setting down a toddler. I know that sounds weird." He looked at his empty tankard and said, "That story made me thirsty, and my glass is empty. Who's buying?"

Later, as Leisil sat at the table, nursing what she'd decided must definitely be her last beer, Peters plopped down across from her.

"Well," he said. There was a long pause as he studied her face. Leisil squirmed internally despite sitting perfectly still, her expression unchanging.

"Well, what, sir?"

"No need for sir in here. You can call me Wayland."

"Leisil."

"Well, Leisil," he started again. "I'm just curious why you did it."

"Did what?"

"Jarly told me a little about your struggles at the academy. I've had my eye on that Borcine for a while now. I can see she's nothing but a ruffian. If she was guilty of half the stuff that Jarly told me about, well, I'm not sure I would've gone out of my way to save her life, like you did this blastday."

Leisil stared into her beer, a little upset with Jarly for sharing her life story with a stranger. "I'm not really sure why I did it. I just reacted in the moment, that's all."

"Are you sure? I've watched you too: that's actually my job. You're extremely deliberate and careful when you aim, even though you're one of the fastest pullers I've ever seen. It's kind of hard to explain. It's almost as if time slows down around you—like you've got your own personal timesmear."

Leisil giggled nervously. She wasn't used to praise of any kind and had no idea how to respond. Finally, she mumbled, "Thank you, sir—I mean, Wayland."

"What I'm trying to say is the most important thing a warrior needs to understand is herself. Our old friend Sun Tzu said something to that effect, you know."

"Sorry, sir, I never met the man."

Wayland sniggered. "Well, I'd be very much surprised if you had, since he's been dead for eons. If you ever run into an Over—or whatever life brings your way, for that matter—it's better to know what you're capable of. How far you're willing to go in any given situation."

Leisil studied her beer intently, as if the pattern of foam on its surface would reveal the meaning of life. Finally, she sighed. "It won't break my heart when karma catches up with Borcine. It's just that I don't care if I'm the one to cause it anymore. I've got enough bad luck as it is. I don't need to tempt the fates. I'm sure she'll get what's coming to her eventually, without me needing to tarnish my soul to achieve it."

"You sound like my shaman friend, always talking about fate and the consequences of intention."

Leisil was silent for a long time. Wayland seemed happy to sip his beer and wait.

She said, quietly, so no one else could hear, "Do you really know a warrior shaman? Is their power real?"

Wayland looked surprised. Perhaps this wasn't the reaction he expected. "Yes, of course. In terms of history, warrior shamans are a fairly recent development, having appeared in a portion of the population only after the arrival. There is even a council of elder shaman who have some kind of power over their ranks, but I get the feeling they're an independent bunch. Why? Do you know someone you think may be coming into the power? Surely not Borcine?"

"Oh no, not her! Forget it. I'm being silly. I've got to go."

In a sudden panic, Leisil made to get up, but a large brown hand held her back.

"Sit."

"I'm not a dog," growled Leisil, before she remembered who she was talking to. "Sorry, sir." To her surprise, Peters laughed good-naturedly.

"That's perfectly all right. We're off duty. Besides, I like a soldier with some gumption, and I'm the one who should be apologizing. You were talking about yourself, weren't you? I guess you just didn't strike me as the type."

"The type?"

"Oh, you know, the navel-gazers, herbal potioners, dreamweed smokers and philosophizers—that type of thing."

Sometimes she just didn't understand a word he said. Perhaps seeing that in her expression, he said, "I know someone you might want to talk to. He's not like some of the others, real down-to-afterarth kind of guy. He works in town. Next time we get leave, I'll take you there."

"Thank you, sir."

"I'm not doing it just for you. We don't want you turning half the unit into toads now, do we?"

Wayland grinned, but Leisil couldn't bring herself to reply in kind. Since the two-headed falcon had first burst out of her, she'd felt it, always ready, trying to peck or claw its way up out of her nightmares and into her waking life. It started as a mild itch, but now it was a roaring, bleeding need.

All she said was, "I'd appreciate that, sir." Leisil studied his face and frowned.

"What is it?" Wayland said. "You look like you have more questions."

"More than you could possibly answer," said Leisil with a snort. "It's just that...I wonder why you're here. There are so few men in the Resistance—at least in combat."

"Ah, yes. I get asked that a lot by newbies. But the real question is, why are *you* here?"

"I don't understand."

"I don't know who first figured it out, or how, and you probably haven't experienced it yet. You'll find that when you're here for a few months, your cycle will start to align with all the other women here."

"My?"

"Your female cycle."

"Oh," said Leisil. She studied her dirty fingernails and tried desperately not to blush.

"It's strange, I know, but the minions only attack at the center point of this cycle every scattermoon. It doesn't even matter if there are timesmears. It happens like clockwork—if we still had any working clocks, that is. Anyway, without it, they'd be here every blastday, or Overs know when. It's one of the few regular, predictable events in this whole fucked-up world."

"So why are you here?" she asked. "You're not secretly a woman, are you?"

Wayland laughed, loud and uninhibited. It was a beautiful

thing to behold. "Not by a long bowshot, girl. But there is a ratio. If we exceed it, the attacks increase and become irregular again. It's approximately one male to every hundred females."

Leisil's smile took on a lascivious slant. "Nice for you, I guess. You get your pick of the women here."

Wayland looked wistful for a moment, then his face hardened. "I'm afraid my match has come and gone. I doubt I'll ever find another like her." He straightened up in his seat. "But that's neither here nor there. We've got a job to do, and that's all that matters now. Time to hit the sack."

Wayland rose and left the tent abruptly. Leisil watched him go, wondering what frightful internal demons had just chased him away from her.

13

LYDARC, NOW

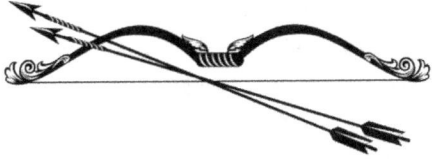

Trust in dreams, for in them is hidden the gate to eternity.

—Khalil Gibran

I use the dreams as they use me, leading me down dark alleys and through fog-shrouded cemeteries, where ghosts of my past weep blood. To see what will be, I must wallow in the undead memories I thought I'd buried for good.

The dream starts out as a perfectly reasonable memory.

Nags, honeydoos, wedding rings, willywags, ass knockers and unseeums fill the sky. We get them all on the front lines. Those are the technical terms. Forget what the facilitators name them in their reports. We know them first-hand. They're what their names sound like, only more intensely so.

The sky is an explosion of vivid birthday party colors. Nags, the delicate flying seahorse-like creatures that spit greenish poison that will turn your skin to simmering, smoking pus, are purple and rust. The flaming melon-colored monsters shaped like a slice of orange are honeydoos. Wedding rings swirl with the brightest pink and citrine yellow, feathered with incandescent cyan where the heat of hell bursts from inside their spiral rings. The willywags? Well, your guess is as good as mine. Most observers see a mass of translucent and iridescent grayish cubes and spheres in ever-shifting positions and warping forms. The only thing everyone agrees on is that they will crush to pulp anything unlucky enough to end up beneath them. The unseeums are just what you might think; invisible, unseen, silently splitting you, forehead to crotch, effortlessly eviscerating and ending you. As for the ass knockers? Don't even ask.

I survive them all, that first blastday on the front, I don't even know how, but I do. Miracle, I guess, if you believe in that crapola. Maybe coincidence? Luck? Is my survival even possible by the rules of statistics?

Professor Wayland teaches me a bit about the science of statistics and other studies of little use in our world now. He says, "Who can foresee what knowledge will be found useful when humanity survives the solstice, and we wake to an entirely new world?" He was known to say crazy, over-under things like that.

My main education before meeting him was in combat, archery and arms creation. It turns out I'm especially good at those skills, but that's a nightmare for another time.

It's my first blastday on the line, and I haven't had a chance to practice much with my newly apportioned bow. I'm at the front of the line, and fortunately, several of the best archers in the fifth regiment stand behind me. If not for this, I'm sure it would be my first and *last* blastday on the front.

"Hey, hey! You. New girl. What the fuck're you aiming at? They're up there. *Up there,* you idiot!"

This is how I meet Peters, my captain; the first words he says to me. He's quite a piece of work, but you know that already.

"I'm trying, all right?" I yell back at him, winging another arrow aloft with unlimited enthusiasm if little accuracy. I'm rattled. It's all so strange. Despite the many briefings I attended at the academy, it was never as disturbingly real as the real thing is now.

To say Peters and I are friends at these initial intersections would be a gross overestimation. We are not. In fact, I'm not sure we ever become friends, but instead skip ahead to something at once less and much more.

Peters shows me how to track the unseeums. He saves my life this blastday, and on later occasions as well.

The soundtrack of my dream changes, becoming ominous, foreboding.

A group stands before me in shades of blue, almost two-dimensional, like a drawing. I know them, yet we've never met. They're tall and imposing. Familiar, somehow: like family? Their lips move in slow motion. They point at me. One steps forward and says, "Lydarc, we're looking for you." But my name isn't Lydarc, it's Leisil, then it's Lydarc again. Who am I really? The largest one continues, making no sense at all, "You must prevent the fall, my son."

As I dream a dark chaos beyond my comprehension, a bit of wisdom seeps into me unbidden.

This, I realize: Time is royally screwed for us all. Matter, too. The world is utterly wrong, and I can't fix it, unless I embark on some ill-advised, surely doomed, and wholly unwanted second journey into the underlands. But if I do, something horrible will happen.

Fate will drag me into the future dark and there is no escape. It's coming for me as surely as grimshade, coldspawn and solstice rising. It hunts me like a willywag, bloated to bursting, unshakably destined to crush me and those I am foolish enough to give the slightest fuck about, squishing us to mushy pulp, no matter how we scrabble and scurry like hunted rats to survive.

Here, the dream veers from what happened into what can never happen. I look away from the arcing flight of my arrow for just a second and I'm in someone else's nightmare. It must be, because it can't be mine.

There on the ground lies the dead body of a girl. I'd never seen her before, not at this point in my mostly worthless life. Despite this fact, her face is quite familiar. Crumpled and broken, her slight form and shriveled limbs are the most pathetic things I will ever see. Her pale, dead face and hollow eyes mock me and blame me for everything. She's right, of course. It's all my fault.

I want to scream, but you can't scream in someone else's dream. So, I pretend at a crooked, ironic smile instead. It's as if I created this fate myself, it's that fucked up.

If I save the world, my apprentice will die.

14

LEISIL, BEFORE

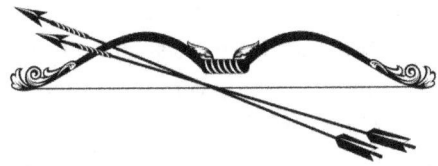

So hand in hand they passed, the loveliest pair that ever since in love's embraces met—Adam, the goodliest man of men since born his sons; the fairest of her daughters Eve.

—John Milton, *Paradise Lost*

Peters and Leisil just happened to end up in the same lottery for leave. She had hoped to avoid her fellow soldiers if she could, but choices for entertainment around the camp were limited, since most of the territory was uninhabitable or lost to the sucking underland breaches, a place no one would willingly visit.

In hopes of some much-needed time alone, Leisil opted for an overnight trip on a riverboat inn. It was much safer than land-based choices, where the afterarth could fall out from beneath you at any moment, or a stray willywag might crush the entire building with patrons inside.

The riverboat captains had learned the hard way that the boat needed to keep moving. There was something about the active water that kept the vessel more stable, away from the disruption fissures. Plus, for whatever reason, the minions generally avoided water.

The voyage wasn't without risks, however. The river might rise above its bed and float in the sky for a time, but it always seemed to make its way back down with few casualties, or more importantly to the captain, little damage to the boat.

She'd signed up for the round trip. The inn would float down-river overnight. Inebriated customers slept it off the next blastday in their cabins, as domesticated grundles tethered to long traces hauled it back to its home berth.

The riverboat she'd chosen had the misfortune to be named *The Leaky Bucket*. Despite the inauspicious name, Leisil felt good about her choice. There was little chance that any of her fellow soldiers would choose a trip on such a floating turd for their leave time.

She preferred to be far away from most of them on her off time. She only wished that Jarly had been selected for leave with her. The girl was one of the few fellow soldiers she could stand. The others all tended to be arrogant, boastful, and unknowingly ignorant. She didn't want to spend another evening listening to how Gristman had taken out three minions at once, or how Kastler was bedding two different female mud soldiers from a nearby camp and managed to incite them into a very entertaining catfight over her. And she'd heard enough of Wayland's stories to write a book, if pen and paper weren't so prohibitively expensive.

After she'd stowed her gear in her cabin, she wandered the deck, enjoying the brisk air and fading blight as the dock receded behind them. After a while, the air turned crisp and cool. She decided to find an ale and maybe a singer to take her thoughts off her thoughts.

The bar was busy, and she had to wait in line for her drink. As she stood, the entertainment began: a woman playing an instrument that Leisil had never heard before. It sounded like a tiny guitar, delicate and tinny, but had a magical character all its own.

As she turned to look, she was startled to see Wayland's grinning face right behind her.

"It's called a mandolin. Nice, huh? There're only a few of them left in all of afterarth. I guess they could be reproduced, but no one has bothered. Makes the music all the more special to hear, doesn't it?"

Leisil sighed. So much for escaping camp. "Is that why you're here? For the music?" She should have known. Wayland was a raging musicophile—another word he'd taught her.

They got their beers and found a table near the stage that a swaying group of patrons had just left. Probably off to their cabins to smoke some dreamweed or engage in another mind-numbing recreational activity. For a moment, Leisil wished she was going with them.

When they were seated, the instrumental piece ended to a smattering of applause, and the lone musician began to sing a new piece as she played. She had an incredible voice, mellow and smooth, without all the shouting that most wannabe musicians at camp seemed to consider talent. Her voice projected effortlessly, even on the quiet refrains.

Wayland, who normally had to fill every space with pontification, was unusually quiet. When Leisil glanced over at him, his eyes were glassy. He noticed her watching him and quickly pulled a handkerchief from his pocket, wiping his eyes.

"Damn allergies," he said through his handkerchief.

"I didn't know you were allergic, and the nearest pollen is probably miles away."

"Water. I'm allergic to open water."

The woman finished her song, saving Wayland from more lame excuses for being human. She stood, saying in a strong accent, "Thank you. I'll be takin' a break now, to wet me parched lips and speak to an old friend here."

There were some grumbling noises from the crowd, but most of the patrons were too busy imbibing and flirting, arguing and making up to notice.

To Leisil's surprise, the singer approached their table. She was long and lean and had an economy of movement that was a pleasure to watch. Her thick mahogany hair was obviously her natural shade, a perfect foil to her equally perfect pale skin.

Leisil hated the woman already.

"Wayland, it's so good to see you again. What's it been? Fifteen years or so? How's Cassander these days?"

Wayland's face collapsed. "We broke up...I..."

The singer was fast on her feet, Leisil had to give her that.

"Oh, no worries," she said, with a hand on Wayland's. "Things change. I just never thought you two would ever part ways— anyway, no matter. Sorry I brought it up. It's obviously bad memories for you."

Wayland regained his voice, but he spoke as if his throat was constricted. "We split up back at the University that last term. She joined the troupe. I don't know why to this day. She never even said goodbye."

His eyes filled with tears and Leisil squirmed in her seat, infinitely uncomfortable. She'd never seen Wayland like this.

The woman, as if finally noticing Leisil, said,

"Nice to meet you. I'm Charlotte O'Reilly. Everyone calls me Charlie. An' you be a captain too?"

"No, I'm Leisil. No captain, just a grunt. It's my first season on the line."

"Just a grunt, are ya?"

Wayland, recovered somewhat and interjected, "Don't listen to her. She's one of the best archers we've ever had."

"An archer? How fascinating. Perhaps you'll be tellin' me the story of how you became a master of this craft at such a young age. Look at ya, you're just a babe! There could be a ballad in this, somewheres."

Leisil frowned until Wayland said, "Never you mind Charlie, she'll milk you for your life story, and the next thing you know she'll be singing about you all over the territory."

"I'm not sure I'm ready for that," said Leisil, "Besides, there's nothing song-worthy about my life story, trust me. I'm more interested in you, Charlie. From your accent, I'm thinking you're not from Nowhere or Hiccup."

Charlie laughed. "No, not by a long shot, girl, but that's a tale too lengthy for an overnight cruise. It involves the *Leviathin*, a sea voyage from hell with century storms, sea monsters, modern-day pirates and a foolish young girl running from a dead-end life of petty thievery, drugs and debauchery."

"Sounds like what the befores used to call a best seller, I think." said Leisil.

"I'm afraid it's more of a cautionary tale that I won't be writing down anytime soon, but 'never say never,' they say. Maybe we could swap tales one of these days."

They both looked at Wayland, who hadn't made any attempt to join the conversation. His expression was distant. Leisil assumed that he wanted to talk to his friend without a third wheel rolling through their conversation.

"I think I'll leave you two to catch up."

Before either could object, though Leisil noticed that neither of them jumped up to stop her, she got up from the table and wandered over to the dartboard. A few patrons stood slumped around the board with darts in their hands, but no one seemed in a hurry to make a throw.

"What's going on?" she asked. "Are you playing or not?"

One said, with a smirk, "We're waiting for the boat to get past the rapids. In case you haven't noticed, darts on a moving vessel can be a bit of a challenge."

"Well, you just need to account for the motion of the boat, and adjust your speed and trajectory, right?"

She held out her hand for the darts.

After a momentary frown, the man grinned and handed her the darts. "Have at it, little girl. You go right ahead and adjust that trajeckery of yours. We'd love to watch." At this, he let his eyes slide slowly from her breasts to her hips. "Let's see what you got."

He obviously expected her to make a fool of herself. While

that was always a possibility, Leisil didn't think it likely. She knew her barbs, rough water or not.

A while later, Leisil was counting her winnings when Wayland came up to her, grinning. "Did you take advantage of those poor boys?" Leisil noted that Charlie had returned to the stage.

"Those 'poor boys' are arrogant and sexist, not to mention uncoordinated, so they deserved what they got."

"No doubt, no doubt. Hey, let's get another round. I've got some sorrows to drown."

Leisil was surprised that Wayland wanted to talk about himself. It was so unlike her captain. As much as he liked to tell stories in which he was the protagonist, he rarely included an emotional arc for himself.

A few ales later, Leisil knew more than she wanted to know about the ballad of Wayland and Cassander. Apparently, the woman had broken his heart.

"Is she why you joined the Resistance?"

Wayland frowned at this. "No, of course not," he said, too quickly. Then he was silent for a moment. "Well, maybe. I never considered that."

For a man who was highly intelligent and excessively educated, Wayland could be an idiot at times.

Later, noticing his bleary eyes and the almost empty room, Leisil said, "Maybe we better get you to your cabin. You look a little tired."

"Tired? 'Course not. Jus' gettin' started. But..."

A blight had leaked into his expression.

"I got one of these we could share," he said with a sneaky grin.

He reached in his pocket and pulled out a too-large tube of pipeweed.

"What's that?"

"Pleasure stick. Been savin' it for jus' the right time."

"I don't think so." Leisil got up to leave. Wayland tried to join her, tripped and ended up on the floor. The barkeep called out,

"Hey there. We don't want none o' that in here. Get him to bed or I'll have him tossed over the side."

"What?" said Leisil, "You wouldn't."

The bartender just glared at her.

"Oh, all right." She helped the big man up with difficulty. He leaned on her like a drunken tomcat leaning on a church mouse, and they lurched their way out on deck. The air was cold and damp. It felt good compared to the stuffy, stale ale-scented bar. The breeze seemed to revive Wayland.

"Over here," he said, leading her to a space behind the captain's lookout. It was dark, narrow, and smelled of fish, but there were containers they could sit on. The deck was empty. As their eyes adjusted, Leisil became aware of a sky bubbling over with stars.

"It's beautiful," she said wistfully. "We never take enough time to notice how lovely the world still is, despite how fucked up it is."

Wayland laughed, "I knew you had the heart of a philosopher." His words were clear, as if the frigid air had leached the drunkenness out of him. Or had he been pretending all along?

He pulled the pleasure stick out of his pocket and Leisil stood hurriedly to leave.

"Oh, come on," he said, pulling her back down. "It's just a cigar."

When she eyed him suspiciously, he said, "Honest. I got it in the market at Nameless just the other blastday. Just pipeweed, I assure you. Come on. We get little enough enjoyment out of our time on afterarth as it is. Let's just sit here and enjoy the sky and the water and each other for a few moments before our shitty lives take over again."

"You make it sound so romantic."

"Ha. Yes, it is! Every iota of enjoyment we can wring out of our miserable existence, we need to do it now, before it's too late."

Leisil was silent for a while, then she said, vehemently, "I agree with you on that."

With a cackle, Wayland put the smoke stick to his lips and, miraculously, it lit itself. A tiny orange coal reflected patches of fire onto their faces in the soothing darkness. He took a deep pull.

"How'd you do that? Are you a shaman?" Leisil was beyond surprised that Wayland might have such skills.

"Naw," he said, exhaling gigantically. "Just a little trick Rapha taught me. You'll like him, I think. A solid guy. Here."

He handed the glowing stick to Leisil, and she inhaled as deeply as he had, immediately erupting in a wracking fit of coughs that threatened to spread her guts across the deck.

"Easy, easy. It's an acquired skill. You might want to start by not inhaling, at least not so enthusiastically."

"I see that," she squeezed out wheezily. Her lungs were screaming vacuums that sucked wildly for fresh air, but the toxic gases she had willingly inhaled left no room for such niceties.

After she'd recovered somewhat, she foolishly tried again. This time it was a little easier, or perhaps her abused lungs had just resigned themselves to breathing without oxygen.

"So," he said, "Are you a virgin?"

"What? Of course not!" she lied poorly. She was so shocked by his sudden attack, she couldn't even remember how to lie effectively.

"It's all right," he said with a chuckle that sounded patronizing to Leisil. "It happens a lot these blastdays. The academies are full of girls, of course. There's no shame in it. I just wondered." He was silent for a moment. "You do like guys, though, right?"

"What the fuck're you talking about? Either way, it's none of your blasted business."

"All right, all right. I was just asking. No harm, no fool, as they used to say."

"That makes no sense at all."

"Little does any more."

With an expression she couldn't quite read in the dark, he put out the cigar and leaned over to kiss her gently.

Leisil flinched, as if in pain.

"I didn't expect a peck on the lips could be quite so painful," he said with an uncertain, teasing frown. "Are you all right?"

Instead of answering, her body took over, and she kissed him back with little of the subtlety he had shown her. Soon they were tearing open each other's clothes, laying hot skin to hot skin. She climbed onto his lap, straddling him. When his cock entered her, she cried out at the sky, but the stars, possibly embarrassed, had turned their backs on them. She later realized that it had been an encroaching cloud cover. Even so, she appreciated the privacy.

There was a painful pressure at first, and then it broke through to exquisite pleasure. For just a few moments, her whole life was worth living. Then, to her deepest regret, it was over. Apparently, she was one of those few lucky women who didn't need time, or coaxing, or foreplay. Thank the Overs for little favors. She was vaguely aware that Wayland had stopped thrusting.

"Oh," she said, pulling up and off him where she'd been skewered on his penis.

"That was nice," she said in a matter-of-fact monotone.

"Yes," he said, grunting as he pulled his pants up.

He turned to her and drew her face close in his warm hands. All she could see in the dark were the glowing whites of his eyes. "But we must never do this again. I'm your captain. I could lose my posting. Are we agreed?"

They agreed, both knowing that it most likely would, and should, happen again.

15

LYDARC, NOW

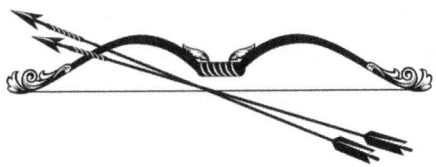

Seneca was wrong. Opportunity is what happens when your preparation sucks and all you have left is blind luck.

—Wayland Peters, as quoted by Sitka Sangashee in her personal journal

Despite an overabundance of foreboding, I allow Sitka's spirit animal to accompany us. As we prepare to leave, I turn to the group and my deliberate silence demands their attention.

"There's one more thing I must require, or this journey is off," I say to the group in a loud voice. "Does anyone have rope?"

"Rope?" asks Wayland. "It's heavy. Why would I carry rope? We're not on a sea voyage, praise Poseidon."

"I have it," Rapha says.

"At least sixty feet?"

"Of course."

Wayland awkwardly tosses aside the pack he's been inspecting. The frustration is evident in his every uncoordinated, one-handed gesture. "What are you two ninnies going on about? These caves—surely we're not going to be climbing? With a bear? What good is rope going to do us with a giant russet bear? And this?" He points at the stump of his arm. Wayland, at least physically, has responded well to my healing. His spirit is what I'm worried about. How do I heal *that*?

"You'll see." I say, calmly. "Everything will work itself out." He looks at me defiantly for a moment, then his expression turns dull, as if he doesn't really care what happens next. Painted on his features is the malaise I've been unable to erase.

My own frustration showing, I say, "Let's get going. Sitka has only a blastweek and we can't waste a moment of it."

As we approach the twisting metal stairs that will take us down to the top of the building, I look back, sparing one last glance at Sitka's body and her protector. Jin is leaning over and delicately adjusting her neck so she can rest more easily. Despite his size he's gentle with her, as if she were a fragile, thin-shelled egg, though I know Sitka to be as strong as steel when she needs to be.

The two older dragons return to their home in the mountains, though Faustina promises to check in on her nephew and his strange new friend as often as her busy mani-pedi, yoga, and reiki schedule will allow. She'll also bring them snacks, which of course Sitka will not need, as her body is suspended in time, but Jin will devour. Apparently, librarianship is a hunger-inducing duty for a dragon.

The stairs shudder and shake under me, and I watch the massive body of the russet bear sway in a frightening state of precarious imbalance in front of me.

"Why does it move like that?" asks bear-Sitka, shooting a look back at me even as she stumbles, looking ridiculous with her giant limbs crammed into the too-small space. Was it a huge mistake, bringing a forest bear into these confined spaces? Again, I show my oft-underestimated skill at stating the obvious.

Wayland responds for me. "The steps were once animated by

contained blightning machines so that the befores would not have to take more than one step. The stairs moved under them until they were deposited at their destination above or below. They had to jump off at the bottom. They even had whole roads like this."

"How odd. Were these people all confined to carts like me?"

Wayland chuckles. "No, not all of them, and they also used moving closets that went straight up and down. Most were just extremely lazy, I think."

The bear giggles, a bizarre sound coming out of her giant vocal cords. "How strange they were, the befores. It's almost no wonder they lost everything. Having no respect for what they had, gobbling up every resource, leaving nothing for their children, or their children's children. Shortsighted and greedy. That's the conclusion we can draw from places like this."

"Or perhaps their rumored experiments with time and space are actually what did them in," says Wayland under his breath, but no one hears him but me, since I stand close behind him.

Rapha has said nothing so far, as is his usual bent, so I'm surprised when he speaks. "The befores were hedonists. You're right about that, but they had advanced in ways that we can only imagine now. If we could reclaim their ancient knowledge and technical skills," his voice rises in excitement, "perhaps we could return this world to its former glory. Humans could be the courageous and industrious beings they were always meant to be."

I snort. "Are you saying we were better off in the ancient past as primitives, having so little self-awareness and initiative we chose to rely on moving steps?"

"No, of course not. But a human engineer designed these steps. I just believe that regaining our former potential is still possible. It is sleeping out there somewhere, our true capacity as a species, waiting for us to evolve into it. Humans need to reclaim their destiny and start living the dream that fate designed for them."

The bear turns back to him sharply. "You are so strange,

Rapha. You teach shamanistic magic yet preach hedonistic prehistory. I will never truly understand you."

Or trust you, I think, but have no idea where the thought comes from. Of course, I trust Rapha. Why wouldn't I? Ever since we first met, I felt a kinship with him. Maybe it was our shared shamanic power, but it feels deeper than that. Perhaps I need to rethink my distrust of everything and everyone. Nah, forget that.

Rapha laughs nervously, or so it seems to my ears. He says, "Oh, it is just a hobby of mine, studying the past and dreaming of a remade future. It means nothing, I am sure."

"Maybe," says the bear as she awkwardly navigates the dismount from the strange stairway. Broken and canted to one side, I have to wonder if it will be intact for our return. *If* we return.

To save our shamanic energy reserves, Rapha brought a lantern, which he now blights.

"What next?" asks the bear.

I say, "Up ahead, there's a rectangular hall of glass and steel that leads to a larger building. The befores called it a sky bridge, but now it's more a bridge of dirt and chaos than anything else. The rooms beyond are a total mess, and there are other, more insidious dangers there. If we can get down to the roof...From there, we will find the caves, if they're still open and not collapsed like the lava tubes."

"Always the optimist," grumbles Wayland.

I just grunt.

As we approach the opening to the underground hall, I fear the worst. I can see where the entrance was, but it's now packed with dirt, sand, and debris.

"Oh no," says Sitka. "What now? Are we doomed to fail before we even begin?"

"It appears to be mostly dirt and sand that has collapsed into the walkway," I say. "There's a chance I can call the afterarth spirits to help us."

"Is it safe to use your powers down here?" asks Wayland. "You could make it worse than it already is. This would not be my first choice for a tomb."

"Now who's the optimist?" I say through gritted teeth as I raise my arms to the afterarth and air spirits. "It's our only chance, unless we're ready to turn back now." I look at the others, whose expressions are resolute, if frightened.

I try to show a little more control than I used on the library. That turns out not to be a problem, since the afterarth spirits are exhausted from my earlier demands on their resources. It's hard to get even a little movement in the obstructing mass. It begins to rattle and shake, but nothing more.

Hit by a sudden wave of dizziness, I fall to my knees. I hear Wayland yelling, but he's far away.

"No! It's too much, too soon. You can't keep this up. Stop before you hurt yourself."

Never known for my obedience—or sense of what's good for me for that matter—I continue straining for a few more moments, until I can see a blight filtering through the billowing dust clouds. Hope flares with it.

"There's an opening!" cries Sitka. "I can see the other side."

"Oh great. I've managed to make us an opening the size of my little finger," I say, but even my own voice is coming from a great distance. I feel Wayland's hand on my back, urging me forward. Somehow, we squirm and scrabble up and over the debris, the great bear pawing and shouldering the steel beams out of our path as we go. Perhaps I was wrong about her usefulness.

The trip across seems to take forever, with the fear of collapse looming over us with every piece of rubble we climb over and under. Finally, the debris pile begins to slant downward, and the space opens up. We slide more than climb down to the floor of a gigantic, high-ceilinged room. Round glowing blights at intervals in the floor—once the ceiling—illuminate the space.

"Artificial blights down here?" asks Sitka. "What power source could last this long?"

Wayland answers, "Obviously it can't be solar. There are

stories about a form of energy that was developed in the later stages of the before times that was perpetual, but I've never seen any engineering papers or even anecdotal evidence that it existed."

Once brightly colored, but now dusty and worn machines litter the floor, where they've apparently fallen, turning it into an obstacle course for the damned. Toppled and twisted, they resemble the broken tin toys of giants.

"What are these things?" asks Sitka in wonder, as she shakes dust from her fur.

"I'm not sure, but I've seen pictures of them," answers Wayland. "One theory is that they were machines that duplicated and dispensed the monetary currency of the time, but that doesn't explain the many working parts, or the whimsical nature of the graphics and their emphasis on fruit."

A wavering voice echoes from distant shadows. "One-armed bandits, the idiot tax, fruit machines. Here perambulate sharks, fish and whales, puppies, pigeons, railbirds, and high rollers. You'll find the fulfillment of your deepest desires right here in the heart of Sin City. From sawdust joints to carpet joints, to the headquarters of Gamblers Anonymous, we've got it all. For just a small fee, we'll sell you hope and possibilities. We'll even comp you a room with a grand view of hell. Ready to place your bets?"

Wayland begins to draw his sword, and the hair stands up on the back of my neck. Then, I recognize them.

"Ignore them," I say, placing my hand on Wayland's. "They're nothing more than ghosts that cling to the past. They're a fungus blighting the rotting remains of a once-impressive waste of time."

Wayland glances at me sharply. "Ah, the soul of the poet is at last revealed."

"Fuck you."

"That's my Lydarc, saved from the depths of scholarly hell by a mundane expletive."

"Fuck you with the largest institute of higher learning that will fit up your ample ass."

"Ouch."

Several hunched figures lurch forward, their clothes in disarray, falling from their bodies in moldy strips and shreds. Their skin is a blotchy blue-gray and their eyes are nothing but blackened, empty holes. A dark perfume wafts over us, the scent of a decaying corpse, with just the hint of regret, as in a bet, long lost.

The diminutive leader, whose name I recall as Nicklaus, steps forward, his arms raised. "Oh, come now, Lydarc, my dear old friend. Please do not malign us. Did we not allow you to pass last time? Did we not show you the safe route down?"

I snort. "Only after forcing me to play your ridiculous games until my fingers bled."

"What are they?" asks Sitka, her bear head tilted in bemusement at the newcomers.

"Gamblers, I think," says Wayland, spitting the word as if it's a curse, "forced to spend eternity in purgatory, playing their ridiculous games."

"Are they unders, or alive in both dimensions?" asks the bear.

I pause to consider. "Neither, I think. Perhaps they once had souls, but they were trapped here eons ago when the Overs arrived and tipped this place on its head. If I had to give them a name, I'd call them undead."

"They're abominations," says Wayland.

Nicklaus pulls himself up and his shoulders back with a cracking sound. "Indeed? You're one to speak, with your group consisting of a talking bear, two clueless shamans, and a burned-out warrior as old as this casino."

"I am *not* a talking bear," states Sitka, despite the evidence. "Chamina is my spirit animal, and you will show some respect if you value your head."

"Well, not that much, I guess," says another of the undead, a stodgy, lumpy woman wearing what must once have been a gold lamé dress. "I'm getting a little tired of this existence, to tell the naked truth. We've been down here for centuries without a break. The bar service is abominable, not to mention the house advantage being stuck on ninety-nine percent. I mean, what do they expect, that we'll just keep playing despite the crappy odds and horrible comps?"

Nicklaus looks back at her with a frown. "Well, yes, Belinda, that's exactly what they expect. We're gamblers, remember? Nothing is gonna stop us, not rain, not gloom, nor blight, nor dropping body parts."

"You're referring to the postman's pledge, I think," says a lanky undead man behind her with a confused frown, "but something isn't quite right about the verbiage..."

"What's a postman?" asks Sitka, as she approaches the group with a curious look on her furry features.

I put a hand to her fur. "Don't get too close. I don't entirely trust them, and they might be contagious. Let's just get this over with and get moving."

Rapha cuts in. "Yes, let us please get past this unfortunate roadblock and on to the underlands, before my patience wears so thin it shatters."

"What are the odds of that?" asks one of the undead gamblers in a nasal, whining voice.

"What are the odds that we can escape this hellhole?" says another.

"Yeah," says Belinda, "we've tried every tunnel, and they all lead right back here. Why is it that Lydarc can come and go as she pleases, and we're stuck here?"

"Lydarc, take us with you," begs the gold lamé dress woman.

Lydarc raises her hands. "No. You don't understand. We're headed deeper into hell, not to the surface. You don't want to go with us on this trip, trust me."

Belinda sighs. "Just our luck."

Nicklaus leans forward with a sly smile. "You know the rules, Lydarc. We'll tell you what routes are open. All we ask is for you to grace us with your company for just a little while. Just a few innocent games. What can it hurt?"

16

LEISIL, BEFORE

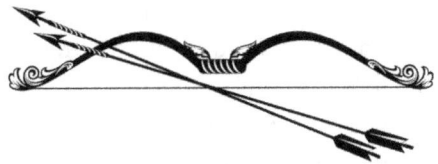

It is a wise father that knows his own child.

— WILLIAM SHAKESPEARE, *THE MERCHANT OF*
VENICE

On one of the rare occasions that all three had leave together, Leisil, Jarly and Wayland rode out to Hiccup to take in the sights. Unfortunately, the sights in Hiccup were few and far between. As they walked their ponies down the empty street, Jarly said, "What a hot bed of revelry this is. I can hardly contain my excitement."

"They just survived a minion attack," said Wayland. "Everybody's probably hunkered down in their basements, if they have them."

"You'd think they'd be out celebrating instead," Leisil interjected. "I mean, what are the odds there'd be another attack so soon after the last one?"

"I'm afraid people don't think that way and—"

Wayland was interrupted by a rumbling and a cacophony of

tinkling. A female voice yelled, "Whoa, there, Beatrice, Bobby. Halt."

They turned to find a highly decorated wagon approaching. It was painted with bright murals in primary colors and festooned with wind chimes, scrollwork and lamps of every conceivable shape and design. Slowly, the sounds died down as the two horses in harness came to a gradual stop beside them. Atop the carriage seat sat a man and a woman in well-worn traveling clothes, their muted colors at odds with the flamboyant wagon. The woman, who held the reins, stared at Wayland.

"Wayland, is that you? It can't be. What're you doing way out here in the wilderness? This place is for crazies; troubadours, vagabonds and soldiers, not college professors."

"Rebecca? Rebecca Westwind and JJ!"

Wayland handed his reins to Jarly and took the man's hand.

"JJ. It's been forever. How are you?"

"Well," said the man in a pleasant baritone voice. "We're surviving. So far, at least. Not much else you can do out here, is there? But let's get out of the street. We're headed for the inn. My ass has had about enough of this rattling torture box, and Beatrice and Bobbie need a comfy stall and a bucket of grain."

As if in agreement one of the horses snorted, making everyone laugh.

At the inn they helped get the horses settled and wandered into the empty tavern. Fortunately, there was a bartender in attendance: a squat woman in a dirty apron who did her best to ignore them until Wayland and Jarly went to the bar. They returned with frothing ales for everyone, except Rebecca, who explained that she was pregnant and avoiding alcohol. For her, they brought a somewhat murky iced tea.

"Congratulations," said Leisil. "When are you due?"

"Oh, she's a few months away yet, I think. But that's why we left the troupe. We're headed back east, to safer territory. I won't risk my little girl just to make a few coins."

"She? You know it's a girl?"

JJ chuckled. "Becka knows a lot of things she probably shouldn't, but that's her job. She tells the fortunes, while I disseminate the news."

Jarly spoke up. "If you don't mind my asking, I'm fascinated by your wagon. Is there a reason it's so...well..."

"Gaudy and loud?" laughed JJ. "That's Becka's idea. She thinks it deters the minions. My thinking is that it deters everything, including my sanity. The things I put up with for my dearest." He leaned over and kissed his partner on the forehead.

"Wayland," said Rebecca, "You still haven't explained what you're doing out here."

Wayland sat up straighter. "I'm a captain in the Resistance now. I left the university."

"It's been so long since we've seen you. I think it was before we lost Cassander—"

Wayland's face took on a look of horror. "She's dead?"

"Oh, no, no. She left the troupe with the baby to go back to the university—and you."

"The...*baby*?"

Rebecca frowned deeply. "You didn't know? But we all thought she was returning to you. That's what she said she was doing."

"I—I left soon after she did. I must have missed her!"

Wayland appeared to be in a state of shock. Rebecca took pity on him and switched the conversation to Leisil and Jarly. After a while, everyone realized that Wayland wasn't going to rejoin them: his attention far away. As they exchanged goodbyes, Rebecca leaned close to Leisil

"Take care of him. I think he needs a friend right now."

Leisil nodded, but she wasn't sure there was anything she could do for Wayland. He was deep in his own personal hell.

17

LEISIL, BEFORE

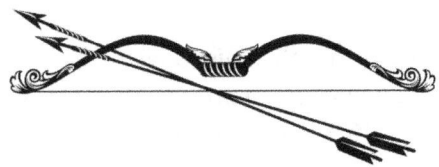

There are more things in heaven and earth, Horatio, than are dreamt of in your philosophy, and every one of them is trying to kill you.

—Wayland Peters, as quoted by Sitka
Sangashee in her personal journal

Again, she'd been fingered to replace a soldier who'd suddenly taken ill.

Leisil had no fear of night watch duty, as some of the others obviously did. She rather liked it. It was a chance to be alone with her thoughts, to deal with the fucking demon bird who threatened to burst through her skin and rip her sanity out along with her precious innards. There was a two-headed falcon inside her, clawing, scratching and screeching to be released. Leisil dared not allow it. It didn't like her. She knew that for a fact. She had no idea what the bastard might do next, and no skills to control it. Wayland still hadn't come through with his offer to take her to a shaman in the town. Maybe this teacher didn't even exist; just another of Wayland's tall tales.

Far less frightening to her were stories of the Overs, whom she'd never seen. They were said to be capable of blasting huge sections of the afterarth into oblivion or tearing your heart out at will. Leisil was beginning to think that it was all a fable: exaggerated, snowballing tales circulated by soldiers with too much leave on their hands.

This night was unusually quiet. Blastnight had only flipped a couple of times, arriving at a gentle blastday with blue sky and no wind, returning with a cosmic snap to this tranquil darkblight after only a few moments.

Mid-scattermoon would be here in a few blastdays, and the camp had been busy with last-moment preparations. A group of the latest recruits had arrived: they needed to be settled in and armored up. The majority of them were mud soldiers, as their ranks were the ones most decimated by the minions. Unfortunately, Borcine hadn't been among the fallen.

Leisil heard a scuffling sound ahead of her in the darkness, followed by an eerie whooshing whistle that made the hair stand up on her forearms. She reminded herself of Wayland's story of meeting an Over out here, then she grunted.

"More likely it was a dreamweed-induced nightmare," she told herself out loud.

A voice spoke in the dark, or in her thoughts. She couldn't be sure which. She knew she should be raising the alarm, but she was paralyzed, helpless to do anything but watch.

I can be many things, but a hallucination produced by mere herbs? I think not. In fact, I am just a tiny bit insulted by the whole concept.

The voice had a tremolo quality, as if the speaker were under-water. A gentle blight shone ahead of her, but it glowed from around an unseeable wall or a door of unknowable dimensions. One side of the sharp edge was total, limitless nothingness, the other filled with soothing blight. Something told her it would be necessary to step through this endless door or around this wall to enter the realm of the speaker.

She hesitated, but only for a moment. Something was drawing her to look. She could only resist it so long. Like her nasty spirit animal, it would eventually scratch its way to the surface with or without her permission.

That is it. Just let it happen. What can it hurt? You are different, you know. More receptive than most. You have the sight. We could use you.

'We could use you.' Later she would remember these words and rue the blastday she stepped past the darkness, into a blight that held no brightness to ameliorate her future dark.

Despite her growing fear, Leisil's legs took her around the wall. Blight met her, but it was blight fashioned from night, motion made of stillness, beauty constructed of the ugliest, most abhorrent, unworldly abomination she'd ever seen. The smell—like nothing she'd ever experienced. It smelled of singed hope, fuming and stinking of what could be, but shouldn't. Yet it was beautiful, of this Leisil would never have a doubt.

She was forced to look at the unseeable. Was it strange and difficult to fathom, or so easily conceived of as to be invisible? Was it a bird, or a bludgeon beast? Was it tall and tasteful, or fat and fetid? As she stepped closer—even as her instincts screamed for her to step back—the thing began to sing. If a thousand angelic voices had chimed together in perfect harmony, it could not sound as sweet. She felt larger than she could be, more complete. Alabaster wings fluttered and danced, each feather sparkling in the blight of its own minuscule sun. Leisil's skin tingled and tears filled her eyes, blinding her, but after all, what need had she to see this thing bursting from inside her?

When, after an eon or so, she'd recovered enough to think words, she whispered, "You're an angel."

How sweet you are, little one, but no, I am no such beatific being of your people's vivid imaginations. I am what you call an Over.

Stupidly, she repeated, "But you *are* an angel."

Instead of answering, the being bent down to her with a perfectly shaped, gigantic human hand formed of molten gold, dripping honey and liquid sunset. Instead of touching her face, as Leisil expected, it reached for her chest and through it, into her being. There it deposited a searing hurt beyond any imaginable agony.

Leisil and the falcon within her screamed in unison and fell to the depths of their own worst imagined hell.

Then Wayland was there, swinging his sword with a ferocious yell and a mighty arcing effort. The sword went through the beast as if it were made of cloud candy, but at the end of his swing, the blade crackled and splintered, disintegrating into acrid, smoking dust. The Over faded away, back to whatever hell or heaven it had come from.

Leisil heard him call her name so distantly it seemed he was speaking from another world. Then all was blessed silence for a very long time.

18

LYDARC, NOW

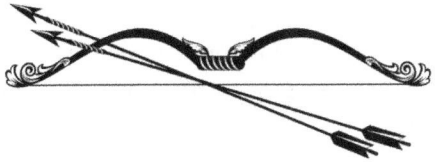

If I had a world of my own, everything would be nonsense. Nothing would be what it is, because everything would be what it isn't. And contrary wise, what is, it wouldn't be. And what it wouldn't be, it would. You see?

—LEWIS CARROLL, *ALICE IN WONDERLAND*

The gamblers do their best to distract us. I must admit, they do a pretty good job of it. Wayland, as ever, is susceptible to correcting sub-par logic wherever he finds it. It's almost as if they know that and use it against us.

First, it's the wheel. They call it the Wheel, with a capital W like it's a proper noun. Who knows what it was originally called?

"Pick a color, pick a number and count your blessings to be so lucky to choose from among all these wonderful chances," says Nicklaus. "Black or red, that's it. So simple, right? Or pick your numbers, one through thirty-six, plus zero, or double zero. How easy could it be?"

Wayland scratches his chin, saying, "Wait just a moment. You mean to get any significant kind of payout, we need to pick one number out of thirty-six, plus one zero and one double zero. That makes the odds one in thirty-eight. That's only a two point six-three percent chance of winning per spin. Those are horrendous odds! Why would anyone play this game? The house is going to win ninety-seven percent of the time, and the longer you play, the more you'll lose."

"Well," says a tall blonde woman with black eyebrows but dirty pits where her eyes once had lived, "It's fun, isn't it? I remember the time my number came up, and I won seventeen hundred and fifty dollars. I was an accountant in the other life, so I remember. I bought rounds for everyone."

"Yeah, she did," says a rotund, grinning man with acne-scarred skin and thick eyeglasses over his empty eye sockets.

"But how much did you spend on bets before you won?" asks Wayland.

"Oh, I don't keep track of that."

Wayland splutters. "You know to the centavo how much you won, but have no idea how much it cost you? And what about food and drinks and lodging?"

"If you spend enough, that's all free. Besides, it's entertainment, isn't it?"

"How can it be free if you have to spend thousands to get it for 'free?'"

The lanky man turns to Lydarc and covers his mouth as if to hide what he's saying, keeping the words from no one. "Bit of a downer, isn't he, this boyfriend of yours?"

"He's not my—oh, never mind. Let's just get on with this."

We surround the Wheel, which, despite the best efforts of the undead, sits at a slight angle on the littered floor of the casino. The faded, broken word *Roule...* encircles the dusty surface. From my last experience here, I know that this slight incline favors certain numbers. "Give me these numbers: red one, two, three, five, eight, thirteen, twenty-one and thirty-four."

"Wait," says Wayland, "Those are Fibonacci numbers."

"Liberace?" croons an elegant undead woman in a once-black, once-elegant gown that now hangs in tatters from her bony frame. "Oh, he was something special on the Strip in his day, I can tell you. I've seen vids. What a charmer, and not a bad piano player, neither."

"No, no. *Fibonacci*, the ancient mathematician. The number sequence follows patterns of nature, like some shells and spiral seed kernel growth, and is related to the golden ratio. He outlined it in his *Liber Abaci*, or *Book of the Abacus*, in the year 1202, in the before times."

"That's just what I said, 'Liberace,' but you're pronouncing it wrong, young man."

"No, no," says Wayland, showing his irritation by the way he nervously fingers his sword hilt.

"Don't even start, Way," I say. "It's just not worth it. Can't you see the logic games they're playing with you?"

"Logic? There's no logic in any of this!"

"I can't agree more. Let's just do this and be gone, all right?"

With a grunt, Wayland steps back to let me place my bet. The wheel spins erratically and at last the stone comes to rest on thirteen with a rattle. I win back slightly more than I wager, and the undead come to life.

"See? You can win. It's easy. Go ahead, play again," says the leader.

"I think not. I believe in the 'quit while you're ahead' method of gambling."

"Who uses that method? I never heard of it," says the gold lamé woman. "No legitimate gambler would quit early."

"That's right," says another, "It's just not done. We play around the clock, or not at all. It's who we are."

"Well, it's not who I am, and we don't have all blastnight. According to our agreement, you need to give me the first clue to the route if I win, so?"

"Oh, all right." says Nicklaus petulantly, like a little child being forced to give up his favorite toy, "The northwest skybridge was open last time I looked. It's your best bet if you stay to the right until about halfway, then it's just a crapshoot from there."

"What's that? asks the bear.

"What, a crapshoot?" he says, "It means your odds are not the best no matter which way you go."

"Oh, great," says Rapha. "Why do we even need these cursed aberrations? How can you be sure they are telling the truth?"

"Oh, they are," I reply. "I learned the hard way last time I was down here. Just follow my lead, and we'll get out of here and make it to the lake in one piece."

"The lake?" asks Sitka.

"It's easier if I just take you there. It's kind of hard to explain, and you might not want to follow us all the way once you understand what it entails. I'd prefer that you wait there for us on the shore of the lake."

"No way! I'm not sitting around while you guys have some grand adventure in the underlands without me. This is my test, right? My initiation into the shamanic way. You did it, didn't you? With Rapha?"

"She has a point," says Rapha, his tone as close to sheepishness as I've ever heard it.

I glare at him. "You're not helping, and, as I recall, you turned my life into the ultimate nightmare on that so called 'shamanic journey of enblightenment.' What a load of grundlecrap that was. Throwing me to the chupacabra was the least of it."

"This is no time to get into that. You survived, didn't you? And came out stronger and wiser from my excellent instruction."

I growl, preparing to launch myself at him.

"Guys, guys," interrupts Wayland. "Let's not lose sight of our goal. You can work through your petty differences another time."

"Petty differences? You—" I say, pointing at him with one sharp finger.

"Please," pleads the bear, "I have no desire to die up there while you all argue down here. Can we continue?" Her beady bear's eyes slice through my rabid, uncontrolled soul with the sharp blade of reason.

I sigh deeply, trying to calm my rampaging temper. "Yes, you're right, Sitka, as usual."

I turn to the leader of the undead, who says with a hopeful grin, "Shall we continue the games?"

With a group grumble, the undead move on to the next trick in their arsenal, the black jacks table. The cards have shriveled to scraps of wispy, crispy cringles, but we make do.

When we finally finish the required number of games to get the information we need, we learn that all the other tunnels are open.

"Why didn't you just tell us that to begin with?" says Wayland, stepping forward, his eyes flashing murderous intent.

Nicklaus puffs out his chest and says, "There is a proper way to do these things. You can't rush the fulfillment of your fate."

I turn to the others. "They crave contact. Can you blame them? If nothing changes, they'll spend eternity down here, playing their silly games."

"The point is, we've wasted a lot of time we can't afford to lose," says Rapha.

I rub my tired eyes. "I know. Let's get moving."

We make it through the skybridge and into the tunnels beyond. At first, they're wide and tall, with plenty of room and air, but that changes gradually as the tunnel leads us ever downward. Soon, we're forced to stoop as we walk. I look back at the bear, who is scrabbling through on her knees. I let the others pass so I can speak to Sitka alone.

"We're almost there, but it gets worse. Are you sure you want to continue?"

"I'll make it," huffs Sitka.

"It would be no shame to turn back now. I'd rather not take you the rest of the way. The underlands are no place for a girl."

"Lydarc!" roars the bear. Everyone turns to stare back at us. Dust filters down from the roof of the cave. "I'm not a child. I need to do this. You can't protect me, nor do I want you to. Not anymore."

"But you don't understand what you're getting into. The underlands, it's..."

"It's what? Our most terrible fate? The worst hell each one of us thinks we deserve?"

I stare at her.

"Yes," she says, "You didn't know I knew, did you? You underestimate me, as usual. I've had visions of my own. I've been studying the underlands my whole life, gathering every tidbit of fact and gossip I could find. Reading every account, fiction or reality—sometimes I couldn't tell which—to ascertain some picture of what we would face. Then, I listened to everything that Wayland and Rapha told me, along with a few things they said when they thought a silly crippled girl couldn't hear or was too stupid to understand."

"I'm sorry—"

"Don't be. I'm ready for this. Let's get on with it now, before I decide to eat the lot of you and carry on alone."

I laugh, facetiously, and the tension in the small space lessens slightly.

"All right," I say with a sigh, "The tunnel will open up soon, or so I remember."

"Good. I'm tired of crawling on my knees. It's unbecoming of a russet bear in her prime."

We continue, the walls getting even closer. The aroma of stale, dripping water, mud, and human and ursine sweat grows ever stronger, until I detect a slight coolness on my face and sigh with relief.

"We're almost there."

Suddenly, the tunnel widens and a blue blight glows ahead of us. We gather before a vertical pane of water facing us like a rippling wall, extending upwards as far as we can see. Our faces open in awe of the sight—even mine, though I've seen it before. Tiny waves dance across its surface and sparks of blight flicker and fidget as we stare.

"What is it?" asks Sitka, "It's beautiful."

"Welcome to the lake," I say, with a smile that trembles just a little at the edges. "Now, get me the rope."

19

LEISIL, BEFORE

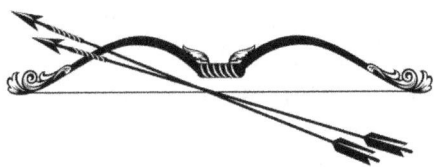

Alexander Pope understood it better than many. He said, "A little learning is a dangerous thing." I believe, had he survived into our present hell, that he would have added, "But a lot of learning will be the demise of mankind."

—WAYLAND PETERS, AS QUOTED BY SITKA
SANGASHEE IN HER PERSONAL JOURNAL

L eisil learned only later that she'd been abed for twelve blastdays, racked by fever dreams and afflicted by a faltering, erratic heartbeat.

No wonder. Her heart was struggling to compete with another power source: an oozing golden goop of alien origin.

The peri-soul.

At least that was Wayland's name for it. When she woke with a scream containing many questions, she sensed Wayland in the background. His presence gave her the strength to live on, despite the pain. After the healers gave up, aghast and baneful of even touching her for fear of some contagion, Wayland stayed.

But the healers need not have worried. The peri-soul was hers and hers alone. She couldn't share it or shed it, no matter how much she wished it gone.

Finally, her body gave in and let the hideous thing take over. The healers said she was gone too long to be revived, so they didn't try. Then, as they were hauling her body out, her heart started up again, jerking into a hesitant gurgling, wheezing *pitter-pat*. It was doing its best, even though it was now second in line when it came to sustaining her life. She woke with a start on the swaying gurney and took a great gasping breath, then threw up a howl that pierced the gray sky.

That was the first blastday of the pain. It filled every corner of her being, throbbing and cutting, poking and stabbing, never letting her be. They gave her poppy-seed tincture, but even that only dulled the most acute corners of her misery.

The pain was made worse by the fact that no one could tell her what was happening. They'd never seen anything like it. The fear of being transmogrified into some kind of Over abomination was almost greater than her terror of being ended.

In those first blastdays, the peri-soul was on the outside. It scratched and scrabbled, trying to burrow its way into her chest. It burned and ached, which then became an exquisite pain as it ate its way through her flesh. She could smell the acrid stench of her ribs and tendons dissolving. The pain went on, it seemed like forever until the horrid mass melted into her chest, where it would reside—supposedly—until her final forever.

Her body was changing too, in subtle ways. She could feel it happening. There were Over bugs crawling under her skin. Her hearing was more acute. In time, she would see that her ears had changed, gotten larger and extended, almost like little wings, from the side of her head. Her eyesight was sharper too, and her eyes, when she looked in the warped mirror in the lavatory, protruded slightly, making her face look even more bug-eyed than it had before. Leisil knew she'd never been pretty, but this was almost too much. What else could fate throw at her? She feared that she was about to find out.

In that miserable time of recovery and adjustment, Wayland and Jarly kept her sane. One of them was at her bedside whenever they could be. She often woke sweating and screaming from some undecipherable nightmare to find Wayland calmly reading one of his books, sitting with his legs stretched out and crossed in the hard-backed chair, the only seating in the room. He wore a bandage on his temple from his own contact with the Over.

As she again laid back from her daymares with a groan, he said, "Squad's doing pretty well, but they miss you."

"Somehow, I doubt that." Leisil stared up at the drab canvas ceiling of the healer's tent, noticing a spider scuttling away from her.

"No, really. Johnson said just yesterday, 'Whatever done happened to that weird Leisil bitch?'" He spoke in a whiney tone that mimicked the speaker perfectly.

Leisil couldn't help but snort as the little-girl voice just sounded so absurd coming out of the big brown man. She said, "It's been what, a fortblight, and she's just now noticing my absence?"

"Well, at least she caught on, eventually. Come on, don't you think it's time you got out of that bed and back to work?" He closed his book with a resounding slap. She noticed the title: *Stranger in a Strange Land*. It described exactly how she felt. She knew that just one book was worth a month's salary to a Resistance fighter. Why was this obviously well-to-do man playing soldier?

Trying to rise, she groaned again as the pain overwhelmed all rational thought.

"I've got an incentive for you. That shaman I was telling you about. He's back in town. I've got leave starting tomorrow, so I thought we'd give him a visit tonight, see if he'd be willing to teach you how to use your shamanic power, control this weird spirit animal, and maybe figure out this Over bit you seem to be stuck with."

"Tonight?"

"Yeah, he's on the night shift at the Nameless tavern."

"Wait, what? A shaman works at a tavern? And it's nameless? You're not making any sense."

"It's not the Nameless Tavern. Nameless is the name of the town, silly. The tavern, well, it doesn't have a name. Just called the tavern, or the inn, as far as I know. There's not much sense in differentiating it from any others, because they don't exist, if you get my drift. And what's wrong with a shaman being a barkeep?"

"I don't know, I just thought..."

"They aren't shamans by profession. At least I don't know any who are. They're warriors and farriers, shopkeepers and drunks. Just ordinary folk, except they have unusual skills, that's all."

"I doubt if any of them also have one of these." She pointed at her own chest, which was emitting a dim glow from the peri-soul within. "Or this." She again indicated her chest.

Wayland frowned. "Oh, you mean that recalcitrant spirit animal of yours? I never heard of such a thing, but I suppose it's possible. Whoever heard of a shaman with a spirit animal that they were in constant battle with? It's just odd, and probably quite uncomfortable as well. He has a temper, doesn't he?"

"That's the understatement of the millennium. The fucker just pisses me off to no end, and I'm afraid of what might happen if I allow him to escape."

"Alright. I think this guy can help you. He knows a little bit about everything, and perhaps a lot about nothing. He'll have an idea, anyway. He always does."

As ever, Wayland was as indecipherable as her strange nightmares.

Leisil made it through her final medical assessment, which consisted of the statement, "We can't help you, but we need the bed space, so out you go." They discharged her from the med tent with instructions to take it slow. She wandered aimlessly, until she ended up at the armory tent. She volunteered to help Cuspis, the acerbic head of archery supplies. He was everyone's favorite bowyer, but not because of his winning personality. Leisil wasn't sure he could qualify as having a personality at all, the man was so dry. His puckered face expressed what appeared to be his one conclusion about life: dissatisfaction.

She tried again to convince him to help develop her idea for a combined longbow-and-crossbow weapon, but he just gave her his signature grunt that she now translated as *I'll think about it.* She was making headway. At first, he'd just laughed at her.

When he grew irritated with her fiddling and constant questions, he set her to work fletching arrows.

As she worked, she listened to the gossip that was spreading through the camp. The minions were attacking more sporadically of late, showing up outside the usual times. Some wondered if there were too many men in the camp. One girl even mentioned Wayland being the possible cause. Leisil wasn't too worried about Wayland. He was probably the most popular captain in the entire camp. Besides, they were far below the quota for male fighters.

She was fletching her last arrow of the blastday when Wayland wandered in.

"I hope that batch ends up in my quiver. You missed your calling; you're a much better fletcher than archer. And that's saying a lot, since you're quickly turning into one of the best shots on the line."

Leisil raised her right hand and observed it critically. It still shook slightly.

"Maybe not anymore."

"Nonsense. You'll get it back. Who knows, maybe this perisoul will only make you better."

"There is no place for optimism in this woman's army."

Wayland just grinned as he led her out of the tent.

The ride into Nameless was uneventful, thankfully, with very few timesmears or weather changes. No minions showed their faces, not that minions had faces anyway, unless you counted the horse faces of the nags. Wayland had procured a couple of ponies from the cavalry for the trip. They arrived well before dusk, even though it had been deepest bitterblight just a moment before.

The tavern was a nondescript, rundown building that probably didn't warrant a name after all. A rickety wooden sign sported faded lettering that read, *Tavren, ale an grog, fifer credet per cuppa.*

"Not much on spelling, these town's folk of yours," said Leisil with a laugh as Wayland held the creaking door for her.

"Ignore that. Former owner was from Winnermucks, I hear."

What being from that long-dead northern city meant for your spelling acumen, Leisil feared to ask.

Inside, the place was so dark that she stumbled, stopping in her tracks for a moment so her eyes could adjust. The bar itself was nothing more than a collection of mismatched wooden tables, laid out in a ragged line. The few dusty bottles behind it stood in rickety crates stacked one upon the other on their sides. One oak barrel appeared to be the centerpiece of this fine establishment, its boar's head tap dripping a molasses-colored liquid onto the grimy, straw-littered floor.

The bar was empty, except for her, Wayland, and the bartender, who was about to pour himself an ale from the tap as they entered. He turned and said, "Ah, Wayland. It has been a while, has it not? And who is this lovely lady who accompanies you?"

He was a handsome man, Leisil had to admit, with black hair and a concise, muscular frame. But it was his eyes that held her spellbound. They were as bright as highburn sky and as deep as a volcanic crater lake. They glowed with an unusual shade of blue, blight and clear, highblighted by specks of gold that sparkled even in the gloom of the ill-lit tavern.

As the man pulled down two more (mostly) clean glasses from a crate, Wayland said, "Rapha, this is Leisil. She's the one I sent you the message about."

Rapha turned to face her and, if possible, his eyes burned an even brighter blue. "Ah, Leisil, it is indeed a pleasure to meet you, valiant warrior. Perchance we can delve into the crux of this peri-soul problem. And there is your mighty spirit animal to tame as well."

Leisil was not a fan of his flamboyant speech. If anything, it was more obscure than the grundlecrap Wayland spouted. Irritated, she slapped her hands on the table. "Jesus fucking crispy christers. Can you help me or not?"

Rapha stared, and the bar was silent for an uncomfortable moment. Wayland laughed, a guffaw that echoed from the wood-paneled walls of the tavern to the slightly open door, where it surely drifted toward the street and into the unwelcoming ears of any passersby, though Leisil had seen none of the "town's folk" as Wayland called them, since they'd arrived.

Wayland smacked his friend on the shoulder and grinned inanely. "I warned you she would be a handful. Are you sure you're up for this, my man?"

Leisil immediately regretted her outburst and spoke before the bartender could respond. "I'm sorry. I'm just a little impatient these blastdays—and irritable," she added before Wayland could beat her to it. "Between the peri-soul and that fucking two-headed falcon, I'm at my wit's bitter end. I seriously need help. Please forgive my rudeness. I know I couldn't make a worse first impression. It's just that..."

As she spoke, Rapha dropped the bar rag and reached out a powerful hand with perfectly groomed fingernails to grab hers. He was silent for too long, and Leisil became self-conscious. She pulled her hand away forcibly and glanced around the bar. It was too quiet. Where were all the town's folk?

Finally, he said, as if the conversation hadn't paused, "Nonsense. You are doing phenomenally well, considering everything you have been through. I cannot say I would have adapted as well as you have, or recovered so quickly. You are a tough one, Leisil Frandling; a real survivor. It would be an honor to teach you what I know about our craft, and help you if I can, to deal with the peri-soul and the bothersome bird as well."

"There, that's settled," said Wayland with a deep breath. "Now finish pouring us those ales. My lips are as parched and puckered as my great-grandmother's arsehole, which I can tell you—"

"That is quite enough information, Captain," laughed Rapha. "Two Bores Not ales coming up."

"Boar's snot? What a horrible name for a beer," said Leisil.

"No, no, my dear. It is Bores Not, B-O-R-E-S followed by the capital 'N' in NOT. The brewmaster wanted everyone to know his latest ale will not put them to sleep. Apparently, the last one was a bit of a snoozer, as they say. After a round or two, half the bar was asleep in their chairs. Not sure what happened with that batch. Said something about boiling the wort too long. Bores Not is an unfortunate choice of name, I will admit, but I could not talk him out of it. The swine-shaped tap was my idea. Carved it myself." Rapha stood up and bowed, waving his arm in a show of mock pride.

"Just lovely," said Leisil, as she plopped down heavily in one of the surprisingly comfortable chairs beside the rough tables, and took a sip of her ale. To her amazement, it was exceptionally good, with a bitter, rich, hoppy taste that she had come to love from the beers in the downtime bar. It was a miracle that anyone could grow hops in the wild seasons of afterarth, but they managed—for the sake of a good brew, and everyone's sanity. Fuck medicinal herbs and healthy vegetables.

"You might want to give up carving," she said.

"Oh, why is that?" asked Rapha with a curious frown.

"I notice you're missing the little finger of your left hand."

"Very observant. But no, it was not carving that caused that. I was helping a friend. I guess you could say I gave it up for a good cause."

Leisil grunted at this strange response but hesitated to ask more. Though curious about this "finger of mystery," as she called it in her thoughts, her own problems took precedence.

Pulling her shoulders back resolutely, she said, "Can we get on with this training you spoke of?"

"Oh, no, not tonight, I am afraid."

"What?"

"Well, this is going to be a ten widder-widths race, not a mad dash for the latrine door, if you understand my meaning."

"No, I don't." Frustrated and tired from her first blastday out of the med tent, Leisil stood abruptly to leave. She weaved as she stood and Wayland put a hand on her arm. Rapha raised his hands. "No, no, please do not misunderstand me, brave woman," said Rapha. "The appointment of an apprentice is no small matter. I must prepare for our journey, and I will need to clear it with the Council, of course, though that will be mostly a formality, considering my standing."

"What council? What journey?" Leisil sat down, but her thoughts were still ablaze with an internal fire that, she had to believe, was the result of her twin curses, the falcon and the peri-soul. Then she paused; told herself to step back and think for a change. If she were honest with herself, wasn't it also the rage and impatience that made up the greater part of her own personality? The man had a point. Had she really expected him to solve all her problems in one night? Well, maybe.

Tugging on her braid, she added, "I'm sorry. I'm saying that a lot tonight, aren't I? I understand that this won't be a quick fix, and I'm willing to do whatever it takes to get these things under control. I appreciate your patience with me. I have a lot to learn, but I'm ready."

Wayland gawked at her with wide eyes, as if she'd turned into a two-headed grundle right before their eyes.

"Wow," he said, "You're different, since..."

"Since I died?"

"Well, that and everything else you've been through. I guess you had to grow up fast, with the life you've led."

"I don't think I was ever a child, to be honest, but I'm not feeling sorry for myself. It's just time I stopped being a victim and started making decisions for myself."

Leisil took a swig of the excellent ale to hide the slight tremor in her hands. Despite her strong words, doubts haunted her. What did training to be a shaman entail? Would she be able to control the fucking falcon? She had a premonition that none of it would be as easy as it seemed, but nothing ever was, was it?

20

LYDARC, NOW

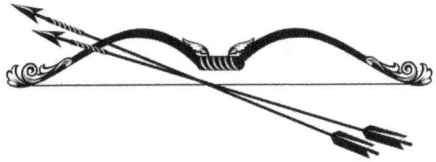

Untethered, adrift in my self-imposed nightmares. Drowning in rage. That is how I would describe my life up to this point.

— LYDARC, AS QUOTED BY SITKA SANGASHEE,
EVOLUTION OF THE SHAMAN MASTER

I 'm forced to explain again how it works, even though the truth is I'm almost as clueless as they are. I give it my best. Still, all I get are blank stares from Wayland and Sitka. Rapha is in his ancient Greek statue mode.

"To reach the underlands, I have to drown in the waters of the lake. The deathguards will revive me once they pull my body from the water. This is how the half-dead are sent to the underlands. Of course, their bodies are already ended in the upper realm when they show up here."

The bear says, "Lydarc, this is insane. How can you be sure they'll revive you? Or that they'll even find your body in the first place? It's just over-under crazy. And the rope. You actually expect us to tie ourselves to it so you can pull us through once you're revived? I've heard some harebrained plans, but this, this—"

I toss up my hands in exasperation. "I don't especially like the idea of being forevered, but if you've got a better plan, I'm all ears."

I regret the ears reference immediately, resisting the urge to push them down against my skull. If I do, they just pop out again. It's so irritating.

Wayland asks. "So, you never found Jarly last time? Rapha hasn't told me much about your trip, except that you made it back alive."

"No, I stayed as long as I could before the place started to get to me. The underlands are as huge as the lands above. In a way, they mirror our lands, but not geographically. They may have the same numbers of lakes and deserts as we do; they're just in different places. I knew the odds were thin that I could find one person among so many sufferers, but—well, eventually I had to give up."

"I'm sorry."

"It's long ago. Let's just forget it and get this over with."

My hands are sweating, and I might throw up. I hate this. I wish we could have gotten here through the lava tubes. This would all be over and I'd be sitting somewhere smoking my homegrown dreamweed and drinking some really bad rotgut scatter moonshine. Sweat beads up on my forehead. Enough stalling.

"The lava tubes and the Fallen City both lead to the same lake?" asks the bear. "How is that possible?" The bear slaps her paw to her own forehead. "Never mind. That was a stupid question. Probabilities, right?"

I turn to Rapha, who has frozen in the act of studying the ceiling of the cave. I say, "I came looking for Jarly, but it was also suggested by the Shamanic Council, or cult, if you prefer. A tiny mistake they and Rapha made was failing to include the fact you have to die to get there."

This pulls Rapha out of his trance, as is my intention. "It is not a cult. We are doing very important work. Work that will benefit mankind."

I huff. "Oh yeah. Work that's so important that sending one inconsequential apprentice to likely oblivion with an almost impossible task is no big deal."

"Obviously, it wasn't impossible. You made it to the underlands and back."

"Except that you somehow forgot to mention the pertinent facts."

Sitka is silent, staring into the swirling waters as if it might give them answers. No doubt she's reconsidering this whole lunatic mission. I don't blame her.

Enough stalling.

I turn back to face the sparkling, gravity-defying surface of the lake. "We're wasting time. I'm going through. You can follow or not; I won't waste another moment arguing about it." Tying the rope around my waist, I hand the end to Rapha. The others are silent, which I take for acquiescence. As I leap forward, I hear the frantic sounds of rope being twisted and tied, then a voice saying, "Wait, Lydarc. I have an id—"

The voice is cut off as water fills my ears with blessed silence. Sideways becomes down, then up. I swim for the blight. I struggle, because you don't just toss away a life. The urge to survive is too strong. I swim hard for the surface until my chest catches fire, and my lungs burn for the caress of precious, cooling water.

My mostly wasted life doesn't flash before my eyes, but Wayland does, the blastday he tells me that he's leaving to be with Cassander, that she's always been the love of his life and we can't see each other again. Well, our relationship had entailed something a bit more intimate than "seeing" at this point. It was the same blastday that Jarly was ended.

I never cried then, but now the memory fills me with unbearable anguish. A sob bubbles up from my throat, and water rushes in. I choke and cough it out, but the reflex is too strong, drawing liquid forever back into my chest. I panic, but it does me no good.

Eventually, my heart stops, and even the peri-soul ceases to function, or at least I stop being aware of it. I burp out a vile taste and my spirit animal, the two-headed gyrfalcon, bursts out of me and swims back toward the cave. It galls me that he will survive, while I must be ended. Did I mention I hate that fucker?

Sometime later, I wake to sheer misery. I can't breathe, but I can't stop trying to breathe, either. It's a conundrum of agony and in-betweens. The world is harsh and unforgiving. The silence is tempting and smooth. I choose neither, but fate chooses for me. Rough hands pound my back until I'm vomiting water. A tiny minnow squirms away in the brackish gunk I spit up.

My stomach heaves and my heart aches, not just for an almost lost life, but for lost love as well. Yes, I finally admit; it had been love, at least the one-sided kind, had not I fucked it up so completely.

Coughing up the last of my onerous regret, and a bit more lake water, I open my eyes. The world is fuzzy.

A blond giant leans over me, a look of concern on his teutonic features. "Thor?" I say, "Is that you?"

"Yes, Lydarc. You cut it pretty close this time. We weren't sure we could get you out. Something kept pulling you under. I had to untie it."

The rope.

I look down at my waist. The rope is gone.

21

WAYLAND, BEFORE

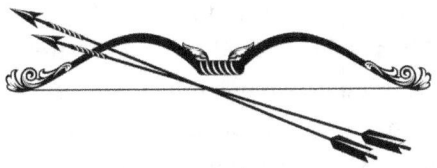

I loved her against reason, against promise, against hope, against happiness, against all discouragement that could be.

— CHARLES DICKENS, *GREAT EXPECTATIONS*

W ayland pulled up on the reins and his pony stopped abruptly, dirt billowing around them.

Ever since the trip to Hiccup he'd taken to roaming the countryside on his leave blastdays when he wasn't with Leisil. It just settled his mind to be moving. Plus, the constant threat of danger kept him alert and less likely to slip into painful thoughts of the past.

Today, his rambling had taken him back to Hiccup without any conscious decision. When he arrived at the town gate and showed his credentials to be let in, he found that Hiccup was dirtier and even less populated than he remembered. The people he did see either hung their heads in apparent dejection, beyond caring if they survived another blastday, or were hyper-alert, looking around frantically for the next minion that might slice them to pieces or squish them to pulp.

He remembered the town had a small inn and made his way down the dirt street toward it. To one side stood a brightly decorated wagon.

His heart thundered. Then he told himself it could be any traveler, the brave wandering entertainers who made their living by singing, performing, telling stories, and sharing news across the territory. Those who worked so near the front rarely had an extended life expectancy. No one might witness their demise out here. Maybe a patron would note that his favorite troubadour no longer showed up every scattermoon, but more likely no one even realized they were gone. They were just erased, taken by a world that offered little comfort and even less legacy when they were dragged into the underlands.

To his disappointment, the tavern had only a scattering of patrons, and the stage, a makeshift affair built of pallets tied together, was empty.

A young barmaid wandered over, cleaning her fingernails and ignoring him, apparently in no hurry to take his order.

"Wadda ya want?" slurred the girl, who couldn't be over fifteen. With intelligent eyes, curly auburn hair and a delicate, oval face, she would have been an impressive young woman, were it not for the deep scowl that seemed to be permanently tattooed on her features.

"What's on tap?" he asked with an affable smile.

"Don' know."

"Well, that informs me that rudeness is at the top of the menu, at least. How about a beer? Can you handle that?"

The girl stomped off. Returning a few moments later, she plopped a foaming tankard of thick ale onto his table, spilling a good quantity of it as she did so.

"Shit," said the girl. "Got it too full again, and the foam is ridiculous."

"You might try holding the cup at an angle and pouring the

beer slowly down the inside. Technically, what's happening is that less contact means less air is allowed into the liquid, thus limiting the creation of foam."

The girl eyed him with suspicion. "What are you, some kind of college-educated ale pouring expert?"

Wayland chuckled. "No. More like a drinking expert. Thanks. I'll start a tab, if you don't mind."

She squinted at him. "You a soldier?"

"Yes. We're stationed at—"

"That's good then. You guys get regular pay, and have some actual morals, is what Kent told me. Anybody else gotta pay as they go."

"I assume Kent is the owner?"

"No. More like the manager slash bartender slash dogsbody. My mom's the new owner. We just got to town a couple weeks ago." The barmaid pushed back her thick hair, and Wayland noticed how her dark eyes shone, even in the meager blight of the tavern. So familiar. Where had he seen eyes like that before?

She continued hesitantly, as if the words were painful to say, "When you asked what was on tap, I didn't... What I mean is, I'm new and haven't memorized everything yet. I didn't mean to be quite so rude. Sorry."

"That's no problem. I totally understand. What's your name?"

"Eva. Eva Winston Peters. Not sure why Mom insists we still tag on the Peters name. Never met my father and I couldn't care less if I ever do. He abandoned us, you know. Don't need him, anyway. We're doing just fine on our own, Mom and me."

He was putting things together; the wagon, a single mom with the last name of Winston, the age of the girl. Could it be? Wayland just stared, doing his best imitation of Lot's wife in the before times Christian Bible.

"Winston Peters? Your name is Peters?" he croaked. It was little more than a whisper.

Before he could say more, a tall, ivory-skinned woman took the stage and sat gracefully, raising a cello to her side. As she played, the space around them was filled with an all-encompassing sense of comfort and pleasure, as if her notes painted liquid joy across every surface in the room.

Wayland felt it in his bones and remembered. Oh yes, he remembered.

As she played, the woman glanced around at her audience. When her eyes lit on Wayland, the music stuttered for just one, almost imperceptible note, then her smile, and the music, resumed.

She played and sang for a time. Her voice was a beautiful counterpoint to the cello. When she finished *Chansons Madécasses* by Ravel, there was applause from every corner of the room. Though there were relatively few patrons this early, they generously filled her tip basket.

When she finished, she came directly to Wayland and sat beside him. She waved a hand at Eva, who poured her a blight ale and brought it to the table. It wasn't overflowing with foam. Quick study, this one.

"You know this guy?" asked the girl.

"Yes," said the woman hesitantly. "I'll explain later."

The girl stared, making no move to leave the table.

"Eva, I think there are glasses that need washing in the back."

"Oh, all right." Eva stomped away and Wayland smiled after her, then turned to the woman.

"She's amazing."

"I can explain—"

"Explain why you left without telling me we had a child on the way? I don't think, with all the time in the world, you could explain that in a way I could make sense of. She thinks I abandoned you both."

Cassander put her head in her hands. She didn't cry, but her hands shook. When she pulled them away from her face, her expression was anguished.

"I'm so sorry, Way. At the time, it seemed like the right thing to do. We were both so young. I had just committed to join the troupe, and you had your position at the university. You loved to teach. I couldn't ask you to give all that up for the life of a traveler. After Eva was born, I thought better of it, realizing how wrong it was to keep you from your daughter."

"Then, why—"

"I went back to the university to look for you, but you were gone, with no forwarding address. We've been searching for you ever since. I'd finally given up. I couldn't believe you'd be out here in the wilderness. The nearest university is—"

"I quit and joined the Resistance. I couldn't stay in the east, with everything reminding me every blastday of us."

"Oh, Wayland. I know I can never make it up to you, but I'd like to try. At least you can get to know your daughter, if that's what you want. I have to warn you; she's a royal pain in the ass."

Wayland chuckled, "Yes, I got a small dose of that already."

They were both laughing when Eva returned to the table. The girl eyed them suspiciously.

"Mom, Kent's back and I need a break. Can I go to the bakery and get a snack?"

Cassander smiled wistfully at her daughter.

"Sure, but there's someone I'd like you to meet first. Eva, this is your father, Wayland Peters."

22

LYDARC, NOW

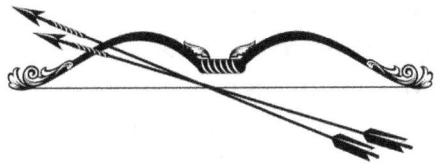

We stared at the soggy, frayed ends of the rope that we'd just pulled from the horizontal lake. I thought we were fucked, until the giant bear said she had an idea. Anyway, try telling this tall tale at your local fine drinking establishment. It's all true, but if anyone believes you, they've had one or three too many.

— WAYLAND PETERS, AS QUOTED BY SITKA
SANGASHEE, *A SHAMAN'S JOURNEY*

T he fact that the rope has come undone bears me down into deepest despair. I sit on the shore of the lake in the underlands, my head in my hands.

After I explain, Thor leaves me to return to his observation tower, in case any of my companions are foolish enough to attempt the crossing by drowning themselves. I hope they don't try it. There's no guarantee they'll reach the surface, or that Thor and the deathguards will be able to revive them if they do. I was twice lucky, but I can't assume that my companions will share that fortune.

Staring out across the still waters, I only hope the surface remains so. Losing any of my friends would be unbearable. Even thinking of them going through the same torture I just barely survived is tearing me apart. I couldn't stand to lose any of them because of my foolishness.

I remind myself that the underlands heighten emotions, especially negative ones, and try to get a grip on my fears. If I let it, self-doubt will overwhelm me here.

The lake and the surrounding forest are deceptively idyllic. Warm eve's dayblight suffuses the trees and swallows dance over the calm surface of the lake, making a fast-food dinner of the abundant flying insects. Loons sing in a distant inlet, and a doe and her two fawns sip at the water's edge.

It's all a deception, I know. While I was focused on finding Jarly and not on the scenery when I was here last time, I remember the chaotic, punishing environment below the surface. There is a reason myths define the underlands as mortal hell.

What now? Can I go on without the others? Perhaps I could find my tribe, but what about Eva, Wayland's daughter? I don't even know what she looks like.

As I rub my aching neck and consider my options, a cry rings out from one of the towers. It's Thor, and he's pointing to the center of the lake.

Oh no.

The water is churning and frothing. Something large and powerful is thrashing toward shore. Thor vaults from his perch and launches himself into the water with practiced efficiency. A couple of the other deathguards follow. Then they pull up, shock dropping their jaws. Standing open-mouthed in the shallow water near shore, they watch as a giant russet bear rises and shakes itself off with a massive shudder. Around its waist is a rope.

I too stare in awe.

"Sitka? How?"

The bear doesn't answer, but continues up the shore,

breathing hard and towing two bedraggled figures out of the water behind her. Wayland and Rapha are coughing up water but appear to be otherwise unharmed.

Running up to the bear and hugging her, I say, "How did you do that? You didn't drown. You're alive!"

The bear, breathing hard, sits back on her haunches and giggles. "I don't know, but I had a theory. The lungs of a bear are far larger than a human's and we're strong swimmers. I thought I could make it. Besides, I'm not really alive, am I, as a spirit animal?"

"You *thought?*"

Knowing me well, Wayland sees my temper blooming and intercedes. "Give her a break. We made it. We're here now. That's all that matters. Besides, Rapha and I were going to try it on our own, anyway. We couldn't stop her from following. She came up with this solution herself. It saved us all from drowning."

The bear lowered her head. "I just wish I'd thought of this a little sooner, before you went through. I could have saved you some pain and misery."

I start to speak, but I'm interrupted by a thud behind me. Rapha, who has yet to say a word, has collapsed unconscious to the ground.

As I kneel beside him, feeling his erratic pulse, I see that he's unusually pale, his breathing shallow.

"What's wrong with him?" asks Sitka.

"I don't know. Maybe he swallowed too much water."

As I watch, Rapha grows even paler. His skin is translucent. Colors and shadows flow under the surface. His image shudders and flickers, reminding me of something I can't quite remember. For a moment, I see...what?

Rapha opens his eyes; after a few gasping breaths, his color returns. I wonder if I imagined what I just saw. I look at the others, but their faces show only concern for the shaman. Sitting up, he says, "What? What is everyone looking at?"

"You collapsed," says Wayland with a concerned frown.

Rapha smiles sheepishly. "Sorry about that. It is a little embarrassing, a shaman who cannot heal himself."

"What're you talking about?" I ask.

Looking away, he admits, "I have severe asthma. It makes swimming difficult, if not dangerous."

I frown. "Well, you hide it well. I had no idea."

"I can control it with herbs and breathing exercises, for the most part. The lake was just a strain on my control. I apologize profusely for my weakness."

"Shut the fuck up. You and your pseudo-humble, heroic grundlecrap." I say, my temper spiking under the stress and, perhaps, the dark influence of the underlands.

Shaking my head, I step away and gaze into the distance. Finally, I say, "We need to get moving. Rapha, if you're up for it?" He nods. "Let's try to get to the Silent Village before blightfall. We need to be inside doors before full dark. You don't want to spend the night out here, trust me."

"Why?" Sitka asks. "It looks perfectly safe to me."

23

LEISIL, BEFORE

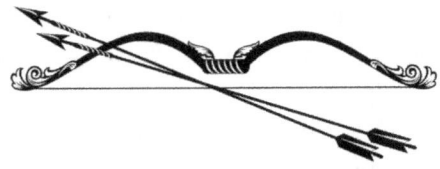

A mule is not an ass, but a hybrid of a male donkey (ass) and female horse (mare). Mules are often considered strong-willed and intransigent, but I believe that is merely the expression of their innate will to survive. In other words, listen to your mule; it may save your life one blastday.

— SITKA SANGASHEE, *EVOLUTION OF THE SHAMAN MASTER*

M y mule, Milton, was almost too much to bear. What kind of cantankerous beast of burden bites his rider, then tries to swipe her off on every low-hanging branch along the bitterway?

How dare you refer to me as a beast of burden? What am I, a mere tool you can abuse and just dump when I go lame? Have you no morals whatsoever?

"Despite your bubbly personality, I would never abandon you like that. I've heard that many parts of the ass are edible."

"Despite what?" Rapha asked. He sat astride Gertrude, the

sweetest pony ever to be foaled. How did he rank Gertrude when I got the jackass from hell?

"Nothing," I replied. "Just imagining things, I guess. For a moment, I thought Milton could talk. Things like that have been happening a lot since the *you-know-what* dropped this fucking peri-soul into my chest. Or maybe it's since you introduced me to the payoton buttons."

I swayed in my saddle, feeling a little nauseous.

You're high as a kitehawk, that's the fucking problem, said Milton in my feverish thoughts.

"It is all part of the journey, apprentice Leisil," said Rapha in his annoyingly perfect diction. "If you are to attain enblighten-ment, you must slide into this spirit journey with your whole being. You must shed who you were so you can grow into your new powers."

"You make me sound like a fucking garden snake. I'm not sure this is working. When does my shamanic training begin?"

"We have been at it for a week, my dear."

I sighed, and Milton snapped to a stop, knees locked. Once I got him under way again and caught up, I said, "Can you explain it one more time, this probability principle? I still don't under-stand it completely."

I say this, but what I mean is: I don't understand it at all, not one little bit.

"We are almost at the lava caves. We will camp outside tomorrow night and enter the next blastday. I can explain more there. It is a power spot, you know. There are ley lines."

"Of course there are. Well, what about my goddamned spirit animal then? You said I'd be able to get rid of the annoying fucker."

"I may have been exaggerating slightly. The truth is that a spirit animal cannot be eliminated, only controlled."

"Help me control it, then."

Rapha said nothing.

This whole trip had been a horrible mistake. I shifted in the saddle, looking back the way we'd come. Could I find my way back to the Resistance camp on my own? Rapha had been using his (admittedly impressive) shamanic skills to keep us safe from the vagaries of the weather, minions, timesmears, Overs and disruption fissures, not to mention all the other deadly monsters that roamed this region. I wasn't sure my burgeoning skills were up to such an onerous task.

Perhaps sensing my inner conflict, Rapha touched his reins ever-so-blightly. Gertrude responded immediately, halting in the middle of the dirt trail as if it were her idea all along. I tried to do the same, but Milton had other ideas. I was far ahead before I could get the stupid mule to stop, only after much tugging and pleading, followed by angry, frustrated shouting.

Rapha urged Gertrude up until they stood beside us. I fumed silently, using all my control not to burst from my skin and explode into a hail of bloody mist.

Looking around, he said, "All right. I think you're ready. Let's dismount. We do not want to frighten the horses. Anyway, it is almost time to set up camp for the night. This spot up here by the rocks will do quite nicely. It will offer us some protection from the high desert wind."

I was worried about more than a little fucking wind.

"First, you must know his true name," said Rapha with a self-satisfied smirk, as I crouched by the campfire.

"Oh, for sucking god's balls! Not that grundle shit," I said. "I can't take it. It's ridiculous. Are you trying to tell me that knowing the name of something is going to give me any fucking power over it? Well, my mother's name is Urpine Jossey Frandling, nee Johannson. Does that give me any say over what that evil bitch does or says or thinks? No, it does not. So, give me some credit. I'm not one of your naïve town whores who falls for your fantastical shamanic crapola because they all want to bed you."

As if I hadn't spoken, Rapha went on, "Second, you must understand *who* he is. Your spirit animal is, after all, a product of your own soul. For a warrior shaman, the spirit animal is a guide and ally, there to fight beside you and help you heal yourself and others. In your case, the spirit animal is an antagonist rather than an aid. Why is this? You must look within yourself for the answers. For you to control him, you must first understand yourself."

"Oh great. Understand myself, so I can know why a two-headed gyrfalcon with the personality of a ghoul and the breath of a gagworm wants to reside inside my psyche? All right, that's done. Next?"

Rapha sighed deeply, adjusting his bony male ass to a more comfortable spot on the rock-hard petrified spine tree stump he'd chosen for a chair.

"Please. This is very important. Do you want to do this, or not?"

It's my turn to sigh. "All right. I'm sorry. It's been a long blast-day. Maybe we can do this tomorrow?"

Rapha gave me a thoughtful half-smile. "I feel that now is the time, when your guards are down. Call him up, please."

I felt the nausea in my gullet again, but I tamped it down and tried. What did it matter now? If the fucking bird ripped out my guts here in no-man's-land, at least the only other victims were likely to be Rapha and the animals. I felt some guilt about Gertrude, but for Milton, I harbored little regret.

Oh sure, my steaming guts are splayed across the desert, and you couldn't care less. Just my luck. I found the only shaman in the afterarth without a conscience.

"Is that you, Milton? I thought I was imagining your sentience. Now shut up and go back to sleep standing up. I have work to do."

Milton snorted, but thankfully stayed silent.

I did my best to call up my spirit animal, but he was nowhere to be found.

Later, as we were settled in our bedrolls, despite my fatigue, all my attempts at sleep failed. I considered masturbation, since that always made me sleepy, but I lacked the energy.

From his own bedroll, Rapha piped up, out of nowhere, "Do not worry about it. Everyone has trouble getting it up on occasion."

"What?" I shot up to a sitting position, aghast at what I just heard from Rapha, prim and proper Rapha.

I could feel the heat of his blush from across the camp. "No, no, that is not what I meant. I was talking about your spirit animal."

"Oh, that." I flopped back down, holding in a laugh with supreme effort.

After that, I slept fitfully, waking a few times to noises that turned out to be nothing more than a desert rodent coming out to feed in the night, and the semi-silent wispy wings of an owl dipping down to snatch up said desert rodent, who had been foolish enough to come out to feed in the night.

Sometime in the early morning, when the ground was cold and my breath steamed where I dared expose my face to the crisp, bright air, I heard a whinny that was suddenly cut off, followed by a slurping, rending sound. Then came a smell that I was reluctant to inhale.

It was a bitter, choking aroma, like rotting potatoes, mixed with the scent of biddle piss and the choking juglone of drying walnuts. Ammonia, juglone and mold, three of my not-so-favorite scents. I'd never yet detected them together, and why would I? This was new to me: therefore, I failed to heed the warning that screamed in my subconscious of impending danger.

I felt a presence, and the hair stood up on the back of my neck, on my forearms—everywhere, in fact.

I dared look, and my heart spluttered, almost stalling. My body started, reeling back in primordial fear and revulsion.

A dire creature crouched beyond the dying fire, creeping out of the dark, glowering at me with carnivorous eyes and a mouth agape with bloody fangs. It stood on all fours, but I had the sickening feeling it had once been human, or at least partly human. Bony limbs jutted at odd angles, and it moved in nauseating fits and spurts, not like any living being should. Its long spine arched downward unnaturally in the middle, revealing beneath it reproductive organs that sagged to the ground, dragging in the dirt as it crept toward me.

"Jesu, Maria, and all the benevolent before gods save me," I uttered under my breath. But the late gods didn't show their faces. They never did.

Skinwalker.

I knew the term from Wayland's stories. Until this point, I had been sure they were just a myth, a tale offering safe and warm tavern patrons a vicarious glimpse at a mythical world they would never be forced to experience. Now, I wasn't so sure. This fucker looked—and smelled—all too real.

"Nice doggy," I whispered.

The glowing viridian blight in the beast's beady eyes flared and more blood dripped from its mouth. From this gaping hole, I detected another fragrance: ruptured intestines, shit with the overscent of succulent grasses and bittlebush. From my stuttering brain, came a random thought: those were the plants the horses munched on out here.

I hoped it was Milton.

No, you don't. You need me.

I risked a glance to the log where the horses were tethered. Poor Gertrude was a mass of torn flesh and steaming, seeping guts. Her lovely bay hide was a tatter of torn fur and glistening underskin fat, all of it weeping blood and viscous chyle fluid. From her severed skull, her huge, lovely brown eyes bulged in utter terror, presumably of the last thing she'd seen before she'd been ended. I didn't blame her. My eyes threatened to do the same, and they weren't even ended yet.

"Rapha?" I hissed, hoping the shaman was still alive and functional. There was no answer.

I think a certain spirit animal could come in handy right now, don't you?

"What the fuck're you saying?" I should have realized how strange it was that I was talking to my ass at a time like this, but I was far too busy to notice. Subliminally, the words reached me and coaxed the ghastly bird upward out of my psyche.

I gaped up at the sky, emitting a mephitic belch of putrid flesh and rotting feathers. The gyrfalcon thrust his two heads out of my gaping mouth, followed by his brittle bird body, and last, the lacerating claws that dragged blood trails across my throat as he thrust forth out of my being. With a keening screech, his mighty wings grasped and held the air in a forever grip, forcing him upward into the ebony dome of night sky. Rarog was soon a spec in the distant blastnight.

Good riddance.

At least, I now knew his name: Rarog. Something to take to my rapidly self-digging grave.

Now, call him back.

That blasted mule again. Why couldn't I get him out of my head?

Because you need me.

"You said that before. What I really need is—"

I was interrupted as I turned to find the face of the skinwalker next to mine. The terrifying creature had moved to my side silently and more swiftly than any mortal could. Milky, blood-adorned fangs and snarling lips reached out to kiss me, and not in an affectionate way. My limbs were paralyzed by some eldritch magic. My neck strained at an impossible angle, away from my eminent end.

"Rarog?" I rasped, almost pleading. A voice so weak I barely heard it myself leaked out of my trembling lips. It was little more than a whispered thought, a drool of hope. But something was listening. Someone.

A whooshing, roaring sound filled my ears, a raging hurricane, followed by crunching and gnawing. Wind washed my face; blood and bits of putrid flesh splattered everywhere.

It smelled of forever, but not recent. It tasted of an end long ago dealt to the more than deserving, a body disturbed in a grave-yard where only the decaying corpses of restless monsters molded.

The gyrfalcon paused in his disgusting evening meal, staring at me with his fierce avian eyes. Bits of skinwalker dribbled from both his beaks. He clenched at the pale, limp body with his inescapable claws and aimed a feral, unrepentant shriek at the star-sprinkled sky. I understood what he said easily enough, but there were no human words for it. Later, the closest I could trans-late it to was: "I revel in the orgasm of killing."

Rapha woke and stepped forward, leaning over me. All he said was, "Good job." No explanation for why his great shamanic powers failed him long enough for a skinwalker to put him in a trance. I considered raging about this, but, exhausted, I decided to save that pleasure for tomorrow.

I leaned back on my bedroll and willed my heart rate to recede into a manageable prestissimo tempo.

At some point, after the waking nightmares ebbed, I slept.

In my dreams, a voice said, *Oh, and by the way, a mule is not an ass, even though his rider may well be one.*

24

LYDARC, NOW

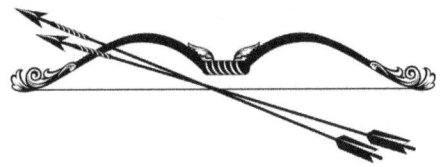

Better to reign in Hell, then serve in Heav'n.

—JOHN MILTON, *PARADISE LOST*

*F*orgive me, for I am sin. These are the words roughly carved above the first door we come to. All the cabins in the Silent Village are equally uninviting: simple, single-room affairs with neither gardens nor porches, nor any signs of life within. There is one small window in the front of each, and on each window, the dirty, drab curtain is drawn.

"How do we find one that's unoccupied?" asks Sitka.

I frown, remembering my experiences here. "We just look. No one will answer their door. They're all...otherwise occupied. Maybe you should wait out here, Sitka."

"Occupied with what?" she asks. "I want to see. Stop trying to protect me from the truth. I can take it."

"All right," I sigh, "but don't blame me for the nightmares."

"They can't be any worse than the ones already playing around in my head every night," whispers Wayland.

I know he hasn't been sleeping well, despite the fact that I've been spiking his wine with the strongest valerian root extract I dare give him.

I open the first door and reel from the smell.

In the center of the room, a man is whipping himself, despite there being nothing left of his back but tatters of shredded flesh and lacerated bone. His ribs are a hollow shell of misery. A pile of flesh and melting adipose fat seeps toward us on the floor.

As I close the door, I hear the words he repeats over and over.

"I will not touch a child again. I will not touch—"

"Not that one," I say, slamming the door.

In the next cottage, a woman is beating her husband. On the wall is a drawing of the happy couple in wedding garb. She looks down, her large hands bloody. The man's small frame shudders with sobs. She hauls him up viciously to hit him again, but the face that greets her is not his, but her own. With a cry, she lets the frail man drop back to the floor and turns away. She stands for a moment facing the wall, then turns back and starts beating him all over again.

As I close the door, Wayland says, "I'm sensing a pattern here. If the next miserable sod is cutting his own balls off, I'm out."

The next cottage is different. As we open the door, extreme cold hits us. The room contains no furniture, just a floor of ice, with a ragged hole in the middle revealing frigid blue water. A boy of perhaps nine seasons leans over the edge, weeping as he cries, "I was afraid, sis. I'm sorry I ran away. I should have helped you. I should have. Can you forgive me?"

A cackle erupts from the pit as a pathetic, dripping figure floats up into the air. A rotting corpse, a little girl in a once flowery dress, says in a fingernail-on-chalkboard voice, "Forgive you? Sure. I forgive you, big brother. But *you* never will. I'm here to make sure of that. This is fun, isn't it? Wanna do it again?"

I slam the door on the boy's screams.

The next cottage is empty.

"Thank the fucking Overs," says Wayland. "But this village is too creepy to spend the night in. Maybe we'd be better off camping out in the trees."

"No," I say, "There are things in the trees you don't want anywhere near you. In fact, we need to stay away from the window. No matter what you hear or feel, do not look outside or open the door. And keep your spirits up. That is essential here."

"Sheesh," says the bear, who has squeezed her massive frame through the door and takes up most of the floor space in the room, "Is it all like this?"

"No, this is only purgatory."

Rapha, who has spoken little and still looks pale, says, "We need to find Aamon tomorrow."

"No," I say, "The Siletzon first, then your fucking 'lord of the underlands.'"

Rapha starts to object until he sees my expression. "All right, but we cannot spend more than a blastday finding them and sending them back through the lake. What did you find out from the deathguards? They would not talk to me."

"They don't talk to anyone."

Rapha frowns. "But they talk to you? That is very odd, but there is nothing about this place I have not found strange."

We spend a restless night, harassed by the wailing and pounding noises emanating from the other cottages. In the morning, when there appears to be a lull in the horrid cacophony, I say, "Let's get moving. The best I could gather from the deathguards is the tribe headed west, out toward the plains."

We hurry out of the village, hoping to put the miserable self-torturers far behind us as quickly as possible.

The way is fairly easy. Once we get through the forest, we come to a rough but wide trail leading out onto a grassy plain. It's a cakewalk until we run into the guards.

"Halt!" screams an officious but immature sounding male voice. A skinny, shortish wannabe soldier in some sort of woven metal suit and mask pulls up a staff and tries to force us back on the trail. He runs into Wayland and bounces back as if he's hit a living wall. One arm or not, Wayland is still the toughest S.O.B. I know.

Wayland faces off with the kid, and I can see him resisting the urge to laugh.

"Well, son, maybe you could show your face, so we know who's manhandling us."

The other guards surround us and raise their weapons, which are composed of sticks and rusty farm implements.

"What's going on here?" I ask. "What exactly are you guarding? It's an empty plain, for Over's sake."

"Leisil, is that you?" says a gruff voice from the back.

A burly soldier clomps forward awkwardly in boots that look too big for her. She removes her mask as she steps in front of me.

"It's Lydarc, the warrior shaman, now," I say, "It's not especially good to see you, Borcine. I hadn't heard that you were here. I would love to hear your story, but I'm sure you saw nothing."

Borcine snarls, "What are you talking about, fool?"

"Well, it's hard to see what's ending you when you're running the other way, crying like a blubbering baby."

Borcine raises her implement on a direct angle to smash my head, but, surprisingly, Rapha is there. He raises a hand and a flash of miniature blightning throws Borcine to the ground. She grunts as the air escapes her lungs. It seems hesitant to return.

"No!" I snarl at him. "What're you doing?"

He stares at me as if I've lost my admittedly unstable mind.

"This is *my* problem," I say. "Let me talk to her."

"*Talk* to her?" says Wayland with a frown. "Are you sure—"
He sees my glare and backs off, his hands raised. "All right, you two have a little visit. We'll just be down the trail, waiting."

The little man soldier pulls up his pants and attempts to stop Wayland, saying, "I demand the tribute you owe—"

The boy's words are cut off as Wayland lifts him with one hand and tosses him into the grass.

"You were saying, you little fuck?" His dark eyes flash with deadly intent. In that moment, even I wouldn't challenge Wayland—and he loves me, or at least he once did, but perhaps I imagined that. The others, who are apparently a little bit smarter than the skinny one, back away.

I watch my friends leave, realizing that they are concerned for me by the hunching of their shoulders, by the hesitant steps. When they disappear around a low hill, I turn to face Borcine. A wide, rust-colored shape grows in my vision until there is nothing else. I later realize that it was the flat blade of a shovel. After a bright flash, there is only darkness.

I wake, my back against a tree, with an irritating throbbing in my forehead. I look down to see that my hands are poorly tied.

Borcine is sitting beside me, munching on a wild apple like a ravenous hog. When she's done, she tosses the core aside and looks down on me with an idiotic grin.

"It seems your friends have left you to me."

I moan as I rub the growing knob on my forehead with my tied hands. Borcine grunts.

I say, "I doubt that, but I don't need them, anyway. I can handle you on my own."

She snorts. "Yeah, I see that. You will, from this moment forward, refer to me as Borcine, the Dark."

"What're you doing here?" I say, ignoring her ridiculous edict. "Why aren't you back in the village, making amends for your shitty deeds? Paying for your sins?"

"What sins? I ain't done nothin' wrong, as I see it."

I'm silent for a while, taking this in. "So," I say, thinking, "Since you feel no guilt, you rank above the less guilty who show some remorse for what they've done?"

"I guess so. Brilliant system, huh?"

I don't see a system at all. It makes no sense. But what did I expect? The afterarth is no holy temple of just desserts where the innocent are rewarded for being fucking naïve. If the underlands is the fate we imagine we deserve, the unimaginative, the psychopaths and the truly evil should do just fine here.

Borcine struggles to her feet, lifting her shovel. "Seems like that fuckin' monster bird didn't come down here with you, did it? You're on your own. No two-headed falcon to bail you out. This is my land. 'Bout time you paid 'tention, probie," she says, "I'm gonna teach you to stay off our patch. After I give you the hidin' you deserve, you can jus' run back to the fuckin land o' the livin' with your tail between your legs. If'n you survive, that is."

Borcine is grinning as she raises the shovel, but something is boiling up in me. It's not the gyrfalcon, but something larger and meaner than he could ever be. It's a fucking puke of indignation and rage that travels up my throat like bloodspore vomit, like volcanic indigestion seasoned with revenge too long denied.

I scream, pulling the full force of the spirit realm, of the arth powers, of raging wind and unfeeling storm. I pull worms from the pits of underland's deepest hell and mold from every grave that ever rotted, plague from the under-ages and sprinkle it with leprosy, the instant kind. Summoning it all to my breast as a tiny tornado, I let it loose on Borcine with an elegant, economic flip of my hand. What's left, I shred with the teeth of a dragon, and bite with mother-in-law's judgment. My burning rage ignites her skin, and it melts like frosting on a hot blastday.

Borcine doesn't have a chance to scream. Borcine doesn't have a chance in hell.

When I catch up to the others, Sitka asks, "Well, did you talk to her?"

"Not so much," I say, "but I definitely put her in her place."

"Finally," grunts Wayland.

Behind us, a delicate ribbon of pestilential smoke rises from the weeping, stinking pile of what was, until a moment ago, Borcine, the Dark.

"What happened to just letting karma take care of Borcine for you?" he asks.

I flash that almost-smile that means I'm extremely amused. "Well, karma wasn't doing its fucking job, so I had to take matters into my own hands."

25

LEISIL, BEFORE

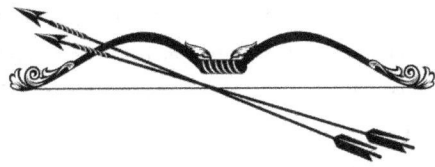

Reality is created by the mind. We can change our reality by changing our mind.

— PLATO, *THE REPUBLIC*

I t took Rapha and Leisil three more blastdays to reach the lava river caves. He had promised it would take one, but that was before the skinwalker ate Gertrude. They put all their gear on a recalcitrant Milton and walked the rest of the way.

When they arrived at the caves, it was getting dark. Leisil was exhausted and thankful they weren't entering the caves until morning.

"Any tests this blastnight, master? I truly hope not. I'm a bit fatigued from the last one," said Leisil, sarcasm dripping from her words.

Rapha pulled his blanket up over his head and mumbled, "I have no idea what you are referring to. Let us sleep now. Tomorrow will be..." But she couldn't hear that last word. No others followed.

"Fuck."

As they hiked into the caves the next morning, Rapha explained to her how underground rivers of lava left the pockets that shaped these tunnels.

"Well, let's hope we don't run into any of these lava rivers," said Leisil. "I'm not up for a dip right now."

"That is unlikely, since the volcano that formed them is long extinct. One interesting side effect was the creation of powerful ley lines where two of these tunnels intersect. There is also an interesting gravitational anomaly that...Well, we will soon arrive. It is easier to show you than explain."

The tunnel gradually widened as they walked. Leisil thought she heard waves lapping on a shore and was certain she smelled water; not just a cup of spring water, but the complex, life-rich scent of a lake or languid river. But that was impossible down here, wasn't it?

They turned a corner and her eyes grew wide. It was, in fact, a lake, but there was something very wrong with it.

"Why is it like that?" she asked, unable to keep the wonder out of her voice.

"I tried to explain about the ley lines and gravity shifts. Reality acts...differently here."

They faced a lake that stood on its end.

As she watched, amazed, the reflected ripples played across their features.

"Why, what, wah..." Leisil couldn't find the words, but Rapha seemed to understand.

"This lake leads to the underlands. There are only a few places on afterarth where one can reach that realm alive, and this is one of them. You dive in and reality shifts. Sideways becomes down, then up. You end up on the shores of a lake in the underlands. There is a bit more to it than that, but I can explain that later."

"But why would anyone want to go to the underlands? Isn't it a living hell?"

"Ah, that too must wait until I show you more."

"More than this?" Leisil was reaching her saturation point for acceptance of the unbelievable.

"Just come a little farther. There is one more thing I need to show you."

Rapha led her further down the tunnel.

As they advanced, Leisil's skin tingled. She felt more alive. She felt...What? Power? Concentrated being? "What is this place?"

"The ley lines create spots where the probabilities are stronger, more accessible. Every shaman has a map of where these areas exist across the afterarth, and even in the underlands. If you pass the final test, when we return, you will receive yours, as well."

"Oh great, another test."

"This one should be easy for you."

"Somehow I doubt that."

As Rapha slowed, a glow came from around a twist in the tunnel, and the intense feeling of hyper-awareness increased. As they turned the corner, Leisil's mouth fell open. Before them was a tall cavern wall. Across it stretched a net of glowing fibers of blight extending from one wall to the next. At each node, where the fibers crossed, there was a glowing orb. There must have been thousands of them adorning the structure, in all colors of the rainbow. If Leisil's eyes weren't deceiving her, there were colors here she'd never seen before. As her eyes adjusted, she sensed other nets, other rainbows, going back into infinity behind the first, ever reducing and growing at the same time. It was gorgeous, amazing, disorienting and eerily frightening all at the same time.

Rapha looked at her wondering expression and nodded with quiet pride. "Only a true shaman can see this. You pass that test, Leisil. Now, tell me, what do you see?"

"It's so beautiful! I see a net, and nodes that shine so intensely, like tiny stars. And the colors... I don't know. Some of them feel almost like...thoughts, or versions of time."

Rapha's mouth curved into a subtle smile. "Good. Your mind

is beginning to unbind. That is a prerequisite. What you see is called a veil of probabilities. There are several still known to us—one here, and one beneath the Fallen City, one in the underlands, another in Waxahachie in what was once Texas. Their locations are guarded by the Shamanic Council. Were they to fall into the hands of a dark shaman like Aamon, it could mean the annihilation of coherence across all realms."

Leisil tore her eyes from the glowing mesh. "What's its purpose? Is it a machine?"

Rapha stepped closer to the net, and the blight caught in his eyes made them seem almost translucent. His voice took on a strange, alien cadence. "The veil is not a machine in the way you understand it. It is a rupture in causality. A lattice of potential. It is what remains of a failed attempt to collapse quantum coherence on a planetary scale."

He traced a finger through the air just inches from the net. "Each node you see is a stabilized probability; a point where one version of reality exists, however briefly. The fibers, or what you might call probability chords, are entanglement paths, residual connections from before the Fall, when all minds were still synchronized to a common framework. The veil holds what the befores called 'pre-blight resonances,' but we call them 'memories of what might yet be.'"

"So you can choose which one to make real?" Leisil asked, a deep furrow between her brows.

"Not precisely. To observe is to disturb. The veil abides by the uncertainty. If you look directly, you collapse it. The art of the veil is not to choose, but to be chosen. You must approach the moment obliquely. It's what the befores once called the observer's paradox."

He touched his temple. "To use it, your consciousness must fragment just enough to exist in multiple potentialities at once, though only one may manifest. You must see all nodes, but none too clearly. You must open the doors of your psyche wide enough that your deeper self—what the befores might call the quantum interpreter—makes the selection for you. The correct thread resonates in harmony with your intent, and only then can it be collapsed into reality."

Leisil squinted. "But how do you know which one is right?"

"You do not know," Rapha said. "You feel it. The veil speaks through instinct, through intuition. That is why only shamans may use it. Machines failed because they required precision. The veil does not tolerate precision. It is built upon the infinite ambiguity between possibility and truth."

He paused. "To attempt to see all paths is madness. To see only one is blindness. The shaman must be both mad and blind and yet walk the single correct line through chaos. When you see it, Leisil, it happens."

Leisil put a hand to her forehead. "But what if I'm one of these dark shamans that you spoke about? What if I choose a reality where everyone suffers?"

"Ah, there you have it. That's how the underlands came into being eons ago. When Aamon arrived there, he found a place where he could rule and mete out what he sees as justice. Only the Shamanic Council holds him back from expanding the underlands to our realm as well. It is a delicate balance. If we could reach the underlands and eliminate Aamon, then his realm would most likely collapse, restoring the world that was lost ages ago."

"What do you mean, 'eliminate' this Aamon character? Forever him?"

"I'm afraid so. I believe it is you who is destined to do it."

"What? No way. Why choose me? You shamans have incredible power. Why don't you go through the lake yourself and take this Aamon out?"

Rapha turned away and paced the cave restlessly. "We tried. None of the shamans we sent through returned. They were forevered, just gone. We think the demon lord detected them, and they were ended by him or the deathguards before they could even get close to him."

"Why do you think I would succeed where other much more powerful shamans have failed?"

Rapha turned back to her and stared into her eyes. She found his gaze disconcerting. "It is the peri-soul. It is a part of an Over. Aamon must have at least some Over in him too, to wield the power he does. We believe it will hide you from him, allow you to get close enough to do the deed."

I raise my arms defensively and look down at the cave floor, which is flickering with patches placed there by the veil's pulsing blights. "I'm not ready for this. I haven't even figured out how to do this probability trick yet, if I ever can. Plus, I've never ended an innocent human being. I'm not sure I can do it. It's too much."

Rapha flashed the knowing smirk that I was beginning to hate. "There is nothing innocent about the demon lord. Perhaps it is too much for you now, but you will grow into your power, over time. You will become more than you can imagine. Leisil, it is time for you to accept your destiny as a warrior shaman and join the Council to fight the demon Aamon and his evil."

He pulled a leather pouch from his coat and handed it to her. "What's this?"

"Your medicine bag. A gift from me. It has only a few basic amplifiers in it for now, but you will fill it with other crystals and power objects as your skills and knowledge advance."

"Thanks...I think." Leisil took the soft suede leather bag reluctantly. It felt worn and familiar in her hands, as if she'd handled it many times before. She opened it and felt the first object inside. It was a soft feather. She pulled it out and blue blight reflected off her hands. The feather glowed as if blighted from within, a cool cyan blight emitted by every barb and vein. Almost in the first moment she touched it, she felt calmer, more in control.

"What is it? It's beautiful."

"It is a molted feather from the alkonost, the loveliest and most spiritually powerful of birds. The feather will soothe your spirit animal, make him more pliable, and reduce some of your own anger and angst as well."

Leisil reflected that this was the first helpful thing Rapha had given her. She emptied the other contents into her palm. There were seven small, rough stones in different colors. She immediately felt warring vibrations from each, ranging from calming to frenetic.

"These are the basic chakra crystals, ranging from clear quartz and amethyst to tiger's eye, carnelian and red jasper. Each stone amplifies a specific shamanic power. For instance, labradorite facilitates your weather control. Carnelian is the truth stone, and clear quartz will increase your healing efforts manyfold."

"Thank you." This time, her words were more enthusiastic. "Can we get out of here? This place makes my hair frizz and my palms itch."

Leisil turned to the tunnel that would lead them back to open air.

"Wait, Leisil. There are a couple more parts to the ritual." He bent down and handed her a pebble from the floor. It was a tiny, porous piece of red lava rock.

"Keep this in your pouch as well. If you ever need to access the veil, this pebble will bring you back for the instant you'll need. But use it only in the direst circumstance. The jump is painful and rips several seasons from your physical life, while advancing you as many seasons forward along the path to true wisdom. You might decide it's preferable to travel by mule—or dragon." He added this last with a sly smile.

She took the pebble, not really wanting it. She had no desire to return here. Both the lake and the veil frightened her in some primal, instinctual manner.

When she looked up from stowing the pebble, Rapha had drawn his sword.

"What now? Does your shamanic ritual also require a human sacrifice?"

"No, silly woman. It is nothing like that. Merely the last thing that will make you a warrior shaman in the eyes of the Council and your peers—and in your own heart. Please kneel."

She did as she was told, feeling foolish. He touched the flat blade of the sword to the top of her head, saying, "You are now a warrior shaman in heart and mind." Then he tapped each of her shoulders delicately. "You are now a warrior shaman in body and soul."

Rapha paused for a second, and Leisil wondered what could possibly be next. She was running out of body parts to pledge to the shamanic cause.

"I now grant you your warrior name, the name you will carry from now on." Here, he paused again, frowning as if in deep thought. "Opposing inclinations divide you, but they also give you strength. Because you are made of blight and dark, from this moment forward, you are Lydarc, the warrior shaman."

As Rapha spoke the word 'Lydarc,' something changed within Leisil. Her awareness seemed to grow with every step she took as they followed the tunnel back to the surface. She'd never believed in the power of names. Perhaps she'd been wrong about that; perhaps she'd been wrong about other things, too.

As her excitement grew, she could feel her spirit animal pushing to be released—but controlling him was easier now, with the alkonost feather in her pouch.

You'll just have to wait. I'm not letting you out inside these tunnels.

The falcon screeched in her ears but settled down. That felt good.

Lydarc wanted to scream too, to proclaim to the mountain-tops that she was someone. She had a place, a calling. That felt good. She reined in her enthusiasm. There had to be a downside to all this, and she was sure it would show its ugly head soon enough.

When they stepped out of the lava tubes, a giant purple dragon greeted them. She stepped back in shock, but Rapha ambled forward to stand beside the creature and placed a hand on its muscular leg. He looked small next to the hulking form that was now stretching its wings and bowing its elegant, curving neck down to her. When the huge, aquiline face was right in front of her, she frowned. Was there something familiar about those eyes?

Rapha chuckled, saying, "Lydarc, I'd like you to meet Milton, my spirit animal."

As they rode the mule-turned-dragon back toward Nameless, Lydarc raised her arms to the sky and let her spirit animal fly. With a sharp cry of being, she loosed the thunder that had been condensing inside of her for as long as she could remember.

"I am *Lydarc*!" she yelled, and multiple bolts of blightning lit the sky, while the mountains shuddered and quaked in shared joy beneath her.

26

LYDARC, BEFORE

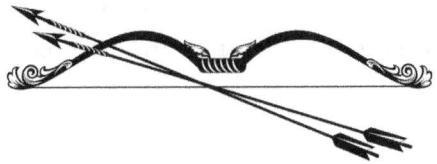

Everything I did was wrong. No matter how I tried to avoid it, people around me got hurt. I should have stopped trying, but I didn't, not ever.

— LYDARC AS QUOTED BY SITKA SANGASHEE,
EVOLUTION OF THE SHAMAN MASTER

W hen she returned to the Resistance camp, life went on as usual—until all fucking hell broke loose.

Though Leisil—now Lydarc—felt as if she were a different person, no one seemed to notice. She no longer slouched or tried especially hard to be invisible. With what she'd learned, it just seemed ridiculous.

"Feeling full of ourselves, are we?" Jarly danced up to join her as she headed for the armory tent. Jarly grinned knowingly when she saw Lydarc's guilty expression. "Your face gives everything away, my friend. You're going to have to develop some deceitfulness. You wear your thoughts on your face like a phosphor worm in heat."

"I'll work on that. It's just that I've discovered so much, even though I've still got a lot to learn. This shamanic grundlecrap, it turns out, can be quite powerful."

"All right, but just don't turn me into a tree, or anything like that."

"Shamans don't do that kind of thing. You're perfectly safe around me."

"So, what's up with you? You're spending a lot of time with Master Cuspis these days. You two aren't secretly involved in a torrid affair, are you?"

"Ugh, no. What a horrible thought. It's nothing like that. But it is kind of a secret."

Jarly's eyes lit up. "What, some clandestine project for the Resistance Strategy and Tactics Board?"

"Kinda. Follow me."

Jarly's excitement was palpable, an electric buzz that fizzled away quickly when she saw what Lydarc was working on in the armory.

"What's this? Some sticks and metal?" She gazed at the pile of parts on the table with a disparaging frown.

"No, look. This is the challenge, see," said Lydarc, her face flushed with an inventor's enthusiasm. "We want to blend the traditional power of a hand-drawn bow with the mechanical precision and stability of a crossbow. It's a recurve design mounted horizontally, like a crossbow, but with a draw system that uses longbow dynamics rather than relying entirely on mechanical advantage. Instead of a traditional crossbow trigger-and-crank mechanism, you draw the bowstring manually via this partial draw-assist lever." Lydarc picked up an anonymous piece of metal. "This allows for faster reloading than conventional crossbows. It requires more strength and skill than simply pulling a trigger, of course."

"The materials are the real challenge." Both women jumped at the voice. Cuspis had crept up behind them silently. "A hybrid like this needs balance, tensile strength and flexibility. We're torn between treated yew and hickory right now. The tiller needs to be a lightweight but strong hardwood like maple or ash, reinforced with brass, aluminum or tin to reduce weight while maintaining durability. We need to carefully manage its size and mass. The goal is to make it portable and quick to aim, with a draw length and power stroke designed to maximize kinetic energy while maintaining enough length for a recurve-like arc."

Jarly raised one eyebrow. She'd never heard Cuspis use so many words in a row. "So, in layman's terms that even a simple soldier like me can understand, what exactly is the advantage of this thing? If you ever get it built, that is."

Lydarc lifted some anonymous parts. "Faster, lighter, more power and accuracy. In short, the perfect bow for the Resistance. Look at the beauty of it: an elegant blend of tradition, craftsmanship and effectiveness."

Jarly's eyes had glazed over. Shaking her head, she said, "All right. Enough of this. I think you're starting to lose it, Frandling. It's time you escaped this hell-hole for a bit. Let's do the O.C.R."

"What? Now? It's almost dark. We'd never make it back in time for mess."

"That's the challenge of it—excel or go hungry. Are you game?"

Lydarc considered. She had the leg-length advantage, but Jarly seemed to possess an endurance overdrive and a parkour-like creativity in action that was almost superhuman. She'd defeated many larger opponents, including Lydarc. Lydarc's eyes flashed. The game was on.

"As long as any skill we possess is fair game."

"No way, you'll just use that shaman magic of yours to turn me into a flopping guppy."

"All right. I will not use any shamanic magic. Fair? What are you willing to wager on it?"

"Hmm," said Jarly, her hand on her chin. "I'll bet ten downtime coins that I can beat you to the gate before you reach the last obstacle."

"Now, that's just insulting. You know I'm faster than that."

Jarly had that sparkle in her eyes. "Well, prove it then, bitch. Meet you at the start."

Jarly was gone before Lydarc could take a deep breath. Putting her precious bow parts away, she headed to her tent to change. The Obstacle Course Run was a challenge on a good day, but this close to darkness it could be downright dangerous. What if minions or Overs-know-what attacked? She debated taking her bow with her and finally decided against it. The extra weight alone could mean she'd lose to Jarly. Who was she kidding? She'd yet to beat her frustrating friend, bow or no bow.

The dusk had cooled the plain to a bearable simmer. Crickets chirped a grim chorus from cracks in the rocks, and a well-cooked wind slid over and through the petrified trees and junk, whistling a dry tune. The course loomed before them—an angry zigzag of piled refuse, rope bridges, and jutting metal beams strung between the broken carcasses of rust-eaten vehicles.

Lydarc stood at the starting line, already regretting her life choices.

"Last chance to back out," Jarly said, bouncing on the balls of her feet. "We can still spend the evening drinking bad beer and swapping trauma stories."

Lydarc rolled her neck, the joints popping. "Tempting. But I'd rather beat your smug ass over a pit full of rusted rebar."

Jarly grinned. "Spoken like a true masochist."

The attendant sounded the horn—a relic from some forgotten emergency vehicle that now served as the course's starting klaxon. They both shot forward.

The first leg was a sprint over uneven shale, sharp enough to slice through worn boots. Jarly bolted ahead, compact and fast, weaving like a rabbit through broken stumps and jagged debris. Lydarc pounded after her, long strides chewing distance, her breath even and measured. She was heavier but more stable. Arth didn't rattle her the way it did the lighter runners.

They reached the first obstacle: a vertical climb up the half-toppled hulk of an ancient school bus. Someone had gutted it, stripped the insides and attached footholds into the metal sides. Jarly dove up it like a squirrel, hands and feet moving in rhythm.

Lydarc followed, slower but more controlled. Her fingers snagged on rust and peeled skin from her palms, but she didn't pause.

At the top, Jarly turned and blew her a kiss before diving headlong through the open back door—now hanging over a twenty-foot drop into an abandoned sewage trench. Several lengths of knotted rope tied to overhead beams swayed in the air like a tease. Jarly did a somersault in the air and grabbed a rope with a "Whoop!"

"Show-off!" Lydarc yelled, but she didn't pause. She jumped and caught another rope mid-air, boots scuffing the side of the trench as she swung into it. Halfway down, she let herself fall and rolled, absorbing the impact. When she stood, her shoulder throbbed. Jarly was already at what the soldiers had named "the jungle," a mess of cables strung over open sky between two skeletons of collapsed buildings.

"Didn't your mother ever tell you not to play in the jungle?" Lydarc called.

"She told me not to talk to freaky girls with frilly ears, and yet —here we are!"

Lydarc snarled, half-laughing. She leapt for the cables.

That's when the air shifted.

A low, almost inaudible hum vibrated through the rocks. The clouds overhead, once pinked by dusk, turned a curdled gray. Jarly froze halfway across the cables, her head snapping up like a deer's. "Did you feel that?"

Lydarc's ears tingled. A shimmer stirred behind the next pile of junk—something vast and ugly and probably hungry. It stepped through the ruin of a billboard, each footfall a wet scrape. The creature was injured. Never a good sign.

Its body, broad and feline, moved with predatory grace, but lacked fluidity—like muscle and metal barely agreeing on how to share a skeleton. Its back bristled with twisted plates and broken armor, fused into scar tissue. A tail like a segmented iron whip dragged behind it, ending in a barbed, oil-slicked stinger that glowed bitter-orange with menace. Its face was *almost* human. Eyes too intelligent. Teeth too numerous. Its lips parted in something that could have been a grin, or just exposed hunger and pain.

Jarly's voice dropped. "Shit. Shit. That's a...That's a..."

Lydarc nodded, slowly. "Manticore."

"Those things nest, don't they?"

"Not if we kill it first."

The beast saw them. Its howl of excitement filled the air with a strange, keening lust for food; human food being the manticore's preferred delicacy.

"Guess the course just got an expansion," Jarly muttered. "Go. I'll draw it off."

"Like fuck you will." Lydarc launched herself across the rest of the cable span and grabbed Jarly's arm.

"Let me go," Jarly growled.

Lydarc's face twisted. "I already have enough ghosts. You're not joining them."

The manticore barreled toward the base of the cables, faster than a thing that size should move. With a dry pop, it launched itself skyward—*toward them.*

"Drop!" Lydarc shouted.

Both women let go at once, falling through the tangled netting. Lydarc wrapped herself around Jarly as they crashed through layers of wire and canvas, finally landing hard on a slanted slab of old roadway. The impact knocked the breath from their lungs.

The manticore landed in the cables above, shredding them like cobwebs. It screeched, panicked to escape the tangled net that had captured it.

Jarly staggered upright. "Now would be a *great* time to cheat."

Lydarc's breath came ragged. Her hand drifted toward her

chest. She didn't summon a storm—not fully. Just a whisper of what lay inside her. The clouds thickened above as she met the creature's eyes.

"Come on then, fucker," she whispered.

The beast had ripped through the netting and was coiled to leap at them.

A crack split the sky. Lightning stabbed down, not at the creature, but into the base of the ancient, rusted water tower behind it. The structure groaned and collapsed with a satisfying screech, metal and stagnant water crashing down on the manticore's back.

"Run!" cried Lydarc, unnecessarily.

The beast shrieked, a forlorn yowling death rattle, then lay still, buried in cables and junk.

"Not magic," Lydarc panted. "Just...climate adjustment."

Jarly laughed, wide-eyed. "That's what you're calling it now?"

They stared at the ruined course, half of it a mess of debris. The finish line, a bent iron gate made from scavenged signs and construction leftovers, stood crooked but inviting

Jarly spit and grinned. "Double or nothing?"

Lydarc groaned. "You're insufferable."

"Yeah. But you love me."

Lydarc didn't answer. But she offered her hand. Jarly took it. They ran for the gate.

Later, she joined Wayland at the downtime tent. Jarly had begged off, saying she needed rest after beating her friend on the obstacle course, which led to another heated debate.

Wayland was in a strange mood; not his usual loquacious self. She even wondered if he was avoiding her. As the tent emptied, she watched him absently sip his beer. Finally, they were alone, giving her a chance to find out what was on his mind.

"What's up with you tonight? You act like you're holding in the biggest dump ever created by man or beast."

"Always the socially appropriate, inoffensive speaker, my Leisil."

"You know it's Lydarc now."

"Oops. I keep forgetting that."

"Out with it. What's up with you?"

Wayland's eyes scanned the room, his mouth tight. He said, "My M.S.O. is up in a couple of months."

"M.S.O.?"

"You might not have signed one yourself, since you started so young. Your parents probably did it. It means Military Service Obligation."

Lydarc was silent for a moment too long.

"I'm sorry, Leisil—Lydarc. I'm leaving the service. I recently found my daughter. She's fifteen now. Her mother, Cassander, she—"

"She's the one you never talk about, isn't she? That one?"

"I'm sorry."

"You keep saying that."

"Sorry. They live over in Hiccup, and I'll be moving there to be with them. It's been fifteen seasons; fifteen seasons that I've already lost with her. I want to make up for that. Get to know my daughter, join my family. Leisil—Lydarc, you and I..."

"You don't have to explain. I get it. I always knew this woman—"

"Cassander."

"Yes. I could tell she was the love of your life, and no one could ever replace her. Whatever we had could never compete with that."

"You're taking this better than I expected."

Lydarc was practicing what Jarly had told her about keeping her feelings from showing on her face. She grinned stupidly. Inside, she was on fire, her life going up in incandescent, raging flames right in front of her.

"Another round?" she asked as she rose, her tone casual.

"No, I think—"

They were interrupted as a soldier, breathing hard, ran into the room.

"Captain Peters! There's a huge attack on the barracks!" she yelled, "Several wounded already. I don't know how many gone. It's a real mess. Sir?"

Wayland was immediately on his feet, giving orders as he moved. Without thinking, Lydarc followed, stopping at her barracks to get her bow. It had started to rain and the drops lashed at her face as she ran. Only later did she consider how odd it was that an attack from the minions was happening so far outside their usual timing.

The barracks looked like a tornado of hellish origins had landed, ripping everything to pieces. Lydarc rushed in, bow drawn, but there were only a few struggling minions left which she quickly dispatched. The rest were dead or dying on the floor of the tent. Above, the canvas gaped open to the stormy sky where the monsters had broken through. Most of the soldiers had been asleep and unaware of the danger that had come upon them without warning. The medics were busy hauling out the wounded.

Outside, bodies under canvas were lined up in the mud. Suddenly, Lydarc recognized these barracks.

"No! Jarly?"

She ran back in, screaming the name of her friend, but there was no answer.

When she gave up looking among the wounded, she found Jarly's body shrouded by a canvas tarp, her mangled form covered in mud and blood. Her pale face looked peaceful—too peaceful, considering the terror and pain she must have suffered.

Lydarc collapsed to the ground, guts churning, refusing to believe what had happened. How could this be possible? They had just defeated a manticore together. To go like this, in her sleep, was too much. Lydarc felt her spirit animal stir and she let him go. Rarog launched out of her chest and took to the dark sky with a deafening screech of pain and loss, mirroring her own.

Rain lashed down on her face as Lydarc knelt in the mud, screaming up at the unfeeling darkness. Even now, Lydarc refused to cry, yielding to rage instead. Life sucked, and this was just further proof of that enduring fact.

She'd just lost the only two people she'd ever been foolish enough to care about in one lousy, fucking blastday.

27

LYDARC, NOW

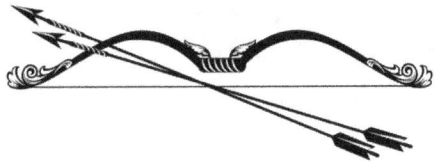

The mind is its own place and in itself, can make a Heaven of
Hell, a Hell of Heaven.

—JOHN MILTON, *PARADISE LOST*

A s we come up over the rise, we're met with a strange
sight.

"What are those things?" asks Sitka.

"I think they're called teepees, but there are too many of them
for it to be our clan alone. Besides, the Siletzon didn't use them. In
the before times, they built cedar plank houses."

As we approach, a rider comes at us through the tall grass,
pushing his mount hard. I hope he—or his horse—knows where
the gopher holes are. He pulls up abruptly and jumps from his
gray stallion.

"Hey there," says the man, "You're trespassing. This is no
place for you people, or your pets." At this, he frowns at Sitka the
bear.

"I am no one's pet," says the bear.

"Forgive me, I meant *talking* pets," says our visitor with a smirk, who I now realize is little more than a boy.

The bear growls.

I step forward before hostilities can erupt.

"Please. What is this place? We're looking for our people, the Siletzon."

"Oh, them. I thought there was something familiar about your aura. They're camped down by the river, thataway," he points, "but the others will have to stay here."

"I am Siletzon," says the bear, "and you can let me through, or I will rip your arms off. Your preference."

As we speak, another group arrives from the teepees, having traveled on foot. A woman with shining gray hair and brightly embroidered overalls seems to be in charge, perhaps the matriarch of this mysterious group.

"Forgive my grandson. He's a bit overenthusiastic at times. Welcome to the underlands. I am Delores the Elder. What is your tribe?"

"I am Lydarc, shaman of the Siletzon, and this is my apprentice in her spirit animal form, Sitka Sangashee."

"Ah, that group," says the old woman. "Very interesting. It's unusual to receive so many at once, but we managed. Follow me."

The old woman leads us to their camp. We pass a collection of teepees, some huge, others no bigger than a two-man affair. Some are rather makeshift in their construction, as if the builders are still learning their craft.

Delores stops before a well-constructed long cedar building with a roof that reaches almost to the ground. She leads us through a circular doorway, above which a brightly painted, carved figure looms over us with wide hips and a scowl. To me, the carving looks a lot like Delores the Elder. As she steps through, she rings a knocker made from a cervid hoof.

Inside, it's smoky and smells of years of human habitation. A long hallway leads us in. We pass by several deerhide-shrouded doorways: inside them, I hear children playing and adults conversing. When we reach the center of the building, the way opens up to reveal a great room with a gigantic round hearth and tall ceiling, beams angling up to a high opening in the roof. Sunblight streams through, creating patterns on the floor.

"This is our central hall," says Delores, "where you will gather with us for meetings and group discussions."

"Oh, no, we're not staying," I say. "I'm here to bring my people back with me."

Delores gives me a long, studied look. "I sent Jeremy to bring the elders from your tribe. Please, sit." She leads us to a long bench. We sit and the bear leans back on her haunches.

After a brief, uncomfortable wait, Delores's grandson leads the Siletzon in. I rise to hug Pegram. The old man has tears in his eyes.

"Welcome, welcome, shaman. It is good that you followed us through. We could use your help here." Pegram turns, as if seeing the bear for the first time. He starts and draws back in fear.

"It's all right, Pegram. It's me, Sitka. I found my spirit animal at last."

"That is indeed an impressive animal, young Sitka, but where are you? I mean, your body?"

"We left me at the Fallen City and need to get back there soon. I can't hold this form forever."

"Back?"

"Yeah, Lydarc can get us back, through the lake that you came here by, to the afterarth above—or below. I'm not sure what's up or down anymore. We're still alive there."

Pegram scratches his head. "Why would we want to go back?"

"What?" I ask, now totally confused. "Why would you want to stay? This place is hell."

"That's just it. We don't have this religious hell in our traditional beliefs. Yes, we lost some that had converted, but the rest of us—it seems we're mostly immune to the three sisters, the Algeans that everyone is so afraid of here. This land is much better for us than the afterarth ever was. No Overs or their minions, very few leshii or ghouls or wendigo. We want to stay."

I stare in shock. "Stay? Are you all over-under crazy? This place is toxic."

"Not for everyone. The Algeans have much less sway over us, and not even the Overs can reach us here. We can have a good life. It's a lot of work, building homes and hunting and gathering for food. But Delores and her people have helped us. It's a good start. We want to stay. You should remain with us, shaman. Send for Sitka and we can be a tribe again."

Rapha, who has so far been silent, pipes up.

"These lands are not stable. The Shamanic Council predicts that the underlands will collapse, or at the very least, be transformed by the coming solstice. You should leave now, while you still can."

Pegram waves a hand in dismissal. "Lydarc has been telling us the solstice is just around the corner since she came to us. It hasn't happened yet. Besides, we're used to life being difficult. How much harder can it be than it was in the bitterwood? We barely survived there, despite everything the shaman and the other hunters did to provide for us. No, I think we'll stay right here."

"Stubborn old bastard," says Wayland under his breath.

I say nothing, because there's nothing I can say. I can't believe that we've come all this way and now my tribe rejects me. It can't be right. Even if I wanted to stay, what about Sitka? We must go back for her body.

"Come," says Delores, leading everyone outside. "There's no need for the new ones to decide this moment if they're going to stay. There's a meeting tonight. You'll have a chance to discuss what Pegram and the Siletzon have accomplished here. Besides, if you decide to go back, you don't want to be traveling at night. It's when the Algeans are most active."

I follow, lost in my own tortured thoughts. What now? Were all my hopes of bringing back the tribe just a fool's errand? If the

Siletzon are not my family, where do I belong? Am I doomed to be alone for the rest of my life?

I hurry away, wanting to put some distance between myself and my recalcitrant clan.

A deadly thought occurs to me: *What if the Siletzon were* forced *to return?*

As if reading my mind, Rapha says from behind me in a hushed voice, "We have to find the demon lord and eliminate him. If we can end the underlands, your people will have no choice but to return with us."

"How can you be so sure any of us will survive the collapse?"

"The end won't happen immediately. Just as the underlands took a while to develop, it will take time for it to disincorporate. I'm sure we will have plenty of time to get your people out."

"I hope you're right."

Wayland, who has hurried up behind us, leans in and whispers, "You'd better be right, Rapha. A lot is depending on it."

As I walk along, the bear sidles up beside me, her great paws touching and placing themselves elegantly in the prairie grass, a giant with a ballet dancer's gentle step.

"Lydarc, I sense your distress," says Sitka. "I too want our people to come home, but what you're considering now—"

"It might be the only way to convince them to leave. They're being idiots."

"Lydarc, you've changed. Ever since Wayland was attacked and you used the veil, you're different."

I frown. I feel the same as ever. Perhaps a pinch more cynical than before. "Different how?"

"I can't believe that in the past you would have tried to make our clan's decisions for us as you are now."

"Rapha told me using the veil would only increase wisdom. Perhaps that's what you sense."

Sitka is silent, but I feel her worry and concern as clearly as if the girl were speaking it out loud.

That evening, Simply Waites pulls me aside.

"I've been talking to some of the younger Siletzon. We don't all agree with Pegram and his hidebound ideas. If what you're saying about the underlands being doomed comes true, it's likely we're too far away from the lake here to make it out in time if this realm collapses. A group of us are planning to move closer to the lake in a few blastdays."

"You've made the right choice. If you can convince anyone else in the meantime, you'll be saving their lives."

With a grim nod, Simply melts back into the group.

I feel better than I have in blastdays. Maybe I can't save all the Siletzon, but if even a few will trust me, I can at least save some of my family—can't I?

28

LYDARC, BEFORE

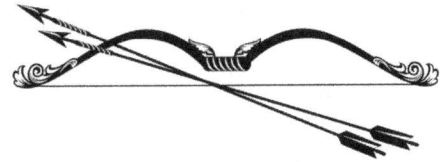

I believed that home was not to be for me, never realizing that I carried it within me all along.

— LYDARC AS QUOTED BY SITKA SANGASHEE,
EVOLUTION OF THE SHAMAN MASTER

After losing Jarly and Wayland, Lydarc thought nothing worse could happen to her. She was wrong.

Although, technically, Wayland wouldn't leave for a couple months, he was effectively gone already, spending all his leave time on trips to Hiccup. What a ludicrous name for a town. But somehow, it fit.

At Jarly's funeral, Lydarc met the deceased girl's parents and two brothers, who had doted on their warrior sister. It was a sad affair, as all funerals must be, but at least Jarly had people who would remember her. Lydarc wondered who would come to *her* funeral, when it eventually happened.

Who're you kidding? Funeral? You'll be lucky if they throw some dirt on your rotting carcass.

Another off-timed minion attack cut the funeral short.

Afterwards, she noticed some of the other soldiers giving her odd looks. When a third person stared at her a little too long and intently, she let her easily ignited temper catch fire.

"Look a little closer, and you'll be staring at me from your new luxury villa in the underlands."

The woman lifted her hands in silent apology and slunk away. Later, Lydarc learned why everyone was looking at her as if she were a pariah.

It was because she *was* a pariah.

～

"Unbelievable!" she shouted at Griffin, the base commander. Griffin had summoned Lydarc to her tent. "You're telling me that the minion attacks are *my fault*?"

"Calm down, soldier," said the doughy officer, hunched behind her walnut desk as if its bulk would protect her from Lydarc's wrath. (It would not.)

"You must admit that, if it isn't true, then it's a hell of a coincidence. The random attacks started just after your encounter with the Over, paused while you were away, and resumed when you returned."

"I still don't—"

"I'm sorry, Frandling, but my decision is the law here. Something about that peri-soul you carry is drawing the minions to us. Seven soldiers died the other night. I can't risk the entire camp because of one soldier. You'll get an honorable discharge with a final rank of sergeant and a season's pay in compensation."

"I don't give a pisser rat's ass for any of that grundlecrap. The Resistance is all I've ever known. What am I supposed to do now? Where will I go?"

"I don't know. Anywhere but here."

"How long do I have?"

The commander pretended to study the papers before her. "If

you could be out of camp by tomorrow morning, I think it would be to everyone's benefit."

Snapping up the packet held out for her, Lydarc said, "Yeah. Everyone's but mine."

She stomped out of the tent and went directly to her barracks to pack.

She had no idea where she'd go or what she'd do. At least when she was sent to the academy, she knew where she was going; when she arrived at the front, it had been inevitable, planned, predictable. Nothing about her future was predictable now.

She couldn't return to her family, if they were even still alive. How could she face them knowing they'd handed her over to the service as a child, without a second thought, like a calf being sent to market to be butchered and served up as veal?

A vague memory popped up of her father talking about distant Siletzon relatives in the Oregon territories. It was a hell of a long way. She might not even survive the journey.

But the Fallen City was on the way. She had the map of waypoints into the underlands that the Shamanic Council had given her. Jarly's half-life was there. Did she have the guts to throw herself into that bizarre lake? Would she be able to find Jarly in the underlands and bring her home? She owed it to Jarly to at least try. If Griffin was right, it was Lydarc herself who had caused her friend to be ended.

What the fuck. There was nothing to lose. She'd buy a sturdy pony with some of her compensation pay and head for the Fallen City, then Oregon if she survived that far. If she didn't make it, no one would miss her.

She had no idea how wrong she was about this.

29

WAYLAND, BEFORE

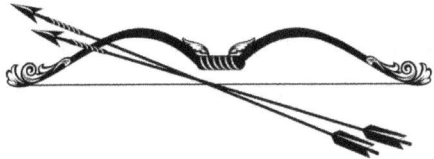

I was thrown into it at a late stage, not knowing what to expect. To say that I was pleasantly surprised by the strong woman my daughter had become without me—well, it was a little embarrassing, really.

—WAYLAND PETERS, AS QUOTED BY SITKA SANGASHEE IN HER PERSONAL JOURNAL

Wayland had been out of the Resistance for almost half a season. Eva still wouldn't call him Dad. At least she was talking to him now. It'd been rough at first: she had rebelled against everything he said or did. He couldn't really blame the girl; she'd grown up believing that he'd abandoned them, instead of the other way around.

At least now they had a home. With his separation pay, they'd gotten a small cottage down the street from the tavern. He went to the inn every blastday to help out—and try to get to know his daughter, if there was any hope of that now. She was almost sixteen and seemed to have no space in her life for a long-absent father.

Eva was wiping down the bar as he walked in.

"Cassander tells me you're interested in learning to be a bowman."

"Bow *woman*."

"Well, I've never heard it phrased quite like that, but whatever you want to call yourself. Maybe 'archeress' would fit you better. Anyway, I was thinking we could go out to the quarry and get in some practice. I could throw a couple of hay bales and a target into the wagon. After lunch, sound good?"

"I guess so. I'm off until this evening."

It wasn't the enthusiastic response he'd hoped for, but it would do.

The quarry was in the hilly forest outside of town. A warm breeze was dancing in the tall evergreen firs that surrounded them, and the trees were whispering among themselves. Bitterblight was in its later stages and had held for long enough that the chamomile was blooming. Tiny daisy-like blossoms covered the gravel where they set up the practice range.

Wayland remembered how Leisil—he kept forgetting to call her Lydarc—had taught him to gather and dry the chamomile blossoms to make a relaxing tea. He missed Leisil—*Lydarc!*—dearly. She'd left without a word. He supposed he deserved that, given how he'd treated her.

Eva was retrieving her arrows. After a brief tutorial on form, she'd taken to archery like a natural. He was unashamedly proud of her, but he should have expected it. The girl was good at just about anything she took up.

"Just a few more, Eva. I want to get back before blightfall."

The girl heaved a theatrical sigh. "Oh, all right. But I was just getting the hang of it, I think." She handed over the longbow and quiver. "I'll just go up in the trees and take a pee first."

"All right. Just be careful."

Eva put her hands on her hips. "Oh, come on. We're just

outside of town. What possible danger could we find this close to civilization?"

"Lots. Just hurry. We need to get back before your mother starts to worry."

Wayland was just thinking she'd been gone a while when darkness arrived with a snap. Thunder growled and blightning flared in the empty quarry, illuminating the towering torsos of the firs—now resembling a group of angry giants glaring down at him.

"Eva?" he yelled. No response.

Fearing the worst, Wayland gathered the sword he carried out of habit and caution, and climbed into the gloom of the trees. As he ran, the rain poured down and the wind increased, swirling and whistling all around him. Leaves, fern fronds, and pine needles spun in the wet whirlwind as it increased in speed and power.

At the top, he came into a clearing where the trees bent down over a form at the center of the maelstrom. Was it a tree, or a giant, or both? Animated branches twisted and twined around a struggling shape. He caught of glimpse of dark curly hair.

"Eva!" The response was a muffled cry from within.

The creature issued a squealing roar of anguish and rage. Glowing, glowering jade eyes stared out from gnarled branches that could have been hair or beard or long scrabbling fingers. The branches tightened around their victim in a constant, squirming movement.

Eva cried out in pain.

"Hang on! I'll get you out of there," Wayland screamed over the whooshing of the wind and patter-pounding of the rain.

"This one is mine now," shrieked a voice shaped of wind and creaking limbs. "Trespassers will be swallowed. This is my wood, my domain. Run away before I take you too, you stinking meatbag."

Wayland ignored the creature's expletives and hacked at the

circling branches with his sword. A great bellow came up from the tree beast and the wind grew in its ferocity.

The sword was doing little to free Eva.

"Hang on," he cried desperately, "I'll be right back."

Without waiting for a response, Wayland ran back down the hill to the wagon, pulling out the ax they used to cut firewood.

Rushing back up the hill as fast as his middle-aged body could carry him, he saw with chagrin that the branches had tightened even more around Eva. Was she already dead?

"No!" He swung the ax over and over. Sweat broke out on his brow, even in the chill of the storm. His arms burned with fatigue, but he kept on swinging. He would not lose his daughter now, not after just finding her. Wayland would die before that happened.

As he made headway on the branches, they emitted a choking smell like freshly turned earth and sickly-sweet pine pitch. The limbs wept a greenish-gray ooze where he'd hacked into them.

Finally, with a great groan of anguish, the tree beast let go of its prize and stumbled backward. Eva's body toppled forward and would have tumbled to the forest floor had Wayland not dropped his ax and caught her in his arms.

She was unconscious, but still breathing. Setting her down gently, he recovered his ax and turned to the forest being, where it crouched, its limbs shaking in fury. The horrid tree-thing's face was cracked bark, its hair and beard slithering branches and swaying moss. Its arms and legs were twisted sprays of root-like appendages as long as a man.

Yateveo.

Wayland had heard of the forest demons but never seen one. He advanced on the yateveo with his ax, but the bleeding yateveo seemed to think better of continuing this particular battle. It shuffled off into the trees, taking the swirling wind and rain with it.

Turning back to Eva, he felt for broken bones and found none, though bruises were already forming on her arms. As she came to, Wayland exhaled a long breath in relief.

"Dad? You—you saved me. What was that thing?"

"Yateveo, I think. A tree beast. How're you feeling?"

In answer, Eva struggled to her feet with a groan.

"Mom's gonna end you."

Wayland smirked. "She can do her best."

Only later did he realize that, for the first time, Eva had called him Dad.

30

LYDARC, NOW

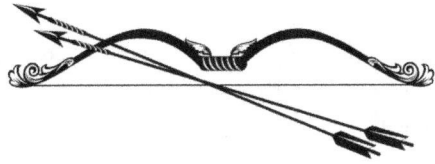

Jean de La Fontaine said, "A person often meets his destiny on the road he took to avoid it." Lydarc's destiny seems to be to avoid that road at all costs, until it—inevitably—runs her over.

— WAYLAND PETERS, AS QUOTED BY SITKA
SANGASHEE, IN HER PERSONAL JOURNAL

We trudge through the underlands. I try to keep everyone upbeat, but I know that the more time you spend in this horrific realm, the more it infects your thinking, dragging you ever downward into depression, self-loathing, and thoughts of suicide.

I have the map showing that the underlands veil is in the hills ahead of us. We're following a stream that will lead us there. Checking the map as we walk, I almost trip over a tent's guyline. Wayland grabs my arm so I don't fall.

A teapot steams on a nearby campfire and wet clothes decorate the shrubs.

A stout woman jumps through the flap of the tent and raises

her staff in the fluid movements of a seasoned warrior. She looks familiar.

"Flossy? Is that you?"

The woman's frown transforms into a wide grin. "Leisil? Leisil the archer?"

"Yes, but it's Lydarc now. I'm a shaman."

"Always knew you'd amount to something. See you grew some too."

I had no idea that Flossy thought I was anything more than a slight irritation to her, but that was the way of the academy. You didn't make friends, only relationships that fed into your survival strategies.

I can see that she's grown some too, if that were even possible. Stiff muscles bulge from her rolled sleeves, and she stands even taller than she had when I fought her at the academy grounds, all those seasons ago.

Flossy yells, "Get up, sleepyhead. There's someone you need to see."

To my utter delight, Jarly, *my Jarly*, crawls out of the tent, rubbing her eyes.

"What is it, dear?" she says, "I was just falling asleep. After last night, I need a nap like a corpse needs lime."

But then Jarly sees me and Wayland, and her eyes go wide. "What? How?" She jumps up to hug me, threatening to bowl me over with her enthusiasm.

"You guys know each other?" asks Flossy.

"Yes," I explain, once I'm able to extract myself from Jarly's grasp. "We both ended up in the fifth regiment together. We were friends."

"Ah," says Flossy, pushing back her long black hair. "She told me about you. I went to the third."

I introduce the others. When Jarly asks if we'll stay for tea, my half-smile turns downward.

"Jarly, I'm afraid we can't. It's a long story, but we only have so much time in the underlands. Once our mission is complete, we'll be returning through the lake back up to the afterarth."

"It's possible to return?"

"Well, I did it one time before. I can talk to the deathguards. They let me pass before, when I came looking for you. I couldn't find you last time, though."

"I can believe that. I've been on the move ever since I got here. It's the best way to stay sane in this terrible place. When Flossy and I found each other, things got a lot easier."

Jarly eyes her companion with a degree of warmth and gratitude that goes far beyond friendship. I'm happy for her.

I continue. "Whether or not we're successful, we'll be leaving through the lake. If you two could meet us there in a few blast-days—if you want to get out of this hellscape."

"Are you kidding?" Jarly scoffs. "We'll be there with bells on."

"I'd pay to see that," I say with a chuckle.

As we leave, I look back with hooded eyes, wondering if I'll see Jarly and Flossy again—then wonder if any of us will survive long enough to escape the underlands.

31

EVA, NOW

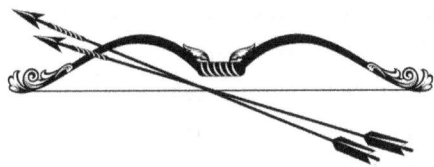

Hope not ever to see heaven. I have come to lead you to the other shore; into eternal darkness; into fire and ice.

— DANTE ALIGHIERI, *INFERNO*

Eva dries her eyes from another session of weeping. It's getting tiresome. Her eyes are raw, her nose red, and the lump in her throat is painful.

She can't get the image out of her head; her mother falling to the unseeum, being ripped apart and left to bleed out, her intestines strewn across the ground. The finality of it, the purple tint to the air signifying that Cassander had been forevered, had no chance of ever living again, not even in the underlands. Then her own intense pain. The expression on her father's face as he reached for her, to draw her back from the second forever, his touch fading as life left her too. It was unbearable. She wails, and the tears erupt again.

"No. I will not be like this for the rest of my life."

What life? She wipes her eyes and looks around. The cottage

they'd brought her to is stark. No family photos, no lacy curtains. Nothing to make it personal, to make it home. No one visits or even speaks to her from across the fence. It's total isolation. Someone delivers food to her doorstep, but she can never catch the deliveryperson.

She'd woken on the shore of the lake, lungs burning and exhaustion making it a chore to even lift her head. The death-guards—she'd later learned what they were called—had led her to a long building with a worn sign that read *Orientation Center*. What a misnomer. It was nothing more than a hall filled with hard, lumpy bunks, where new arrivals were dumped and left to recover from their ordeal on their own. Then she'd been led along a trail of misery. She'd tried not to look, but apparently some hadn't made it to the village before the underlands took them.

One woman was surrounded by gold, silver and jewels, but when she tried to touch the pile, which she couldn't resist, the objects burned her. Her hands were stumps of charred flesh.

There was a man who cut himself endlessly, his flesh in tatters down to the bone, his blood a congealed puddle at his feet. Yet nothing could stop him from abusing himself as he wept, saying "I'm sorry, I'm sorry," over and over again. She'd tried to talk to him, tell him to stop, but he wouldn't listen.

After that, she did her best to keep her eyes on the path.

Ordeal is a mild term for what had happened to her. Dying in the afterarth and being brutally revived here, in this strange land, without family or friends, with no hope of ever returning home. An intense and constant ache, unlike physical pain, never leaves her. No wonder so many go back to the lake to drown themselves in earnest. Ended in both realms. *Forevered*. It's tempting. She feels the tears coming again and fights them back.

She doesn't deserve this.

At this thought, a giant bell rings in her head. At least that's her impression, as if the idea is changing everything for her from that moment forward. She packs up her meager food and belongings in a bedsheet and leaves the cottage, slamming the door behind her. No one notices. No one tries to stop her. They're all lost in their own personal hells.

Eva heads for the path. It's not really a road, but it's the only route out of the village. The trail is rocky and steep, but she keeps on, her bare feet developing blisters that grow into sores. She travels through woods and along streams, but there are no houses, no villages where she might find more talkative residents. She begins to wonder if there are any such people in all the underlands.

Several times, she thinks she hears a snuffling, snorting sound in the bushes behind her, but she moves on quickly, not knowing what strange beasts might inhabit these woods and not wanting to find out. At night, the sounds get worse: she stuffs torn pieces of the sheet in her ears and pulls the rest of it over her head.

After what must have been several blastdays, her food runs out. Her stomach growls until she finds a stream and a patch of wild berries.

She lies in the grass, considering what to do next—if anything —when she hears a *chuff* from the bushes. Sitting up with a start, she looks around, but the little meadow where she sits is empty. Eva rises to her feet, wincing. Could she even run if she needed to? She's sure her feet are becoming infected. Is it her fate to die like this, eaten by wolves? Or worse, from an infection that turns her feet into green, smelly stumps of death?

"Hello. Are you all right?"

Eva whirls at the male voice. A nondescript man in patched canvas pants and a worn leather vest leads his horse out of the trees toward her. She realizes that these are the first words spoken to her since her arrival in the underlands.

"You...you're talking to me."

The man laughs. It's a pleasant sound. While not especially handsome or tall, he has a winning smile. "Why yes, I am."

He runs a hand through longish brown hair. Eva likes long hair on a man. Contrary to logic, she thinks it makes them seem more masculine. She looks at his hands, noticing his fingers lack a wedding band.

Just stop it, Eva, you idiot, she tells herself harshly. *Not every man you meet is a prospective boyfriend.*

"It's just that no one has spoken to me since I got here," she says. "I find it quite annoying."

The man tilts his head. "Out of curiosity, how long have you been here? In the underlands, I mean."

"I don't know. A couple of blastweeks maybe?"

The man raises his thick eyebrows, whispering as if to himself, "That's not possible."

Eva is offended. Truth is important to her. She's been told before that she could be brutally honest, not always as if it were a virtue. She doesn't like it when someone calls her a liar.

"I assure you I'm telling the truth," she says through gritted teeth. "Besides, why would I lie about that? What does it even matter?"

The man is silent for a while. Eva wonders if she has offended him. That's another of her vaunted skills. Finally, he speaks.

"Forgive me, you just took me by surprise. My name is Aamon. And you are?"

"Eva. Eva Winston Peters."

"Eva. That's a beautiful name."

His eyes take in her tousled hair, ragged and dirty clothing, and berry-stained fingers. They come to rest on her feet.

"Oh boy," he says, concern twisting his features. "That looks bad. Please let me help you. My cabin is just over the rise. We need to clean those wounds and bandage them before they get worse. Infections can be deadly out here."

Depression sweeps over Eva. She's dying, she knows it. She just wants to lie down and let it happen.

"It's all right," she says in a flat voice. "I can't walk any farther. I'll just sit here and see what happens next."

"No, no. You've come so far already—farther than you know. Don't let the Algeans take you now. It would be such a shame after what you've accomplished. Here, let me help you up on Shelly. Don't worry, she's gentle as a baby bidden. Careful now."

Eva isn't sure what Algeans are but allows him to help her onto the horse. She'd ridden a lot as a kid and has no fear of the mare, so she settles into the saddle and lets him lead them up out of the meadow. When the horse pricks up her ears at a scrabbling sound in the brush, she pats the mare on the neck and says a few soothing nonsense words.

"You seem to know horses," he says. "Are you a rider?"

"I was."

The man studies her with a frown, then throws a quick glance into the trees. "Don't let them warp your thoughts. You can ride here—you can do anything you want in the underlands. It just takes a little more resistance, a little more determination than you're used to. You're already fighting them off instinctively. With a little training—"

"What the hell are you going on about?" She's immediately regretful for her tone. *This man is trying to help her, isn't he?* She says, "Sorry. This is all new to me. I just don't understand what you're saying."

"No, no. I'm the one who should apologize. It's a lot to take in so soon. We'll talk about it later, once we patch you up and get some warm tea and food into you."

Eva wants to cry out of gratitude, but she refuses to start weeping again. "Thank you. I suspect you just saved my life."

Aamon laughs again. It's a welcome, soothing sound that spreads a protective barrier around them. Eva imagines she can feel the strong, shining melody of it pushing back the darkness that presses on her thoughts.

He says, with a thoughtful smile, "Then I guess we're even, because I think you just saved mine."

32

LYDARC, BEFORE

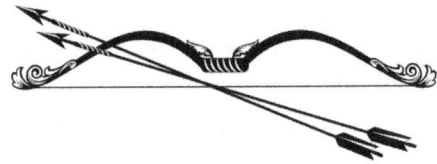

Nothing ever comes free, but when it came to the Council, the price for their gifts turned out to be far, far too dear.

— LYDARC AS QUOTED BY SITKA SANGASHEE,
EVOLUTION OF THE SHAMAN MASTER

Lydarc didn't look back as she left Nameless. She had the supplies she needed for the arduous overland journey to the Fallen City and, eventually, the Oregon territories. She was in no hurry to start this phase of her life, but she had even less desire to remain in the vicinity of the Resistance camp, Nameless, or Hiccup.

The road was dusty and hot, the rains having stopped when the sky shifted to highburn and stayed there over the last several blastdays. When she heard thrumming behind her, she thought it might be a disruption fissure opening up.

Just her luck. Exiled one blastday and ended the next. But the pounding came from a large bay horse that was being ridden hard toward her. Who could be in such a hurry out here? The nearest town was blastdays away.

As the figure approached, she recognized Rapha. When he reached her, he smoothly set his horse to a walk beside her.

"Glad I could catch you," he said. "I heard what happened. It is indeed a shame that you are leaving us."

"You're so good at stating the obvious, you should make a profession of it."

Rapha never laughed at her lame jokes and slights, if he understood them at all.

"It is just that we wanted to talk to you about something of grave importance before you go."

"We?"

"The Shamanic Council. We are gathering in the grove. It is where we always meet. You were invited anyway. That is how I learned of you leaving the service. I went to your camp to find you and they told me you had already gone."

"Why would I want to talk to the Council now?"

"As we discussed before, you are instrumental in advancing our goals. If not now, then in the future. It is important that you understand your pivotal role in saving humanity."

"Oh, give me a break. I've barely started to learn this shamanism thing. Surely you have far more powerful magickers at your disposal. I can't even work the veil."

"But you have the peri-soul and great potential. Lydarc, please. The grove is close to your path if you're headed north, as it appears you are."

"There you go with that obvious shit again." I shift in my saddle, uncomfortable. "Oh, all right. But this had better not take long. I want to reach Pahrump before blightfall. Who makes up the names of these towns, anyway?"

"I believe that one is quite ancient, surviving even from the before times. You will find it a very quaint and inviting little town."

"Somehow, I doubt that. Everywhere I go, the 'inviting' runs out quicker than a cheater from the bed of his best friend's wife."

~

Lydarc was getting impatient. The grove was turning out to be a lot farther off the trail than Rapha had intimated.

"How much further?"

Rapha smiled at her indulgently, as if she were a child asking if they were there yet. "It is right around the next bend in the trees."

Was Rapha losing his mind? They were in the middle of nowhere, with nothing to see but low scrub and sandy, unfertile soil as far as the eye dared travel. There was no bend, no trees at all.

Suddenly, Lydarc felt a pressure on her body and in her ears. Her hearing was muted as if she were underwater. Were they passing through an invisible bubble? It stretched as they forced their way through. Her pony's eyes grew wide; he fidgeted and fought her urgings.

"Calm, little one," said Rapha in that voice she'd heard him use before on animals, and a couple times on her. The pony stilled at once and carried her the rest of the way through the barrier with no more hesitation.

Her ears popped. Lydarc was shocked to find they were now in a grove of tall mesquite trees that hadn't been there before. A tinkling stream meandered through this impossible forest. The smell of the place hit her, an intoxicating scent with an almost tropical headiness.

"How did we get here? What is this place?"

"We call it the grove. It is a mystical place of healing and knowledge. The trees are always in bloom here. Just being within this wood brings one clarity of thought and expression, making it the perfect meeting ground for us. No one but a shaman may enter, so our conversations are protected."

Lydarc wondered why the Shamanic Council needed to keep their discussions so private.

Soon they reached the center of the grove, where several men and women sat around a fire on roughly carved benches. She noted they weren't built of mesquite: perhaps it was sacrilege to cut down one of these magical trees.

She had expected the Council members to be dressed in white robes, maybe with oaken staffs and long beards, even the women. These people looked like ordinary shopkeepers, housemaids, farmers, and workmen. Their clothes were worn and clearly chosen more for comfort than ostentation.

She was quietly impressed.

Rapha sat on a bench, introduced her and offered her a seat next to him, saying, "Shall we begin? I know that many of us have other pressing duties, but nothing is more important than what I am about to say."

Lydarc dismounted and took her place. The group looked at Rapha with a shared expression of concern—perhaps even a hint of fear.

"As some of you are aware, I have been using the veil to monitor the underlands to the best of my abilities. The underlands are difficult to penetrate, much less fathom. Aamon's influence on the underlands is a continuing problem. We must eliminate him. If we fail, the underlands will continue to grow and will eclipse the afterarth entirely."

"How do we eliminate this threat?" asked a stately gray-haired woman in farmer's coveralls. "We know how deadly the underlands are. How do you propose to get there and back? No one we've sent has returned. They stopped communicating almost immediately. It is likely they were forevered soon after they went through."

At this, Rapha rose and started pacing. "You've all heard the theory that the underlands and the Overs have more in common than first thought. I believe we have a unique opportunity in our newest member, Lydarc. She alone possesses a piece of an Over inside of her. They are calling it a peri-soul. With it, I believe she will be immune to the evil perpetrated by this Aamon. She might be able to take one or more of us through with her, undetected by the underlands lord, to aid her in this quest."

"Now wait just a fuckin' moment," said Lydarc, rising from her bench abruptly. "I didn't agree to any of this. I've barely started on my journey to be a shaman. I'm certainly not going to dive into this hooey-looey lake that leads to the underlands, just to forever some fella I've never met."

Rapha turned to her, his piercing blue eyes even more intense than usual. "Yet you are planning a trip into the underlands anyway, are you not?"

Lydarc stared, stunned. "How did you know that?"

"Merely a guess, that you have now confirmed. The Fallen City lies along the route you have chosen. That is the nearest underlands lake location on your map. Then there is the unfortunate demise of your best friend, who may still have a half-life in the underlands that could be retrieved. Perhaps the guilt you feel for being responsible for her untimely forever is a catalyst. And I assume that you decided not to use the pebble I gave you, but to travel there overland."

"All right, all right. You guessed correctly, but I have no intention of committing a random murder for people I just met while I'm down there."

"Of course not. You need time, and Aamon is just coming into his power. The future is dark and cloudy yet, but it will become clear. We merely wish to provide the tools you will need to survive your trip into the underlands, which is no small feat in itself."

"What 'tools?'"

"There is nothing material we can give you. You can carry very little with you when you dive into the upside-down lake. The dangers of the underlands are to the mind, foremost. We can give you psychic tools to fight the overwhelming malaise and depression you will feel there. A strong will is the greatest requirement of anyone who wishes to leave the underlands unscathed."

"I think I already have that."

"You do. But we can give you more. If you will allow us—and if my associates are willing—we will each give you a bit of our own life-force, a smidgeon of our individual shamanic talents. Not enough that we each will notice the loss; combined, it will make you a much stronger shaman. I fear it is strength you will need in the underlands if you are to succeed."

As Rapha looked around the circle with a raised eyebrow, every shaman nodded their assent.

"I don't get it," said Lydarc "Why would you all do this, even though I already said I'm unwilling to forever this man for you?"

Rapha studied the high mesquite blossoms, his vision targeted far beyond.

"Think of it as an investment," he said. "All we ask is that you agree to go to the underlands at some point in the future, perhaps taking me with you, nothing more. If you say no, that will be the end of it. Do we have a deal?"

"That seems like a deal too good to be true, but I guess I have little to lose. Let's do it. Is the transfer painful?"

"Not at all. You won't feel a thing."

Lydarc discovered then that Rapha could lie when he felt the need.

Later, as they were leading their horses out of the grove, Rapha was quiet, but that wasn't unusual for him. There was something else about his silence that set Lydarc's nerves on edge. When she glanced over at him, he was frowning.

"What is it?"

Rapha stroked his horse's mane. "There is one more thing we need to discover."

"What do you mean? Discover about what?"

"Your abilities with the peri-soul."

"Abilities? What abilities? As far as I can tell, it's a miserable curse that cost me my place in the Resistance."

"No. I suspect there is more. Why would the Overs do this to you? What is their plan? I have given this much thought, and I have a theory. Let us tie the horses and step away. I do not wish to spook them."

"Well, you're doing a pretty good job of spooking *me*. What's this all about?"

Rapha didn't answer as he led her away from the horses. After a brief hike, they approached the edge of a steep arroyo. He paused, looking back at her with an expression of mild regret.

"I know they are monsters, but I believe it damages the soul to take even a semi-sentient life."

Lydarc approached the edge cautiously and looked down. A figure was stooped at the tiny creek, drinking from the muddy trickle of water. It was hunched over, its leathery, scaled back bristling with nasty-looking spines. Bat-like, featherless wings supported it as it leaned over. Muscled limbs flexed as clawed feet dug deep into the sandy ground. Lydarc stepped back, dislodging a pebble that rattled down the steep incline. The beast turned abruptly, and a primitive reptilian face with smoldering eyes locked on to Lydarc with infinite malice.

Chupacabra.

Lydarc had heard of these mythical beasts but had never seen one in the flesh. They were almost as rare as your chance of surviving an encounter with them.

"Sorry, my friend," whispered Rapha, as he pushed her over the edge.

33

THE ALGEAN SISTERS, NOW

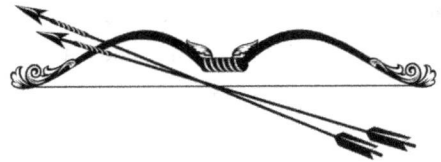

Double, double toil and trouble; Fire burn, and cauldron bubble.

— WILLIAM SHAKESPEARE, *MACBETH*

Ania leans over to spit into the fire. Instead, the anemic gob of foul drool catches in her tree-moss beard and dribbles down the fungal conks jutting from her bark-encrusted chest, *plop, plop*, like a zen fountain burbling with gut-rot pudding.

Sitting across from her, her sister Lupe cackles and sucks up a churning ball of mucus. She spits, doing a far more commendable job of it than her sister. The fire sizzles and splutters as the wad of vile pitch splats. A noxious odor rises from the flames, and Lupe nods her massive antlers in self-satisfaction.

"Vat are you athes doing?" hisses Achus, the third sister, from where she sits cross-legged, skinning a muskrat with her formidable, if rotting, teeth and jagged fingernails. Her words are distorted by the animal's screams, plus the fur and stringy membranes that stick to and gather between her teeth. "Vee need to conthentrate on the tathk at hand."

"Spit out the water rat, sister. I can't understand a thing you're saying. You need to *annunciate*," says Ania, emphasizing the last word. She is the most articulate of the bunch and loves to show off her prowess with words.

"I'll anunthiate your thorry ath into the lake of eternal thuffering. I'm holding a plathe just for you, dear thither."

"Oh, fuck you and your eternal promises, Achus. We've heard it all before. Save your misery and anguish for the living. They need it far more than we, your loyal sisters."

"I've got plenty enough to go around," says Achus, her speech improving as she spits and picks threads of membrane and fat from her teeth.

Rising, she throws the squirming, skinned rodent into the flames. "That'll be tasty-wasty topped with pond slime sauce and the deathcap mushrooms we gathered this morn. 'Tis all the better when the flesh is imbued with the exquisite agony of being skinned alive, don't you think? A gourmet genius, am I not?

"Now, down to business. I think it was a mistake, letting the strange human pass. She could be trouble for us down the long road."

Lupe, whose idea it had been to let the woman go, bristles. A cloven hoof scritches at the dirt where she crouches. Her eyes are the sickly green hue of phosphorescent sludge worms, and their glow flashes bright with annoyance as she speaks. "We needed to figure out what she has. Is it some disease? She seemed almost totally immune to the delicious waves of pain and distress I sent her. What if there are others with her affliction on the way? We need to find out before we take her."

Ania sits back and the gnarled branches that protrude from her forehead creak, like an old oak talking to itself in a storm. "I tried to send her trouble and corruption, but all I could reach were her feet. I couldn't get it to spread any higher. What's up with the girl? Could she be part Algean?"

"What? No," scoffs Achus. "There are only three of us, as it always was and always will be."

"Then I just don't know," says Ania. "It might take a full-blown, concerted effort by all three of us together to get her thinking straightened out, the poor thing."

Lupe says, "Then I say we move camp nearer the human structure, so we can observe her more closely. Then, if we decide, we'll rip her heart out and cook it with my delectable amanita sauce."

"That's the spirit," says Achus. "The sisters who slay together stay together."

"Amen," says Ania. "After all, it's for the greater doom of everyone concerned."

34

LYDARC, BEFORE

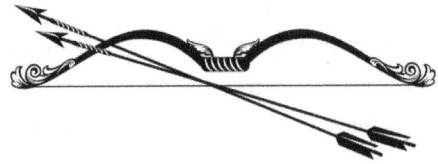

I'm glad he's hungry. Not that I want him to suffer, poor chap!
But then he'll enjoy eating me much more. There's a cheerful
side to everything.

—GEORGE BERNARD SHAW, *ANDROCLES AND*
THE LION

Lydarc must have lost consciousness as she rolled down
the slope, as the first blurry sight that hit her was the
face of the chupacabra, way too close for comfort.

Its glowing neon eyes burned a searing pain into her head.
She scrambled back in terror as a strange chittering sound echoed
across the little canyon. As the beast opened its mouth, Lydarc
could clearly see the hollow in each fang where the blood was
sucked from its living feast.

Not living for long, I assume.

"Una soldado out here, and alone? What luck for me." The
voice was rich and deeply accented. Lydarc noted this even as she
contemplated her brief future. Was this it? Dying alone in a gully

without even a soldier's honor? Betrayed by her own shamanic mentor?

The chupacabra raised its fetid, dirt-and-blood-encrusted claws to strike, and a fire rose in Lydarc's chest. Not anger, or even gyrfalcon-induced indigestion, but something new. A pressure built between her upper ribs. She felt her sternum splitting, delicately and perfectly centered, down the front of her chest. The pain was incandescent. She screamed, but it was too late. Whatever was about to happen had already begun, like a levy bursting, and there was no turning back from this flood of power.

Knowing she needed space, she scrabbled away, pulling her bow from her shoulder. As quick as lightning, she notched an arrow and aimed. Time slowed, then stopped. She stared. Chupacabra were notoriously hard to kill. About the only way they died was at the natural end of their lifespan. Was she about to die here, betrayed by Rapha? Why would he do this? Unless…

Instinct directed her next actions. With trembling fingers, she reached to her opening chest and into the golden pit of viscous goop that had resided in her since the Over had touched her. A dollop of it adhered to her fingers. She applied it to the tip of her arrow. It glowed and smoldered. Her chest reassembled itself with a slap like the door to hell closing, and she faced the beast. Its expression had changed. Gloating had transmogrified into trepidation, even fear.

"No, mi querido, this is not possible. The realms cannot cross over in this way. It will mean the end of all of us."

Before she could respond, the chupacabra lunged at her with a desperate cry. She loosed the arrow. As the barb reached its target, the chupacabra exploded into a hail of bloody mist that floated away on the breeze.

Wow.

She had learned what use the peri-soul could serve. She couldn't wait to try it on Rapha.

When Lydarc climbed up out of the arroyo, confused and exhausted, she discovered that Rapha was gone. Just as well. She really didn't have the energy to kill him just then. Besides, he *had* helped her learn what power the peri-soul gave her. That could be useful.

When she'd gotten as far away from the arroyo as she could, the shock of what had happened hit her hard. She pulled her pony up and sat, just staring, until the horse wandered toward the weeds in the ditch.

Lydarc sat up in the saddle. "All right. Let's stop here for a bit while I get my head straight."

She dismounted and let the pony graze on what meager offerings it could find as she gazed into the distance. "What're we gonna do, girl? It's such a fucking big-ass territory. I don't have the foggiest idea what I'm doing. I'll say it, just cause you're not gonna tell anyone. I'm a teensy-weensy bit scared to go on alone. There, I said it, but if you tell any of your horsey buddies, I'll have to take punitive action. You guessed right. Wayland taught me that word."

This pony wasn't like Milton, the mule-turned-dragon. She remained silent and unhelpful. Lydarc pulled out her medicine bag and felt for the small volcanic pebble, already having decided not to use it. She wasn't ready: she didn't know if it would deposit her in solid rock, or a widder-width up in the air, only to fall to her death.

Help me, whispered the pony. Then Lydarc realized the sound wasn't coming from the pony. Instead of a tiny voice nearby, it was an enormous voice far away.

"Hey, did you hear that?"

The pony continued to munch.

Lydarc thought for a moment, then rummaged through her pack until she found the hobbles.

"All right. You stay here and I'll check this out. Be right back."

She wondered why she was conversing so casually with a

stupid horse, then remembered her extensive conversations with a mule called Milton.

Lydarc headed off in the general direction of the sound. As far as she knew, she had fairly good directional hearing. Not everyone did, but it came in useful when hunting an elkin or other prey. What little hunting she'd been able to do in her off time at the Resistance had taught her that all her senses were needed to be successful, and then they had to be on high alert every moment, without exception. A moment of inattention could cost you dinner for a month.

One time, she'd been out with Jarly hunting the elkin during the rut, when their bugled grunts and whistled squeals filled the air. That proved beneficial to the hunters, as the horny elkin broadcast their locations in their lust for a mate.

"There," Jarly said, her voice high with excitement. "Did you hear that? He's over there."

Jarly pointed in the exact opposite direction from what Lydarc had heard.

"I don't think so. I think he's that way," Lydarc replied, pointing.

Jarly laughed. "Alright. It's a contest. I'll go my way, and you go yours. We'll see who has the bragging rights tonight in the downtime tent."

Jarly hurried off, sure she was right and keen to beat Lydarc to the kill. Soldiers of the Resistance were nothing but competitive. That was a fact you could bet on.

When Lydarc came looking for Jarly to help her haul out the elkin she'd just shot in the heart with her bow, Jarly was livid.

"How'd you do that? I was sure it was up the ridge and when I get up there—nothing."

"Well," Lydarc said with her now trademark half-smile, "I have the ears for it, don't I?"

She was yanked back to the present as a whining, wheezing sound flowed up from the ravine below her. At the bottom was a strange dark blob of stone that was...*steaming?* It emitted a noxious, cloying odor that reminded her of over-cooked snake.

"Ew. What is that smell?"

I do not smell, young human, and I will devour anyone who countermands me on that, or anything else, for that matter.

Lydarc stared. "Are you...are you alive?"

For now, said the voice in a sardonic tone. *If you could help me with this minor problem of mine, we're all likely to survive the blastday and go on our merry ways.*

"Marry...What?"

Listen, girl. I'm feeling extremely fortunate—and therefore forgiving—that you are so receptive. What are the odds that a shaman would wander by just when...Well, you get the drift.

"No, not at all."

The stone sighed. It looked like the arth was breathing. It raised its head.

Lydarc backed up too abruptly and tripped over a rock. When she sat up, she was face to face with a giant reptilian head.

"You're a... Are you a..."

Dragon? Yes, said the giant creature. It was so close Lydarc could touch it, had she wanted to. She restrained herself. The stink and the heat made her feel like throwing up. Now that she was closer, she realized that the creature's skin was more metallic than stone, ebony scales glinting in the available light. Its lips didn't move when it spoke, and its mouth was partly open. A gelatinous red fluid dripped from giant, craggy lips.

Yes, now we're starting to figure it out, are we? Dragons and shamans can communicate through the spirit realm. We have an ancient pact. We help each other, rather than one eating the other. You can guess which is which. I do for you and you do for me. Get it?

"I still don't understand. How are you talking? I can hear you, but—"

The great beast blew a torrent of air through giant nostrils. In the subsequent gale, several bushes were dislodged from the ground, rolling along in the breeze: the first tumbleweeds in the afterarth, perhaps.

Now, back to my problem. Are you going to make me beg? Lady Faustina the great does not beg, I can tell you that right now.

Lydarc was coming to her senses, or perhaps the unreality of it was taking over, like an unpleasant dream that keeps coming back every time you nod off. "All right, Lady Faustina. Just tell me what it is you need from me, and I'll do my best to comply."

Much better. If you look closely, you will see I have something lodged between my teeth, just a little toothpick of a thing. There, just there, see it? The dragon pointed a brown-tinted claw as sharp as a razor toward her gleaming molars.

I've tried to pry it out, but it's stuck like a fat rodent in the gullet of a tiny snake. It's so tightly lodged that I can't even get my jaws apart. I hope I don't need to tell you what happens if I can't do that. I will die of thirst or starve. An entirely unbecoming end for such a grand being as myself. Do you agree to help me? Do you see it?

Lydarc foolishly got close enough that she could peer into the reeking slit of the beast's mouth. Trying not to faint from the dragon's overwhelming halitosis, Lydarc squinted at the thing that was causing the dragon so much distress.

"Is that a human leg bone stuck in there?"

Oh no, I'm sure it's not. That's pork, is what it is.

"I don't think I can—"

Oh, for Over's fucking rum balls, just pry it out, will you, please?

Lydarc closed her eyes as her trembling fingers reached for the greasy, tendon-slick bone. At first, it slipped through her fingers, and she was sure she couldn't continue. At a grunt and a shudder from the dragon, the primitive part of Lydarc's brain decided it would be wise to do this quickly. She yanked at it with all her might, urgently wanting this bad dream to be over.

Nothing happened.

You might need a lever and a fulcrum. My jaw might suffice for the fulcrum, as it is made of quicksilver and adamantine, on a poultry DNA base. All our other bones are hollow, you know, to facilitate flight, but that wouldn't work for the jaw of a predator, now, would it? said the dragon in her mind.

"A what? Made of what?"

Has this Wayland fellow taught you nothing, girl?

"You know about Wayland? How? Yes, he's taught me a lot, but not much about things like adamantine, or quicksilver, or chicken genomes."

The dragon laughed, a chortling, clucking sound that seemed to emanate from her belly. *Ah, so you're not as stupid as you pretend. Excellent. We may have use for you yet, shaman wannabe.*

It was Lydarc's turn to be offended. "I am not a wannabe. I'm a fully recognized warrior shaman and I—"

I get it, child. I had more than my share of hubris back in the blast-day. It's curable, but it takes time. Now, can we get on with this? I'm so hungry I could eat a stringy, underfed shaman.

Lydarc stared. Was this really happening? Maybe she'd accidentally ingested some psilocybes last night. Oh well, better to get this nightmare over with. Looking around, she found a stout stick and lodged it as best she could under the bone.

"All right. This might hurt a little, but it's going to take some force to dislodge this puppy."

Oh, no, it's not a puppy, I assure you. That was last week.

"No, it's just a turn of phrase from the olden times that Wayland—"

Taught you?

"Yes. Hold on," she hissed in exasperation. With all her might and not-inconsiderable weight, Lydarc yanked on the stick. The bone, as if in slow motion, popped out and danced through the air gracefully, arcing and landing with a *splat* in the dirt.

Blood spurted from the wound in her gums, but the dragon inhaled forcefully and opened her mouth wide, revealing rows of ragged teeth. As she exhaled, a sound like a hurricane aspiring to be a bad jazz horn player split the sky.

When Lydarc picked herself up from where she'd landed—

what felt like a quarter widder-width away—she foolishly made her way back to the dragon.

"Are we good then?" she asked with a slight tremor in her voice that she tried her best to still but couldn't.

This time, the dragon spoke outloud. "No, shaman. Unfortunately, I must now deliver the recompense you deserve."

"Oh no, that won't be necessary," said Lydarc, backing away.

"Don't worry, frail human. There are no bones, no rending or tearing involved."

"Oh good. What is it?"

"Dragons keep their word. If ever you need me, just call. I owe you my life and I'd like to even that score as soon as possible. I don't like owing a shaman anything, much less one as scrawny and inarticulate as you."

Lydarc climbed up the ravine, relieved that she had survived a conversation with a dragon. Most did not.

She was just starting to relax when a voice echoed up from the valley behind her. "Yoo-hoo! Wait up shaman, I'm not quite done with you."

35

EVA, NOW

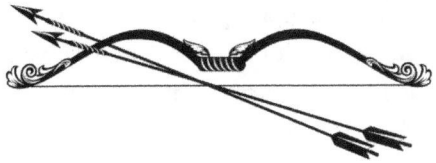

Oh what a tangled web we weave, when first we practice to deceive.

— SIR WALTER SCOTT

Eva sits on the deck of Aamon's cabin, her healing feet propped up and a cup of wild mint and rose hip tea cradled in her hands. It still isn't easy to stay upbeat, but with Aamon around, it's getting easier.

Why he lives alone, up here in this cabin, is a mystery to her. At least, until the blastday she finds the door to an unused room, and she goes in.

She decides to confront Aamon with what she's found.

"What is all that in the spare room?"

He just stares at her for a moment, his smile flash-frozen in place.

"Oh that. It's nothing. I call it the veil. Just something I found here when I first arrived. Must have belonged to the former resident."

"So, you don't use it at all?"

"Why do you ask?" He pauses in mid-stride, still as a watching owl.

"Because the room is dusty, but not under that thing."

Aamon sighs. "You are an observant one, aren't you?"

"That's a question, not an answer."

Aamon, who'd been clearing the dinner bowls, sets them back on the wooden table, plopping down heavily beside her. "All right. I guess you deserve an answer. You're the only one but me who's ever made it up this far, except of course for whoever built that room, and this cabin."

"And you didn't create it?"

"Me? No. I'm clueless about anything like that. I'm no shaman or magicker either, that's for sure. I just found it there. It took me months to even figure out what powered it. Still not exactly sure about that. I think it runs off blight or maybe air or even thought. I don't know.

"Then it was a while before I got her to show herself."

Eva frowns. "What do you mean, show herself?"

"Well, it kind of talks to you, in a strange way—like thoughts in your head, but not in language. It shows the underlands, but actually—and it took me a while to realize it —all realms, even the Overs. Those are hard to understand. The images are so strange. I watched what was going on. Then—"

"Then?"

A muscle in Aamon's face twitches. "Maybe I should just show you. How are your feet?"

"Fine. They're almost healed now. I want to see what this thing does."

As they enter the room, Aamon waves a hand. A fine netting of blue blight swirls and grows before them, emanating from a metallic box hanging from the ceiling in the room's center. It settles gently like a fisherman's net in still water. At each intersection point of the net, a tiny orb glows. The whole thing forms a half-sphere that grows to fill the entire room, containing them within it.

Eva pulls away but Aamon grabs her arm. "It's all right. It's harmless."

"You're sure?"

"I've been in here many times, and I've never even gotten a twinge of pain. Slight headaches at first, before I learned to understand her."

"You keep saying 'her,' but I don't see anyone."

"Hang on. It takes some concentration."

Aamon closes his eyes and is silent for so long that Eva wonders if this is all his imagination. Yet she can't ignore the network of blights flickering around them. Aamon finally opens his eyes and smiles. "She's here."

Eva looks around, seeing nothing but the blights. Then she sees it. A glimmering, silver shape is fading in and out before them. The fluttering female form is liquid quicksilver, sliding and slithering through her vision. Eyes of purest violet form, large as bird's eggs, staring at her, through her. Eva gasps.

"She's so beautiful."

"I know, right? I don't think she's alive. Some kind of projection, maybe. But she shows me things. I'm betting that you can see it too, with a little practice."

But Eva doesn't need any practice. It's a simple matter for her. She's a natural. She doesn't even need the interface; that is for newbies. She goes straight into the net and sees what needs to be seen.

Later, she cries on the floor, hugging her knees. Aamon tries to comfort her. "Eva, it's all right. It takes time, is all. You're gonna be fine."

"No, I'm not," she sobs between gasping breaths. "Someone or something is coming for you, for us, and they have no compassion, no understanding anymore of what it means to be human. They're going to end you, Aamon. And there's nothing I can do to stop it. Everything is about to change for the worse."

36

AAMON, NOW

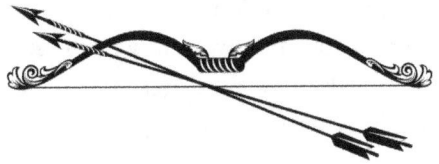

Lovers don't finally meet somewhere. They're in each other all along.

— RUMI

"Tell me more about that thing." says Eva one evening as they sit drinking Aamon's bitter homemade wine on the porch.

"What thing?" Aamon knows what she means but is stalling for time, so he can come up with a way to explain it that's just true enough.

"You know exactly what I'm talking about. That thing in your room."

'That thing,' she calls it, yet she'd been in there every day since she'd found it. He wasn't as fast at it as she is, but he isn't envious of her ability at all. He's tired of the job. She can have it. He's happy to chop wood and gather herbs and berries, preparing for the solstice that's supposed to arrive any blastday now. Well, at least he's met an amazing woman.

He feels like he's shirking his duty, but he doesn't care anymore. It had been like that with his father in the long ago. His dad had always been the intellectual, the scribe, and the eternal student, while all Aamon wanted to do was ride his horse across the estate or hunt with his falcon, Percy. Instead, his father wanted him to read book after book.

Thinking of his father triggered a memory. That would do.

"My father had many unique manuscripts. Books are quite rare nowadays, you know, but my family had the means. My dad, well, the passion of his life was arcane knowledge. I haven't known anyone quite like that since. Anyway, I remember an especially ancient one, from the later before times. It talked about otherworldly beings and parallel realities."

"What did the book say? What does this 'veil' do?"

"I don't know, exactly. I only read it because my father insisted, and I'm afraid I didn't pay as close attention as I should have." Aamon runs a hand through his hair. "I think it gives you the power to see into the realms of otherworldly beings and influence what occurs there—and here."

Eva heaves a massive sigh. "You might be right. From what I've been able to see with the veil, as you call it, it gives me the ability to see things that are happening in times and places I've never experienced and gives me the ability to change them for the better, but it all mystifies me. I'm not sure I should be messing with it at all."

"Nonsense. You took to it immediately. I wonder why...Any shamans in your family?"

"Not that I know of. My mom was a musician and my dad, well, he left us before I was even born. I guess my mom has always been my hero."

Aamon bursts out in a laugh, unbidden.

"What?"

"Oh, I just remembered my own dad. One time, my mom was in the shop cleaning and accidentally poked a broom into a wasp's nest. The entire swarm erupted from the hive. She called for him to help, but he was obviously terrified. Even at the age of nine, I could see that my father was no hero. He turned and ran."

"Oh, no, what did your mother do?"

"She had a bucket of soapy water for cleaning windows and threw it all over them and me. She got stung a few times, but the wasps never got to me. My mom was my hero, and I was spared a bath that night, too."

Eva smiles broadly and openly, and her eyes twinkle with humor. Aamon notices for the first time just how lovely she is. All right, maybe he'd noticed before, but this time, it hits him hard. His pulse races. He starts to sweat.

"Aamon, there's something I've been meaning to ask you."

"Huh?" For some reason, his brain isn't working quite right.

"When you found me, you said I'd saved your life, too. What was that all about?"

His hormones take a steep dive into shockingly cold water.

"Oh," he says, stupidly.

"You can tell me. We're friends, right?"

Aamon suddenly realizes that he wants to be so much more than friends with this beautiful, talented woman. She smells amazing, and her skin...

"Yes, we're friends, of course, but things have changed since I found you."

"What do you mean?"

Aamon leans forward and grabs his knees. "It's just that it can get lonely out here. Not seeing anyone for so long. You start to lose it, you know?"

"I can imagine, but—"

She looks at him with those doe eyes as deep as eternity; eyes that insist he stop lying to her right now.

"I was going to drown myself in the lake."

"What?"

"I know. I don't know what I was thinking. The moment I saw you—"

"Everything changed?"

245

He nods.

"For me too." She sets down her glass and reaches for him. When her lips touch his, Aamon's hormones come roaring back with a vengeance.

~

Afterward, Aamon knows it's time to tell Eva more. He takes her out on the porch and refills her glass.

"Eva, we need to talk. I didn't tell you everything I know about the veil. It's just that I've been alone for so long. At some point I stopped trusting. The underlands is a dark place, full of regret, sorrow, and evil thoughts."

Eva frowns. "You lied?"

"No, not exactly. What it does...The way it works..."

"Just tell me, Aamon. How bad can it be?"

Why is it so hard to just tell her?

"Edwin Ross, the physicist who invented the first veil, was my granphater. I don't have any special talent with the veil, but I grew up with it—at least, the later experimental versions. That gives me some ability with it, but you're much better at it than I ever was. I just managed to ameliorate some of the worst effects of the underlands on its residents. I guess, because of my granphater, I feel kind of responsible for the veil. When we met...What I was doing by planning to drown myself in the lake was much worse than just killing myself. If the veil isn't tended, then the underlands will devolve into a much more miserable place than it already is. A true fire and brimstone hell."

"You didn't go through with it, though, so it doesn't matter now, does it?"

"No. Because of you." He puts a hand on her shoulder. "Eva, I really like you. That's why I need to give you the choice I didn't have. You don't have to stay here if you don't want to, but if you do...It's a long-term gig, is what I'm trying to say, and it gets lonely out here. I've been here longer than you would think—much longer."

Eva smiles but he's not sure what it means. Does she know how much hinges on her next words?

"Well," she says, "I'll have one advantage you didn't have."

"What's that?"

"I'll have you to share it with, if you'll have me."

"Then you'll stay?"

She sets down her wine and hugs him. "Of course, silly man. Where else would I go? Besides, I like you too. In fact, you're the best thing that's happened to me since I died and went to hell."

37

LYDARC, BEFORE

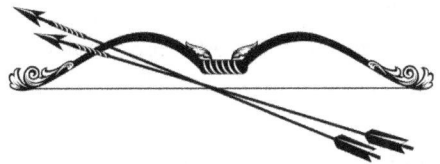

Someone said, "No good deed goes unpunished. I contend that every deed goes punished, especially the altruistic ones."

— LYDARC AS QUOTED BY SITKA SANGASHEE,
EVOLUTION OF THE SHAMAN MASTER

"I'd be happy to give you a lift. It's not far to the Fallen City, at least as the dragon flies."

Lady Faustina was cleaning her scales with her tongue as she spoke, and Lydarc was not sure she heard correctly. The dragon had a tongue like a bidle, scratchy and loud.

"You'd give me a lift? You mean I could ride on the back of a dragon?"

"It's not unheard of, dear. You don't look like you weigh much more than a goat carcass."

"Unlike the goat, I would hope to be breathing at the conclusion of this proposed ride."

"Of course, of course. Do you take me for a mere beast?"

Something occurred to Lydarc. "I'm sorry, Lady Faustina. I

forgot about my pony. I can't just leave her out here to die of thirst or fall into a disruption fissure."

"We can bring her too. I'll carry her in my claws."

Lydarc frowned. "I'm sure your intentions are noble, my lady, but the pony is apt to die of a heart attack along the way. The fear of dragons is built into the very essence of equines, you know."

Lady Faustina had finished cleaning her scales and leaned down to scrutinize Lydarc.

"You've come into some powers lately, have you not?"

"Powers?"

"Don't be cute. You know perfectly well to which powers I refer. You can put the pony into a hypnogogic trance. She won't remember a thing. Maybe she will experience occasional nightmares for a month or so, but nothing worse."

"A hypno-what? Faustina, I can't. I was just gifted these powers. I don't have a clue how to use them yet. I need time to learn."

"Nonsense. It's in you and you know how to use it, instinctively. You're a natural. Give it a try. Go to the pony and do your thing. I'll be there in a bit. I just need to find a snack to carry me over."

Lydarc wandered over to the road in a daze, where her pony was still grazing. She stared at the animal, not sure what to do next. From the hills, a sharp scream echoed, perhaps from a dying cervid or other prey animal. The pony started, looking skyward with the whites of her eyes flashing.

"Shush. It's just a dragon eating anything but us."

Lydarc closed her eyes, trying to call up the abilities granted her by the Shamanic Council members. Unbidden, she saw a face: that of the gray-haired woman in coveralls. Her piercing eyes looked right through her. Lydarc knew what she needed to do.

She spoke to the pony, "Quiet, dear one. Be still in mind and body. You're going to have a dream. Not a bad dream at all. You're with your mama and the night is mellow and cool. You're running with the herd, swift and sure and filled with the freedom your kind so love to share with each other."

To Lydarc's amazement, the pony closed her eyes and was soon snoring gently.

Later, a whoosh of unnatural wind announced that Lady Faustina was done with her dinner and ready to travel.

Next to being attacked by an Over, the ride to the Fallen City on a dragon was the most frightening thing Lydarc had experienced. The ground flew by beneath them while the stars encroached upon them, too close for comfort yet too far away to grab for balance. Every time the dragon dipped as its wings raised to gather more air, she was sure they were falling out of the sky. When they finally landed, Lydarc climbed off, shaking and breathless. The dragon set the pony down gently. The little horse weaved as she stood, then fell back into a deep sleep. Lydarc realized that she may have used a bit more power than was necessary on the poor little beast.

"Our time together is almost over for now, shaman," stated the dragon formally. "We will meet again when I can fully repay our debt."

"No, no, I'm sure this makes us even. I appreciate your help getting us here, but we won't need the assistance of a dragon again."

"Don't be so sure, young shaman. Your full visionary power has not yet evolved. We will meet again; for this I cannot wait, as owing a skinny little shaman is not a comfortable state of being for one such as myself, a queen of the sky, knower of all things and scorcher of the arth beneath me."

Lydarc thought this statement a bit over the top but tried her best not to smirk or laugh. She liked the heat well enough, but being toasted to cinders by dragon's breath was not an immediate desire.

"Thank you, Lady Faustina, but I hope there is never a need for us to meet again."

"Hope is a vain thing, silly girl. Hope leads to nothing but disappointment."

"A bit of a negative view of life, isn't that?"

"No, shaman. I'm a realist—a higher state you shall eventually achieve as well."

Without another word, the dragon spread her wings, and they captured the sky. In a spray of dust and dragon scent that inundated the sandy plain, Lady Faustina was gone.

After setting up camp, Lydarc spoke to the pony, who had woken long enough to eat her allotment of grain, then fell back into a deep sleep. "She's a bit theatrical, don't you think?"

The pony responded in her dreams. *A regular thespian, that one.*

"How do you know a word like 'thespian,' little girl?"

My former owner was a bard, or at least a fool-in-training. Used to go on and on about how brisket is the soul of wit and how the wisest man knowest himself to be a stool.

"I don't think that's quite right—"

And 'All the world is hay, and all the men and women mere hay makers.'

"That's not right, either," said Lydarc. The pony snorted loudly in her sleep.

Oh, hell. It's better your way, she thought, wondering if she hadn't put a bit too much dreamweed in the pony's grain that evening. The poor horse was going to have to fend for herself while she was below in the Fallen City. At least time above moved more slowly than it did below, at least according to Rapha, and hopefully the pony would be fine while Lydarc took the blastdays or weeks she needed to find Jarly.

She let the pony sleep it off as she considered her next move. She didn't know what she'd find on this journey, or how far down it might be to this lake of the underlands. All she wanted to do was find Jarly and get the fuck out of there before hell froze over.

As she sat in the darkness, with the fire crackling and the pony snoozing, she felt peaceful for the first time since returning to the

Resistance camp after becoming Lydarc. It was always a bad sign. A wind came up; a foul, desperate, grasping gale. With it came wings and claws. In a flash, the pony was gone, dragged up into the sky.

"No!" she cried. "Why would you end the pony, you foul wyrm? She was innocent..."

In her mind, she heard the strange clucking sound that is draconian laughter.

I changed my mind, shaman. I decided to show compassion. Did you deceive yourself into believing a prey animal could survive out here for a moment without you? If not me, then the wargles or the gastrins or the billabogs would have had her, and they would have shown far less mercy than I. Would you prefer the poor thing be eaten alive, slowly and painfully, or go quickly in my claws?

Grow up, shaman. The world is not a pleasure garden designed for your leisure, and the sooner you learn this fact, the longer you'll survive.

38

EVA, NOW

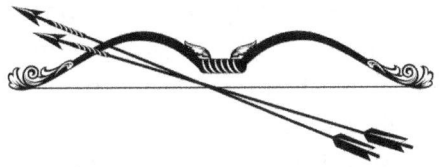

At first, I was so angry over what I'd missed. Like I planted a garden and never got to watch it grow. Then I realized that I was given the greatest gift of all: the chance to see it blossom.

— WAYLAND PETERS, ON FATHERHOOD, AS
QUOTED BY SITKA SANGASHEE IN HER PERSONAL
JOURNAL

Despite the pounding of their hearts, Aamon and Eva hear footsteps at the front door. They look at each other, both questioning the other with their eyes.

Aamon frowns. "Someone else made it all the way up here?"

"Apparently so. Should we go see who it is?"

To their surprise, they find three visitors at the door.

"Hello, we're looking for a man named Aamon. Does he live here?"

Eva stares at the strange woman. She is tall and powerfully built, but her bulging eyes and strange, frilled ears made her look like a fae creature from her mother's ancient book of fairy tales.

On top of that, she carries a strange, elegant bow fashioned of hardwood and polished metal.

Aamon whispers, as if to himself, "I didn't see you coming. How is that possible?"

Peering behind the tall woman, Eva can't believe what she sees. "Dad?"

Wayland pushes his way past Aamon and into his daughter's arms. The big man lifts her up with one arm and swings her around, laughing as she sobs. For Eva, it's too much to believe.

"What are you doing here?" she gasps. "How'd you find me?"

Wayland laughs gleefully as he sets her down. "Actually, we were looking for this demon lord. With a little encouragement, some of the more communicative residents said he lived up here in the hills. This was the first cabin we came across."

"Demon lord? What're you talking about? The only ones here are me and A—" she stops talking abruptly. Behind Wayland, Aamon shakes his head almost imperceptibly, but she sees it.

"Adams," interrupts Aamon. "Elric Adams. Come on in. It must have been a rough trip up here, with the Algeans being so active right now. I'm not sure what's going on, but it's been crazy."

Aamon, who, for whatever reason, wants to be called "Elric" among these visitors, leads them all into the cabin. Eva notices a massive, dark form moving in the brush: the warrior woman explains that this is her apprentice in spirit animal form, hanging back to avoid the usual questions and subsequent lengthy explanations. At the time, this makes perfect sense to Eva, but she later reasons that she'd probably been in shock from the blastday's events, and had invented the entire, extremely unlikely conversation. That is, until the bear speaks to her.

Right off, Eva notices how the second man, handsome and dark-haired with bright blue eyes, squints at Aamon with suspicion. In turn, Aamon locks onto this new arrival with a deadly gaze, as if they are mortal foes, members of two warring tribes who, though they have never met personally, know each other for the enemy with only a glance.

Finally, she notices her dad's arm—or rather, the lack of it.

With wide eyes she asks, "Dad, what happened to you?"

Wayland manages a weak smile. "Dinner invitation from a wendigo. Turns out they're not the pleasant hosts everyone makes them out to be."

"Oh, no. That's so awful." Eva feels like she could cry again.

"It's all right, honey. The moment I found you... Well, I feel fine now."

"Oh, Dad. You look like you need to sit down. Come in. Here, sit there."

She pushes Wayland down into a chair, which he sinks into heavily.

To everyone's surprise, evidently including Wayland's, he begins to cry.

"Oh, Dad."

Eva hugs her father and starts sobbing herself.

Wayland sits up straight and roughly brushes at his face. "It's these damn underlands; they play havoc with my allergies."

Eva grins through her tears. "Yeah, they sure do. You've got to be upbeat all the time, or it just gets to you. I really struggled at first, too. Aamon helped me."

Aamon gives her a look that could torch a dragon's skin.

"Elric, I mean Elric," she blurted.

Wayland chuckles and leans over to whisper in her ear. "It's all right. We all know this is Aamon. He just doesn't look like the evil lord that Rapha described."

"He's not an evil lord!" she shouts.

Everyone turns to stare at Eva and her face burns red.

Wayland stands and pulls his daughter up. "Hey, sorry to spring this group on you for dinner at the last moment, but we've been hiking all blastday and we're starving. How about I help with dinner? Lydarc bagged a wild turkler on the way up here and—"

Eva feels her face transform into a sly smile. "You? Cook? Are you kidding? Remember that time you offered to make breakfast for Mom and me and cooked up those atrocious clam pancakes? Ugh. I still can't get that taste out of my mind. So no, Dad, you will not be helping us with dinner."

Wayland gives her the mock hurt look that's his signature expression with her.

Seeing this, Eva is truly happy in the underlands for the first time since she'd kissed Aamon. *It turns out hell isn't so bad,* she thought, not realizing that she would soon be forced to revise this assessment.

Later that evening, when Aamon has been on the porch talking to the shaman woman for what seems like forever, a horrific howling and screaming erupts outside. It sounds like war has broken out in their front yard.

It has.

39

LYDARC, NOW

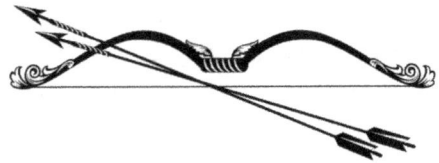

Man's enemies are not demons, but human beings like himself.

— LAO TZU

I'm surprised that we find Wayland's daughter here at the cabin, but not surprised to learn that we've found Aamon. "Elric" has to be Aamon: the map to the veils of probability led us directly here. It must be in the cabin, or very near it. If the veil is here, then the lord of the underlands is here too.

But a lord? Forget it. This guy looks nothing like the devious mastermind of a mortal hell. For one thing, he isn't much more than a kid. How could he have had time to set up this evil empire that Rapha keeps going on about? Something is horribly wrong with this whole scenario.

I'm surprised that Wayland lies, too. We didn't learn the location of the cabin from talkative locals, because there are no talkative locals, except the deathguards. But they only talk to me, and they know little of the goings-on in the countryside, as most of their time is spent at the lake, saving the souls that float up to them as limp, unbreathing bodies.

It seems that Wayland understands the need to keep the existence of the map of veils secret. Perhaps he knows more about our mission than he's letting on. If so, he might also know that I'm supposed to end this Aamon. Now that I've met him, I'm even less inclined to do it. Sure, I've done my fair share and more of killing, but this doesn't seem right. Besides, by the way Eva is looking at Aamon, she's become attached. Wayland will not be happy with me if I end his daughter's new boyfriend. *Now* who is being Sergeant Obvious?

As I watch Aamon and Rapha, I become increasingly concerned. The atmosphere is tight with tension, if not downright animosity. The two men sit across the room from each other, glaring daggers at each other as polite conversation continues around them.

"Have you two met before?" I dare to ask.

"No, never seen the man," says Rapha, not once taking his eyes off Aamon.

Aamon rises and comes over to me.

"You are Lydarc, the shaman that Eva mentioned?"

"Yes, probably. I'm surprised Wayland would have told her about me."

"Oh, yes. You are quite the celebrity with your peri-soul and all. That's why I didn't see this coming. I'm just sorry it took me so long to figure it out. We need to talk. Alone."

After dinner, he leads me out to the porch. He jumps when he sees a giant russet bear sleeping in the grass at the base of the stairs.

"Oh, don't worry," I say, "That's just my apprentice, Sitka."

Aamon shakes his head distractedly, then straightens, as if something even more important than a man-eating bear is eating at him. He's trying to frame something difficult to express. "Your friend Rapha is not who he claims to be. He's lied to you, I'm sure."

"If that's so, then he's not the only one claiming to be someone he's not."

"I'm sorry about that. I'd hoped that I could remain anonymous a little longer."

"Then you are this Aamon, demon lord of the underlands?"

Aamon snorts, "Don't be ridiculous. I'm no demon or lord, just someone with a minimal talent for using the veil. I try to keep peace and bring some light to the darkness of the underlands. It's a full-time job, just maintaining a semblance of control and fighting off the Algean sisters. You can't know how relieved I was when I found Eva. She's much more adept at using the veil than I am."

"The veil is here, in the cabin." It's more of a statement than a question.

"Yes. Just as I found it many seasons ago."

"But you're so young. Rapha told me that the veil ages you by several seasons every time you use it."

"That's not true, In fact, it's quite the opposite. But what it does do to you is perhaps even more insidious."

I frown deeply now, lost in all the contradictory information. Who is telling me the truth? Aamon or Rapha? Or are they both lying?

Aamon gives me a look verging on pity. "I can explain what the veil does to you over time, but it might be easier if I just show you. Eventually, if I continue to use the veil, I will be forced to leave this realm. I'll miss Eva, though. She's something special."

He takes my hand and leads me down into the gloom of the trees. A dappled scattering of moonblight creates a patterned wallpaper of ferns and fir branches on the walls of the forest room as we enter. The cooling air smells of mushrooms, fir boughs and damp earth. I hear the almost silent padding of the bear behind us.

In a flash of blinding blight, Aamon is gone, replaced by an abomination and a miracle. Silver-white wings flutter all around me, each feather sparkling with multitudes of tiny suns.

Goosebumps prickle my skin, and tears stream from my eyes. I can see nothing and everything all at once.

Aamon is an Over.

At that moment, the Algean sisters attack.

40

LYDARC, NOW

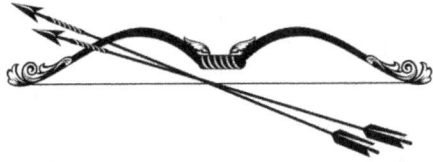

By the pricking of my thumbs, something wicked this way comes.

— WILLIAM SHAKESPEARE, *MACBETH*

I've seen many incredible and horrific abominations in my journeys, but nothing as atrocious and foul as these three beasts. Or the sounds they make. The screeching and howling, the caterwauling roars tear at my sanity. Sadness and horror, regret and fear emanate from each of them in waves, like they're spewing their vile guts on us, spraying us with the excrement of anguish with every belched word. If they are words. They sound more like bestial grunts, screams and primitive yelps.

Aamon returns to his human form as quickly as he transformed into an Over. I have no time to unpack my reaction to this improbability, as we face a new and possibly greater threat in these three attackers. I raise my bow and loose arrow after arrow into their bizarre bodies, but I only manage to push them back for a second. One is some kind of rank-smelling human/cervid clone with ragged antlers, another a howling, furry, black-clawed beast, and the third an equally malodorous, rotting tree creature with a curvaceous woman's figure, from which grasping tentacle roots squirm as they grasp at us.

"What are they?" I cry at Aamon. "I can't end them."

He screams back at me as he runs for the cabin, "You can't take them that way. We need the veil. These are the Algeans. They're pure horror. I don't know why they're coming after us like this now, unless...Follow me."

I turn and run, almost beating him to the door. As we rush inside, we slam the door: the fury of the beasts smashes against it like a wave of solid dread. Dust billows and splinters fly. The door shudders but holds. For now.

The horrified faces of Wayland and Eva stare back at us as we put all our weight against the door.

"What now?" I ask, panting.

"Eva," says Aamon, "We'll need all three of us if this is going to work."

"I don't understand," she wails, but Aamon is already running down the hall to a closed door. He throws it wide and I see the veil within. It throbs and flutters, as if responding to the presence of the three vile beasts at our door.

"I don't know what to do," Eva cries. "I just started learning how to use this thing. I can't—"

Aamon grabs her by the shoulders. "Yes, you can. You must. Just follow my lead."

He takes each of our hands and directs us to stand in a three-point position under the veil.

"Concentrate. The sisters are immortal. We can't forever them. We must undo them throughout time, remove them completely from the web of reality."

"What?" says Eva.

"Eva, you take Lupe. I'll concentrate on Ania. Lydarc, Achus is yours, since you're the strongest of us."

I doubt this, but do as I'm told.

At first, it seems impossible. The sisters are strong, and Achus is the strongest among them. I'm drowning under an overwhelming sense of defeat. This is never going to work. A wave of despair washes over me and I can't breathe. I start to panic.

Then I sense Aamon. He smiles in our thoughts, possessing a bright strength to fight the malaise and terror these beings emanate. I concentrate on his lead and face Achus. Her vile essence threatens to overwhelm me. But I'm used to pain. It's almost as if my whole life has primed me for this moment. I'm in constant anguish from the peri-soul: there's nothing she can do to me that could be worse. I laugh out loud in my vision, ripping my chest open to reveal the peri-soul. Achus, who I sense fears very little, stumbles back, her trembling, furry, claw-tipped arms covering her wolverine's face.

The peri-soul responds to the net, increasing the power of both. The feeling is heady: I can barely control my ecstasy at wielding it. Achus whimpers, as if knowing what I'm about to do. I channel the power of both the net and the peri-soul and direct it at her. I could forever her, or rather unmake her in all times and spaces, but I almost think she would enjoy that. The surge within me threatens to explode if I don't use it soon. An idea occurs to me.

"Achus, for all the pain you've meted out to the poor, weeping souls of the underlands, you deserve only the worst punishment imaginable."

"Oh, please end me, great shaman. I will gladly suffer whatever torturous ending you have devised for my crimes."

"That's the problem. I think you would enjoy it, at least for a moment, until I obliterate you. A beast like you deserves no less, but I've changed my mind."

I focus the power at her, and a beam of pure blight streaks toward the elder Algean sister. With a pop, Achus is gone, replaced by a harmless bunny who squeals in fear and hops off into the forest.

"I'm sure you'll get your wish in time, Achus, when an owl or hawk invites you to dinner. For now, enjoy being a harmless prey animal, cowering in fear in the bushes."

I return my awareness to the net, only to find that the other two have successfully eliminated their sisters. I realize that our work has just begun.

In horror, I see what we've done.

By eliminating the Algeans, we've shattered the structure of the underlands themselves. Now, in order to save its inhabitants, we must rebuild the underlands from the ground to the underside sky, *without* the Algean sisters. We need to harness all our concentration just to keep the underlands whole. I call to Aamon, but he suddenly disappears from the net. I hear a *thunk* of something landing hard to the floor. Aamon does not respond to my calls. Why would he abandon us now when we need him most?

I call to Eva, and she channels all the power she has to me, but it's not enough. Without Aamon, we're royally fucked. Where has he gone?

I've lost control. I feel the reality of the underlands shattering. Its end takes the form of a wall of ice, spreading faster than a thundering herd of racing elkin, straight toward us.

First, a deceptively delicate hoarfrost forms, waves of silver beard-like crystals growing and spreading to every tree and every rock, instantly freezing the surface of every stream, every river.

Then comes a horrible cold, an unsurvivable cold. Whatever it touches explodes as every iota of water is forcibly ejected from within and the crystals shatter. I see it crossing valleys and tearing through villages, an advancing army of nothingness. Screams are cut short, faces freeze solid, locked in a moment of utter terror. Then they shatter and spray the space the underlands once occupied with the desiccated white dust of lost hope.

Hell freezes over.

It's then that I call for help to my brother, Rapha, but he is nowhere to be found.

41

LYDARC, NOW

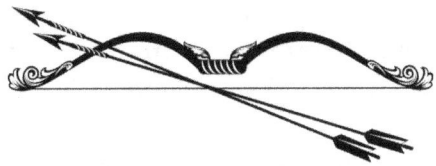

Long is the way and hard, that out of Hell leads up to light.

—JOHN MILTON, *PARADISE LOST*

I do my best to keep the spreading ice storm at bay, but without Aamon or Rapha to help, it's a futile struggle. I'm able to protect us for now, creating a corridor around us, a safe path to the lake. There's a chance we can get ourselves out if we run like hellbeasts are pursuing us.

Coming out of the veil, I look around. To my dismay and horror, Eva is weeping as she kneels beside a body on the floor. Aamon lays there, an arrow in his chest. His eyes are open and staring at the ceiling. I recognize the particular shaft extruding from his body as one of mine. A froth of bubbling pink fluid burbles from the corner of his mouth as his final breath escapes this world.

Lung shot.

Whoever forevered Aamon was not especially versed in anatomy. If it had been me, I wouldn't have missed the heart.

Eva launches herself at me, yelling that she'll end me. I know I didn't do it, but I can't blame her; the circumstantial evidence is somewhat damning, were it not for the obviously poor aim.

"Wait, Eva. You know I couldn't have done this. I was inside the veil with you the whole time."

"Besides," says Wayland as he steps into the room, "Look at the angle of the arrow. It came from below rather than above. This barb was thrust by an arm, rather than shot with a bow. Lydarc would never abuse one of her arrows in this fashion."

When Eva just stares at him in horror and shock, he pulls her to him as she sobs.

"Perhaps this is not the best time to play detective, Way," I hiss. "We need to get out of here *now*. The underlands are collapsing. I can only hold the corridor to the lake for so long before the whole thing freezes over."

"All right," says Wayland calmly, always the rational one under pressure. "I already put our packs on the porch. Sitka is there, but I can't find Rapha anywhere."

"Forget him. If I'm right, he's why all this is happening."

Wayland looks at me with a quick frown but says nothing as he leads a vacant-eyed Eva out to the porch.

Sitka is there. "Good job on the weird sisters. They just exploded—well, at least two of them. The other one transformed into some little forest beastie and scampered away. I let it go. The other two—it was kinda messy, and the smell...It's getting cold out here," she interrupts herself to say, "Is it time to go home now?" The bear paces nervously, lifting one paw after the other from the cold ground in a very amusing way, had I the time to appreciate it.

I say nothing, though I'm sure my expression says everything I'm thinking as I lead them down the path in the limited blight.

Can we make it? I'm not sure, but I'm going to do the best I can. I use a fraction of my power to raise a spirit blight. It burns fiercely, illuminating the path and reflecting my fear with every pounding step we take. I think I hear a rustle of wings behind us.

Turning, I see nothing but freezing darkness and decide it's just my overactive imagination.

I realize we're not going to make it.

With the last droplet of my peri-soul and the probability power of the dying net, I snap us forward to the lake. If I don't survive, at least the others will. In the second before life deserts me, I see a crowd surrounding the deathguards, who are using their power to hold the desperate underlanders from jumping into the last unfrozen body of water in the entire realm.

I wake. A deathguard is leaning over me. Thor is behind him, leaning down with a concerned frown on his handsome blond features. "I think she's coming around. Lydarc, we need you. The cold is advancing too quickly. You need to use your shamanic skills to hold it off, or we'll all be forevered."

I struggle to sit up, head spinning. The deathguards must have revived me. Neat trick, saving someone even if they didn't die by drowning. I remind myself to keep these fellows close on the other side. As I look around, I see no one has entered the lake yet.

"What're they doing? Why is no one going through?"

"We can't let them," says Thor. "If we allowed passage through the lake back to the afterarth, the underlands would be emptied. No one would willingly stay here."

I stand, swaying slightly, more from rage than fatigue. "I think you need to take a new look at your job descriptions, in lieu of the fact that the underlands are dissolving. Can't you see it? You've got to let us through and follow yourselves. Your positions have just been eliminated."

Thor spends a few seconds longer than I can handle, gazing back vacantly at the encroaching wave of ice and nothingness that is bearing down on us.

"Come on, you idiots. We've all got to go. Now."

Thor turns away and consults with his fellow deathguards. I'm about to take violent action when he turns to me. "All right, shaman. We'll let these people through, but we must remain to ensure that the way is closed after that. It will be our final duty."

"You'll be guarding a gate to nothing. Please come with us."

"We cannot."

I want to argue with them, but there just isn't enough time. We get the crowd organized and watch as they dive into the lake. Jarly and Flossy are there. Simply Waites and a group of the Siletzon made it, too.

I send Sitka the bear through next. Wayland and I are the last to go. As I dive, I feel the ice storm licking at my feet. The surface crackles and groans above me as the freeze advances. I say a psychic goodbye to the deathguards, who served their purpose to the very end.

Going back through the lake is easier than coming down. Or is it going up? Like everything else about the underlands, nothing follows any train of logic. Going up, the lake is shallow, and the water pushes us instead of dragging us down. In just a few seconds, we surface in the cave, which is now filled with others struggling to their feet on the floor of the tunnel.

Wayland takes charge, directing everyone through the tunnels.

It all goes well until we're almost to the library. The ground begins to shake and dust filters down from the roof of the cave. As exhausted as I am, I call on the arth spirits to hold back the collapse just a while longer. I worry about Sitka and Jin on the surface. Will the library collapse too?

Despite how tired everyone must be, I urge them to go faster. Through copious groans and complaints, they speed up. For a group of people in shock and disbelief, they do an incredible job of helping each other upward. Perhaps the joy of being out of the underlands is their incentive. They say the sudden absence of pain is the greatest joy. I wouldn't know.

I begin to think we're going to make it. That's our undoing. Never think a thing is done before it truly is, or your hope will jinx it. Superstitious? Me?

With a creaking noise that grows into thunder, the tunnel collapses in front of us. When the dust settles, I see no one was crushed, but the blockage looks complete. My shamanic powers are exhausted. I can do nothing to move this mass of arth.

"Well, we tried," says Wayland, as he plops down in the dirt.

"Don't give up yet," says Sitka. "I made some arrangements before we left."

"*Arrangements?*"

"You'll see. Everyone," she shouts, "get away from the cave-in. It's going to get a little warm."

We all scoot back as the rock begins to glow. The stones are melting under an intense heat. At first, I fear a lava tube has appeared and is spewing molten magma into the tunnel, then I see a flash of golden scales on the other side.

"Jin!" cries Wayland, "You little sucker. For a dragon, you're all right. Good job."

I wonder if we can wait for the puddling rock to cool when Jin steps right onto the melting floor of the cavern and lays down. I expect him to scream and turn to ash, but nothing happens. He says, in a jovial tone, "Everybody can climb over me. My scales are the ultimate heat insulators. Just step carefully, unless you want to be barbequed."

We don't need the advice to be careful. Everyone makes it across with only a few minor burns. We're all sweating as if we've been in a sauna. As we get to the library, the shaking has lessened, and the building appears relatively unharmed. The bear wastes no time returning to Sitka, who sits up, looking stiff and sleepy.

"Wow. Tha was qui a journey," she mumbles as she rubs her eyes.

"That's an understatement. I think we should get up to the surface now. Everything looks stable here, but I don't want to take any chances."

"Besides," says Wayland, "it's going to feel awfully good to get my feet on solid ground that isn't anywhere near the underlands."

As we scrabble up the bank to the desert floor, I notice an odd glow reflected on the sand. Almost purple or violet. Glancing up, the sky is a shade I've never seen before. Not a darkblight, or high-burn, not a graduation of these, but a sickly swirling color unlike anything I've ever seen.

When we get to the top, Wayland stares at the cloudless sky above us and states the obvious.

"The stars are gone."

42

LYDARC, NOW

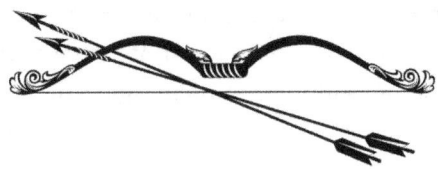

I always try to find the good in people, and someday, I hope to succeed.

— LYDARC AS QUOTED BY SITKA SANGASHEE,
EVOLUTION OF THE SHAMAN MASTER

S taring at the bizarre sky, which has just flipped back from bitterblight with a grating cosmic screech, Wayland asks, "What happened to Rapha's claim that eliminating the underlands would bring balance back to the world? It looks to me like it's more chaotic than ever."

It's only a short while since we returned to afterarth. I've just finished telling Wayland Rapha's whole story; his threats and promises. I needed someone to discuss it with, and Wayland already knew more than he should, anyway. It's just too much to handle alone.

"It's pretty obvious he lied, isn't it?"

"But why? What purpose could it serve to deceive us so completely?"

I pull Wayland away from the group so we can talk privately. "There's something I haven't told anyone yet." I hesitate.

"Tell me. I don't think this whole thing can get any weirder."

"All right," I say, fingering my crystals. "Just before the Algean sisters attacked, Aamon showed me what—he claims—happens to those who overuse the veil of probabilities. He transformed into an Over right in front of me. Maybe Rapha is an Over too, or more probably a minion, since, as far as I know, Overs from the upper realm cannot enter the human dimension. Yet. I imagine that with a little more time using the veil, Aamon would also have been relegated to the realm of the Overs."

"Aamon transformed into an Over? That's unbelievable."

"I wasn't smoking any dreamweed or taking poppy-seed tincture at the time, if that's what you mean." My indignation flares. I turn to walk away, but he grabs my arm.

"That's not what I meant. I believe you, of course. It's just so over-under crazy. If Rapha is actually a spy for the Overs, what do you think his agenda is?"

"I don't know, but I have an idea. The Overs have been trying to get into our realm all along. I mean, it seems obvious that's their plan, sending the minions to attack us as they do." Wayland nods. "It hasn't gotten them very far, so now they're trying a new tack. What if destroying the underlands weakens the division between the Overs' realm and our own, giving them physical access to our world? That would mean—"

"It could mean a major attack from the Overs is coming soon," says Wayland.

"And it's all my fault," I whack myself on the head with the heel of my hand. "If I hadn't taken Rapha to the underlands, none of this would be happening."

"Don't blame yourself, woman. If it hadn't been you, they would have chosen someone else." Wayland reaches out to comfort me, then thinks better of it. "I wonder if there are more spies in our midst."

"I hope not. If there were, you'd think we would have known about it by now. Look at the chaos that just one has caused."

"I wonder what all of this has to do with the peri-soul." Wayland muses.

"What do you mean?"

"I was just thinking about it. Perhaps Rapha hid behind it—or within you—to enter the underlands without being seen and intercepted by Aamon. That means they've been plotting this for countless seasons. Patient cocksuckers." Wayland shakes his head.

The thought of carrying Rapha in my chest makes me want to throw up. When the nausea passes, I say, "I wonder if..." I pause, not wanting to voice this thought.

"Go ahead."

"Well, if the peri-soul got Rapha into the underlands, I wonder if it would get me into the realm of the Overs."

Wayland frowns. "What would you do there?"

"Well, it appears I have a talent for taking down realms."

"No. Don't even think about it. We barely survived the unraveling of the underlands. Besides, we're a long walk from the front. I assume that's where you'd need to be to get close to them."

I rub my neck. My whole body hurts on top of the aching fatigue, but pain's nothing new. "I know, and I need to get these people to safety, not lead them into more danger. The Siletzon who survived—I should take them west, back to the Siletz Valley. There's an abandoned town there. It's really just a flat spot in the forest now. The befores called it Valsetz. It would be a great spot for a walled village. Easily defended. Close to water."

"It sounds like you've thought this through."

"I certainly have. Our blastform is gone, but with the Siletzon who survived, I think we could make a new home in Valsetz. At least if I can wrangle the idiots into working together."

Wayland smirks, and I'm tempted to cut off a body part he prizes highly.

"No, no, don't misunderstand me. I'm just amazed that, no

matter how hard you try to be a dickhead, I just don't think it's in you, Lydarc."

"Exactly. I'm darkness and blight, just as Rapha named me. I know what you're thinking; there's a good portion of arsehole in there too, but just this once, I'll go against my first inclination and *not* plant an arrow in your nether regions."

I catch a flash of gold in my peripheral vision. Jin is approaching us with Sitka nestled in his claws.

"Shaman, the Lady Faustina has given me permission to travel on with you, if you would allow it." Sitka looks at me with hope written on her features. I hate to disappoint her, but I can't trust a dragon. As if reading my thoughts, Jin dips his head down to gaze into my eyes. I still find it disconcerting to be this close to one of the beasts, even a smaller one like Jin.

"I think there's something I need to tell you about my aunt," says Jin.

"I know more than I care to about your kind. Dragons are unpredictable killers. Faustina especially."

"That's just it. Sitka told me about your experiences with my aunt when she first gave you a ride to the Fallen City—and what happened to your pony."

I hate thinking about it: that poor creature being ripped apart by the claws of a dragon. Jin's expression softens, as if waiting for me to come to some conclusion I couldn't quite reach on my own.

"What're you trying to tell me?"

The little dragon sighs. "Faustina has occasional lapses from the defined nature of dragons, as do I."

"What are you talking about?"

"She doesn't like me to discuss it, but she occasionally falls victim to human failings, such as compassion. Faustina spared your pony."

I frown, confused beyond reasoning. "But that can't be true. I saw her—"

"You saw her performance. She is the consummate actress, is

she not? Your pony still lives, part of a little herd in a high mountain valley near our Cascadian lair. She is fat and happy still."

My mind is spinning. Can this be true? Thinking back, I realize that I didn't actually see Faustina eat the pony.

"I'm sorry. I just can't believe it."

Jin tips his elegant head, as if considering. "If you will open your mind, I can show you."

I hesitate, but Sitka says, "Please listen to him. We're going to need the dragons, especially Jin. I know it."

I close my eyes, opening my thoughts to the spirit realm. I jerk away at first as I find myself falling, then realize I'm seeing through Jin's eyes as he flies over the mountains of his Oregon high mountain home. The bright white Cascade peaks surround us as we wing down into a lush green valley. A herd of wild horses runs free and happy, fierce and powerful in their element. One mare looks up; I see the face of my pony, older now but strong and wise. A first-season colt runs beside her, and I feel her pride. She whinnies, and the joy of it echoes through my soul.

I pull away from the vision and rub my eyes. Tears of relief are streaming down my face.

"Damn allergies," I say.

43

RAPHA, NOW

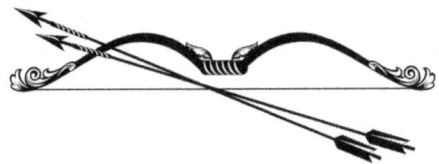

I could never forgive Rapha for what he did, but more than that,
I couldn't forgive myself for falling for his lies.

— LYDARC AS QUOTED BY SITKA SANGASHEE,
EVOLUTION OF THE SHAMAN MASTER

What have I done?*
We were almost there. After seasons of planning, then waiting for many more, all the sacrifices,
the hopes that we could reverse this nightmare at last. I only
wanted to help them, these primitive, pathetic souls.
But what have I done?
The masses of the egregores have woken. Even now they bear
down on the inferiors unchecked. No, that is not exactly correct.
They are not inferior at all; they are my friends. But do I even
know what friendship is?
Am I the classic example of the spy who gets too close and
loses sight of the objective? The spy who goes over to the other
side? I worked so hard not to be assimilated that it happened
while I was not looking. And because of my attachments, I made
mistakes. Big mistakes.

By ending Aamon as I was instructed, I set in motion a series of events that will lead us all to ruin. At least that is my best prognostication, based on the spheres, the whispers of the spheres, the agonized screams of the spheres. Yes, I hear them, even though I cannot weep with them.

All right. I'm not sure when they started talking to me, between their cosmic burps and interstellar hiccups. I did not even ingest the copious amounts of herbal concoctions that Lydarc uses to get relief from pain and bring on her visions. Visions, which I must admit, have been and continue to be amazingly accurate, unlike my own sight, which failed me catastrophically. I assumed that when the underlands were eliminated, balance would return to the world and the Overs would regain their rightful place—I would return to my rightful place. Do I even know what that is anymore? Was I lied to? That now appears to be the case. Even as I lied to Lydarc. I was used by the Overs. What can I do now? How can I repair the damage I have done?

There has to be a way.

~

It all becomes clear. A group of ancients sit in a circle. There are uncomfortable folding chairs, rock-hard donuts and coffee so bitter-strong and thick they use the leftovers to dislodge rusty bolts the size of hippos from ocean carriers.

I stand and say, "Hello. My name is Rapha and I have been taken over by the inferiors. I can almost feel some of them," I add in a whisper.

I start to cry, which is, of course, impossible.

A big-haired blond man says, "It's all right, Rapha, just let it out. You can share anything here. It's a safe place."

"But I was wrong," I cry. "Everything I did was wrong. It is all chaos and I cannot fix it now. It is an avalanche I started by kicking a pebble, and Lydarc was that pebble. Why did I not see it coming?"

An attractive woman with a wave of luxurious mahogany hair and tattoos around her dark eyes stands and says, "You just need to ask for forgiveness, my dear. It's the twenty-seventh step to salvation. And it's incredibly empowering, trust me."

An antique blightbulb appears with a flash above my head. "That is it. That is what I will do. I can fix everything. Lydarc will forgive me. She is the forgiving kind, right?

"I will just go to her, and we will work it out. I will tell her about how I had her discharged from the Resistance, and the finger, and how I forevered Cassander, and sent Eva to the underlands. Because I knew Lydarc could not refuse Wayland if he asked, but when she did anyway, that is when I had to end her tribe. I had to get her to the underlands at all costs, you see."

I turn to the mediator, a stout man with a mouth that turns only one direction—down.

"Good luck with that," he says. "Would anyone else like to share?"

44

LYDARC, NOW

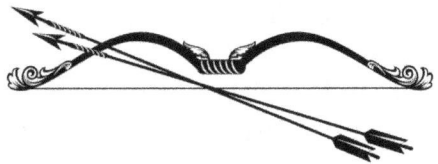

Hateful to me as the gates of Hades is that man who hides one thing in his heart and speaks another.

— HOMER, *THE ILIAD*

A s we lead the survivors north, my mind is lost in thoughts that I don't want to share, much less think.

What now? How am I going to get all these survivors to safety? Can I just leave them to make their own way back home to the Siletz?

What about Jarly and Flossy? Will they want to come with me on some ill-advised and poorly conceived plan to infiltrate the realm of the Overs? Do I even want them with me, risking their lives again? Or will they agree to go west with Simply Waites and the others, if I ask? It would be a relief to know a couple of seasoned warriors are accompanying the survivors.

A cry from ahead interrupts my disquieting internal conversation.

My eyes threaten to jump out of my skull. Wayland, who took the lead, jogs back to me, his hand—the extant one—on the hilt of his sword.

"What is that ahead of us?" I ask him stupidly.

"I don't know," he says, his breath rasping, "but it looks like a horde."

"A what?"

"Like in *The Last Hurrah of the Golden Horde*, you know? That kind of horde."

"What the fuck are you talking about?

"Norman Spinrad? It was cataloged next to the *Book of Lamentations* in the university's ancient wisdom section. Forget it. What I'm trying to say is, there's a swarm of horrible monsters coming this way, right now."

As I watch, individual beasts stand out from the advancing forces. I recognize a minotaur, a satyr, golem, bloody bones, basilisk, chimera, a fury, banshee, bogeyman, carbuncle, harpy, siren, firebird, Ratman, thunderbird, and zhenniao. Then I register a bugbear, chupacabra, Bael, manticore, sharabha, yali, kishi, kushtaka, yeti, ammut, cockatrice, wendigo, ghoul, harpy, hydra, centaur, and Krampus, of course. Charro Negro, the headless horseman, and a killer clown follow. Behind them are a cyclops, manananggal, medusa, penanggalan, Kappa, Nian, Ammit, Mothman, werewolf, vampire, ogre, orc, Pontianak, zombie, hydra, gorgon, Godzilla, kaiju, Baba Yaga, a demon who causes house fires and there, pulling up the rear, is what appears to be a rabid jackalope.

"Wow," says Jarly, coming up beside me. "What the fuck kind of attack is this? I'm not sure whether to defend myself or slit my own throat. It looks like all the monsters of afterarth are showing up to dine on us. Who ordered takeout?"

In my buzzing brain, I realize she is taking this with more equanimity than ever I could muster. I guess if you've lived in hell as long as she has, you can take a lot and not show a crack.

Wayland is beside me, sword out and shining in the moon-blight like the tiniest star, a little prick, far too ineffectual to do us any good against this horrendous mob. I mean to tell him that his little poker is just too small, but I think better of it.

"I think they're called egregores, or cryptids," explains Professor Wayland. "They didn't even exist for real until afterarth was born. Because they arrived at about the same time the Overs did, it is thought that the Overs created them from our own myths. The wendigo that ate my arm? Allegedly just a figment of Over imagination, though it felt quite real at the time." He looks down at his stump with an expression of longing and loss.

Jarly says, "Whatever the fuck they are, we need to do something. Now would be good."

They all look at me as if I have the answers. I do not.

"Run away," says Flossy, as she steps up to join us.

Wayland yells, "In the Monty Python language, that means *retreat!*"

We all ignore him. We're used to the nonsensical things he spouts.

But this seems like as good a plan as any right now. I look back to see that Sitka is safe in the arms of her dragon. As we retreat, I pull the lava pebble from my pocket. I hate to leave the others in mortal danger, even for an instant, but I see no alternative.

The jump to the underground veil in the lava caves is no picnic. When I'm done heaving up my guts, I look around at the glowing net of probabilities. As ever, it's lovely—and scary as hell.

I'm not alone.

"Lydarc, I would like to explain."

I turn on Rapha, pulling a knife from my belt and lunging in a single smooth movement that Mrs. Ghandi would have been proud of. My aim is perfect and the knife slices through Rapha, followed by my body, as the lack of resistance takes my balance off guard. I fly through him and hit the floor, dropping the knife and skidding in the gravel, implanting a good portion of it into my palms.

"Fucking Christ." Only now I notice that his body flickers, patches of blight playing across his translucent skin.

"Sorry about that. We need to talk, but I could not be here in person. I am afraid my superiors are not happy with me right now. Our time is short."

"You forevered Aamon."

"I am afraid that is not the worst of my sins."

When he explains what he's done, I want to forever him even more.

"Why are you even explaining this? You know the moment I get the chance, I'm going to forever you, in the flesh and every other way I can imagine."

I rise and start picking pieces of gravel out of my bleeding palms. The pain feels good. It's the only thing keeping me from launching myself at Rapha, the hallucination, again.

"I would not do that, if I were you."

"Try to stop me."

"It is not that." He observes his left hand and the missing little finger with an expression like loss of something more than precious.

A horrendous idea occurs to me.

"No."

"Yes, Lydarc. I was the one you met all those seasons ago. Posing as an Over, I implanted a part of myself inside you. You cannot end me without ending yourself. We are entangled, a couple."

"No bleeding way." I feel like throwing up again.

"I am afraid it was the plan all along to implant a part of a minion into an inferior. As a minion, I have the ability to enter your realm, while still retaining the qualities of an Over. As time went on, my essence melded with yours, making you invisible to Aamon, who was on his way to becoming an Over himself. He was trying to maintain the underlands and its people, not destroy them as my superiors wished. We had to eliminate him—at least that is what I was told. I rode with you into the underlands. It was not an easy trip. Once we got through, I almost disincorporated right there on the shores of the lake. It was touch and go."

"I still don't get it. Why are you telling me any of this? The Overs have won. Our reality is destabilized, the underlands are gone. Their monsters, the egregores, are attacking my people right now."

Rapha studies the glowing net, not looking at me. He takes a deep breath.

"The Overs are out of touch. They cannot feel emotions. They do not know what it is like on this realm or understand the extent of the damage they are causing. It took a while, but I realized that what we were doing was wrong, and might lead to..."

"To what?"

"I believe if we continue this aggression into your realm, both our dimensions will suffer."

"Suffer in what way?"

Rapha seems reluctant to continue. "Reality itself will destabilize completely. The word you have for it is 'the apocalypse.'"

I can't believe my ears, and they're usually more reliable than my thoughts. "Are you fucking kidding me?

"Lydarc, you should know by now that I lack a sense of humor."

I sit down hard on the gritty floor with no regard for the shooting pain it delivers to my ass and up my spine. In fact, I can't feel my body, as if it's far away and long ago, lost in regret and hopelessness. With my head in my hands, I mumble, "It doesn't escape me that the only reason you want to help us 'inferiors,' as you call us, is that your own ass is on the line now, too. Is there any hope?"

Rapha leans down, offering me his hand to rise.

"It is you, Lydarc. You are the last hope of mankind."

"Oh, that's just great," I say as I try to take his hand, but mine just slips through this shadow limb, the hand of a friend who never was one.

Grunting as I stumble to my feet, I say, "If that's the case, we're all totally and royally fucked."

Optimist all the way. But that's just me.

45

LYDARC, NOW

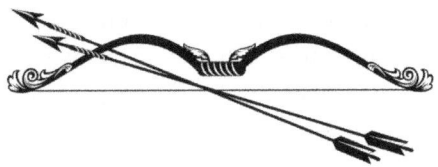

They carried me to a lofty spot, to a mountain, the top of which reach to heaven. And I beheld the receptacles of light and of thunder at the extremities of the place, where it was deepest. There was a bow of fire, and arrows in their quiver, a sword of fire, and every species of lightning.

— *THE BOOK OF ENOCH*

Rapha hands me a pair of clunky, black-framed eyeglasses. They flicker at first. As I reach out for them, they gain weight and solid form.

"What's this for?"

"The monsters that gather to attack you. They are not real. Not really."

"Did you just say that?"

"What I mean is, you can negate the power of many by seeing them as they really are."

"You mean, if I see them eliminated, they will be?"

"Something like that, but I am afraid it is a little messier. You still must eliminate their corporeal existence, but to do that, you need to see them. That's where the glasses come in. You will be immune to their powers while you wear them, and you will be able to see through their illusions."

"I get the feeling you aren't coming back with me to help."

"I cannot. I must return to the upper realm and try to dissuade the Overs from using the access to your realm that they have gained with the destruction of the underlands. I may fail. It is possible that I cannot return, but I will do my best to do so."

"You sound like you actually care a little."

"Lydarc, I could not spend seasons with your people and not become attached. It is just that my kind do not feel or express emotions as you do."

"Well, you've fucked us over enough that we're practically family. Just get out of my sight before I figure out a way to forever a hallucination."

With a grim look, Rapha fades, as gently as a nightmare forgotten on waking. As he fades, another image intrudes. It's the group I've seen before—the tall, majestic fighters and their leader. Wide eyes and ears like...Suddenly, I recognize them, despite the fading image. Elves. Why would elves have any interest in me? As quickly as they appear they're gone, and I wonder if I'm hallucinating. No matter. Even if they do exist, they can do nothing to help us now.

I put the glasses on and, activating the net, return to a time just before the horde arrives.

It has turned bitterly cold, sharp and brittle dark. The scattered blight litters the desert with shadow demons. When Wayland sees me in the odd glasses, he breaks out in laughter.

"Keep that up and you won't be able to pee standing up anymore," I growl.

"All right, it was just the shock. They just popped onto your face, and you look so studious, like someone in my Ancient Tropes and Trivialities class. What's the deal?"

"You're about to explain to me what a horde is. We need to get ready to fight. The glasses will allow me to see them. Stay close and follow my lead, but look none of them directly in the eyes."

"I think I learned my lesson with the wendigo. I won't make that mistake again, ever."

We run forward, facing the leading attackers. I draw my bow and fire into them. The glasses allow me to see their weak spots: they fall more easily than I would have expected, but I run out of arrows quickly. Wayland, Jarly and Flossy are there, wielding sword, staff and bow with the grace and power of seasoned warriors, which, of course, they are. I pull my knife and fight hand to hand.

I glance to my side, and there is Sitka in Jin's claws, but the glasses show me something impossible when I look at Jin. Instead of the small golden dragon, a human knight in gleaming armor wields a glowing sword and advances with dire intent on the hordes of monsters. I quickly pull the glasses down and Jin returns to dragon form. With no time to figure out this vision, I return my attention to the battle at hand.

A hulking form approaches me. The stench of sweat, piss, and worse makes my eyes water.

"Throat Slitter is me," growls the giant, who swings a weapon I've never seen before. It's a long, flexible wire with a stone crudely tied to the end. In his other hand, he wields a knife with a rusty, pitted blade. "Who are you, pathetic little elf," he roars, "to challenge one as great as me? I hates elfs. Just hates 'em." The brute spits into the dirt with so much force the dust flies up in a miniature fountain.

Orc.

I've never fought one, but I've heard about them. There aren't many stories, because there are few survivors to tell the tale of their encounters with these brutal, inhuman beasts. I don't bother to correct him, that I'm no elf. Perhaps it's my ridiculous ears that have misled him.

The wire whistles at an increasingly high note as he swings it faster and faster above his head. I'm worried about the wire, though the knife is also of concern, as is the fact he weighs several times what I do. Thick muscles twist and ripple in his massive arms and thighs as he rushes me.

For a second I see no way out, and panic drains my initiative. I stare dumbly as the stone approaches my head. Wayland shouts at me as he delivers a mortal blow to the cyclops he's been battling. That pulls me out of my funk. I will not allow Wayland to rescue me, not one more time. This is my fight.

Pulling up the arth spirits, I fill the stone with heat until it shatters. Losing its driving force, the rusty wire falls limply to the ground. Enraged, the orc screams and swipes at me with the knife, which I evade by falling backward. He grabs my ankle as I scrabble out of his reach. His grip is like an iron vice and the pain draws out my own scream. I stick my knife into his forearm and twist. Releasing me with a roar, he arches his knife and throws himself onto me. At the last moment, I twist out from under him, but the blade slices my forearm to the bone. Blood spurts between my fingers as I try to stop the gushing fluid. There's no time to access the peri-soul; I'll need to use my wits and remaining strength if I'm going to survive this encounter. As I scrabble backward, my feet tangle in the discarded wire. Ignoring my bleeding arm, I gather up the wire just as the orc lunges at me again. I wrap the wire around his thick neck as many times as I can and jump on his back. He scrabbles to knock me off, reaching back to grab at me as he bucks and shudders like a wild grundle being ridden for the first time. Pulling with all my strength, I heave on the wire until it digs deep into his thick neck. It seems to take forever, but the beast finally ceases his struggles and thuds face-first into the dirt, still at last. From the smell, it seems the creature's bowels were released along with his life.

I tear off my sleeve and bind the wound in my arm, returning to the fight, despite how hopeless it looks.

Just as I slice the neck of a banshee with my remaining good arm, my ears pop from a disconcerting negative pressure in the air, as if the world is trying to suck in its breath. The ground shudders and shakes. Something huge and deep-space black rushes upward from the ground like a giant beanstalk from hell, filling my vision.

We're all thrown to the ground as a looming shape, dark and jagged, erupts from the arth, right in the center of the horde. I see other similar structures rising in the distance, hundreds of them, ranging as far as I can see in the scattered moonblight. The air stinks of burning flesh as anything touching the growing shapes sizzles and fries. Screams, growls and screeches of terror surround us as the surviving beasts run past us in a thunder of panicked escape. Intense heat on my face gives me an instant blastburn.

As we stumble away, the structure nearest us morphs as it rises, developing jagged stairs, parapets, battlements, barbicans, spires, turrets, and towers, all of the darkest obsidian stone. On every flat surface, a human figure stands. Some are desiccated skeletons, but others retain some flesh, hanging in ragged tatters like rotting cloth from their bones. All are waving arms and stomping legs as if in great anxiety or pain. Some lose their footing and crash to the ground, where the bones scatter, yet keep moving, writhing and twisting in the dirt.

"What the hell are those things?" yells Flossy.

I have no answer for her. I look to Wayland, whose brows are scrunched in thought.

"They're coming from below—" he begins hesitantly.

"From the underlands? But how?" I ask, not wanting to hear more, but riveted to his words.

"There's a theory from ancient scientific knowledge that no mass is created or destroyed, only changed from one form to another."

"Well, fuck me bloody. You think the material of the underlands is intruding on our realm as these, as these—"

"Dark fortresses, I would call them," he says, as we all stare in disbelief at the destruction these terrible towers are causing. I worry about the towns and military bases. How many will be obliterated? How many people will die this blastnight?

As we watch, the fortresses keep rising. Instead of developing a solid base, as I would expect, the bottom grows ever thinner as they rise, until there remains only a single point of contact with the dirt. Defying gravity, the evil things pose on a spear point, barely touching the ground.

Shapes erupt from the base of each structure. Poking out from either side is a jointed length of articulating stone. Each leg grows claws that grab the dirt ferociously, biting through sand and rock. The black legs push upward, uniformly raising the structure from the ground. The nearest fortress lumbers toward us slowly, inexorably.

"Correction," says Wayland in a dry voice, "I would call it a *walking* dark fortress."

We avoid the walking fortresses, which, despite their size, are slow and lack any obvious aggressive intent. The only problem, besides the fact that they've torn up the landscape, is that they're here, and look as if they're going to stay.

As we approach the encampment of the fifth regiment, I am again reminded how I miss Jarly and Flossy, but I'm grateful that they agreed to accompany the remaining Siletzon back to the Oregon territory. I'm hopeful, knowing that they'll be there to defend the people along the way. The hordes of monsters are terrified of the walking fortresses and haven't bothered us since the structures erupted.

I wish I was going west with the others, instead of facing a horrid, unknown conflict with the Overs. I did my best to convince Sitka to go with the Siletzon, but she can be so stubborn; she also has a dragon to protect her, so she's probably safer than any of us. Over time, I have to admit that I've come to trust Jin, at least a little. Unlike Faustina, he hasn't pretended to eat any of my horses.

Griffin, the base commander, is now gray-haired and dowdier than ever. She isn't happy to see either of us.

"We're not a retirement facility, in case you haven't noticed, Captain," she says upon seeing Wayland enter her tent.

When the commander sees me, her eyes turn to slits.

"Well, that explains this weird walking fortress problem we've been having. Frandling, I know it's been many seasons, but I never forget a troublemaker."

Wayland steps forward with a grim face. "Lydarc didn't cause the fortresses to appear, and I have my doubts she caused any of the things you accused her of in the first place."

I'm thinking *Oh yes, I did*, but say nothing.

"Besides," continues Wayland, "we're here to help."

Griffin slumps into her seat. "All right, I guess I owe you a few moments. We're running out of ideas. The minions have been worse than ever, the timing of their attacks more erratic. We can't know when or how severe they will be. This damn war has gone on too long."

"I'm afraid we've got some bad news on that front," I say. "The Overs are planning a massive incursion soon."

Griffin rises and stalks around her tent. "Please don't tell me that. We can't handle the attacks at the level they are now. Recruitment is down and the academies can't send enough troops to replace the ones we lose to...well, I guess *attrition* is a good word for it."

"There's no good word for it," says Wayland. "You're going to need all the hands you can get. And Lydarc has a crazy idea that she can..."

He looks at me to continue.

"The peri-soul gave me access to and from the underlands," I say, "and I was able to bring some of our people back. There's a chance that it will also allow me to get into the realm of the Overs—"

"And do what?" scoffs Griffin. "They're other-dimensional

beings. The Followers of Enoch call them archangels. What could you possibly do against them?"

"I'm not really sure about that part yet, but I have to try. We need to do whatever it takes to end this war."

Griffin stops her pacing abruptly and eyes us both critically. "All right. I'll provide you and your people with lodging while I take this to my superiors." She points a stubby finger at me.

"You. Do nothing until I get approval. Understood?"

"Yes, ma'am."

"And keep the goddamned dragon away from camp. It's spooking the horses."

"Yes, of course."

The next few blastdays are quiet as we make preparations. An air of apprehension shrouds the entire encampment in a soupy stillness flavored with fear and foreboding.

In the downtime tent, Wayland looks at me over his glass of ale.

"Maybe there won't be an attack, after all."

I snort. "Don't even start. If bad luck didn't have a home before, it's surely found one with us."

Just as I'm speaking, we hear a rumble. The tent shakes with a powerful gust of wind.

"See what I mean?" I say as we rush outside.

"What is that?" asks the commander, who's exiting her own tent in her long underwear. She squints into the sky. "Another of those black fortress things?"

Wayland says, "I don't think so. For one thing, it's white, or crystal, or..."

It's hard to define what is forming to the north of camp. It isn't coming out of the ground, as the dark fortresses had. It is flickering into being before us. I see great arches or portals all around the perimeter, different colors and shapes swirling within each. Hot wind blows at us from the nearest portal. The structure is square, with what appear to be three arches per side. White and crystal spires and towers jut up from the center, sparkling and glowing in the setting sun like some imaginary palace of dreams, bad dreams.

Unlike the dark fortresses, no skeletons adorn the parapets.

"Where are the minions," I ask, "or masses of Overs rushing out to destroy our world?"

"Hold on, Ly," says Wayland. "There's time yet for Armageddon. It's still early in the blastday. Let's just be thankful we're catching a break this time, whatever the reason."

"I guess you're right. Now... do you think one of these arches will take me to the realm of the Overs?" I ask.

"Maybe," muses Wayland. "Those arches. There's something familiar about them."

"I'm trying to remember too. Something from an ancient book."

He snaps his fingers. "That's it. The Book of Enoch."

He quotes, "*And at the ends of the earth, I saw twelve portals open to all the quarters of the heavens, from which the winds go forth and blow over the earth.*"

"Enoch?" I ask. "As in the Followers of Enoch, the protesters who believe the Overs are angels?"

"Yes, they use the book to support their crazy, over-under theories."

"Maybe not so crazy, after all. Do you remember anything else it says about the portals?

"A little." He frowns as he calls up the text. "*Through four of these come winds of blessing and prosperity, and from those eight come hurtful winds: when they are sent, they bring destruction on all the earth.*"

"Oh, great. So how do we tell which portals are hurtful and which aren't? If I take the wrong one, will I end up in a new hell, or better yet, bring down hellfire and brimstone on the afterarth?"

"I think hell is already here," says Griffin in a dazed voice.

"I'm sorry," Wayland fingers his sword. "That's all I can remember. We'll need a copy of the book to get the rest. We should be able to find some of the Followers in Nameless. The Book of Enoch is practically their Bible, so they're sure to have a copy."

"I'll send Eva, Sitka, and Jin to find one."

"Great, just tell Jin to land outside of town and let the others do the talking."

"Why?"

"Because we don't want the entire town running away to escape a dragon. Most people don't count them as friends, as you do."

"They're not my friends. Jin is just less of an enemy than the rest."

46

LYDARC, NOW

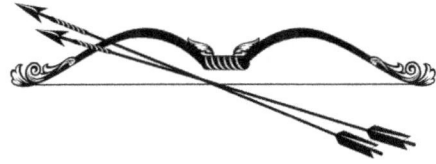

War is cruelty. There is no use trying to reform it. The crueler it is, the sooner it will be over.

— WILLIAM TECUMSEH SHERMAN

When the others return with a copy of the Book of Enoch, Wayland spends more time than I would like to decipher it. I pace nervously as he sits at the makeshift desk the commander set up for us in the armament tent and pester him relentlessly.

"What does it say? Which portals are safe? Any idea which one will get me to the Overs?"

Wayland slaps down the thin leather-bound book and rubs his eyes. "Well, so far it seems we can choose between rain, fruitfulness, prosperity and dew, or locusts, drought and desolation."

"What does any of that mean?"

"The ancients weren't known for their succinct turn of phrase, but what I've gathered so far is that the central arches in each direction are the prosperity portals. The others all bring death and destruction, and a few locusts for good measure. Of the four beneficial ways, I can't decide which will lead you to the Overs. They're so similar, just varying versions of the same phrase."

"Is there one that's any different? Even a little different?"

He picks up the book again and peruses it carefully. "Well, the text on the east central portal adds the phrase *comes what is fitting.*"

"'What is fitting?' Does fitting mean what is correct? That it's the correct path?"

"Maybe."

"We're risking a lot on a maybe."

Wayland sighs, again throwing down the book. "Well, the ancient Navajo peoples also valued the east-facing direction as the sacred birthplace of the sunrise. That's the best I can come up with. But I don't like the idea of you doing this alone. I think I should go with you."

"Why? To protect me, like you did the first time I faced an Over?"

"Yes, if need be."

I study the worn surface of the table, noticing that someone has carved *Jennie loves Wenthine* in crudely jagged letters in the wood. "No. A sword is less than useless against an Over. I should do this alone. In a den of Overs, you would only be another soul I'd need to protect. This isn't a jaunt through the countryside to bag a brace of conies. Despite the appearance of blight everywhere, it's a foray into the heart of darkness."

"Outstanding novel, that. Explores the dark spirit of man."

"What?"

"Oh, nothing. I understand your need to protect those around you. It's a virtue, if not your higher calling."

I splutter an unintelligible reply, never good at accepting praise.

Wayland sniggers. I find this offensive, and I consider removing his head with my bare hands.

He says, "Stop that. You're glowering at me. It's just that you're so endearing."

"I am not, and if you ever repeat that remark anywhere, I will remove your head, after some of your more treasured organs."

Wayland raises his hands in supplication. "All right, I get it. You're determined to do this alone. I would too. Just be careful. Eva wants to get to know you."

"Just Eva?"

Wayland looks me in the eyes. "Ly... yes, I'd like us to try again."

Embarrassed, I splutter a gruff, disrespectful reply.

Neither of us is aware of the bear outside, who hunches near the tent, listening.

It happens gradually. The space between the minion attacks lessens, very slowly. At first, no one notices, not even the commander, who keeps a detailed record of every attack in a spreadsheet she calculates by hand, her military school degree being in math and statistics. She and Wayland often spend an evening going over the figures, drinking Griffin's imported port wine, until neither can make a coherent sentence that begins with, "The statistics show that..."

"Der statistics sow hat..."

"Statisticums does shoe dat..."

They laugh together and give up the pursuit of numbers to a discussion of relationships. Griffin has a husband in New St. Louis, who refuses to brave the front to be with his beloved wife but enjoys the perks of being a commander's spouse; the dinners with her female lieutenants and all the expensive clothing and other perks her stipend can purchase for him.

Wayland has memories of Cassander that he doesn't discuss with anyone, and his daughter Eva, who he loves completely but understands to an equally opposite degree.

"What're you two gonna do, Peters, once this conflict is over?"

"Don't know exactly. I think Eva and I will go west. There's a viable section of the Oregon Territories we might want to settle in."

"This wouldn't be the same place that Frandling ran off to, would it?"

"It might be, yes."

Griffin smiles. "Happy for you, Peters. Few o' us gets a second chance."

"Yes ma'am. I hope so. We just gotta survive this fucking war first."

"Amen, Captain. Amen."

A siren sounds outside.

"Here they come again," says the commander. She reaches for her glass, but misses it, almost falling out of her chair.

A second siren blares over the first.

"What's that?" asks Wayland, attempting to shake off the alcohol as he stands.

"That means at least one Over, on top of the minions."

"Has that ever happened before?" Wayland is almost out the tent door as he turns back to ask.

"Not in my knowledge."

Wayland shuffles off the cloak of a drunken man and replaces it with that of a warrior ready to act. He pretends to enjoy the sickly-sweet port, but the truth is, he prefers a bitter ale.

"How d'you do that?" slurs the commander, as she pours herself another blood-red portion, spilling half of it on the once-white tablecloth. "You act like you barely had a tipple." Griffin wipes a hand over her face and breathes a sigh of resignation. "My second in charge tonight's Carlahan. See her if you need anything."

Wayland exits the tent and inhales a brisk draught of the evening air. It's tainted with the faint smell of sulfur.

"Damn it. That means unseeums."

Wayland joins me, my apprentice and the dragon, who has snuck into camp during the uproar, in gazing up at the crystal citadel.

"What's happening?" he asks, though he looks like he knows.

"I think this is it," I say, turning to him feeling already defeated.

Jin says, "There are so many of them."

Minions stream out of all but the central portals, an almost constant barrage of the bizarre creatures. The soldiers muster, forming the traditional lines of defense, but we are hopelessly outnumbered.

I take my place in the line, anyway, sending arrow after arrow into the mass of attackers. I smell sulfur and taste metallic blood on my tongue. Before I can say it, Wayland leaps forward, yelling, "Unseeums!" He waves his sword frantically until it hits something invisible. The unseeum shudders, a flickering disturbance in the air. It screams as Wayland's sword splits it neatly in half.

"That's for Cassander, you cocksucker!" he yells. There's a wild look in his eyes I've never seen before. He's always been so controlled, so predictable. This is a new Wayland. I guess this fucking war gets to everyone, eventually.

I feel a hot wind at my back: the minions above us are tossed and twisted, thrown to the ground. The mud soldiers rush up to dispatch them. Looking behind me, I see Sitka in Jin's arms. Her eyes are closed and a look of concentration grips her features.

Good job, Sitka! Why didn't I think of that?

A few arrows won't be enough against the forces we now face. I shoulder my bow and call on the wind, arth, storm and blightning spirits with all my will, adding to Sitka's attack.

I think we're making inroads in their numbers when the air thrums. A wild screech of unnatural dissonance echoes across the battlefield, painful to hear. The minions scatter. A giant patchwork creature is forming above us, a contortion of scrabbling arms and legs, claws and wings. Spiraling tentacles churn into the dirt, anchoring the thing to the desert floor. Several beaks sprout from its chest, and I see that these are the source of the grating yowl. None of it fits the rest, like a hundred bodies were sliced up and stitched together randomly into a Frankenstein's monster far worse than anything Mary Shelley could have imagined. Just looking at it makes me feel sick.

As I listen, I realize that the howling voice has been emulating human speech, but the words are so distorted, I can't make out a bit of it. I turn to Wayland.

"Can you understand it?"

But Wayland's face is a mask of horror and confusion. "What?"

Sitka is beside me in Jin's arms. "I thin is tryin to communicae wi us, bu I can't unerstan it."

"But you can see it, right? What do you see? Is that an Over?"

"Jus a mass o st...strange pars cobble togetha."

"Well, at least we're seeing the same thing. It's like no angel I can imagine, that's for sure. The Followers of Enoch are going to be disappointed."

"It doesn't seem aggressive," says Wayland, "Maybe it's just having trouble materializing. I thought the elimination of the underlands would make it easier for them, but it doesn't look so good."

As we watch, the Over shudders, as if in pain, or struggling to hold the jumble of parts together. With a final screech, the thing explodes.

"Run!" I cry as parts rain down on us. There's a disgusting *plitter-patter* as gobs of flesh hit the dirt near us.

After the last splats of fat, gristle and bone hit the ground, the battlefield is silent.

"That's encouraging," says Wayland.

I glare at him.

"What?"

"It is *not* encouraging. They may have failed at taking over our world on the first try but look at the facts: the Overs have built a citadel in our reality. They've also been able to take on corporeal form, if only for a brief time. What do you think is next? Do you think they'll just give up? Have they ever?"

"You're right, of course. I was just trying to be optimistic, for a change."

"Well, don't. It's just a bloody waste of our precious time."

47

SITKA, NOW

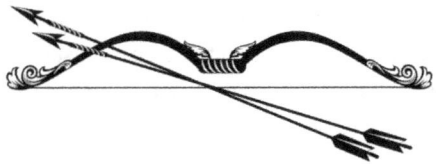

In any moment of decision, the best thing you can do is the right thing, the next best thing is the wrong thing, and the worst thing you can do is nothing.

— THEODORE ROOSEVELT

To *Lydarc, I will always be just a child. She takes so much upon herself, not realizing that I have the capacity and the desire to help. What can I do? We have a decision to make.*

I've told no one that I can communicate with Jin this way, through the spirit realm, but it saves time and miscommunications. Dysphasia sucks.

I stare up at his elegant, aquiline features. Dragons can't frown very effectively, with their metallic scales, but it seems he is frowning at me now.

"I don't think I like where this is heading," he says. "You are indeed a talented shaman, Sitka, but you do not possess a peri-soul. Let Lydarc do what she does best."

What's that?

"Challenge, disrupt, destroy."

That's a little extreme, but perhaps true. I still think it's time we did something to help. I found out which portal will lead us to the Overs. Let's just check it out, do a little reconnaissance. Maybe we can even delay the next attack.

"I don't think it's wise, Sitka. You could be ended. Or worse. I will not assist you in this folly."

All right, then stay here. I'll go in as my spirit animal.

I close my eyes and concentrate on the russet bear.

"No, wait!" cries the dragon. "I can't let you do this alone. I will go to my death with you, if I must."

How can you be so sure going through the archway will lead to your death?

"Because, even if we survive the citadel of the Overs, when Lydarc finds out that I assisted you, she will surely end me."

48

LYDARC, NOW

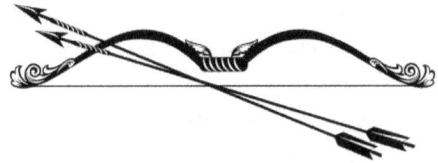

When you look into an abyss, the abyss also looks into you.

— FRIEDRICH NIETZSCHE

The next morning, we wander the battlefield. The minions are gone, many of them carcasses on the field, but there were more human bodies earlier. Many more.

"A feast for buzzards," says Wayland beside me, his expression dark and closed.

"Nonsense. All the human bodies have been removed. The buzzards can have this lot, for all I care."

"I know that. It's just such a mess, and we don't know if they'll send more, or when. At least the Over couldn't stay very long. If they thought it was going to be easy for them to enter our realm, I hope they were dissuaded of that notion last night."

"Maybe, but I think I need to go through the eastern portal soon. Tonight."

"Let's talk about that. We need to do some more research—"

"Excuse me." One of Griffin's assistants runs up, panting. "I think we have a problem."

"What is it, Matthews?" asks Wayland.

"Earlier this morning, one of my guards saw someone go into the central east portal, actually a couple of, a a c-couple ..."

"What are you saying?" I lean into her as I grow impatient with the stuttering and delays.

She pulls up and straightens, as if gathering herself to face my wrath. "One of the guards saw the dragon carrying a girl enter the east gate."

"What? When? You're just telling us this now?" But I don't wait for her answer as I run back to the tent to gather my bow and quiver.

Wayland chases after me. "Wait, Lydarc, you can't just rush in there."

"I've got to catch them before they do something really stupid."

"I think that's a fait accompli."

Normally I would ask him what the fuck he's talking about, but there's no time.

As we approach the portal, I turn to Wayland. "Way, please don't follow me in. I'll be a lot safer with you out here, guarding against anyone else entering."

He looks at me and for a second, I think he'll say no. He takes a deep breath and his shoulders relax.

"All right. I'll stay and guard the entrance until you return." I turn to go, but he grabs my arm. "But. If you and Sitka aren't back by this time tomorrow, I'm coming in for you. Understood?"

I want to argue, but again, there just isn't time. It occurs to me that this might be my last chance to tell Wayland how I feel. Fortunately, I stop myself before anything asinine spews out of my mouth. Instead, I give him a companionable peck on the cheek and step through the portal.

Lame, lame, lame.

Inside, I feel a disquieting lurch, as if I'm stepping through more than space, farther than a step. Stumbling into nothing, the floor turns to mush under me and I'm floating, spinning, falling into the Over realm headfirst. My stomach threatens to come out through my clenched teeth. I can't take it one more moment, but somehow, I make it through to the next existence.

I'm in the barn at home, a three-season-old with a lot of attitude and non-existent self-control. The sun is warm on my skin. The blight flows through the dirty six-paned window above us. I'm kicking my legs as I sit on the bench where my dad is fiddling with some kind of doohickey, poking at it with another doohickey.

He says, "You know, I never wanted to let you go to that school. The only reason I allowed it was because your mother said you could come home on weekends. Well, we know how that worked out. You never knew, but I died right after that—before I could tell you how I felt, how much we all missed you and loved you."

"Daddy?"

"Yes, hon?"

"Why you fibbin' me?"

He laughs, but it's Wayland's laugh, not his. I never heard my dad laugh.

"Look, it's not that big a deal. I knew even then that you were different—probably not mine. But I loved you just as much as any of the others. I'm sorry for what happened. You can have a family again. Just because ours was fu—messed up—doesn't mean you can't have a good life now."

Shifting, I stand behind him in my battle gear, as an adult.

"Dad, it's too late. My life is almost over, and I don't care if I ever have a family now. I'm a warrior shaman. I don't need your platitudes or your lies, so you can just fuck off."

Slow clapping sounds behind me. I hate that. As I turn, the barn floats away, making me dizzy and sick.

When the swirling stops, I'm in a circular room or office. Blighted bookcases surround us, but they're empty. There are no books, no windows, no chairs or desk. A tall, almost regal man stands erect and unmoving before me. His hair is gray, as are his eyes. He wears a thing I've seen in faded prints. Wayland calls it a three-piece suit.

"Are you an Over?" I ask. "I'm looking for Sitka, my apprentice. You'll know her by the golden dragon attached to her ass."

He smiles, ever so slightly. It's a cold smile, lacking feeling, lacking humanity.

"Welcome, Lydarc. Rapha has told us so much about you."

"I bet he has, the fucking spy." I look around for a door. There are none. No big deal, I'm not really expecting to exit this place. but I've got to find Sitka and get her out somehow. "Is Rapha here? Can I see him?"

The stiff man says, "I'm afraid Rapha is not available right now. He may have spent too much time with the inferiors—with you and the others with your affliction, I mean. We're understanding that it may be contagious."

"Affliction? You think being human is an illness?"

"I'm not sure what else you can call it. So much suffering, hatred, and pure malice. Your first instinct, when encountering something new, is to kill it."

I shuffle my feet and snort. "Yeah, especially when these new things just happen to end us with a touch, like your minions."

"We won't be sending any more envoys. None of them have been successful in opening talks with your kind. Now that the underlands are gone, we don't need them, anyway. As you've seen, we can enter your realm now. We'll work through the slight technical difficulties."

"Slight difficulties? Your first infiltrator exploded before our eyes. Do you really think it's going to get any easier? And what are you going to do if and when you figure out how to stay longer? Your very presence is toxic to us. We can't exist together. We'll keep fighting."

The man turns from me and faces the empty shelves. When he turns back, his expression has changed. I step back in horror. His face is twisting, collapsing in on itself, his eyes expanding, bleeding as his eyeballs are squeezed out of their sockets. When he speaks, the words are garbled, like his face. "The way things are going for your kind, that might not be a problem soon. There have been severe inroads in your population numbers since the afterarth first came into being. We'll just wait you out: you'll take care of our problem all on your own. With a little help from the egregores, that is. We took control of them when you destroyed the underlands for us. It was you. Lydarc. You made it possible for us to eliminate the inferiors, once and for all. We should be giving you an award, rather than killing you."

Without warning, the Over reaches for me, his arm extending as if it's made of rubber. I knew it was coming, but it catches me off guard all the same. He almost touches me before I draw my knife and lop the hand off. It drops; halfway to the floor, it rises and reconnects to the arm. He reaches at the same time with the other hand and grabs my bicep.

The Over screams as his hand sizzles and cooks. Soon there is nothing but a smoking stump.

"I thought something like that might happen," I say with a snarl. "You can't harm me because, thanks to Rapha, I'm part Over myself."

The Over flickers and flutters. Hands, arms, legs all recede into its body, which grows squat and bulbous, like a giant segmented worm. Out of its mouth, or whatever orifice it might be, comes a howling screech of ultimate pain. The whole being starts to smolder and fry. As it shutters out of existence, it thinks at me, *Maybe I can't touch you, shaman, but your apprentice has no such protections.*

I add my scream to his, but he's gone, and someone else is there, the figure I've been seeing but not recognizing all along. But who is he? Nothing is clearer.

We are expelled back into our own realm.

Jin is there, staring past me at a lump on the ground. We're outside the portal, and I see what he's looking at, tears running from his elegant dragon eyes. I look down to see Sitka's body, just as I saw it in that long-ago vision. She isn't breathing.

49

LYDARC, NOW

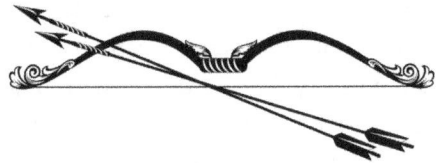

They say that if you wait long enough, justice will prevail. I call grundlecrap on that. All I've known is sorrow and loss. There is no balance in the world, no justice, and no reason to expect it.

— LYDARC, AS QUOTED BY SITKA SANGASHEE IN
HER PERSONAL JOURNAL

I kneel next to Sitka, searching for a pulse, even though I know I won't find one. How long has she been gone? Is there time to use the veil to save her?

Pulling out the little lava rock, I waste no time transferring myself to the veil, but when I get there, something is wrong. I try time after time, my panic rising. Finally, I realize that the palace of the Overs may be outside the range of the veil. The time that Sitka was in the crystal palace is missing. How can I return her to a timeline that doesn't exist?

I try to go back further, but by then it's too late. I need the time of her death, and it doesn't exist in our realm. Did the Overs know this? Did Rapha know it?

My fury grows as I return. We're now at the encampment, Jin standing over the prone body, wringing his clawed front limbs. I immediately draw and launch an arrow at his heart, but his metallic scales just deflect it. It falls with a pathetic *twink* at my feet, enraging me even more.

Wayland and Eva are there, trying to hold me back. My anger is so consummate that I don't stop to ponder the impossibility of a human ending a dragon with her bare hands. I struggle in their arms, unaware of the sobs that wrack my body until Jin speaks.

"Lydarc. I am so sorry. They attacked with blightning speed, before we could respond." The dragon gazes at the sky for a moment in thought. "That's it. Blightning. It might work. Lydarc, cool your anger for a moment if you want Sitka to live."

This gets my attention at least.

"When we were in the library, I read a book on—"

"Sitka is gone, and you want to quote to me from a fucking book?"

"Please listen. There was an ancient medical device that—"

"That no longer exists," I interrupt.

"Yes, but the device delivered a pulse of electrical energy to the body to shock the heart into restarting. We don't know exactly how much power is needed, but it was only a fraction of what a blightning bolt releases. According to the book, a blightning bolt can produce a billion joules of power, while the defibrillator delivers no more than one thousand joules. As a shaman, you have power over blightning. I've seen you wield it. Use your instincts and your shamanic vision to gauge the voltage. You can do it."

I stare at him. My rage solidifies into icy determination.

"All right. I'll try. Everybody, get back. I don't want to end anyone else trying to save her, compounding stupidity with recklessness."

The problem, as Jin rightly guessed, is how much power to utilize. I don't know why electricity is measured in jewels, but I know I must control the storm beings, or I will fry Sitka's body to cinders. Not a pleasant thought. I enter my trance state, but fear and anger are pulling me back. I know time is running out, but panic won't allow me to fully enter the trance. I string my best line of swear words together, an underappreciated art form. This calms me somewhat, and I can access the power I need.

The sky roils. Thunderheads gather in double-time and thunder rocks the arth. Too much. Way too much. I pull the tiniest thread of blight into my hands and touch it to Sitka's silent chest. Her body jumps and I'm sure I've done too much, but nothing happens. I hear a voice that I think is Jin's say, "Just a little more. It needs to be enough to shock her heart back into action."

I recalculate as best I can and try again.

Nothing. It must not be enough. Either that or this whole idea is shit. In exasperation and desperation, I let loose a larger charge. Sitka's body jumps off the ground and I cry out in agony, sure it's too much, but when her spasms stop, she pulls in a huge breath and plops back down, unconscious, but breathing.

"Sitka!" I cry, but her eyes remain closed. I listen to her heart, and miracle of miracles, it thumps evenly, if weakly.

"Let's get her to the med tent," a distant voice says.

Fear tempers my relief. Was her brain starved of oxygen too long? Will Sitka ever wake?

50

LYDARC, NOW

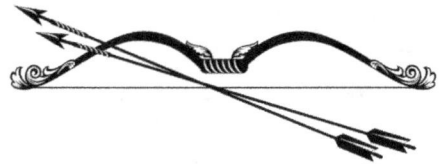

Yesterday is but today's memory, and tomorrow is today's dream.

— KHALIL GIBRAN

I have trouble getting into my vision state, even though the dreamweed is potent. I add a few dried psilocybes, and the goodly portion of a fifth of gin for extra measure. Finally, after I toss myself around the lumpy, creaking cot for hours, I sleep.

I wake to a different world. The season is not one I've ever experienced before. Honeybees buzz, tiny flitting birds dance and sing. The sky is a shade of blue I've never seen. It's so bright it hurts my eyes. A warm breeze gentles my face as I meander through tall grass studded with wildflowers. The scents are a cornucopia of pleasure. I pick a daisy-like flower and taste it. It has a rich, chocolatey flavor, with a hint of mint. When I notice that I'm wearing a long, flowing cotton dress, I know this has to be a dream, a fantasy.

"No, it's real," says a voice from behind me. I turn and find that Eva has intruded upon my dream. But she's different. Older. More assured.

"How'd you get in here? This is my dream, and I was kinda enjoying it before you intruded."

"I'm not in your dream; you're in mine. This is the dream I've had since I was a kid. I never knew what it meant before...before we went to Waxahachie."

"Wax-a-what?"

"You'll find out soon. I came here to warn you, though. There's another dream."

"Of course there is. I take it the second one is not quite so sunny."

In answer, Eva morphs into a giant, pus-covered arachnid, with eight furry legs and a mouth that dribbles stringy slime. The grass is gone, replaced by an echoing tunnel. It smells of iron ore, rusting machinery and neglect. Oily scum covers dank puddles at our feet. The tunnel is taller than any I've ever been in, at least twenty heights of a man, and it goes on forever in both directions until it curves out of sight many widder-widths away. Along the walls, pallid blights weep, their flashing pattern at odds with a normal heart rhythm. The cold and damp inject themselves into my bones.

"What is this place?"

The spider speaks in Eva's voice, "It's where we'll end up, if the Overs take the afterarth from us. What's left of humanity will be forced to crawl underground, where we'll all die, gradually. Every last one of us."

"That's a cheery thought," I say, as I rip off the flowery dress. My battle gear grows back onto my body, like budding brown leaves in fast motion, and I feel more at ease.

With a deep breath, I say, "But what of Sitka? Will she be all right?"

"I can't tell you that, but if we don't succeed in our quest to defeat the Overs, her life won't matter. None of our lives will matter."

"Oh, great. No pressure, right?"

I turn to Eva, but she's gone. The spider and the tunnel are gone, replaced with a howling shitload of nothingness. No hope. No dreams. No regrets.

There had to be an upside to this place. At least the suffering is over.

I want to puke, but I have no stomach and no last meal to power it. Is this our ultimate fate? The end of everything?

I've been here just a moment, and I'm bored already. There's no beer.

And where have I heard the name, Waxahachie before?

51

LYDARC, NOW

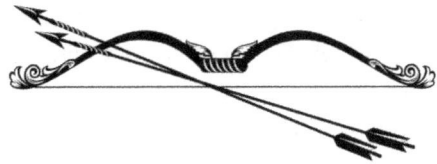

We saw what could be done, and we did it. How could we know
the horrific damage we would cause?

— EDWIN ROSS, PHYSICIST AND INVENTOR OF
THE FIRST VEIL

Wayland looks at me with an expression of concern.
He says, "Are you sure you're all right? You haven't
talked about what happened inside the crystal
citadel except for that truncated report to Griffin."

I rub my forehead. "Because it's so hard to explain, and I feel
like such an idiot. I didn't realize how powerful the Overs were.
My idea that I could go in there and somehow fight them, defeat
them—it's not gonna happen. I don't know what to do next.
They're just going to keep trying to break into our world, and
when they do figure it out..."

"I know. It doesn't look good."

An alarm sounds. It's the modulated whine that means an
Over has been spotted.

"Here we go again." Wayland grimaces as we rush out of the tent.

When we get outside, there is no Over, or rather the Over is no longer an Over. Rapha walks toward us in his human form. I see rage ignite in Wayland's eyes. I'm the cause of this fire, having told him that Rapha was responsible for what happened to Cassander and Eva.

When he lunges for Rapha, I throw an arm up to stop him, which is somewhat like trying to stop a raging grundle with a feather and a polite "please."

"You motherfucking—"

"Please," says Rapha, stepping back quickly and running a hand through his dark hair. "I am so sorry for everything that has happened—what I did. I did not truly understand the impact my actions would have. To the Overs, you are just tools to be manipulated for their own ends. I want to help. Please, just listen to what I have to say. We have little time." Rapha looks back at the crystal citadel. "Can we go into one of the tents? Do you have maps?"

I see Wayland hesitating.

"Way, I want to end him too, and I don't trust him worth a fuck, but what choice do we have? If he has anything that will give us an advantage against the Overs, we have to take it. We owe it to humanity. Don't you want Eva to have a chance at a future?"

Mention of Eva seems to bring him down to arth. At least he's paying attention now.

"Let's just listen to what he has to say. After that, we can end him together."

That brings a sad smile to his face.

"That sounds like a plan," he grunts.

Rapha is pale as Wayland leads the way to the makeshift desk in the armament tent. I blight a lantern and pull out the maps.

"How large an area are we talking?" I ask as I rifle through them.

"Large," says Rapha. He plucks out a map of the entire region, all the way to the southern ocean. He spends several moments searching until he pokes at a location far south of our present position.

"Here it is. Waxahachie, a town in the old Texas territory."

That name again. "That's a long way from here. What's there?"

Wayland says, "What's so special about this Waxa Cheese place?"

"Waxahachie. There is indeed something very special about it. The ley lines are stronger there than anywhere in the entire afterarth, except perhaps for Cern in Switzerland, but no one knows if that still exists. Waxahachie started out, back in the before times, as a supercollider site."

I frown. "What's a supercollider?"

"That does not really matter right now. Just know it is ancient technology. What matters is that it is the largest veil of probabilities in the world. It's over fifty widder-widths in circumference."

"The largest—and the most powerful?" I ask.

"Always a sharp one is our Lydarc," says Rapha, with his ridiculously smug smile. "If it is still functioning, I believe that the Waxahachie veil will give us the power to hold off the Overs—perhaps permanently ban them from this realm, or even destroy them, if all else fails."

I say, "How can we believe you, Rapha? You lie as easily as you breathe."

"I admit that I have bent the truth in the past, but I assure you that this is all true. As far as I know."

"Bent the truth? More like you've completely broken it, then stomped it into tiny pieces at our feet. You made these assurances before. How can we trust you now? Why are you helping us and turning against your own kind? What's in it for you?"

"I merely wish to make amends—at least in part—for the destruction of your home and the death of your loved ones. Regret is not something the Overs experience, but my time on arth has changed me. It has, for lack of a better term, made me more human: open to concepts like friendship, compassion, and sacrifice."

Wayland is shaking his head ever so slightly. I finger my crystals, navigating to the lapis lazuli, the stone of truth, but it tells me nothing. I stop when I realize I'm doing it.

"What do you think, Way? Should we choose to trust someone who has proven over and over that he is untrustworthy?"

To my surprise, Wayland says, "I don't know, but we're running out of ideas. If there's even the slightest chance you could use this veil to repair the rift in our world, I think we need to try. I don't trust Rapha any more than you do, but he seems sincere this time. I've heard rumors of this site. I thought they were just myths, but maybe there is some truth to it, after all."

I say, "My guess is that, as usual, he isn't telling the whole truth."

"You are correct," says Rapha, with a contrite expression, "but the only reason I'm not telling you everything is that it would take more time than we have, and it's likely that you would not believe me, at any rate. Please. We need to go soon. The Overs are even now planning another incursion."

"But how will we get there? Jin is too small a dragon to haul all of us to Texas, and he's not my favorite person right now,qq anyway. Taking Sitka into the citadel was the stupidest thing I've ever seen a dragon do, and I'll never forgive him for it."

"He did come up with the idea of using blightning to revive her," says Wayland.

"I'll give him that, but with Sitka still unconscious, I would rather leave someone here to guard her, even if it is a dragon."

Rapha raises a hand. His face goes blank for just a moment.

"What is it?"

"The other dragons are here. Faustina and Krimsena are offering to ferry the three of us to Waxahachie."

"Four," says a new voice.

Wayland turns and sees his daughter at the opening of the tent. "No. I forbid it."

Eva's eyes blight up, tiny fires in each iris. I get the feeling that Wayland is outmatched by this woman.

"No, Dad. Lydarc will need me. You know that, if you think about it. I have a talent with the veils. I just know that I'll be needed."

Realization hits me. My vision last night. Have I underestimated Eva all along? What power does she have?

"She's right, Way. We need her. She's meant to come with us."

The trip to Waxahachie is uneventful, except for the deep depression that overwhelms me at the sight of the devastation the dark fortresses have inflicted on the land and the people. Whole towns are ripped apart from the inside out, their buildings and residents spewed across the tortured landscape. I'm not sure we can recover from this level of destruction.

Have my actions led to the end of the human race? It's not a pretty thought, so I bury it deep and carry on. What else can I do?

When the Waxahachie facility comes into view, I'm not impressed. It's just a sprawl of ugly gray buildings, designed for facility rather than aesthetics.

The dragons set us down in front of a broken sign poking out of the ground that reads, *2275 Highway 77 North...Supercollider central facili...*

The rest of the words are unreadable, half the sign ripped away by some ancient calamity.

The low, dirt-encrusted buildings look as if they've been alone for a long time; no visitors, no maintenance, nothing but dust and wind and the erosion that our bluebird weather inflicts on people and places.

I hope the inside is a little more impressive.

It is not.

Empty offices, broken windows, decaying signs and debris-ridden hallways that smell of rat piss prevail. It's a real pleasure palace.

"Where's the veil?" asks Wayland.

"I do not know exactly," begins Rapha, "it is a huge facility. The veil will be on the perimeter, but this one differs from the others. Because it is so large, there will be a central hub: the control center or bridge, as they called it. That is where we should go."

"You seem to have a lot of details about something you know nothing about," I say.

"I did some research. I did not want to lead you astray. Again."

"Again? Wasn't it your plan all along to get us into the underlands and kill Aamon?"

Eva winces, then glares at Rapha. If looks could end someone...

Rapha studies the dirty floor. "I am so sorry about that. I was told that it was the only way to stabilize our reality."

"Well, you were told wrong. It destabilized it instead. What are the Overs thinking?"

"Anymore? I do not know. Perhaps I have been too long in this realm. Their blind ambition and willingness to cause any degree of collateral damage, I now see for weakness, rather than strength."

"There may be hope for you after all, Rapha."

"Which way now?" asks Eva.

We've come to the junction of three hallways. They're so long that the ends are shrouded in shadow. I call up a blight being to show the way.

We could each try one hallway, and come back to report, but an undefinable panic rises in my gullet like a bad meal. I have the feeling that time is running out, and any delay now could mean disaster. The Overs could even now be invading our realm.

I notice panels on the wall. Though the blightning that

powered them is long dead, there are a series of raised dots below them. I touch one, feeling the patterns.

"Braille," says Wayland, "It's touch lettering for the blind."

"Can you read it?"

"No," he says, "I always meant to learn."

Despite our dire situation, I giggle. "Finally. Professor Wayland meets a question he can't answer."

"Perhaps he doesn't need to," says Eva as she fingers the symbols. "The word 'bridge' has six letters, and only the sign to the center hall has six symbols. This must be the way."

"Who's the smart one now?" I say to Wayland as I pass him, a stupid grin on my face. I enjoy harassing my old friend. It's one of the few pleasures left to me.

Eva is right: the hall leads us to a large circular command center. Any locks have long ago been blown by teenagers and looters looking for a place to fuck and stuff to sell, or maybe the other way around. The doors stand open.

Inside are rows and rows of panels along the walls. There are more buttons and switches and knobs in one place than I've ever seen, even in one of my wilder, drug-induced spirit journeys. At the center is a metal and leather chair. The rats have eaten most of the leather, but a little stuffing of some unnatural material remains. More buttons cover the arms of the chair.

"How am I going to operate this? I don't have a clue how any of it functions." I say, fingering my crystals.

Wayland steps by me, laying a hand on my shoulder as he moves. I wish he wouldn't do that.

"Don't worry," he says. "We'll figure it out, but we're going to need some power. Do you think you could do your blightning trick again?" As he talks, he wanders the perimeter of the room, feeling along the walls.

"What're you looking for?"

"There will be an auxiliary energy source, in case of a power failure. I'm hoping they would have placed one nearby. Here." He opens a panel in the wall. Inside is a squat piece of equipment with multicolored rod-shaped nodules surrounding it. They balance in the air.

I look at Wayland questioningly. He shrugs.

"Some kind of wireless technology is my guess. Do you think you can give it some juice?"

"I'll try, but it's the same problem as the defibrillator: I don't know how much power to deliver. This isn't exactly a science, at least on my end."

"Let's hope this mechanism has some kind of regulator to control the current. Just start out slow and I'll signal when to stop."

"I'll try," I close my eyes to call up the storm spirits. It's a little harder to get past the bulk of the building, but it's only a perceptual problem. In reality, the sky is as close to me as the earth and the thunder that lives in my heart, as much as in the sky.

Thunder booms and the walls rattle. A bolt obeys me and snakes raggedly down into the power generator. Blights flicker and flash, then stabilize. The floating rods blight up and wriggle wildly. The generator hums. The hum turns into a rumble, the rumble into a roar.

With a celebration of sparks and smoke, the generator explodes, throwing fire and debris at us.

Just in time, I call up a pressure front that protects us from the worst of the blast. Even so, I smell the acrid scent of my eyebrows burning.

The fates give us one more flash of blight, then the room fades to black.

The blight dies, along with the last of my fragile, fading hopes.

A shaky voice in the dark says, "Well, that didn't go exactly as I had hoped."

52

LYDARC, NOW

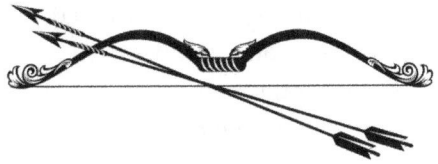

Our world will die, not as a hero, wielding a sword, but as a beggar, whining pitifully at the door.

— LYDARC AS QUOTED BY SITKA SANGASHEE,
EVOLUTION OF THE SHAMAN MASTER

"**W**hat are we going to do now?" says Wayland. "I can't fix that."

We stare down at the smoking pile of crap that used to be a power generator. I kick it hard for good measure and turn away, hiding a wince of pain. The blight being at the tip of my finger flares, responding to my anger and frustration.

Eva says, "I think the only alternative is to get to the veil itself and try to activate it without the controls."

I look to Rapha. "Do you think that's even possible?"

Rapha throws up his hands. "I have no idea, but we are running out of options and time. I think we have to try."

Without another word, I head out of the control room, taking the first hallway I see. We're lucky: eventually we come to a door marked *Danger. Authorized Personnel Only.*

"This looks like a good a way in as any." I try to open the sliding metal door, but it doesn't budge.

Wayland says, "Wait, we passed a fire station just a ways back."

He disappears back down the hall and returns with a large red ax. Instead of trying to hack his way in, he uses the back of the ax head at an angle to the locking assembly and delivers a powerful one-armed blow that takes off the entire device. Neon blue sparks fly, and the door slides gently open.

"Nice work," I say. "I know who to call for my next break-in."

As the door opens, the scent of damp stone and machine oil hits us, and I am reminded of my vision. As we enter the tunnel, I see it is almost identical to the one I saw in my dream, but it feels even larger. Our words echo in the vast space.

As we reach the middle of the tunnel, I see it goes on for many widder-widths in both directions, only disappearing from view in the far distance, where the gradual curve of the tunnel hides it at last. The blight apparatus on the far wall is dim, as if dying. This veil is nothing like the ones we used in the north.

"I don't know about this," I say. "It looks like this veil is failing. What do you think, Rapha?"

"All we can do is combine our shamanic abilities and try to access the power that still lives within it."

We form a triangle below the blights, Rapha, Eva and me. Wayland finds an old piece of equipment and leans on it to wait with his legs crossed.

I close my eyes and enter the trance state. Unlike my struggles last night, the vision state arrives almost immediately. Perhaps there is more residual power left in this thing than we thought.

As the power grows, I can feel the blights above us brighten and speed up. They're flowing in waves now, faster and faster, around the whole circumference of the tunnel. I can feel it happening, even though I can't see it.

Swirling images come to me. I relive many visions of the past; the destruction of the underlands, the last attack of the Overs. The Over morphs again as I saw it in the crystal citadel, but this time, I feel its agony as if it's my own.

A sudden realization almost knocks me over. The Overs are living in their own hell. They're no angels, nor are they beings from some parallel universe. I suddenly grasp what the Overs really are.

The shock of it pulls me from the trance. I fall on my butt to sit awkwardly in the mud and muck of the tunnel. Eva reaches me first and kneels beside me.

"Are you all right? What did you see?" she asks.

For a moment, I cannot speak. Then slowly, my tongue thick, I say, "We can't end the Overs. The Overs are us."

"What are you saying?" asks Wayland, who is also now by my side, trying to help me stand.

In a fog, I ask, "Rapha, did you know about this?"

"No, Lydarc. Know about what?"

"That's strange, if not even the Overs remember it...The memories must have been stripped when the accident happened, and reality was shattered. The catastrophe that created this fucked-up world we live in now. It all started here." I point to the veil in awe and horror.

"You're not making any sense," says Wayland.

"The befores were playing with forces they didn't understand. This device caused a rupture in our reality. The egregores—they're not creations of the Overs, but rather a product of human myths, brought to horrible life by our own collective imaginations. The broken seasons, the timesmears, and cosmic instability are all a result of the accident. The underlands is the hell we think we deserve, a manifestation of our guilt.

"The Overs—they're part of us. The human psyche was split in two. We got the more humane side, but lack drive and ambition, the will to better our own lives. The Overs have the ambition, but they lack compassion and humanity. We can't end the Overs. They're part of us, or at least they once were."

"I can't believe this," says Wayland as he paces the floor. "If the Overs are sundered parts of our own souls, then why do they attack us?"

Rapha has his hands on his face and he's mumbling something unintelligible. When he pulls his hands away, there are tears in his eyes and his face twists in a rictus of anguish. "We did not know. How could we have known? All this time we were subconsciously trying to repair the split, but our efforts were deadly. What are we going to do now?"

Eva, who has stepped away from us, turns abruptly and says, "We need to tell the Overs. If they understand, maybe they'll call off the attack."

"But will they believe it?" asks Wayland.

"I will make them believe it," says Rapha, with deadly resolve in his tone.

Wayland says, "Then what? Lydarc, do you think the results of this accident can be reversed with the veil? Can you do it?"

"No. The damage is too extensive, the capacity of this veil is greatly diminished. We need to get the power back on and try to understand how it works. If I mess with it the way it is, I could make the situation even worse. I won't do that again, like I did when I destroyed the underlands."

"I would like to study and repair the veil, if I am deemed an acceptable candidate," says Eva. "I think this was my destiny all along."

Wayland frowns. "I'm sure you would be at the top of the list. You've got a talent for understanding these veils, that's obvious, but nothing needs to be decided right now. First, we need to get the message to the Overs, before all hell breaks loose. Again."

We rush out of the building, intent on making a quick return to the encampment, but when we get outside, everything changes.

Gentle flakes are falling, and the ground already has a lovely dusting of pure white powder.

I gasp. "Snow. The white dust from my visions—the sign that the solstice is here!"

These are the last words I say or think before I cease to exist.

53

LYDARC, AFTER

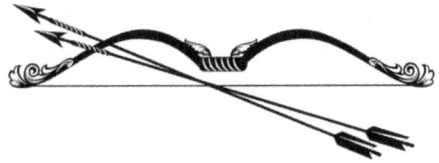

Only the wisest and stupidest of men never change.

— CONFUCIUS

W ho knew there could be so much pain from being reborn?

Lydarc is gone. I know this for a fact. What has replaced her? Well, I guess that would be me. Whatever or whoever I am. I guess I'll keep the name. It's pretty gender-neutral, right?

At first, the agony of the change kept me in an almost constant state of waking to a reality I couldn't accept, then falling back into unconsciousness. Over and over, the cycle repeated. Until a few mornings ago. The pain finally eased, at least to the point where I can function and communicate. If you can call this function, or communication. All I do is mutter under my breath and cough when I realize how much lower the register of my voice has fallen.

My body is different. It's almost impossible to describe how it feels. It even smells different. From what Wayland has told me, the solstice brought many changes, not just to me and the climate, but even the landscape. The big mountain range has moved east, and the Texas territory is now closer to Oregon. I know because Rapha sent the dragons to survey the damage.

It's not all damage. Apparently, Sitka has recovered and can walk and speak normally, though she has aged a bit. Wayland has his arm back and Jin got his wish to be human. He's now a handsome blond man who plans to spend the rest of his blastdays with his love, the powerful shaman Sitka. Rapha and Eva are unchanged. All while this... *this* happened to me.

They chose not to take me back to the encampment until I had woken and they could figure out how I had changed, and if it was permanent. Krimsena brought back supplies and a tent, while Faustina stayed with me. I find her presence oddly comforting, especially considering the abrupt change in my attitude towards her. Perhaps I can be wrong. On occasion.

Now, I'm not sure I want to return to the front at all. It's too difficult to explain. Everyone else seems to have gotten what they wanted out of the solstice. Had I been subconsciously unhappy with who and what I was? Well, maybe, but I never asked for this.

In some ways, I haven't changed. I was never the delicate princess type, anyway. I still tend to internalize my feelings, and I can be just as insensitive and demanding as I always was. Gender was never as important to me as it might have been to someone who had lived a more normal life, someone who played with dolls instead of weapons as a child and shopped at the village market instead of hunting for it in the bitterwood. Someone who could wear a white dress and be given away by her father. That was never me, but is this?

And then there is Wayland.

Wayland and I are over. He doesn't lean that way and neither can I. I know he's having almost as much trouble adjusting to the changes as I am. He only visits for a little while before he gets a strange, queasy look and comes up with some excuse to be anywhere else immediately.

Rapha was able to convince the Overs that what I discovered in the veil was the truth. They've ceased trying to enter our realm, at least for now. They've assigned Rapha to be their liaison and help Eva repair the veil, if it's even possible. Knowing the Overs, we'd better come up with a solution within a reasonable time frame, or they'll most likely return to their aggressive ways.

I don't know what I'll do. Probably return to the Siletz, but will they accept me? They only knew me as Lydarc, the warrior woman. Will they even recognize me now? It was hard enough to break into their insular community the first time.

Simply Waites, Jarly, Flossy and the others made it to the Siletz Valley without incident. At least they all survived the trip. Before we split up, I drew them a crude layout of the walled village I planned for Valsetz, and according to Milton, they've already begun construction. I'm not sure we'll even need the walls now. The fortresses and the monsters we called the egregores have disappeared—except for the dragons, who may have escaped annihilation because of their advanced development and intelligence. Or maybe it's just because of their fucking giant egos.

The climate is warmer and milder. There are fewer timesmears and other anomalies. We're not sure what to call the new season. I voted for bitterburn, but Wayland vetoed that, saying we needed something more hopeful. Fuck hopeful.

In the meantime, I try to adjust to being able to pee standing up. It's not as easy as it looks when you're forced to learn as an adult. I don't know how many times I've dribbled onto my pants or failed to adjust for the wind.

Then there is the nod. I never realized it before, but it's something males of the species communicate with. So much is shared in the slightest tilt of the head. Prospective rivalry is assessed, equals recognized, and superiority shared. As a woman, I never received that nod, not once. Why would I?

So much to learn. Shit. I guess I have the rest of my fucking miserable life to adjust to being a dick.

54

LYDARC, AFTER

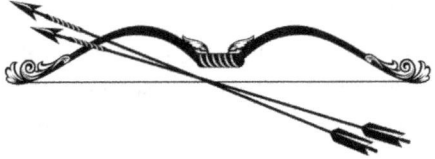

Whoever, at any time, has undertaken to build a new heaven
has found the strength for it in his own hell.

— FRIEDRICH NIETZSCHE

I take aim at the stag, surprised that I could get so close. The
hunt has been more of a challenge since the change. I know
it might just be my imagination, but I believe prey animals
can smell testosterone.

As a woman, I could walk right up to a cervid and they would
just stand there sniffing me, wondering what kind of animal I
was. Then I killed them.

Now it's a struggle to get within a widder-width of the
critters.

My arrow flies, a perfect arc, swiftly delivered. The stag bucks
and spins, his heart bleeding out inside his chest. Within a couple
of awkward leaps, he stumbles and falls dead. I've never had to
track an animal. I'm not that cruel. If I ever miss a heart or lung,
it'll be time to hang up my bow, my precious Spike.

I always made fun of idiots who give terms of endearment to their tools. That was before I created Spike.

In the Resistance camp, I learned everything I could from Cuspis, the master bowyer. I watched him shape the wood and metal with a degree of loving care the dour old man could never shower on a fellow human being. I shared with him my idea, to create a hybrid weapon that had the best attributes of a crossbow and a recurve bow.

At first, he grunted at me. Cuspis never laughed. The grunt was his expression of substantial amusement. I kept at him until he offered objections, then suggestions. Then we built weapons. The first one wasn't Spike, not by a long bowshot.

Spike was number seven. Lucky number seven. One through six all had problems of accuracy, while the speed and range of the bolt was consistently amazing. As my shamanic skills increased, I saw that the wood was flawed. When I left Leisil behind to become Lydarc, the way became clearer to me. I could coax the tree to grow into the perfect balance of resiliency, strength, and flexibility. The same for the metal. I had, after all, a deep communion with the arth spirits. From this, and Cuspis's craving for a legacy of greatness within the bowyer community, Spike was born.

I finish dressing the deer, then hear a lame bird whistle from the forest to the south, the direction of Valsetz.

I whistle back, knowing it's Simply Waites by the off-key signal. He never could learn to whistle in tune, or effectively imitate a bird, for that matter.

"Yo, Lydarc. Whoa, that's a nice one!"

"I assume you're here to help me pack it out."

"Well actually, I came looking for you 'cause we have visitors. They arrived by dragon."

"Really?"

The dragons only work with a few people, and there are only a few of those from the Resistance who know where we are. I'm not eager to talk to any of this select group. I consider taking my time getting back. As if reading my mind, he says, "They're asking for you specifically. They say it's urgent."

"What could be so urgent after all this time?"

Waites knows better than to answer this question. Back at Valsetz, we haul out the carcass, hang it to season and skin it before I head to the meeting hall. We tailored the building after the cedar longhouse in the underlands, though ours doesn't have the chubby carved figure of Delores the Elder above the door. Instead, there is a carved sign that reads: *Life begins with creating yourself.*

I enter the long hall then pause in the gloom, remembering a time long ago, when I entered a similar room to find Wayland and Rapha waiting for me. Then, one of them had my heart, while the other, well, I possessed a piece of *his* heart—or finger, as it turned out. How odd life could be, how melodramatic. I have no patience for drama of any kind anymore.

I step forward, my bootheels clicking on the floor rhythmically, until I reach the central chamber. Eva turns and almost runs into me. She stumbles back and emits a startled shriek. I can't blame her. Behind her, I see my premonition was correct. Wayland and Rapha are here.

They all stare.

Rapha is the first to speak.

"Lydarc. Is that you? You have changed."

I know my appearance has changed, but I'm different inside as well. My explosive anger is muted, replaced by a dire intent that shines in what has been described to me as a piercing, ever-evaluating gaze. I no longer display my inner life on my face. What a strange place to hide it. These blastdays, I embrace my purpose with the focus of a starving weirdog pack on the hunt.

I've also found a certain degree of inner peace. With everything that I've been through, I now realize that a sense of family and belonging is something that starts inside you. I just have to trust in the love I am being offered, trust in myself to be strong enough to accept it, no matter how long it might last. I'm still working on that.

Physically, I've grown a few inches: it turns out that testosterone has its uses, like building muscle. I no longer braid my hair, but let it flow freely until it gets too tangled. Then I chop it off and start again. It grows back more quickly than I would like, but that's just me. My eyes are still buggy, and I make no effort to rein in my frilly ears. If my appearance offends someone, fuck 'em. It is what it is.

I'm still Lydarc the warrior and shaman, just more so, and at the same time, less. Less fear. Less guilt. But that would have happened had I retained my given gender. I'm sure of that, though that's also a work-in-progress for me.

Wayland steps forward. I find it odd, looking down on the top of his head instead of up into his chin.

"Lydarc, it's good to see you. You've been such a recluse up here. But it looks like it's been good for you. You look well."

"I am well, as are the Siletzon," I say. "I would like to keep it that way."

Perhaps he senses the threat in my voice. I make no effort to conceal it, after all.

He touches the hilt of his sword. I give him the benefit of the doubt. Having known him for such a long time, I know it means not the threat of violence it seems, but is his way of dissipating tension. "We bring no danger this time. In fact, I think we bring good news," he says, glancing back at Eva with a tentative smile.

Eva, too, has evolved. Not physically. She's still the lithe young woman I remember, but something has changed in her eyes. There is a darkness and gravitas there I never would have expected. Perhaps the insight of one who has dived into hell and survived, then spent the last few seasons trying to find a way to patch a rift in reality—a rift I caused.

Looking into her eyes, I say, "I'm sorry," before I can stop the words from escaping.

"Sorry?" she says. "Sorry for what? As far as I can remember, you did all you could to prevent the destruction of mankind by the Overs. In fact, I suspect you're the main reason humanity still exists."

I pretend no modesty. "Perhaps, but I left you to deal with the aftermath. It couldn't have been easy."

Eva smiles, more of a grimace than a grin. "No, it wasn't, but Rapha and I took it on willingly. That's why we're here. With Jin and Sitka's help, we restored power to the veil at Waxahachie. We think we've found an answer." She raises her hands in warning. "Not a way to reintegrate the Overs into the human psyche. I fear that may never be possible, but we can repair the net. When we destroyed the underlands, we tore the fabric of the veil. If we don't fix it, it will continue to unravel. But there are..." She trails off and I am at a loss to continue her sentence.

"There are what?"

I look to Rapha, who, just like the last time I saw him, has not aged a blastday.

"Complications," he says. "There are complications. We think there is a way, but we need your help. We will need to combine all the shamanic magic the three of us can muster. We will need to work together. In fact, we'll need to become one being to achieve this feat."

I breathe deeply. I saw this in a vision, of course, and hoped it would never actually come to pass.

"I must join with you and Eva inside the veil," I say, "and trust that it won't end the lot of us. I saw this coming, and have had time to think about it, but I still haven't decided that it's the best solution."

"We think it is. It won't be easy to unite within the veil," says Eva. "I don't believe it will be fatal, though." Her face is a distorted kabuki mask of fatigue, hope, and something else.

Subterfuge spiced with regret? What else does she know or suspect?

"Well," I say, putting hands to my hips as the old Lydarc might have done, "I guess we might as well give it a whirl. After all, what do we have to lose, except everything?"

Wayland breaks out in a shit-eating grin, despite the dark mood in the room. "That's our Lydarc, always seeing things on the bright side."

55

SITKA, AFTER

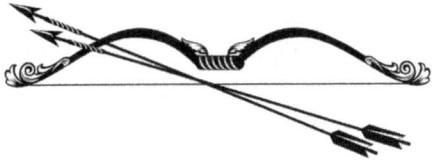

When the shamanic power awakens in you, it's as if the after-arth is remade. You are born anew into a world where your deepest dreams are possible, indeed, where everything is.

— SITKA SANGASHEE, *A SHAMAN'S JOURNEY*

I set down my pen, blow on the page, and close my journal. The library is unnaturally quiet at this time of night, especially with Jin off on one of his book-finding missions.

The stacks of the Fallen City library surround me as I walk. I trail my fingers gently along the spines, like a blind librarian, teasing out images in my mind from these, my dear two-faced friends. My hands know every book, every report and pamphlet in this building, as well as they know the landscape of my lover's face.

After the solstice, Jin and I reverently restored the library. First we sealed it against the weather, replacing windows and rebuilding shelves. But just restoring what was here wasn't enough for either of us. We decided the library would be the repository of knowledge for all of afterarth, an archive that would one blastday herald a new scientific and cultural renaissance.

It's a lofty goal, but if you're going to dream, why not dream the impossible?

I pause as an odd sensation tingles under my fingers. The feeling creeps up my arm and induces a shudder. It's not right. This book wasn't here yesterday, and no one has been in here but me since then.

Calling up a spirit blight, I study the room, but nothing moves. There are no sounds louder than my own breathing. All I smell are the wonderful scents of sixty-pound book paper, glue, linen and leather.

Tentatively, gently, I ease the mystery book from the shelf. It has an ornate leather cover with embossed lettering and gilt-edged pages. The words are in a language I don't recognize, runic and artfully drawn. Beautiful in a rugged, wild way.

How strange. What kind of magic is at work here?

I hesitate for only a moment. Introspection and caution have never been my virtues, as Jin so often reminds me.

"What the hell?" I say out loud as I open the cover. An intense blue blight blinds me, stabbing my eyes with needle-sharp pain. In my temporary blindness, I'm left with my other senses: smell, hearing, taste, touch and my inner eye. I smell a forest glade, deep in the passionate throes of a never-before-seen season; bright and open lavender and goldenrod, spicy arrowhead and aster, new green grass and just a hint of lemon trillium, all carried to my nose by a warm breeze over a fresh flowing stream.

I hear the rustle of clothing, some sections as delicate as silk, sliding almost soundlessly against each other like two breezes meeting. Others are roughly woven, like reeds for a basket. They creak with a leathery croak as the being moves. I also hear breathing, strong and deep.

When I recklessly reach out a hand to touch, I feel a beating chest, a heart too strong to be human, too slow to be monster, too warm to be undead or cadaver ghoul.

With an intake of breath, my tongue detects the tang of citrus and the warmth of cinnamon on the air. All these things tell me what I face long before my inner eye shows me. Yet, how can I believe?

I open my physical eyes, hoping the flashing blight has passed. Before me stands the shadow of a broad-shouldered figure, probably male, with long hair and ridiculous ears...

Of course, I've seen those ears on someone else.

"What are you?" I dare to ask, hearing how squeaky and childish my voice sounds. "Who are you? Your species is just a myth, and besides, all the egregores are gone."

"Nice entrance, don't you think? I've been working on that, just for you," says a deep, mellow voice, followed by a melodious laugh. "First impressions are so important with your kind. As to what I am, I think you know already. Always brighter than the average human, is our dear Sitka. And I am not an egregore, at least not since the solstice."

"You're an elf."

"Bingo."

I see it now, the frilly ears, the violet eyes. But it can't be.

"Yes, my dear, you're two for two. I am Lydarc's father, Elneroth."

He stands up straighter and I see how tall and massively built he is. His bearing is regal, one of those beings who immediately commands attention and obedience. I know it's elven pheromones. Even so, I'm tempted to fail to resist.

"So, the farmer Lydarc knew as her father wasn't..."

I wonder if that's why her mother sent her away at such a young age. Not everyone reveres the elves as I do. There is a great deal of superstitious fear out there.

"Elneroth. That name is familiar. You're elven royalty, and if you are, then Lydarc is..." I whisper this to myself in awe.

Elneroth taps his leather-booted foot impatiently.

"Time is short, my dear. It has taken me far too long to find you, and now you must carry me into her shamanic vision. My daughter and her friends are about to take actions that will affect all our futures. Shall we try to save her from herself—or is it himself, now?" he says with a sardonic tilt of his head. "I can't keep track of what these kids are doing with their bodies these blastdays."

56

LYDARC, AFTER

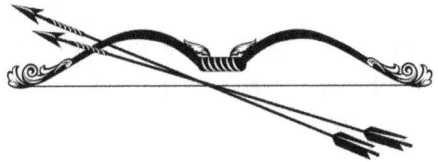

Autumn is as joyful and sweet as an untimely end.

— REMY DE GOURMANT

I'm on the wide sleepy river, rowing a dug-out canoe. I'm alone, but I sense watchers in the surrounding forest. The trees along the verge are dressed in their best autumn hues, orange, rust and mellow yellow, even though this is a season I've never seen in the waking world. A blacktail stag starts as he sees me, water dripping from his muzzle as he turns blightning quick and disappears into the woods.

A roaring grows in the mist ahead. Gravid with power, the air sparkles and thrums. The noise reaches a crescendo, and the water surges faster and faster. Something is approaching. Something inescapable. Suddenly, the arth falls out from under me.

I wake sweating and breathing hard. My dreams have been strange tonight, even stranger than usual. My already tenuous self-identity is sliding, slithering between Sitka and me and someone who could be, but shouldn't. He is odd, yet strangely familiar. My...*father*? But he's different, or perhaps he was someone else all along... His very scent is alien, yet it speaks of home. A home I've never known. Emotions I've yet to experience fully. Home. Family. But these self-centered thoughts are torn from me by need, someone else's desperate need for me to listen. For a change.

A man, Elneroth—no, not a man at all, but something very different—stands before me now, solidifying as I stare dumbly. Suddenly, it's perfectly clear. This man is my father. My real father. I have a real father?

When he speaks, it's as if I've heard his voice all along in my deepest dreams.

"Son—or is it daughter—you will develop the power to choose what you are at any moment, as need dictates. You can be one or the other, or perhaps something totally new, the best of all your experiences."

"What? You mean this gender change isn't permanent?"

"That's not what I said. I said that it's up to you. If you continue to work with the veil, you will evolve into something this world has yet to see; a true shamanic force. More than human, more even than elven."

I snort. "What, some kind of monstrous super hero? That's not me."

Elneroth crosses his arms and emits an exaggerated sigh. "Oh, Lydarc, will you forever underestimate yourself? It's time for you to step up and embrace your destiny.

"Lydarc, you must listen carefully. The fourth season must not be allowed to arrive. It will bring disaster. If you and the others fail to repair the veil, it will set in motion a series of events that can only lead to the destruction of our world. I'll be there to help you, but the onus of fixing the veil lies on your shoulders. You have the shamanic power and the peri-soul. It's time for you to use it."

I have used it. It didn't always turn out so well. For the first time, I'm terrified to sleep, to dream, to let the future in. The fourth season. What lies in wait is like a skinwalker creeping toward mankind in the moonless night, scraping stunted claws in the dirt, bleeding our probabilities away along with its dragging entrails. This rough beast is worse than nothingness, darker than the total absence of blight.

I've made choices in my life, mostly bad. Should I step onto the path that Wayland, Rapha, Eva, and now Elneroth have scratched out for me? And if I don't, will the fourth season be born anyway, perhaps trailing behind it something worse than death, not just for me, but for us all?

Yet, how can I say no? They're my friends, he's my father, and they've worked tirelessly to save humanity, not destroy it. Their arguments are sound. I just need to trust. No problem.

I know this: the next season, the one the ancients called autumn, has not graced this world for centuries. If I do this, the destruction—or salvation—of everything will rest on me.

Out of nowhere, a laugh burbles up from my churning guts. From all this chaos and uncertainty, there's only one thing I know for sure. I'm not ready for this responsibility, but it's coming for me, anyway. I have as much choice as the canoe as it tips over the edge of the waterfall and into the abyss.

57

LYDARC, AFTER

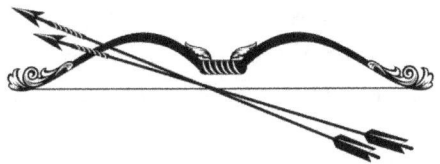

Never underestimate the strength and adaptability of the human spirit. He had the potential for greatness all along. The only one who couldn't see this was Lydarc himself.

— STKA SANGASHEE, *EVOLUTION OF THE SHAMAN MASTER*

We stand below the glowing, flickering wall, the giant veil of probabilities in the intimidatingly huge and echoing tunnel of the Waxahachie site. There is the circle: me, Rapha, and Eva. Sitka, Jin and Wayland are here to watch. I don't like having an audience for this most intimate and revealing of interactions, but I'll just have to deal with that. Sitka, despite her shamanic power, chooses not to join us. She and Jin have found a different path, through her writing and this experiment called "science." I can't fault her for that. In the end, it may prove the real salvation of mankind.

My father, my real father, Elneroth, is also here. Behind him stands a goodly portion of my newly discovered elven family, though they're not really here. Their two-dimensional, translucent blue shapes smile at me. Well, most of them, at least. Apparently, I have some cousins whom nothing and no one can please, and they are especially unwilling to welcome an unconfirmed, unconforming and, most of all, unproven member of the elven tribe; *their* tribe.

But Elneroth is a leader nonpareil, a character larger than his own life, who shapes the elven zeitgeist of his time just by being himself. It is he who has drawn down the veil the elves have hidden behind—a totally different kind of veil—revealing their existence to humanity at last. Though of course my mother knew him, at least in the Biblical sense. I've always wanted a reason to use that term.

If he says I am his daughter-turned-son, then so I am. I can't wait to meet my new family, though I will never desert the Siletzon. It just feels slightly fiddley-widdley and definitely wonkers to think that there are others like me in the world. Like me, of all unimaginable outcomes.

I smile, then frown. This is serious business, and I need to concentrate with all my will. Everything hangs in the balance here. Either we can patch this rift that I caused, or we're all doomed to suffer the continuation of this untenable world order. The Overs only half alive above, forcing their way through the tear in the realms, while humans suffer beneath their boot and the weight of our own lack of ambition. And then you have the underlands. Who knows what will happen down there? Will it be reborn? Will something even worse than hell be birthed in the melting placental ooze we left behind after leveling it?

I must take excruciating care not to upset the balance, but I don't have a clue what that really looks like. There has been no balance in this world for the long ages of the afterarth. The chaos stampedes through my fluttering heart and peri-soul with tortuous intensity; balance is a tiny shape in the distance, a shred of gyrating, diving hope, a toy kite in a hurricane.

The veil hums, and I clench my wide eyes shut, feeling the

rushing waves of it, as the power source Eva, Sitka and Jin have devised comes onboard with a whoosh of electric air. The ominous power of this machine must have been amazing when it was newly operational. No wonder the befores couldn't control it. It's beyond this world. Ingenious really. What ambition and talent and unmitigated drive the befores must have possessed to accomplish this insidious machine that incidentally destroyed our reality?

As the vision state encompasses me, I dive into the swirling mess that we are here to fix. It feels impossible. Too much time has been lost and there are too many random tears in the net, ever expanding now. Like a glass of incompatible compounds, forced to mix, entropy increasing until nothing is left but the fecund mud of existence, being forced to entwine in a coitus that no one desires. Rapha, the liar, I have no wish to be close to, even though we share a soul. He could never be Wayland in my heart. Sitka is tied to Jin in a way that I can't even conceive of, coming from the dark place of general mistrust and fear of being hurt that I do. And family. Are they family to me? Will the elves be?

This ultimate sludge of existence spirals, creating a hole in its center that grows deeper and deeper as it spins. I'm being sucked down and under into this maelstrom of muck when a hand grabs mine and pulls me up. Elneroth.

Dad.

"Hey, kid, get a grip, will you?"

I emit a breathless laugh as he launches me up with super-human strength. I'm flying toward a lake, a body of being like the lake in the underlands, but instead of leading into hell, it takes me somewhere unheard of. I land with a splash and struggle, thinking I need to swim, to try. Panic sets in.

I'll have to let go of all this bric-a-brac if this is going to work. I'll need to be vulnerable, if only for a moment. Can I? Probably not, but we have to try, anyway.

The waves of the veil lake wash over and through me, and I

feel the weightlessness of being suspended in a clear, bright pool of enblightenment. I take hold of the rope that holds me to this despicable life and, with a deliberate motion, let it fall from my fingers.

As I fall, I feel pure joy for the first time in my life. Not the joy of sex or the joy of the hunt, but an ecstasy of letting go, of letting myself become. I'm everything I ever wanted to be, and less, because I didn't need most of the trappings of human success, or the weight of assumed guilt and unbridled dread.

I roll and dance and spiral in the liquid veil, laughing and singing. Rapha and Eva are there with me, and they are clear, winged beauty to my inner eye. I pull them to me and into me. Together, we are a joy to behold. Together, we see what needs to be done: we repair it, just like that. Or at least almost just like that. It takes time, but we make more as needed. We mend the net, heal and soothe the suffering, guilt, and blame. We sigh together and with the world that just narrowly escaped a bitter end. Now it has room to be, for perhaps a millennium or so longer. Someone else will have to deal with the next apocalypse. After this, I'll be fading into retirement. At least, that's the plan.

We separate reluctantly to float for a moment in relief, looking down at our bodies below in the harsh blight of reality. Sitka and Jin glow with the intensity of their future achievements. She's no longer my apprentice but will always be a daughter to me. Wayland is at my side, where he has always stood. I realize that his friendship is the better part of me, and will always be, no matter who we think we are.

I realize too that this is my family and has always been; this random troupe of misfits and overachievers, warriors, dreamers and thinkers. I was just too pig-headed to see it. No matter where we are or what we do, we are one family now.

Soon this voyage will be over, and I'll land hard to the arth like that hurricane kite in its pathetic death spiral, but for a moment, I am just a bit more; more complete, more able to breathe. Brittle pessimism and hidden hope fall away. I don't need them anymore. Everything I've done and will do is just a whisper, a sigh, a gentle updraft floating away from me. I have only what's left.

I'll take that.

.

EPILOGUE

The tavern on the *Leaky Bucket* is full to bursting. The barmaids wipe their brows as the din of arguments, demands and tipsy laughter overwhelms all attempts at rational discourse—or thought, for that matter. Smoky clouds of pipeweed, stale ale and sweat distill themselves into the drunkard's perfume.

On the makeshift stage, Charlotte O'Reilly tunes her mandolin as she talks.

"This is a requiem for a name. It's called *The Ballad of the Bow*, and it's in honor of our dear Leisil."

She begins to sing, softly at first, as the noise around her subsides in response to her mesmerizing voice. Slow, clear and mournful, the song grows surer with every note.

She came from the wilds, herself just a youngling,
Into a war she had no hope of surviving.
With a bow on her back and a ghost in her eyes,
She leaned into life and refused to die.

She fought for the hopeless, the broken, the small,
She stood when the mighty refused every call.
No herald, no banners, no balm for her pain,
But the wind follows her footsteps and whispers her name.

Hail, hail, Leisil, bravest of the bold,
Fire in her bow flight and steel in her soul.
In darkness cloaked, she shone for us all,
She answered the evil and let us not fall.

She never asked tribute, no crown did she seek,
But her deeds are the stories that drunkards still speak.
The war may forget her, her tombstone may lie,
But our songs will remember and praise her on high."

THANK YOU

Thanks for reading *Darkness and Blight*. You're officially a member of my tribe.

This book was an experiment in risk: in structure, in process, in trusting my subconscious to take the wheel. I'm usually a plotter (that's writer-speak for "control freak"), but this time I started with only a sliver of a concept: a troubled shamanic warrior, born in the ashes of a quantum disaster, clawing her way through a broken world. Easy, right?

I wrote the first chapter in a kind of fever dream, as if Lydarc herself had slipped me one of her tinctures and whispered, "Why not, fucker?" After that, I was left to clean up the mess, to build a fractured world from scraps of intuition, navigate alternating tenses, shift between first and third person, and wrangle a whole lot of trauma. Thank the Overs for my brilliant editor, Kevin Eddy, who somehow kept the thing from imploding.

If you made it this far, you're the reason I keep going. Books like this—wild, weird, and defiantly non-commercial— don't survive unless readers speak up. I don't have a marketing budget or a team of interns. What I have is you.

If you enjoyed the story, please leave a review on Amazon or where you received this book. It doesn't have to be long—a sentence is gold. Reviews are the lifeblood of indie fiction and help other readers find stories like this one.

And if you want to reach out, debate quantum metaphysics, writing, book and cover design, or just to say hi, I'm at **gardlandbooks@gmail.com** or **dapdahlstrom.com**

Thanks for reading, for risking the weird with me, and for keeping Lydarc alive.

See you next time,
—Dap Dahlstrom

Shop ***Darkness and Blight*** on Amazon (Available as Epub, Paperback and Audiobook)

ABOUT THE AUTHOR

Dap Dahlstrom writes speculative fiction for readers who suspect reality is overrated.

Influenced by the raw, tangled wilds of Oregon and the Chippewa region of Wisconsin, Dap's fiction blends myth, madness, and the kind of speculative science that might actually be true in a parallel universe—or our own—if you squint hard enough.

A certified Oregon Master Hunter, martial artist, and unapologetic book (and idea) hoarder, Dap spends time catching halibut in the Pacific, studying the obscure and improbable, and muttering about entropy. When not dodging eldritch monstrosities of the imagination, Dap wonders how the hell we got here as a species.

Awards include three finalist nods from the National Indie Excellence and Wishing Shelf Awards, Three Firebird first place awards, A Bookfest Silver medal and a Literary Titan Gold award, all meaning that at least a few people out there get the joke.

ALSO BY DAP DAHLSTROM

DRAKONIA SERIES:

Book One:

Chronicles of the Drakyn War

NIEA Award Finalist

Wishing Shelf Award Finalist

—

Book Two:

Born of the Lesser Moon

—

Book Three:

Thief of Destiny

NIEA Award Finalist

Shop Titles on Amazon

www.ingramcontent.com/pod-product-compliance
Lightning Source LLC
Chambersburg PA
CBHW062004170626
46813CB00001B/31